TOXIC SPHERE

VOLUME 3:
ENEMY APPARENT

C. N. SKY

MINDSTIR MEDIA

Published by Mindstir Media, LLC
45 Lafayette Rd | Suite 181| North Hampton, NH 03862 | USA
1.800.767.0531 | www.mindstirmedia.com

Printed in the United States of America
ISBN: 978-1-958729-43-4

DEDICATION

Not all who inspire us are of the human variety. Some of our greatest teachers and friends are forms of life different from ourselves.

I dedicate this book to very special flying squirrels who shared their lives with me.

 My beautiful little girl taught me that love lasts forever. Once in our hearts, true love never dies or fades.

 My precious little boy taught me that there is no limit to the number of souls we can love. Our capacity to love expands beyond the confines of the universe.

Though both little angels have left the physical world, their spirits light the way through the vast voids of uncertainty and fear.

FOREWORD

"When evil leaders take the mantle of power, people of good intent have no choice but to stand against them. Looking the other way only serves to inspire sinister ambitions.

"Today, our world finds itself in such a state. The men rising to the top of our political, religious, and commercial structures mean to take us down a path that can only lead to destruction. The very cornerstones of our freedoms are at stake.

"Their treachery reaches around the world. Billions are at risk. Clouds of prejudice, hatred, and arrogance hover over us all.

"With great sorrow, I've come to accept that, this time, the rot is centered in Cadona, the nation I love.

"People of Cadona, people of the world, let us join together to end this regime of death."

Bob Fullerby, Investigative Journalist
Andecco News Service
Year 1007 of the Enlightened Epoch

CONTENTS

MAPS OF THE WORLD

The Primary Hemisphere

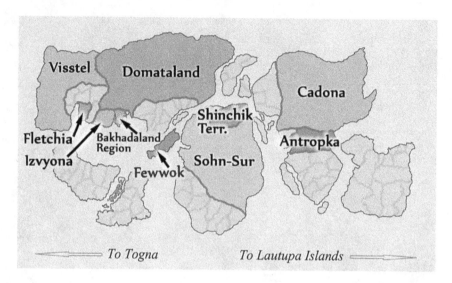

Visstel
Domataland
Cadona
Shinchik Terr.
Fletchia
Bakhadaland Region
Antropka
Izvyona
Fewwok
Sohn-Sur

To Togna
To Lautupa Islands

The Lost Hemisphere

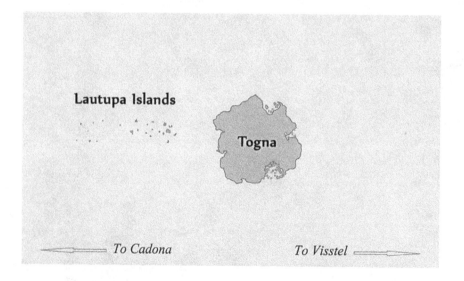

Lautupa Islands
Togna

To Cadona
To Visstel

Cadona

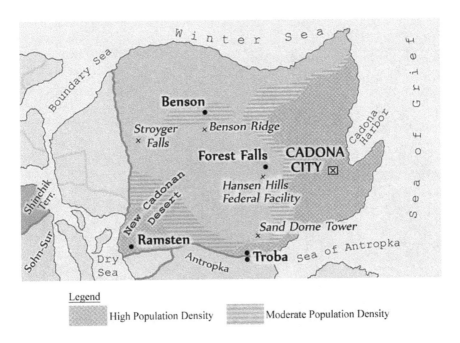

Legend

High Population Density   Moderate Population Density

Population: 1,998,000,000
Capital: Cadona City

Domataland

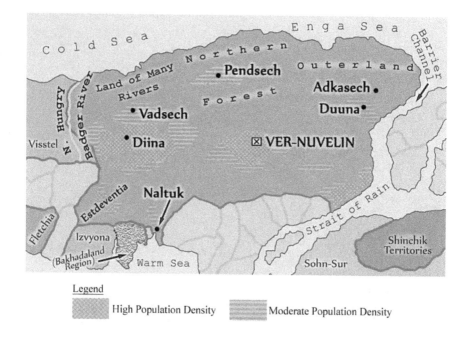

Population: 780,000,000
Capital: Ver-Nuvelin

Izvyona and Bakhadaland

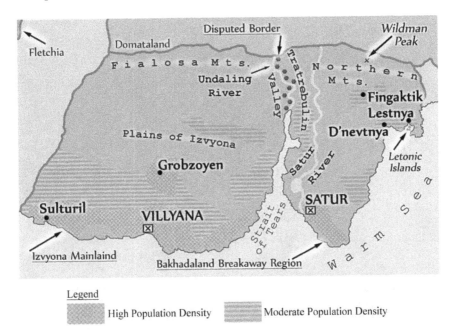

Population: 122,000,000
Izvyona Mainland: 70,000,000
Bakhadaland Region: 52,000,000
Capital: Villyana

Bakhadaland Region considers itself an independent nation and names Satur its capital. Only Domataland, Fletchia, and a handful of other nations recognize Bakhadaland's independence.

Visstel

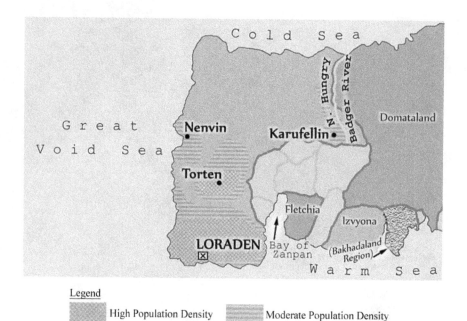

Population: 1,500,000,000
Capital: Loraden

PART · ONE
HUNTED

1

THE GUIDING LIGHT DOCUMENT

Cadona City, Cadona
TUESDAY, APRIL 25, YEAR 1007 EE
5:40 A.M., EAST CADONA TIME

Dazzling light struck Leeha Ritsagin's face when she opened the door of the rattling refrigerator. She shielded her eyes from the appliance's glaring bulbs and reached for the meal she'd prepared the previous evening.

Her hand bumped into an unfamiliar bottle. She squinted into searing brightness and saw all sorts of groceries. Some of the goodies were sure tempting! They might be for a catering event, though. Her boring food would have to do.

She longed to sit down to a relaxing breakfast, but a pile of work was waiting at the office. If paychecks stopped coming, she'd be in terrible trouble. Her mother and Cookie Davis were depending on her, too.

Leeha leaned against the counter and shoveled fruity yogurt into her mouth. Toast sounded good, but the time had come to leave for work.

She washed the bowl and spoon. As she set them in the dish rack, her elbow brushed against the refrigerator. The door slammed shut, drenching the kitchen in darkness.

Her hands groped the countertop. Where had her purse gone? She felt something hard, but it was the spice rack, not her handbag.

She mustn't waste more time.

Leeha tapped the personal device attached to her left arm. A thin beam shot out from the luminaire.

Instead of shining on the counter, the amber light shone on boards at the base of the kitchen cabinets.

A chill fell over her, for she knew what lay hidden beneath the cupboards. A few weeks ago, a mysterious document had found its way into the back seat of her old, brown Monarch sedan. To keep the odd text out of sight, she'd stashed it in a secret place in the kitchen.

Like beguiling chants from the netherworld, the peculiar manuscript called to her.

What was she thinking? Work was more important than reading some goofy document.

The lure was too strong.

Five minutes … she would allow herself five minutes to thumb through those pages, but she mustn't let Cookie catch her. Leeha pointed the faint light into the living room. Rays danced over her roommate's curvaceous form. Cookie appeared to be sound asleep on an air mattress.

Leeha crouched down on the kitchen floor.

One strip of wood at the bottom of the cabinets was loose. She removed the board and pointed the luminaire beam into the hole. Dust bunnies cast shadows, but no spiders or roaches scampered in the dirt.

She rolled up a shirt sleeve and stuck her hand into the hole.

Icky dirt tickled her skin as her arm slid deeper and deeper into the gap.

Her fingertips bumped into the strongbox that protected her important financial papers. The miniature safe, though, was not what she sought.

Her shoulder was pressing against the cabinet frame when at last, her hand touched soft plastic. She grasped the paper-towel-roll-sized package and dragged it through the skinny opening at the base of the cupboards.

To be on the safe side, she peeked in Cookie's direction. Everything was still.

Leeha sat upright on the kitchen floor. She pulled the bundle from the plastic sack.

The document appeared just as it did when she'd first laid eyes on it: folded in half and concealed inside an ordinary, brown paper bag.

The bound stack of papers flopped open as she set it on her lap. The passage on the right looked familiar; she'd read it before.

A shiver flowed through her as she reread the words *justice executions*. The next words conveyed a terrifying message: one hundred women were sentenced to die at the hands of the Soldiers of God Justice Group. A list of women's names and addresses followed the bizarre sentences.

She stared at the first name on the list: Mary Kronvelt. Three weeks ago, a woman with that name had been tortured and murdered. The name *Nancy Pitman* followed Mary's. Was Nancy still alive? Leeha hoped so.

The most frightening sentence of all revealed the name of the person overseeing the executions: Senator John Rineburg, one of Cadona's most powerful politicians.

The craziness of what she read chilled her to the bone, so she flipped to another page. The words, *Toxic Sphere weapons system*, caught her eye.

Leeha heard noises coming from the living room. She slammed the book shut.

Cookie's voice flowed through the darkness. "Leeha, why are you sitting on the floor? Is something wrong?"

"No, I ... I ... was trying to be quiet. I didn't want to wake you. I know you worked really late last night. How did the party go?"

"It was kind of fun," Cookie said. "There were some snobby people there, but a few were nice. Best of all, they paid well for hostessing. Did you look in the fridge?"

"Yeah, I saw all the food. Where did you get it?"

"It's leftovers from the party. Those of us on the catering team got to split it."

"You get to keep it?"

"Yep! We'll be eating like queens for a while. Do you want me to make you breakfast?"

"Thanks, Cookie, but I have to head to work."

"Okay. I'll make us something yummy for dinner. Do you mind if I invite Mrs. Furley and Toofy?"

"Not at all. It'll be nice to see them. Go ahead and get more sleep. I'll give you a call when I leave the office."

"Thanks, Leeha. See you later." Cookie snuggled into the air mattress.

Careful not to make too much noise, Leeha rewrapped the document and pushed it back into its secret spot. She pressed hard on the nail that held the floorboard in place. The last thing she needed was for Cookie to find the strange manuscript.

It was past time to go. Leeha rolled down her sleeve, found her purse, and slipped out the apartment door.

The emptiness of the long, windowless hallway soothed her, as did the quiet stairwell.

Standing in the foyer, though, wasn't relaxing. Beyond big windows, currents of smoggy fog rolled along empty streets. No one stirred in the gritty haze, but the streetlamps' glowing halos didn't reach all the nooks and crannies. The wormy guy might be hiding out there. He'd been stalking her for a long time. Perhaps today was the day he would attack.

She tapped her personal device. A viewplane formed in the palm of her hand. The security system Toofy had installed in her Monarch showed images of the parking lot and street. The pictures revealed no threats: no wormy guy or other predators of the night.

Leeha stepped out of the apartment building. Her pulse raced as she looked for signs of danger. Nothing moved except drifting, tepid fog.

A clang shattered the silence.

She dashed across the road and into the parking lot.

The sound of her own breath wheezed in her ears as she swerved around parked automobiles.

She was almost there! Her old, brown Monarch sedan was waiting for her. She jumped inside. The doors locked. The engine started. She was safe!

Leeha drove onto the street.

Her office building wasn't far. Traffic was sparse, as was typical at this hour. Yet, the littered, deserted highway gave her the creeps. Since her last early morning commute, two more streetlamps had burnt out, adding to the sense that something terrible was about to happen.

A traffic signal turned red. She pulled to a stop.

A deep noise, faint at first, grew louder. The ground trembled.

Driverless delivery trucks appeared. Their massive, greasy bodies crossed the intersection. The world fell silent once again.

Why hadn't the light turned green? Sitting in the dark wasn't safe. Any number of criminals might be waiting for an easy target.

Leeha glanced around. She didn't spot any weirdos, but the sight of the dingy factory gave her shivers.

It wasn't always like that. Before the assembly plant went out of business, light would flood the complex. At all hours, workers came and went. Now, only inky silence spilled onto potholed roads. The industrial buildings, menacing in appearance even when people worked in them, had become an army of misshapen, brooding monsters lurking in the dark.

A convoy of bigger trucks approached. Giant, grimy wheels sent tremors through the earth. The huge vehicles towered over her Monarch.

She needed to distract herself. Leeha turned on the sound array.

Investigative journalist Bob Fullerby was speaking. She loved his voice, but he often reported bad news. Today was no exception. He talked about sand storms and wildfires that were raging in the south and across neighboring Antropka. The bad weather was forcing airlines to divert flights to northerly routes.

The trucks crossed the intersection. The clanking of the motors faded.

The signal turned green. Leeha raced away.

She didn't get far before another mechanical roar juddered her body.

Now what? Did a driverless truck go rogue?

She looked in every direction but didn't see a vehicle.

Flashes caught her eye. Where the heck were the flickers coming from?

She looked up. A huge aircraft loomed overhead. Fog churned like smoky plumes around the metallic sheen and blinking lights of a passenger plane. She recalled an old film she'd watched a long time ago. In the story, a mysterious phenomenon swallowed an airplane full of people.

Just like in that scary movie, the jet floating above her, along with its booming rumble, vanished into the clouds.

An unearthly aura hung over familiar streets. What a spooky morning!

The Monarch topped a hill.

She saw a comforting sight. Rows of intense, blue-white lamps gleamed from atop tall poles. A big sign for Franklin Technologies glowed on the concrete wall of a sprawling building.

Her body relaxed into the seat; she was almost there.

Leeha turned into Franklin's driveway and tapped her personal device. A chain-link gate opened. She parked in a slot near the employee entrance—one of the benefits of starting work early.

She shut off the headlights. The world grew dark. Prickling fear returned. Getting out of the car didn't seem a good idea.

However, she couldn't sit there forever. She clutched her purse and jumped out of the Monarch.

Droplets of fog brushed against her face as she hurried to the employee entryway.

She held her left arm near a sensor.

The sensor hummed as it read the nodes embedded in her flesh.

Why was it taking so long?

Finally, the door slid open. She rushed inside. The door closed. She'd made it!

The reception area's white walls, bright illumination, and shiny floor contrasted with the spookiness of the shadowy streets.

Her troubles weren't over, though. One gauntlet lay behind her, but another arose: she must face the path to her cubicle.

The sound of footsteps clicked on the smooth floor. Someone was coming.

It was Oscar Olsen. He walked around a corner by the reception desk. His security guard uniform was tidy, but a mat of grease glistened on his black hair. He smiled, but it did little to widen his narrow face. "Good morning, Ms. Ritsagin."

"Good morning, Mr. Olsen."

She took a few steps, and an alarm buzzed.

"Ms. Ritsagin, don't forget the J2 scanner."

"Oh, yeah, sorry." She placed her forehead near a translucent bar suspended in a white frame. The scanner let out a happy chirp.

"You're all clear," Oscar said.

Leeha headed straight for the hallway leading to her work area. The last thing she wanted was a drawn-out conversation with Oscar. He seemed friendly enough, but something was creepy about him, as if he would loiter outside a lady's dressing room with the hope of catching a glimpse inside. She heard his voice. "I hope you don't have to work too long today."

Bummer! Now, she was forced into a chat. Leeha prepared her excuses, and she didn't have to lie; after all, she was running late.

She turned around.

Thank goodness! He was speaking to Stacy, not her.

Something seemed odd, though. Stacy had a huge smile on her face. She met him at the edge of the reception desk. Both she and Oscar made the Mark of the Compass.

Leeha felt a wave of fear, the tingly kind that visited when the threat was hidden, but hidden in plain sight. Over the past year, the True Followers of God Church had sucked in many Franklin employees. Proof of it was found throughout the company. Instead of shaking hands or offering a simple *good morning*, people crossed their forearms in front of their faces—*making the Mark of the Compass* as the church called it. Now, the crazy religion had taken Oscar and Stacy, too. How could intelligent people like Stacy fall for such bizarre beliefs? Leeha headed to her cubicle. Once there, she could lose herself in her work.

The wide corridor was empty, which was another advantage of working the early shift. The only human voices came from videos playing on giant wall monitors. Senator Bradley Seldortin appeared on one of the viewplanes. He was an awesome man! He'd make a great president.

She stopped to watch the report. Real-Time Broadcast showed him at his worst. Stark lighting accentuated lines on his aging face. Rills of sweat trickled down his flushed cheeks as he gingerly picked his footing over stony ground in the scorching New Cadonan Desert.

The image changed. Senator Mitch Fischer appeared on the screen. The clip portrayed Senator Fischer at his best. He strutted along, confidently flashing his youthful grin and flaunting a steady gait. The lighting cast a healthy glow on his smooth skin.

Somehow the news crew managed to make Pastor Leon Walls look dashing, too. The camera followed him as he bounded up a wide set of stairs. He joined Senator Fischer in front of a large, impressive building.

Leeha's stomach turned. Real-Time Broadcast was so biased! They did everything they could to make Senator Seldortin look bad and Senator Fischer look good. Would she ever learn? She should only watch Andecco News. All the other agencies were in the Freedom Party's pocket.

She ignored the other wall monitors lining the hallway. The last thing she needed was to make herself sick.

Her cubicle was close now. She held up her left arm. The door to the Business Systems Lab swung open.

So far, so good. Jilly was facing the other way. Rebecca was nowhere in sight.

Leeha tiptoed inside. With luck, Jilly wouldn't notice her.

Luck ran out. Jilly spun around in a swivel chair. "Hi, Leeha!"

"Morning, Jilly. Is Rebecca here, too?"

"Yeah, she's getting coffee. I'm going to run to the cafeteria and get something to eat. Do you want to come along?"

"No thanks, I'm a few minutes late. I better start working."

"Okay." Jilly grabbed her purse and rushed away.

As Leeha walked by Jilly's cubicle, she noticed a new photo. Between a picture of a True Followers of God Church Compass and a photo of Pastor Leon Walls, hung an image of Leon Walls' son, Pastor Mark Walzelesskii. A similar photo of Pastor Walzelesskii rested on Rebecca's desk. Good grief! Her coworkers' hero worship was flippy.

Leeha settled into her own unadorned cube. She sent music to her ear-piece and activated the structural data display. As the root- and bit-plates loaded, she checked the police blotter. Thank goodness! None of the alerts was about a person warning ninety-nine women that someone may be coming to kill them.

The music volume lowered. An automated voice said, *Load complete, Leeha Ritsagin.* Finally, she was able to leave her worries behind and drown herself in a sea of data.

Cadona City, Cadona
TUESDAY, APRIL 25, YEAR 1007 EE
8:00 A.M., EAST CADONA TIME

Pastor Leon Walls looked out the tinted limousine windows. The hulking, gray-stone face of Cadona's Department of Defense building was a magnificent sight. God had truly blessed this country!

The limousine pulled to a stop behind a concrete barrier.

The bulletproof glass separating Leon from the driver compartment glided open. Mr. Garzell, the chauffeur, twisted in his seat. "Pastor Walls, are you sure you don't want us to drop you off inside?"

"No time for that. The confounded security takes too long."

"Very well, Pastor." The window closed.

Leon watched as three bodyguards jumped out of the vehicle. Such a shame it was that extreme precautions were needed to keep him safe. The world was not changing for the better.

The chief bodyguard twirled a finger in the air—the all-clear sign.

Mr. Garzell opened Leon's door. "It's safe to come out now, Pastor."

The moment Leon stepped out of the car, he saw a swarm of anti-Freedom-Party protesters. Why on earth did the National Police allow riffraff scrum to get so close?

A second armored limousine arrived. Senator Mitch Fischer climbed out from the lush back seat. He appeared calm, almost buoyant, despite the string of obscenities coming from the raucous mob.

Mitch reached out his hand. "Good morning, Leon. I see your chauffeur drove you here. I came with mine, too."

"Yeah, I do like having Mr. Garzell around. With the streets as dangerous as they are, it's good to have a human behind the wheel. Who knows what those lunatic protesters will do? What a bunch of worthless idiots! Heck, they look as crazy as their dimwitted slogans sound."

A fist-sized press drone swooped in. Leon swatted it away.

"Be careful," Mitch said. "That drone belongs to a friendly news agency."

"Sorry, I should've looked. Andecco News Service is here, stirring up trouble as usual. That blasted Scott Walters! I'm starting to hate that guy as much as stinkin' Bob Fullerby."

"Don't forget, Leon, we have allies in the crowd. They're better behaved, so they're harder to notice."

"That is true. They don't stand out as much as Senator Seldortin's rowdy Allegiance Party groupies."

Mitch said, "Let's show them how gracious people behave." In his polished, politician's style, Mitch waved at the mob.

Leon wanted nothing more than to get away from the barrage of insults the protesters hurled at them, but appearances were important. He waved at the troublemakers in the same way he waved at his congregation.

"Leon," Mitch said, "let's go inside and see why Dougy called us here."

"Gladly."

They walked into a dark, concrete-walled bay. The shouts of the scrums quieted with the slamming of the door.

A shuttle cart rolled up. A military policeman stepped off the vehicle. "Good morning, Senator Fischer ... Pastor Walls. Please climb aboard. General Willirman is expecting you."

The cart came to a stop in front of a door with General Douglass Willirman's name printed on it.

Leon followed Mitch into a spacious office.

Doug was sitting behind his shiny desk, but he stood as they entered. "Mitch, Leon, come on in and take a seat. John got here early. I've already filled him in on the main points."

Senator John Rineburg didn't bother standing or saying hello. His long body slumped into a chair. A grouchy look covered his face.

Mitch settled into a seat and said, "Dougy, I like your new office. It suits you and your position as commander of the Combined Armed Forces."

Doug grasped the edge of his desk as he plopped into his chair. "Thanks. I'm getting used to it."

Leon sat down. Anxiety crept over him. Something was up. John's sour demeanor and Doug's obvious fatigue meant only one thing; something terrible had happened.

"John," Mitch said, "good morning."

"Trust me, Mitch. There's nothing good about it."

"I'm sensing bad news. What's happened?"

John said, "I'll let Dougy tell you. I don't have the full story yet."

Doug appeared nervous. "We have a rabid dog, Mitch—a bad one."

"Ex ... Excuse me, gentlemen," Leon said. "Rabid dog? Dougy, I don't get it. What does that mean?"

John fidgeted in his seat. His voice sounded angry. "You've read *A Quiet Soldier*, haven't you, Leon?"

"Yeah, back in secondary school, but it seems an odd question. Why do you ask?"

"In the book, the term *rabid dog* means a sudden and serious threat to national security."

"Dougy," Mitch said, "what's our rabid dog?"

"Not *what* ... *who*. He belongs to a defector group called the *Cadona Guardians*." Doug took a sip of water before saying more, probably to buy time to choose his next words. "Mitch, we have an issue with an aircraft."

"A military aircraft?"

"No, a civilian passenger plane—International Flight Ten Seventy. It's heading for Bangtangsu, Fewwok. It took off from Cadona City Airport early this morning. We're in luck; it had to fly up north because of the dust storms down south. The plane is still well within Cadonan airspace."

Mitch's voice was stern, but measured. "Dougy, why are we lucky because it's still in our airspace?"

"Because we have time to respond. We need a decision. There's no good answer ... no easy answer. No matter what we do, we can't let Senator Seldortin, Richard Karther, or Bob Fullerby get wind of this."

Leon raised his hand. He couldn't make it stop trembling. "Sorry, Dougy, but I'm confused. What exactly is the problem with Flight Ten Seventy?"

John squeezed the arm of his chair so hard that his knuckles turned white. "Don't you get it, Leon? Our rabid dog is on the plane."

"Dougy," Mitch said, "what does the rabid dog have?"

Doug rubbed his stubby thumbs together, a sure sign of unease. "The dog works at the Stanton Weapon Research Facility. He stole information about Toxic Sphere and is attempting to sneak it out of the country."

"Dougy," Mitch said, "do you know this man personally?"

"I do. We all do. It's Air Force Captain Timothy Becker."

Leon couldn't believe it. "Dougy, do you mean the *Timothy Becker* who's Rosie Stanton's fiancé?"

"The same."

"Dougy, it can't be! Tim's a patriot. He and Rosie asked me to officiate at their wedding."

"It took me by surprise, too, Leon, but the evidence … there's no doubt."

Mitch said, "Dougy, did Captain Becker have accomplices?"

"He had to. Without help, he would've been caught before he put one foot outside the facility. We have reason to believe he's involved with a woman who's a Cadona Guardian ringleader."

Leon said, "Wait! Wait! Dougy, are you saying Rosie helped Tim steal secrets from the company her family built?"

"No, I'm not talking about Rosie Stanton. She's not involved, but we do think Becker hooked up with her to get his hands on information about Toxic Sphere. There is a woman helping Becker, though. We're still trying to figure out who she is."

"Dougy," Mitch said, "do you think Becker is connected to our Guiding Light document?"

"It's possible. Becker is a Cadona Guardian. The Guardians have links to people close to Senator Sandra Pettock, so—"

"Sandra!" John said. "That witch is a Cadona Guardian?"

"We can't prove Sandra herself is a member," Doug said. "But we're pretty sure the Guardians have contacts in her staff. Sandra and a couple of her buddies got a glimpse of the Guiding Light a few months back. If they happened to stumble upon passages about Toxic Sphere, word might have gotten back to the Guardians. Here's the danger: if the Guardians have Toxic Sphere details from both the Guiding Light and from what Timothy Becker had access to at Stanton Weapon … let's just say an enemy would pay handsomely for such data. An enemy can use that information to figure out how Toxic Sphere works."

Mitch leaned back in his chair. "All right, Dougy, what are our options?"

Leon felt a rill of sweat drip down his face. "Mitch, wait a minute. Why do you fellows need me?"

"If Dougy's right," Mitch said, "and we don't have any good options, we may need your help communicating with the public."

Leon's stomach burned, but his colleagues were doing God's Will. "You can always count on me, gentlemen. Whatever it takes, I'll support you."

TRUE FOLLOWERS OF GOD CHURCH

Cadona City, Cadona
TUESDAY, APRIL 25, YEAR 1007 EE
8:40 A.M., EAST CADONA TIME

Leeha Ritsagin pressed a virtual button on the viewplane. A message appeared: *system processing; please wait.*

She stretched her stiff neck and pulled the ear-piece away from her head.

A tapping sound came from behind her.

She swung around in her swivel chair.

Rebecca and Jilly stood at the entrance to her cubicle.

Jilly's face beamed. "Leeha, are you taking a break?"

Uh-oh, what did they want now? "Yeah, a short one. My changes are compiling. Do you need something, Jilly?"

"We went to that new gift shop across the street. Have you been there?"

Leeha didn't know what shop they were talking about. "Um ... not yet."

"You've got to go," Rebecca said. "They sell lots of awesome stuff."

Jilly pulled something from a small bag. "We bought you a present, Leeha."

"Thanks, but you guys shouldn't spend money on me."

"Don't worry," Rebecca said, "it wasn't expensive, but it'll cheer you up when you get stressed out."

Jilly set a miniature view-display on the edge of the desk. Images of Pastor Leon Walls and his son, Pastor Mark Walzelesskii, popped on. The father and son stood in front of a shining picture of the True Followers of God Church Compass. A short video of the two pastors smiling and waving at the camera played over and over. Jilly placed her hands over her heart. "Aren't they the handsomest, Leeha?"

"Um, yeah. Thank you for thinking of me." She watched the video awhile. Leon Walls was wearing one of his weird, light-colored suits that made his flabby body resemble a painted egg. His smile seemed artificial, almost as if his lips were taped to the roots of his overly white teeth. His son, Mark, had nice features, but something wasn't quite right about him. His gangly look wasn't the only problem. His movements appeared uncoordinated and floppy, as if puppet strings controlled his limbs.

Jilly glowed. "Do you like it, Leeha?"

"Um … yeah. I like the cheery colors."

An automated voice came from the computer: *compile complete.*

Leeha said, "Um, I gotta get back to work. Thanks for the gift."

Rebecca and Jilly headed back to their desks. Jilly's voice carried through the room. "Pastor Mark is so good looking! You know, if he ever actually spoke to me, I think I'd faint."

"Me, too," Rebecca said. "I'd faint, wake up in his arms, and faint again."

Leeha saw her eye roll reflected in the golden-hued plates of the view-display. With luck, no one noticed.

She wanted to turn off the video, but that might hurt Jilly's and Rebecca's feelings. Instead, she tilted the view-display so she couldn't see it, but people in the hallway could. She considered other benefits for letting the clip play again and again. Other people besides Jilly and Rebecca had tried to convert her. Maybe if those people saw the video, they'd think she'd already joined the church. Even better, big shots at Franklin Technologies were church members. If managers thought she was a True Follower, it might help her keep her job.

All this religious stuff, though, was wearing her out. If only she didn't need a paycheck!

Leeha reattached her ear-piece.

She would play a few songs. After that, she'd listen to Andecco News Service. Bob Fullerby would have good things to say about Senator Bradley Seldortin.

A grin crept across her face. Bob also had an awesome habit of revealing Pastor Leon Walls' bad side to the public.

Cadona City, Cadona
TUESDAY, APRIL 25, YEAR 1007 EE
11:00 A.M., EAST CADONA TIME

Andecco News Service Investigative Journalist Bob Fullerby dragged a wooden chair up to the old, scratched table. He stabbed a fork into the last chunk of his breakfast burrito and stuffed the morsel into his mouth. The food had dried over the course of his busy morning, but a mouthful of strong, hot coffee softened the bread and beans.

Red lights flickered. Bob glanced at the print shop's security monitor. He recognized the gray, dented pickup truck rolling into the rear parking lot.

Two of his teammates, Angela Thirgal and Kever Carsen, climbed out of the vehicle and strode with springs in their steps toward the rear entrance of the old print shop building.

Bob recalled long-ago days when he had such boundless energy. Ah, to be young!

The door opened, flooding the windowless back room with daylight.

Angela stepped inside. She smiled. A happy face suited her. For her age, her crabby side came out too often. "Good morning, Mr. Fullerby."

"Morning, Ang. Hello, Kever-o."

Kever seemed his typical, carefree self. "How's it hangin'?"

Bob raised his mug. "I'm on my fourth cup of java, if that tells you anything."

Angela sat down at the wooden table. "Mr. Fullerby, is Row back yet?"

"She's on her way. Carl picked an odd place to meet with her. He didn't want to talk in his office."

Kever took a seat and poured himself a cup of coffee. "Uh-oh, that means Detective Brunish has news he doesn't want to share with his fellow cops, at least the crooked ones."

Again, red lights flashed. "Speaking of Row," Bob said, "here she is."

The camera tracked Rona Betler as she drove into the back lot, parked, and climbed out of her tiny car. She swung a sparkly handbag over her slender shoulder. The purse was large for her petite frame, yet she carried the bag with grace. At nineteen years of age, Rona had already found her own style.

The print shop door swung open. Rona walked in. Her cherub smile and soft voice exuded innocence and hope of a bright future. "Good morning, Mr. Fullerby. Sorry, I'm late."

"No worries, Row. We're just getting started. What did Carl have to say?"

Dangling bracelets tinkled against the tabletop as Rona settled into a chair. "Detective Brunish says he has evidence linking the Mary Kronvelt murder to the Agel Yungst shootings at Hughes Medical Center, but he's afraid if details get out, the Soldiers of God Justice Group will go into hiding. He wants to catch Justice Group ringleaders, the ones who take orders directly from the Back-to-Basics Club. He'll let us know when he learns more."

"Thanks for the update, Row." Bob tapped an autopad. A long list of topics displayed on the viewplane. The Mary Kronvelt murder topped the list. The Guiding Light disappearance was second. Despite weeks of effort, the mysterious document had not been found. "Let's step through the Drop Case sequence of events again," he said.

Angela rolled her eyes. "Why? Mr. Fullerby, we've already gone through it a boatload of times."

"I know, but I just get the feeling there's something staring us in the face that we're missing. Row, would you run the Hatchets Bar bug-eye video, please?"

"Sure." She unrolled a computer and touchpad. Rona had a way with gadgets. In seconds, the first frame of the Drop Case video appeared on the wall monitor.

The bug-eye footage showed three well-dressed, middle-aged women walking along deserted sidewalks. Each lady carried shopping bags. The women were heading toward Hatchets Bar, but they disappeared down a side street. Moments later, an old, brown Monarch sedan lumbered down the road and pulled to a stop along the sidewalk in front of the bar. The driver, a young woman with light hair, stepped out of the automobile. A look of shock covered her face, an expression people often had after an accident. She walked around the vehicle, checking the car's many dents and dings. The woman climbed back into the driver seat. What looked like a map popped up on the dashboard monitor.

Bob put his coffee cup on the table. "Pause video." The video stopped. "Were you able to figure out what the driver was looking at on the monitor?"

"It's a standard WorldLink Direction Finder map," Angela said. "Of what, we don't know. We went to Professor Durban for help, but he couldn't figure it out either. There's too much glare."

"Resume video," Bob said.

The three female pedestrians reappeared. They headed down the street but stopped when they reached the Monarch. One of the ladies dropped a paper bag filled with something about the size and shape of a squashed roll of paper towels. Another pedestrian picked up the package and tossed it through the open, rear passenger side window of the Monarch. The bag landed on top of other sacks that were resting on the back seat. The three women walked away, heading west. Soon they were out of bug-eye range. A few seconds passed; then, the brown Monarch drove away, heading east.

"Pause video." Bob took a sip of his hot drink. "Okay, let's review what we know. The lady who tossed the bag into the back seat is Pam Urzin. Mirgit Vespez appears to be a lookout. Do we know the lady who dropped the bag on the sidewalk?"

"Yeah," Angela said. "Row and I finally identified her. Her name is *Cindy Coraway*. She volunteers as a grief counselor with the True Followers of God Church in the Hillside District."

"Anything special about her, Ang?" Bob asked.

"Nope. Just like Pam and Mirgit, she supports the Freedom Party and is a Back-to-Basics Club member. All three ladies participate in Club events, but they're not leaders."

Bob's frustration grew. Almost a month had passed since the Guiding Light went missing. Based on all available evidence, the bag that Pam Urzin threw into the Monarch contained the Back-to-Basics Club's prized text. Many questions remained. Who was the mystery woman driving the Monarch? Who hired her to steal the Guiding Light? Why was the document so important to Senator Mitch Fischer, Senator John Rineburg, General Douglass Willirman, and Pastor Leon Walls?

"Resume video."

The video displayed the deserted street in front of Hatchets Bar. Leaves hanging on a few scraggly trees fluttered, but he saw no other signs of movement.

A few seconds passed; then, a different car appeared. Like the first one, it was long and painted the same muddy shade of brown. It came to a sudden stop in the place where the Monarch had been parked. The driver swung her head around as if she was expecting someone. She made a call with her personal device. A short time later, she sped away. The bug-eye recording ended.

"Okay," Bob said, "here's what we know. Our Drop Case informant identified this driver as Annetta Longstreet. Her car is a fifteen-year-old Cavalier. This is the type of car that was supposed to be used to pick up the Guiding Light at Hatchets Bar, yet the pedestrians threw the package into the first car—the Monarch. Any thoughts?"

Kever leaned back into his chair before speaking. "A Cavalier looks a lot like a Monarch. My guess is the pedestrians couldn't tell the models apart. The ladies threw the document into the Monarch by mistake."

Angela said, "Also, the pedestrians must not have known what the driver looked like. If they did, they wouldn't have thrown the Guiding Light into the first car."

"I agree," Rona said. "Both drivers are about the same age and have long, light hair, but, other than that, they don't look anything alike. The mystery woman is tall and a little overweight with wavy, reddish hair; Longstreet is petite with straight, yellowish hair."

"One thing's for sure," Kever said, "the mystery woman looked upset while she was walking around her Monarch. The way she was behaving makes me think all those dents and scratches happened shortly before she parked at Hatchets. Mr. Fullerby, has your informant learned anything new?"

"No. The only thing we're sure of is that Leon Walls, Douglass Willirman, John Rineburg, and Mitch Fischer are frantically trying to find the Guiding Light document and the driver of the first car."

Bob felt a twinge in his stomach. He was losing the race. "If the Club gets to the mystery woman first, we'll never learn the document's secrets, and I hate to imagine what Rineburg and his buddies will do to her if they catch her. With luck, we'll beat the Club to the Guiding Light and the woman. The Monarch is our best chance of tracking her down. Row, how's the search for the car going?"

"Slow. Ang and I have gone through stacks of traffic cam images. So far, no matches, but we have a long way to go. The pile is huge."

Bob's personal device buzzed. He read the message. "My apologies, I have to run. Richard's preparing a news release. If I leave now, I should make it there on time."

"Do you mean *Richard*, as in *Richard Karther*?" Angela asked.

"Yep."

A look of concern covered Kever's face. "Mr. Fullerby, why is the defense secretary giving a news release?"

"I'm not sure. A passenger airliner ran into some kind of trouble. It's one of the flights that was diverted north because of dust storms down south."

"Mr. Fullerby," Angela said, "what do you want us to work on this afternoon?"

"I want you and Kever-o to keep working on the J2 virus story. By the way, the boss thinks you're doing a great job, and so do I. However, Bill wants to make sure you don't openly challenge General Willirman on his bio-weapon theory."

Angela sounded irritated. "Why not? Willirman is lying! Doctor Sinje has officially stated that the evidence proves J2 mutated into more dangerous forms on its own. A foreign power didn't turn the virus into a weapon. Why doesn't Willirman listen to the health director?"

"I know, I know," Bob said. "It's frustrating, but remember who our adversaries are. General Willirman is the commander of the Combined Armed Forces. Senator Fischer is the Freedom Party candidate for president, and, come July, Senator Rineburg will likely be sworn in as the head of the legislature. The Back-to-Basics leaders are already powerful, and it's likely they'll be more powerful before the year is over."

Kever rested his feet on an empty chair. "Let's not forget Pastor Leon Walls. He's right there with Willirman, Fischer, and Rineburg. For someone not in an official post, Walls has an awful lot of power."

Bob worried for his team members. "Listen, keep researching the virus: its spread, mutation rate, and progress on a vaccine. But let Doctor Sinje and the defense secretary fight the germ-warfare claim. Those guys are paid big bucks. Let them take the heat. Do not challenge Willirman."

"We'll be careful," Kever said.

"Mr. Fullerby, what about me?" Rona asked.

"Keep plowing through the stack of traffic cam photos. When the mystery woman drove the Monarch to Hatchets Bar on March twenty-sixth, she had to start the trip from somewhere and end the trip somewhere."

"Will do, Mr. Fullerby."

Bob longed to linger in the chair a little longer, but duty called. Soon, the defense secretary would release information about an aircraft. "If you need me, give me a shout, but I may not be able to respond until after Richard's briefing."

3

FLIGHT 1070

"I can confirm the worst. Domataland has shot down a civilian airliner, International Flight Ten Seventy, after forcing the aircraft into Domataree airspace. Over twelve hundred souls, mostly Cadonan citizens, lost their lives."

General Douglass Willirman
Address to the Nation
Year 1007 of the Enlightened Epoch

Cadona City, Cadona
TUESDAY, APRIL 25, YEAR 1007 EE
2:30 P.M., EAST CADONA TIME

Leeha Ritsagin reached her hand into the structural data display. She grabbed a virtual data bucket and moved it into another layer of schematics. The schema realigned. A pinging sound accompanied the appearance of a huge, green check mark.

Yes! The computer confirmed the code was clean. The system still needed to save the changes, but that wouldn't take long. One by one, the bit-plates closed. Only three root plates remained.

A root plate flickered away. Her face reflected in a bare corner of the back plate.

Just great! Facial oils had stripped makeup from her pimples. A giant zit jutted out from the side of her chin. A scarlet blemish marred her cheek. She dug in her purse. Thank goodness! She hadn't forgotten her makeup stick.

Leeha glanced out the window. Her old Monarch sat in the parking lot. Soon she'd leave work and have a delicious dinner in her little apartment. She was starving, and Cookie was an awesome chef.

Thumping footsteps broke the silence. Jilly's shrill voice echoed in the hallway. "We've got to tell Leeha! Maybe now she'll believe us."

"I hope she's still here," Rebecca said. "She's got to know before it's too late."

Leeha wished the computer would finish saving her updates. She had to get out of there, else Jilly and Rebecca would bug her about True Followers stuff again.

Red and blue lights flashed against her cubicle window. Three police cars were zooming down the street.

Panic stole her breath. What if the police were coming for her?

More than two weeks had passed since she'd sent warning messages to the women on the justice execution list, but maybe the cops had just tracked her down. She tapped her personal device. She didn't find news reports or police bulletins about weird messages, but she still might be in danger. Maybe the cops wanted to arrest her before releasing the news to the press. Why, oh why did she ever look inside that crazy document?

Jilly and Rebecca dashed into her cubicle. Did they know the police were coming for her?

"Leeha," Jilly said, "can you believe what's happening?"

Leeha glanced outside. The racing cop cars turned down a street leading away from the office building. The police weren't coming for her after all. Her body relaxed. "Jilly, what's wrong?"

"It's an act of war!"

"What is?"

"Leeha, haven't you heard?" Rebecca asked.

"Heard what?"

Jilly was near tears. "Domataland shot down Flight Ten Seventy."

"Flight Ten Seventy?" Leeha said. "What's that?"

"A civilian airliner with over twelve hundred people on board. Domataland destroyed it."

"When?"

Tears misted Jilly's eyes. "Just a little bit ago. It was going to Fewwok. It had to fly up north because of the dust storms. The Domats forced the plane to fly to Domataland. Then, they shot it down."

"Why?"

Rebecca said, "Because the Domats are the sons and daughters of Bezgog, just like the prophecy says. You can't bury your head in the sand any longer. The End of Time is upon us, Leeha!"

"What would the Domats gain by shooting down a passenger plane?"

"I don't know," Jilly said, "but the attack is all over the news. You should come to the break room and watch it with us. General Willirman is going to make an announcement. This could be it, Leeha! This could be the start of the Last War of Prophecy."

Leeha knew she had to get out of there. She was too tired to deal with more True Followers prophecy nonsense. "I got the data cleaned up," she said, "and I have dinner plans, so I have to get going."

"Hey," Rebecca said, "do you want to come with us to the service on Friday night? Pastor Townly will be speaking. It'll be really interesting to hear what he has to say. The war's beginning, Leeha. The Last War! Bezgog is making his move."

"Um, I'm watching a movie with friends Friday night." She was glad she didn't have to lie. She had plans to watch *Too Many Goodbyes* with Cookie and Mrs. Furley.

Jilly wagged a finger. "Leeha, God is more important than a movie."

"Look, Jilly, I believe in God, but I don't believe in this End of Time Prophecy thing."

"But, Leeha," Rebecca said, "look how it's all coming to pass! Demnar Tarish is the King of the Nastebyans like the Holy Books predicted. You can't deny it!"

"Um … Demnar Tarish is the new president of Domataland."

Rebecca put her hands on her hips. "Leeha, you need to read the Holy Books! Modern-day Domataland is the ancient Nastebyan Kingdom."

"Um, if you say so, but I have to go. See you tomorrow."

Leeha hurried to the Monarch. After touching up her makeup, she tapped her personal device. "Hi, Cookie, it's me. I'm on my way home."

Cadona City, Cadona
TUESDAY, APRIL 25, YEAR 1007 EE
2:50 PM, EAST CADONA TIME

Pastor Leon Walls rushed down a Department of Defense hallway reserved for those with a sensitive compartmentalized security clearance. His pulse raced as he walked into the waiting room behind the briefing hall. General Douglass Willirman, Senator John Rineburg, and Senator Mitch Fischer were already there.

Doug looked tense as he stared at an autopad.

A muscle twitched in John's jaw as he spoke. "Leon, did you hear Karther's press release? Our twit defense secretary is causing us grief."

"Yeah, John, I listened to it."

Given the threat hanging over them, Mitch seemed surprisingly composed. "Thank you for helping us out on short notice, Leon."

"Glad to help."

A military officer in a dress uniform poked his head into the room. "General Willirman, sir, the briefing hall is secure." The door shut.

"Don't worry, Dougy," Mitch said. "You'll do fine."

"I hope so. Dealing with the public is the worst part of my job." He drew a deep breath. "Well, I guess I'd better get out there." Doug made his way across the stage and to the podium.

Leon felt Mitch's hand on his shoulder. "What's wrong, Leon? You seem uptight. Are you worried about speaking after Dougy finishes?"

"No, I'm ready. I'm going to leave Domataland and politics out of it today. I'll focus on the families who lost loved ones on Flight Ten Seventy."

"Sounds good, Leon. So, what's troubling you?" Mitch asked.

"I'm still having a heck of a time believing Timothy Becker betrayed Rosie Stanton ... and Cadona. He seemed like a decent young man. It's hard to imagine him stealing secrets about Toxic Sphere. I bet this other woman he was involved with led him astray."

John said, "Whatever happened, it's over now. We did good work. With one blow, we killed our rabid dog and discredited the Domats. It paints Domataland as a rogue state bent on violence. It helps our cause."

Mitch faced the stage as he spoke. "You're right, John. What we've done is done, but we're taking a great risk. We have a mountain of cleanup work ahead of us. Keeping the truth about Flight Ten Seventy under the rug will be more difficult if enemies have the Guiding Light."

Leon said, "Why would that be, Mitch? The document vanished a long time ago. We didn't know Timothy Becker would steal Toxic Sphere schematics, pose as Paul Stanton, and hop on Flight Ten Seventy. There's no link to the Guiding Light."

"You're right, Leon, we didn't write specifically about Flight Ten Seventy or Timothy Becker. However, we did say plenty about discrediting Domataland. If our defense secretary can prove what really happened to the airliner, and if the Guiding Light resurfaces in unfriendly hands, one may deduce we framed Domataland—which of course, we did."

John said, "I'm not too worried about it. If there's one thing all Cadonans agree on, and, frankly, it may be the only thing, it's hatred of Domataland. Even our staunchest internal enemies in the Allegiance Party will rejoice when those Domataree pissants turn to ash."

4

SINKING OF THE GOODWILL SHIP

Cadona City, Cadona
TUESDAY, APRIL 25, YEAR 1007 EE
3:30 P.M., EAST CADONA TIME

Leeha Ritsagin wondered what was worse: driving to work in the spooky void of zero-dark-thirty or commuting home in gridlock.

The featherweight fabric of her shirt stuck to her sweaty back. She rolled down the driver side window, but the muggy air did little to cool her flushed face and sticky hands.

Traffic stopped. Air no longer flowed in. Perspiration trickled down her cheeks. She peeked in the vanity mirror. Just great! Dripping sweat washed away her zit-concealing makeup. Blemishes glowed bright crimson in the sweltering heat.

What a time for the Monarch's air conditioner to die!

Traffic moved again.

She was almost home, but four lanes of back-to-back vehicles stood between her and the exit.

Like a miracle, gaps formed in the lines of cars to her right.

This might be her only chance. She gunned the engine. Horns honked and tires squealed, but she was too hot, hungry, and exhausted to care.

She squeezed into the last lane just in time. The turnoff was only a mouse's tail away.

The short off-ramp spilled onto a rutted road. Despite the rough pavement, vehicles zoomed about at a frantic pace.

There was another way home—a risky one. A maze of alleys twisted and turned along the grimiest sides of buildings. Gunky dumpsters, tendrils of litter, rills of mucky water, and makeshift human dwellings cluttered the passages.

Taking the main road was even more fraught with danger, as she'd have to face speeding cars and the wrath of grumpy drivers.

Leeha clenched the steering wheel and turned down an alley.

She'd made the right choice; the path ended at a quiet road. Her apartment building lay just ahead.

She turned into the parking lot.

The moment she climbed out of the car, circulating air cooled her back, underarms, and thighs. The trials of another workday had ended.

Just as she stepped onto the sidewalk in front of Pineland Apartments, she saw it: a figure lurking at the far end of the building. Was it the wormy guy?

In a blink, he vanished.

She rushed into the lobby.

The familiar, automated voice said, *Welcome home, Leeha Ritsagin.* Cool air flowed around her. The quietness of the lobby, stairwell, and fourth-floor hallway comforted her.

The impact of the day's trauma had waned by the time she reached unit 413.

She knocked on the door. No one answered. She walked in. "Cookie, are you here?" Lovely silence greeted her.

A scrap of paper sat on the countertop. Cookie's graceful handwriting curled and angled like fine lace. The note bore good news: "*Hi Leeha, Mrs. Furley and I went out. Food is marinating in the fridge. Dinner will be at six o'clock.*"

What could be better? She would enjoy some quiet time and then eat a delicious meal.

Leeha stripped off her sweaty work clothes.

After a cool shower, she dressed in the most comfortable clothing she could find.

In the calm of the living room, her old sofa was waiting for her. Undulating bumps and lumps made the secondhand couch cozier than any brand-new piece of furniture.

She turned on the viewing monitor, but she would skip the news tonight; current events were too upsetting.

A calming scene appeared on the viewplane. Sunlight glistened on the gentle waves of an aqua sea. An occasional seabird glided beneath a blue sky dotted with billowy, white clouds.

Her body sank into the sofa as image after image of spectacular vistas floated by.

The camera then showed white sand. Beyond the beach rose tall hills covered in dazzling shades of green.

She sat upright. That place looked familiar.

Oh, no! What she was watching *was* the news!

Andecco News Service reporter Scott Walters' voice came through the sound array.

> "Yesterday, in the sunshine and fresh air of D'nevtnya, Bakhadaland, people gathered to remember the men who died on the Domataree Goodwill Ship. It has been two days since the sailing vessel's destruction, but sorrow, anger, and disbelief remain high in Domataland and the Bakhadaree Breakaway Region. While the people of Domataland and Bakhadaland come to terms with the disaster, celebrations continue throughout Izvyona. The sinking of Domataland's flagship marks the latest tragedy in an area ripe with turmoil. While Izvyona and its separatist Bakhadaree Region prepare for war, Cadona and Domataland take opposing sides as tensions escalate."

Why, oh why did she listen to the news report? It reminded her of the weird document hidden beneath her kitchen cabinets. Like haunting visions, Leeha pictured the passages about Izvyona, Bakhadaland, and Domataland. An unseen force begged her to read the words again.

Leeha pulled the document from its hiding place. She flipped through the pages until she found the paragraphs she was looking for.

> The Domataree race is unstable, unpredictable, and violent. We must use this to our advantage. We must provoke Domataland. They must lash out before their advanced weapons are ready. Domataland must be defeated.

> Our first strategy: Bakhadaland. We will take advantage of the long kinship between Bakhadaland and Domataland. We are justified to do so. Many Bakhadaree citizens are infected with Domataree blood. If nothing else, by association with evil, they are evil, spirit-blood or not. What better place to light the first fire! Our fuel is the long hatred between Bakhadaland and Izvyona. Our spark is to persuade Izvyona to lash out against the Bakhadaree separatists. We will provide weapons and training to Izvyona, but not enough to overpower the separatists. The goal is to create conditions that will force Domataland to help their Bakhadaree allies.

She slammed shut the book.

This whole thing was nuts! A month ago, she'd found the document in the back seat of her Monarch. The goofy manuscript had been tormenting her ever since. Besides, what could she do? She had no power; she couldn't stop a war. And it wasn't war alone that troubled her. The justice execution list was hanging over her head. What a fool she was to think she could protect the women on the list! She should've never sent those warning messages. What did it get her? Worried sick that the cops might arrest her—that's what!

Enough was enough! She must destroy the document.

She put it in the kitchen sink and grabbed a book of matches. Her heart pounded as she pulled out a matchstick and lit it. Curling, gray smoke rose upward. The smell of sulfur filled the air. Her pulse raced as the flame neared the papers.

A noise! Her hand jerked. The match dropped into the sink.

Someone was calling. She checked her personal device. It was Cookie.

"Hi, Cookie. What's going on?"

"Hi, Leeha, are you okay?"

"Um … yeah. Why?"

"Your voice sounds shaky."

"Oh, um, my PD startled me when it went off."

She heard Cookie's laugh. "You are so funny, Leeha. Did you see the note I left on the counter?"

"Um … yeah."

"Mrs. Furley and I are almost home. We're just coming around the side of the building. I wanted to let you know in case you needed to get dressed or anything."

"Okay, thanks for letting me know."

"See you in a minute, Leeha! We're in the foyer now."

"Okay."

The call ended.

Leeha looked in the sink. The match flame had died. The document didn't have a single scorch mark on it.

Her heart sank. Her plans to destroy the weird manuscript had failed.

She stuffed the document back into the paper bag, sealed it in the plastic sack, and hid it once again under the cabinets.

The sulfur odor of the match floated through the room. She must do something about it; Cookie would notice the smell.

An idea came to her … the perfect alibi!

Leeha grabbed four tall candles and set them on the table. She'd used the candles before, so the wicks were already blackened.

She heard a noise coming from the hall. The door opened. Cookie and Mrs. Furley walked in.

Cookie set a bag of groceries on the table. "Hi, Leeha! We picked up a few more things for dinner." Cookie sniffed the air. "Do I smell smoke?"

"You do. I thought we'd break out candles. I made sure the wicks were clear."

Cookie hugged her and didn't let go. "What a nice idea, Leeha! Thank you."

"Well ... um ... you're welcome."

At last, Cookie released her.

"Hey!" Mrs. Furley said. "I hear Andecco News." She darted into the living room and stared at the viewing monitor. "Darn! It's that young fellow, Scott Walters. I was hoping to see Bob Fullerby. Have I told you girls how sexy I think he is?"

Cookie let out a cheery laugh. "Many times, Mrs. Furley. We know you have the hots for him."

Mrs. Furley stood in the living room and stared at the viewplane as she spoke. "Well, girls, we should get dinner ready. Toofy will be getting home soon."

"Leeha," Cookie said, "go ahead and rest. You worked hard. I can tell you're tired. Mrs. Furley and I played all day. We'll take care of dinner."

Mrs. Furley tapped the sofa. "That's a good idea, Leeha. You rest. I had too much caffeine, and I need to get rid of the buzz. Running around making stuff will be good for me."

Leeha plopped down on the sofa. "Okay, it's better I stay out of the kitchen anyway ... the way I cook."

Mrs. Furley headed toward the kitchen. She stopped walking after having taken only a couple of steps. Her eyes fixed on the viewplane. "Aw, that's too bad. There's a new widow in the crowd."

All Leeha saw on the viewing monitor was a sundrenched structure made of white stone. The camera panned, showing people sitting outside on chairs that were draped in dark cloth. "How do you know there's a widow?"

Mrs. Furley pointed at the image. "See, there's a lady in a purple robe and headscarf. That means she's in mourning. New widows do that. It's a thing traditional Lotish believers do. Most of the people over there in Bakhadaland are Lotish."

"I see her now," Leeha said. "She looks too young to be a widow."

Mrs. Furley's voice sounded sad. "That's how it works. Disease makes old widows. War makes young widows." She then joined Cookie in the kitchen.

Leeha found a different program to watch, a happy one showing beautiful scenery, pretty plants, and cute animals. A stray thought came to her; many of those amazing things no longer existed. She forced herself not to think about it. She stretched out on the sofa and gazed at the lovely photographs.

D'nevtnya, Bakhadaland
TUESDAY, APRIL 25, YEAR 1007 EE
4:15 A.M., WARM SEA TIME

Ina Ruzh-Venkina's body twitched. Even though she was lying down, the intensity was jolting, as if lightning had struck. An unexplained weight pressed on her. Visions of ancient tales came to mind. A demon would sit on a victim, suffocating the unfortunate soul.

She put her hands on her chest. A demon did loom over her, but not the kind from those old stories. This evil spirit had a name; it was called grief. The pain it caused was physical, yet there was something deeper about it, as if it poured into a river filled with every despair ever felt by living beings.

In a heartbeat, consciousness replaced the fogginess of sleep. Reality proved more terrible than any nightmare. She was a widow.

The smell of aromatic spices wafted through the air.

She remembered where she was. The narrow bed on which she lay was in a back room of Pada Rammak's Shinchik restaurant.

In the quiet, dark bedroom, thoughts of her husband's death haunted her. She opened her eyes, but still, she saw the Domataree Goodwill Ship as it burst into flames. It had happened so fast! In one moment, Rosik was waving to her from the deck of the old sailing vessel. In the next moment, he'd been blown to bits.

If she lay there much longer, she'd lose her mind.

Perhaps madness was a good thing; it offered an escape from reality.

As tempting as insanity seemed, however, she'd made a promise to herself—a vow she must keep. It wouldn't be long now. Izvyona, backed by their mighty Cadonan ally, would make their next move. She must be ready to avenge Rosik's death.

Recollections of the Goodwill Ship engulfed in flames faded, replaced by childhood memories of war. Thirteen years ago, during the Great Invasion, the Izvyonsk military had nearly broken Bakhadaland. She'd lost many loved ones in those battles: Aunt Tisha, Uncle Motek, her big brother's fiancée, her best childhood friend, and so many more. Then, just five years ago, Izvyona attacked again. A treaty ended the fight, but a blockade was strangling Bakhadaland.

Images of the past slipped away. Visions of her husband's death returned. Izvyona must pay—for Rosik; for his friend, Captain Garrett Dartuk; and for all those the Izvyon had stolen from her.

She envisioned the future. When sweet revenge was complete, she'd die on the battlefield. Rosik would be waiting for her on the other side. Never again would they be apart.

To get her wish, she had to clear her head. Sorrow sapped her strength. She was in no condition to fight.

Faint light seeping around window blinds called to her. Somehow, the answer she sought was waiting outside in the predawn shadows.

Her feet had just hit the floor when she heard a soft breath. Someone was in her room.

It was Tarma Nedola! Pada had set up a separate room for Tarma, yet there her friend lay, lost in sleep, using a rug as a mattress and a scrunched sweater as a pillow.

Careful not to make noise, Ina pulled her widow's mourning cloak over her head. Her toes were in her house slippers when she heard someone at the bedroom door. She threw herself onto the bed and buried herself under blankets.

Her little brother, Zerin, tiptoed into the room. He carried a quilt in his arms. He knelt beside Tarma and stretched the thick blanket over her.

It was a touching sight. Zerin and Tarma had always been close, but something had changed. No doubt remained; her baby brother and her dear friend were in love.

Zerin stood, but he didn't leave. He walked toward the bed. Did he suspect she was about to sneak away? Ina shut her eyes and lay stone still.

She heard footsteps. A door closed. She listened for telltale sounds of people moving about. Only silence met her ears.

She got up and crept out of the bedroom.

The restaurant and kitchens were dark. The hallways were empty.

Her outdoor shoes were just where she'd left them—by the private entrance.

Although no one stirred, it wasn't safe to use the family door; someone might hear her leave. Instead, she pulled on her shoes and headed for the delivery bay.

She opened the door and stepped outside. At last, she was where she longed to be: lost in the silence of the damp, dim morning.

Pebbles poked through the thin soles of her purple shoes as she made her way along a sheltered alley.

A breeze fluttered her mourning cloak when she reached a paved street.

Ina loved the hillside view. Below her—illuminated by pumpkin-colored streetlamps—stretched the roofs and treetops of D'nevtnya. At the bottom of the hill lay the harbor. Beyond rows of docks, starlight glistened on the gentle waves of the Warm Sea.

She shivered in the cool, dawn air as she strolled down a quiet sidewalk. Her heart ached. Not long ago, she and Rosik had walked that same route. Tarma, Garrett, and four other Domataree sailors from the Goodwill Ship were with them. Ina wiped tears from her cheeks. How quickly joy had turned to despair!

Bundles of fog floated by like sleeping ghosts as she made her way down the hill. The ground flattened. She stopped at a street corner. It was a special—and tragic—place, for she and Rosik had embraced there. *Ina, you're my wife,* he had told her. *We have legal standing to be together. I have family here, and you have family in Domataland. I want so badly for you to see my home in Vadsech.*

Ina clutched the Holy Triad pendant that lay hidden beneath her cloak. Even as a child, she'd admired the uncomplicated theology of the Lotish faith. The rituals, though, had seemed a waste of time. Now, as a widow, those practices had meaning. She would observe the Remembrance Rite by reliving her last journey with Rosik.

The journey's path was a short one. She arrived at the docks where the Goodwill Ship had cast off for its final voyage.

At this hour, only a few people—appearing as shadows in the faint light—wandered about. On the day the ship sank, however, a multitude of her Bakhadaree countrymen had come to bid bon voyage to the Goodwill Ship.

She cringed as sorrow ripped at her stomach. This was the place she stood when Rosik climbed the wooden gangplank. This was the place she stood when the vessel pulled away from the slip. This was the place she stood when Rosik and Garrett waved at her and Tarma from afar. This was the place she stood when the ship burst into flames.

Thumping sounds caught her attention. Farther down the harbor, a few people moved about on a fishing boat. Then, in a mix of starlight, harbor lights, and patches of fog, the vessel moved away from port and into open water.

An image popped into her mind. In the vision, sea life nibbled at pieces that had once been part of Rosik, Garrett, or other seamen from the Goodwill Ship.

Her thoughts darkened—the fish ate the bodies of Izvyonsk sailors who also perished in that short battle. She retched. What could be worse than Izvyonsk blood tainting Bakhadaree waters?

She heard Tarma's voice. "Zerin! I see her!"

Ina wished she could hide, but there was no place to go. Tarma and Zerin joined her on the dock.

"Ina!" Tarma said. "What on earth are you doing out here, all alone in the dark?"

"I had to get away. I just had to."

"Ina, if you needed to talk, why—"

"No, Tarma, I don't need to talk. I need to get ready."

Zerin said, "Ready for what?"

"I'm a widow, so I can't be a full-time National Defender. They told me I have to wait three months before I can apply again. Three months! I want to fight now! This pain I feel … I need to turn it into anger so I can make the Izvyon pay."

"Ina," Zerin said, "anger won't defeat the Izvyon."

"Anger's better than this sniveling sorrow. Look at me, Zerin. I'm pathetic."

"No, Ina, anger may seem powerful, but it's not. It makes you sloppy. The way to win is through logic and planning."

"What's wrong with you two? Can't you understand? Grief keeps me from focusing on what I need to do. It's in the way."

Tarma said, "That's why the National Defenders want you to wait three months. Rosik died, Ina. You need time to mourn. It's natural."

"How dare you speak to me this way! You're going to be a full-time National Defender. And, Zerin, you're going to be an officer in Civil Defense. An *officer!*" Ina's heart was breaking. What was she doing? She was shouting at Zerin and Tarma, two people whom she loved. A great fatigue swept over her. "Oh, my goodness! Poppa was right."

Tarma seemed confused. "Right about what, Ina?"

"Poppa warned Rosik and me that our love would bring nothing but pain. I didn't believe him."

Zerin said, "Ina, if you'd broken up with Rosik, he would've died thinking the woman he loved enough to marry, didn't love him back. Imagine how terrible that would've been for him."

Her little brother was wise. She wished for him to be a child again. That way, he could go to Domataland as a refugee as he had done during the Great Invasion. Instead, he was about to become a soldier like Rosik and Garrett.

Ina's whole body trembled. "I miss Rosik so much! As long as I live, I'll never see him again. How can I go on living knowing that?"

"I don't know, Ina," Zerin said, "but I can say this: we'll fight Izvyona on every front however and wherever we can. We'll make Cadonan scum like Senator Mitch Fischer and General Douglass Willirman regret they sided with the Izvyon. And this I believe: Domataland will stand with us. Our brothers to the north will avenge the sinking of the Goodwill Ship."

JENTON'S AUTO BODY
AND REPAIR

Cadona City, Cadona
TUESDAY, APRIL 25, YEAR 1007 EE
6:00 P.M., EAST CADONA TIME

Leeha Ritsagin heard a knock. She glanced toward the kitchen; Mrs. Furley and Cookie were busy preparing dinner.

The sofa creaked as she pushed herself upright. "Keep working, guys; I'll get the door."

Toofy had arrived. The T-shirt he wore lacked holes or stains. His large, wide hands choked the stems of fluffy, yellow flowers.

Leeha had no doubt; the bouquet was meant to impress Cookie.

Mrs. Furley's thin arms flexed as she set a big, steaming pot on the kitchen table. "Dinner's almost ready. Why don't you two worker bees sit down and rest a bit? Oh, look! Toofy, you brought flowers. How gentlemanly of you!"

A big, goofy grin and a scruffy afternoon shadow made him seem silly. "Pretty flowers for pretty ladies." He took a seat. "Whatever's in that pot smells yummy."

"It does smell awesome in here," Leeha said. "I'm starved. I'll set the table and get a bowl for the flowers."

Mrs. Furley feigned a stern look. "You will do no such thing, young lady. Setting the table is my job."

Leeha obeyed and settled into a chair. Toofy paid her no attention.

He rested his rough elbows on the tabletop. With a goofball grin still etched on his face, he stared in Cookie's direction. Leeha watched her, too. Cookie was hard to ignore. She moved like water. Her skinny waist pivoted above a firm and rounded bottom. Her uplifted bosom pushed out the top of the apron that she wore. Kitchen lights reflected on her raven hair as a moon glistened in the night sky.

Something flashed.

It was just Mrs. Furley lighting the candles. "Sorry, Leeha. I didn't mean to startle you. You looked like you were on the other side of the Earth. You must be exhausted."

"Yeah, I am pretty tired."

"A good meal will refresh you, dear."

"Yeah, food usually does that for me." Leeha peered at her round belly. No doubt it was her love of food that kept her from having a waistline like Cookie's.

Mrs. Furley finished setting the table. Cookie brought more food.

Dinner reminded Leeha of a fancy restaurant. The big, steaming pot contained homemade soup. A pile of spicy rice and colorful shish kebabs filled a platter. An array of leafy vegetables rested in a shiny bowl.

Every bite was as delicious as the last.

She heard Cookie's laughter-filled voice. "Leeha, are you ignoring Toofy's question?"

"Sorry, Toofy, what question?"

"I was wondering how the security system in the Monarch is working out for you."

She wiped soup oil from her lips. "Great! It works great. I always scan the parking lot before getting in and out of my car. I feel lots safer."

"How's the car running?" Toofy asked.

"Seems good."

"You're fibbing, Leeha," Cookie said. "The air conditioner has been out for days, and the weather's already getting hot."

Toofy grabbed another shish kebab. "Heck, that's easy. I can fix it for you ladies."

"Thanks," Leeha said.

Soothing background music stopped. Andecco News Service's lively melody blared through the room. A voice came through the sound array.

Mrs. Furley let go of her fork. "Oh! Oh! That's Bob Fullerby!" She dashed into the living room.

"Grandma," Toofy said, "if you're going to watch the news, then turn the viewplane so we can all see it."

Mrs. Furley adjusted the position of the viewing monitor stand. She zipped back to the table. "Bob's talking about Flight Ten Seventy. It sounds like General Willirman is lying about what happened to the airplane."

Cadona City, Cadona
TUESDAY, APRIL 25, YEAR 1007 EE
6:30 P.M., EAST CADONA TIME

Andecco News Service Assistant Investigative Journalist Rona Betler turned the cardboard sign so the word *closed* would face outward. Beyond the big, front window of the print shop building, a few fat raindrops fell from a gray sky. The drops struck the cracked, concrete walkway and weedy lawn. A handful of cars chugged down the street. Not much happened in this dying neighborhood.

Yesterday, one customer—a little, old lady—asked for a glossy print of a beloved dog who had died. Three days ago, an elderly couple wanted several copies of their wills. But today, not a single patron had visited.

Most of the time, a lack of customers was a good thing. They pulled her away from the real reason she spent so much time in the print shop: researching stories for Andecco News Service.

On this day, though, a customer would've been a welcome relief. Searching for a photo of one particular car in a huge stack of traffic camera images was about as stimulating as watching a snail race.

Rona returned to the windowless back room and settled into a chair by the big wooden table.

She picked up a photo from a pile of printed pictures and held it up to the reader. Two red lights popped on. The brown car in the photograph was not a Monarch. She added the photo to the tall, *no* pile.

The next image was also a *no*.

The third—*inconclusive*. She put the grainy picture in the short, *maybe* stack.

Her personal device buzzed. Bob Fullerby was calling.

"Hi, Mr. Fullerby."

"Hello, Row. I'm sending a couple of files your way."

"What are the files for?"

"Two topics: Flight Ten Seventy and the unrest in Bakhadaland."

"What do you want me to do with the files?"

"Save them offline."

"Nothing else?"

"No, you need to focus on finding the mystery woman's Monarch."

"Okay, I got it covered, Mr. Fullerby."

"Thanks, Row." The line went silent.

Rona stored the files and tapped her personal device. News alerts scrolled on the viewplane.

The J2 virus, upcoming elections, and growing hostility between Izvyona and Bakhadaland took second stage. The hot topic: an airliner, International Flight 1070, bound for Fewwok, exploded deep inside Domataland's Outerland Region. General Douglass Willirman blamed Domataland. Defense Secretary Richard Karther said the cause of the explosion remained unclear. Whatever happened, over twelve hundred passengers and crew members had been killed.

Rona switched off the streaming ticker. Reading it was distracting her from her assignment.

She took a long drink of coffee and grabbed another printed photograph.

Something was different about this photo. The vehicle in the picture had a familiar dent in the hood. Also, this car was a Monarch, no question about it. She held the photo up to the reader and tapped the touchpad. The words, *match in process,* appeared on the viewplane.

A wave of excitement ran through her as the computer compared the traffic camera picture to their Drop Case bug-eye images of the Monarch.

A green light popped on. Progress at last! The dent in the hood captured in the traffic camera picture matched the dent caught by their bug-eyes.

Software next compared other characteristics. Scratches on the automobile doors—match! Smashed taillight—match! Crushed rear license plate—match!

This might be the mystery woman's brown Monarch! It really, truly might be!

Rona tapped the touchpad. The computer's comparison of the drivers came back as inconclusive due to the quality of the traffic camera photo. The woman behind the wheel, however, did have long, light hair, just like the mystery woman in the bug-eye video.

The next step ... figure out where the traffic camera picture was taken.

She sent a map to the wall monitor. A blinking light pointed to a narrow street in the Warrenton District.

Now, she needed to check the timing. Rona found a date timestamp on the traffic camera image. She compared it to the date and time the mystery woman was parked by Hatchets Bar, as captured by the bug-eyes.

The sequence of events fit! The mystery woman could've easily driven from Hatchets Bar to that Warrenton District street in the allotted time.

Next question ... where would the mystery woman have been going? The Monarch was damaged. Maybe the driver was heading to a repair shop. It was worth a look.

WorldLink found a garage in the area where the traffic camera photo was taken: Jenton's Auto Body and Repair.

Rona grabbed her personal device, but decided against calling. People responded better to reporters who showed up in person. Jenton's was open until eight p.m. If she hurried, she would be able to drive there before the garage closed for the day.

She sent an encrypted message to teammates Angela Thirgal and Kever Carsen: *Got a lead on the car. Going to Jenton's.*

Rona didn't bother her boss. Bob Fullerby, no doubt, was up-to-his-eyeballs busy with the downing of Flight 1070.

When Rona arrived at the garage, only a few customers were waiting in line.

She spotted two employees.

A tall, slender man with blond hair stood behind a counter. He was busy helping patrons. Another employee, a middle-aged man, was explaining to a couple what Jenton's options were for automotive decals.

An old guy emerged through a repair-bay door. "Young lady, have you been helped?"

"No, not yet. I hope I'm not too late. I realize it's almost closing time."

"Nonsense! I'll find someone to assist you." The man disappeared from view.

Moments later, another employee appeared. He was young and tall. His grumpy expression vanished when he looked her way. His gorgeous, dark eyes sparkled. "May I help you?"

"Yes, I have a few questions."

The man plopped an unruly stack of papers on the countertop and headed toward her. He walked with a swagger. "I'm Degio Ellis. How may I be of service?"

"Degio, good evening. My name is Rona Betler. I work for Andecco News. I'm investigating a story." She showed him her press badge.

"Andecco? I love Andecco!" he said. "So, what kind of story would involve Jenton's? Not much exciting happens around here ... not until you walked in the door, that is." He flashed a giant smile. "Whatcha need?"

"Degio, if there's something you need to finish—"

"Nope, Ms. Betler, I'm done for the day."

The last customer left.

The blond guy behind the counter said, "Hey, Degio, I'll close up in back. See you tomorrow."

"Thanks, Ray. Have a good night."

Degio was now the only person with her in the lobby. Rona felt his stare. He knew how to do it, where it was impossible to ignore his splashy eyes and smile.

"Say, Ms. Betler, the Axe Grinder Pub is just around the corner. It's not fancy, but they serve good brew. The coffees and teas aren't bad either. Neither is the food. We can talk over drinks or snacks. I'm buying."

"Sure, the Axe Grinder sounds great."

Degio pushed open a glass door. "My lady, after you."

They walked outside. A mist was falling.

"It's raining," Degio said. "The pub's only two blocks away, but I'd hate for you to get wet. We can take my car. It's a classic Dynamo Roadster, completely rebuilt. Did the overhaul myself. Get lots of good offers for her, but, hey, she's my baby. I know when to hold on to a good thing when I find it."

Rona unfolded her flowery, lavender umbrella. "I'm up for walking. Are you?"

"Whatever you wish, my lady."

Raindrops tapped against her umbrella as she sent a message to Angela and Kever: *Having a drink with Degio Ellis, an employee at Jenton's.*

Degio opened the Axe Grinder's heavy door. Boisterous laughter and loud voices rolled out.

"Looks like there are two seats at the end of the bar," Degio said. "Do you want to sit there or wait for a table?"

"The bar's fine with me."

Rona was aware of Degio's stare as they made their way across the sticky floor. Her skirt rose high on her thighs as she climbed onto a barstool. Degio kind-of-sort-of pretended not to gawk at her legs.

A barmaid approached. Thick mascara fused her eyelashes together. "Degio, you back again?"

"Hello, Penny. I can't seem to stay away."

"Do you folks know what you want?"

Degio said, "We'll take menus, please."

Penny handed them menus. They were dog-eared and stained. "Take your time. I'll check back in a minute." She strutted away.

Rona watched as Penny leaned on the bar to chat with guys wearing paint-splattered work clothes. Penny's generous cleavage peeked out from the old, checkered shirt that she wore. Despite the size of her bosoms and derrière, her waist was tiny and firm. She was tall, her hair was too blond, and the red of her lips too bright. Rona liked her. Penny reminded her of women from Cadona's rugged past, the kind of women who, even at eight months pregnant, could swing a bale of hay as well as any man.

"Ms. Betler," Degio said, "if you're uncomfortable here, we can go somewhere else. I mean, if this isn't your kind of place …."

"Are you kidding? I love it here. There's no pretense."

In a booming voice, a drunk guy a few stools down told Penny, "I've been waiting for you all my life, doll."

Rona leaned against Degio's muscular shoulder and said, "Well, I guess I should've said there's no *serious* pretense. Working class and laid-back. This is exactly my kind of place."

A smile covered Degio's face. "Ms. Betler, you are my kind of woman."

Penny swung her hips as she approached. "Okay, kids, what can I getcha?"

"I'll have the usual," Degio said, "and those pretzels with the gooey cheese in the middle."

"You got it. And how 'bout you, sweetie?"

"I'll try cinnamon hot chocolate," Rona said. "As unsweet as you can make it, please."

"Oh, I can make it as sour as you want, hon."

"Good, I like it *way* unsweet."

Penny gave her a wink. "I'll bring you a side of sugar just in case." Penny walked away.

"Ms. Betler," Degio said, "I know we came here because of a story you're working on. How may I help?"

"I'm trying to track down a car, a brown Monarch sedan. We believe it's a seventeen-year-old model."

Rona saw a look of surprise on Degio's face. His voice turned serious. "You're the second one to ask about a brown Monarch."

"Someone else was asking?"

"Yeah, yesterday. Three suits showed up at the garage. They said they were military intelligence special agents. They had badges, but something didn't seem right about those guys … not that I know many intelligence special agents."

"What did they want?"

"They asked if we'd seen a brown, year-nine-ninety Monarch in the last six weeks or so. They want to find the car and the owner."

"Did they say why?"

"All they said is it was a matter of national security."

"What did you tell them?"

"Nothing. Our computer's been down. It's quite a mess. Our local backups are fried, and, come to find out, our backups to WorldLink Remote Storage quit happening over a year ago when our tech provider changed ownership. So, lately, we've been making do with whatever paper files we can scrounge up."

"Is the data permanently lost?"

"Apparently not. We got tech guys working on it. They think they can recover most of the data, but it'll take them four or five more days. I told the suits I'd contact them when our records are restored."

"Degio, do you have any memory of a brown Monarch in your shop?"

"At the time the agents came in, I didn't. I mean, Monarchs aren't exactly unforgettable. But after the guys left, I did kind of remember working on an old Monarch."

"What kinds of repairs did you make?"

"I'm not sure, but somehow, I remember a window. Candy thought it was weird that the window wouldn't roll up, but the glass didn't break."

"Who's Candy?" Rona asked.

"Candy Fellerman. She's been out. Her grandpa's really ill. She's away visiting him."

"What did Candy have to do with the Monarch?"

"She assists me with repairs, and she does a courtesy cleaning after the repairs are made."

"You haven't told the agents what you remembered?"

"Not yet," Degio said. "I'll have to contact them when the computer's fixed, but, like I said, I didn't like the looks of those guys." He flashed a smile. "However, I do like the looks of you. I'll give you a call when I know something."

"Thanks, Degio, I appreciate it."

"Anything for you, pretty lady."

Rona's mind raced. What a thrilling moment! Hours of hard work had led her and Andecco teammates to this point; a month-long investigation might be nearing its end. The brown Monarch that Degio worked on might be *the* brown Monarch. Many pieces fit. A lady named Pam Urzin from the True Followers of God Church had thrown the document into the car's back seat through the open, rear passenger side window. Degio and Candy might have fixed that very window.

She felt Degio's hand on her shoulder. "Hey, it looks like the band is about ready to play. Wanna dance?"

"Sure, sounds fun."

BAPTISM

"The True Followers of God Church Compass can be seen far and wide all across Cadona. By God's hand, our church has become the largest religious body in our blessed nation. The Compass lights the way."

Pastor Leon Walls
"Celebrate God's People" Service
Year 1007 of the Enlightened Epoch

Cadona City, Cadona
TUESDAY, APRIL 25, YEAR 1007 EE
9:30 P.M., EAST CADONA TIME

Leeha Ritsagin savored the taste of a poached pear.

She remembered that she had friends over for dinner when she heard Mrs. Furley's voice. "Leeha, what do you think? Do you think Bradley Seldortin can beat Mitch Fischer?"

"I don't know; I hope so."

Cookie said, "I believe he will. People will eventually see the Freedom Party for what it is. People will realize Senator Fischer is a liar and Senator Rineburg is insane."

Toofy spoke before swallowing the food in his mouth. "I agree, Cookie. People will see that General Willirman is turning the military into Fischer's private army. I wouldn't be a bit surprised if Willirman's lying about Flight Ten Seventy. Do you want to hear something crazy? That jet might have flown right over us, since it had to fly up north because of those nutty dust storms."

"What do you think about Flight Ten Seventy, Leeha?" Mrs. Furley asked. "Do you believe General Willirman? Or do you think he's fibbin'?"

"I ... I don't know. I just heard about the plane as I was leaving the office. Two girls I work with told me about it, but they're into really weird religious stuff. I never know when to believe what they say."

Mrs. Furley shook her head and clicked her tongue. "Oh, are the girls True Followers?"

"Yeah, they're totally into it."

"Oh, you poor dear. Do they carry on nonstop about the world ending?"

"Boy, do they ever. They spend more time preaching than doing their jobs. Seems like more and more people at work are getting into that crazy stuff."

"I run into a lot of them at the casino, too," Mrs. Furley said, "and at the bingo hall."

Toofy sighed as he leaned back in his chair. His wide, hairy hands rested on his pudgy belly. Crumbs and shiny grease covered the afternoon shadow circling his lips. "The True Followers may be crazy insane, but this chocolate cake is crazy delicious."

"It sure is," Mrs. Furley said. "Cookie, you work wonders in the kitchen. You could be a professional chef."

A big, goofy grin crossed Toofy's face. "I second that."

"You're embarrassing me," Cookie said, "but I'm glad you enjoyed the meal." She rose and stacked dirty dishes. Toofy never took his eyes off her.

Leeha felt an urge to be jealous, but she was too tired to pay attention to such an energy-sucking emotion. Besides, Toofy wasn't her type. He seemed a nice guy, and he had his talents, but Mrs. Furley's grandson was too boorish for her tastes. Leeha stood and picked up her plate.

"Leeha, no," Cookie said. "You worked a long, hard day. I've got this; you rest."

Mrs. Furley scooted her chair away from the table.

Cookie wagged a finger. "That goes for you, too, Mrs. Furley. I can handle it myself."

"You sure, dear?"

"Yep. Go ahead and have more tea while I get the plates out of the way."

Mrs. Furley flashed a big, yellow-toothed smile. "You truly are a sweetie, dear. Those bruises of yours are healing fast. I can barely see 'em."

"Yes, thank goodness. Most of the swelling is gone. Makeup hides the weird colors."

Toofy fidgeted in his seat. "I can't believe that fricken idiot hit you. I swear, if your ex ever bothers you again, I'll crush his skull."

"Thanks, Toofy. With luck, he'll never find me here."

Mrs. Furley rested a hand on Toofy's arm. "Toofy, mind driving me to the casino? I'm feeling a tingle; luck is with me."

"Now? Grandma, I have to work the early shift tomorrow."

"Okay, okay. Work, work! That's all you young people do. Tomorrow, then. You'll drive me to the casino tomorrow afternoon."

"We'll see, Grandma. You should be careful. Those places get crowded. What if you catch J2?"

"What's the use in worryin'? I'm old. I'm bound to get sick sometime. *Live while you're alive,* that's my motto."

Leeha couldn't keep herself from yawning.

Mrs. Furley said, "Cookie, dear, are you sure you don't need help cleaning up?"

"Nope, I got it covered."

Mrs. Furley blew out the candles. "Come on, Toofy. Let's let Leeha rest. She started work at the crack of dawn."

"You don't have to rush off, Mrs. Furley," Leeha said.

"Yes, we do. You're sleepy. In any case, Toofy has to be an early bird tomorrow."

Toofy grabbed a dessert bar before standing. He and his grandma strolled to the apartment door. Mrs. Furley said, "Good night, girls. Cookie, thanks again for dinner. Next time I'll bring wine."

After they left, the room grew quiet except for the sounds of clinking dishes and water running from the faucet.

Leeha yawned again. Her eyelids felt heavy.

"Leeha," Cookie said, "why don't you relax?"

"I am relaxing." Her body slumped into the chair. As her mind wandered, worries crept from the shadows. She tapped her personal device.

Cookie gave her a scolding look. "Leeha, are you working?"

"No, I'm checking to see if the computer identified the wormy guy."

"Anything?"

"Nope, nothing yet."

"It'll take a while," Cookie said.

"Yeah, I know, but he gives me the creeps." She stared at his picture. "He's so gross! And I bet he's stronger than he looks. Cookie, doesn't it bug you that he might still be out there?"

"A little, but I'm sure if he comes around, Toofy will chase him off again."

"Yeah, you're probably right. Well, I'm going to brush my teeth." Leeha had not yet risen from the chair when her personal device buzzed. Her brother, Jeremy, from New Cadona, was calling.

"Hey, Leeha," Jeremy said, "glad I caught you at home. When I called on your birthday, I wanted to talk more, but Sonna and I had stuff to do."

"Not a problem. What are you up to?"

"I know this will surprise you, sis, since I've never been much of a religious person, but I'm really lovin' our new church."

"Oh, is there a new Kettish church where you live?"

"No, Sonna and I left the Kettish faith. We started going to the True Followers. We were baptized this morning. We got Skyla baptized, too. And we got our unborn son blessed."

True Followers? Did Jeremy say *True Followers*?

"Leeha, you still there?"

"Um, do you mean the True Followers of God Church?" Her heart was pounding. No way was Jeremy that crazy!

"Yeah! We're really into it. I'm telling you, Leeha, this church has really opened our eyes. We started doing volunteer work for the Family First Initiative. Have you heard of it? The Back-to-Basics Club program?"

"Yes, I heard of it." She hoped to hear a laugh or the words *just kidding*.

"Leeha, have you ever gone to a True Followers service?"

"Um, once."

"Pretty awesome, don't you think?" he said. "Was it Pastor Walls' Sunday Sunrise Service?"

"No." She thought she might vomit. The thought of Jeremy joining the True Followers ....

Nothing about his voice suggested he was joking. "Man, if we lived over there, we'd go see Pastor Walls every week. You are so lucky to be in Cadona City! Who's the pastor where you went?"

"I ... I don't remember who the regular guy is. They had a guest speaker when I went. A total cuckoo called *Pastor Townly*."

"Pastor Townly! I've listened to him. Ah, man! I'd give anything to see him in person."

"Jeremy, please tell me you're joking."

"What do you mean, sis?"

"You are kidding me, right. You didn't really join that band of crazies, did you?"

He didn't say anything.

"Jeremy?"

"Leeha, I'm ... I'm serious. These people know what they're talking about. We've been called to battle, Leeha."

His words reminded her of the weird document hidden beneath the kitchen cabinets. Written inside those crazy pages were Back-to-Basics Club plans to start a war with Domataland. On top of that, there was all the bizarre stuff about killing one hundred women on the justice execution list, taking over the Cadonan press, and silencing Bob Fullerby. She forced herself to speak calmly. "Battle? What battle?"

"The *Last War*, Leeha! It's coming! Bezgog's children are preparing to kill us."

"Us?"

"Yeah, us! God's children. We Cadonans are God's children. It makes so much sense. The End of Time is upon us!"

"Jeremy, you cannot possibly believe this stuff."

"It's all true, Leeha! My eyes have been opened. Everything fits. Domataland is the modern nation that was once the Nastebyan Kingdom. Demnar Tarish is the *Last Ruler* of the Nastebyans, just like the prophecy says. He's Bezgog's chosen king. All the signs point to it. It's written right there in the Holy Books: *'The King of the Nastebyans shall raise his lightning-sword against God's holy people.'*"

"And … and Sonna's with you on this?"

"Oh, yeah! Totally! And Skyla loves it."

"Jeremy, Skyla's a little kid."

"I know! Amazing, isn't it? God's moving through Skyla, Leeha. And when God moves through you, you'll know what it's like. They treat us so well, sis. They're helping Sonna pay her medical bills. They helped us find a great pediatrician. And we refinanced our apartment through the Back-to-Basics Club lenders program. Sonna, Skyla, and I are going to a Life March that's coming up soon."

"Life March? W … what's that?"

"We're going to stop abortion, Leeha. Stop it all! It'll be death for anyone involved in abortion. When Mitch Fischer becomes president in October, he'll make it happen. He'll line the abortionists up and shoot them. I tell you, when I hear True Followers pastors speak, I hear God's trumpets."

"Jeremy, what did they do to you? Give you some kind of drug?"

"The Blessed Drug, Leeha! God is my drug. And he can be your drug, too."

"Jeremy, please tell me you're joking because it is not funny."

"Leeha, for the first time in my life, I *understand* life. It's miraculous!"

"How could you believe this crazy stuff?"

"It's not crazy. They're right."

"Who? Who's right?"

"The True Followers of God Church, the Back-to-Basics Club, Pastor Leon Walls, Pastor Townly, Pastor Phillip Walls, Pastor Mark Walzelesskii. They're God's prophets put here to show us the way."

"Jeremy, listen to me. You need to talk to a Kettish priest."

"The Kettish faith is a false faith, Leeha. All these long years, we've been deceived. At last, The Light has come to free us! God has chosen Cadonans to be his people in his fight against Bezgog."

"Jeremy, how can you believe this?"

"Leeha, look at the terrible things Domataland is doing! They've weaponized the J2 virus and infected us with it. They shot an airliner out of the sky with over a thousand people on board. Domataland is building up its troops along the borders with Izvyona and Bakhadaland. They are sending weapons and supplies to Bakhadaree separatists. What more proof do you need? Look, Leeha, I can tell you're surprised; I get it. I was once where you are. I understand. I will pray for you, Leeha. I will pray that God leads you to Pastor Leon Walls and Pastor Mark Walzelesskii. They'll fill you with the True Followers' Light, too. Listen, I need to go. I'll call back soon." The line grew silent.

Leeha heard Cookie's soothing voice. "Leeha, what's wrong? Is your brother okay?"

"No! He … he and Sonna joined the True Followers of God Church."

"You're kidding!"

"I wish I were. They were baptized this morning."

Cadona City, Cadona
THURSDAY, APRIL 27, YEAR 1007 EE
8:00 A.M., EAST CADONA TIME

Investigative journalist Bob Fullerby stepped off a city bus. Despite the crowd, more travelers packed into the outdoor platforms of the Central Commuter Train Station. In what seemed a choreographed, umbrella-carrying ritual, people paraded down concrete walkways. Several individuals in the crowd wore respiratory paper filters in the faint hope that the thin masks would shield them from the J2 virus.

Bob trotted through drizzle to Platform Number 7. He hunched inside a shelter and waited for his contact.

The ground shook; signals clanged. Wheels squealed as a train came to a stop. Passengers poured out from the wagons.

One of the passengers, a tall, lanky fellow, caught Bob's eye. The man wore a ratty rain jacket. Shoelaces—held together by bulky knots—laced through grungy footwear. At a glance, the man seemed a typical Cadona City bum, but something was amiss. The fellow's smooth, straight-backed gait betrayed the story the ragged attire attempted to tell. His black hair, although long and uncombed, recently had a barber's touch; the strands were too shiny and too even to belong to a person of the street.

The man zigzagged through the crowd, but his path took him toward the rain shield at the end of Platform Number 7. Despite the cheap mask hiding most of the man's face, Bob recognized the fellow: Pastor Mark Walzelesskii, the Drop Case informant.

"Mr. Fullerby, good morning."

"Pastor Walzelesskii, hello. You do know that the thing on your face can only do so much to protect you from J2, right? The virus can go through the skin."

"Yeah, but the mask may prevent someone from recognizing me."

"Good point. You're learning how to be sly, I see."

"I … guess you're right, Mr. Fullerby. I hadn't thought of it like that. It's a shame the world must be this way."

"Yes, it is a shame. You have news for me, Pastor?"

"I do. It's about the Guiding Light."

"Has your father recovered it?"

"No, the document is still missing, but I've learned more about the warning messages."

"What warning messages?"

"Do you remember me telling you about a justice execution list in the Guiding Light?"

"Ah, I believe I do, Pastor. As I recall, the messages were sent from the Hughes Medical Center. You told me that someone warned the women on the list that they may be in danger because Mary Kronvelt was on the list, and she was murdered. What's the new info?"

"My dad got an auto-mail from Zoff, whoever he is. Zoff and another person called *Hands* figured out that the warning messages were sent from the public communications hub at Hughes. And there's something else; whoever sent the messages made it look like they went out on April eighth, a day earlier than they really did."

"Hmm, that means our sender is tech-savvy," Bob said. "Do they have a lead on the sender?"

"Not really. Zoff was ranting because tracking systems inside the hub were turned off at the time. But he did get his hands on a security image of the Hughes parking lot. You'll never guess what's in the picture, Mr. Fullerby."

"What?"

"A brown Monarch, can you believe it?"

"Does Zoff think it's the mystery woman's vehicle?"

"There's a chance it might be, but only a part of the car is in the image, so they can't be sure."

"That Monarch gets around," Bob said. "What else you got?"

"Zoff's been trying to figure out if Senator Sandra Pettock and Detective Carl Brunish were involved with the warning messages or the Guiding Light's disappearance. So far, he's found no link."

"You bring interesting news, Pastor. Our mystery woman not only stole the Guiding Light, she may have also sent the warning messages. It appears Pettock and Brunish aren't helping her, so who is?"

"I don't know, Mr. Fullerby, and I don't think my dad does either. I read something else on my dad's computer that you may be interested in; some guy named *Randy Beller* mentioned a drug called *Mind-One*."

"Mind-One? Wow! I haven't heard that term in a long time."

"Do you know what it is, Mr. Fullerby?"

"Yeah, it was a truth serum the military experimented with a long time ago. They dropped the program because the drug had mixed results and made people sick."

"Well, Mr. Fullerby, the military must be using it again because Randy Beller says they're making Mind-One at Hansen Hills."

"The Hansen Hills Federal Facility?"

"Yeah, they're running low on doses, but they're six to eight weeks from producing more batches. They've tested it on three prisoners so far."

"What?" Bob said. "The military is holding prisoners at the Hills again?"

"It sounds like it, Mr. Fullerby."

"Wow! This is disturbing news. The only activity that's supposed to take place at the Hills is urban warfare training."

"I'm glad you find the information useful, Mr. Fullerby. I'll see what else I can dig up. I wish I could get the info to you faster. Security is tight. The only way I can read my dad's auto-mails is to use the computer in his office in the True Followers headquarters."

"Pastor, that fact alone proves how important your dad and General Willirman think this information is. Be careful. I can't stress it enough."

"I'll be careful, Mr. Fullerby. Sorry, but I've got to run. I'm on my way to the homeless shelter in Westville. I need to assess the J2 situation there since I'm in charge."

"In charge of what?"

"Senator Fischer and my dad want me to lead a medical response to the J2 crisis in Cadona City."

"You?"

"That was my reaction," Mark said. "Maybe I'll bring you good news one day, Mr. Fullerby."

"Knowing you will take charge of the J2 crisis is music to my ears, Pastor. You're a dedicated young man. You'll get things done."

"Thanks for your confidence in me, but I haven't the slightest idea what I'm doing."

"If it's any consolation, Pastor, I've been doing my job for over thirty years, yet every day I face new situations where I have to wing it."

"I find it hard to believe," Mark said.

"It's the truth, Pastor. Take the Flight Ten Seventy thing. I have no idea what happened to the airplane, except that it blew up. Someone's lying, but I can't tell if it's General Douglass Willirman or President Demnar Tarish. General Willirman loves crafting his nutty conspiracy theories, and Domataland has a long history of playing deadly political games."

7

KING OF THE NASTEBYANS

Cadona City, Cadona
THURSDAY, APRIL 27, YEAR 1007 EE
8:30 A.M., EAST CADONA TIME

Leeha Ritsagin heard footsteps in the hallway near her office cubicle. The sounds came to an abrupt halt.

Jilly said, "Hey, Leeha! Guess what?"

Leeha swung around in her swivel chair. Both Jilly and Rebecca stood at the entrance to her office.

Rebecca said, "Leeha, knowing you, you haven't heard the news."

"Probably not, I've been working."

Jilly spoke in an excited voice. "This is really, really important. Senator Mitch Fischer made an announcement; our military figured out what Domataland used to shoot down Flight Ten Seventy."

Leeha knew what was coming—more True Followers of God Church nonsense. "That's good. Now, the matter will get resolved." She was about to turn the chair around to face the viewplane, but Jilly had more to say. "Rebecca, tell Leeha what Domataland did."

Rebecca spoke in a slow, deep voice. "Domataland used an old, really small rocket called *BDM-Fifty*. It's launched from the ground. It's usually not used for shooting down high-flying aircraft."

Leeha knew she should end the conversation, but the urge to argue got the better of her. "Hmm, that seems odd. I heard the airliner was flying way up high when it exploded. Why would Domataland use a weapon not made for high-flying aircraft?"

After several silent seconds, Rebecca said, "Because BDM-Fifty rockets are little, so they're hard to spot."

"But how did they hit a high-flying aircraft with a weapon that isn't designed to go high?" Leeha asked.

Irritation filled Jilly's words. "I don't know, but that's what happened. Senator Fischer says so. General Willirman agrees with him."

Once again, Rebecca's voice turned ominously deep. "Leeha, we need to remember that we're dealing with Domats; they're Bezgog's offspring."

Jilly's eyes widened. "I bet Bezgog guided the missile!"

Leeha fought to keep her eyebrows from raising. Jilly and Rebecca were getting goofier every day.

Jilly said, "This is so exciting! Don't you think, Leeha?"

"Over a thousand people were killed, Jilly. How can you think it's exciting?"

"Because it proves the End of Time is upon us! Demnar Tarish, the King of the Nastebyans, is making his move just like the Holy Books predicted."

"Not only that," Rebecca said, "it proves President Meyfeld and Defense Secretary Karther are catering to President Tarish instead of standing up to him. Senator Seldortin is doing the same thing. We need Mitch Fischer as president. He'll send Bezgog's son, Demnar Tarish, straight to Hell where he belongs."

Leeha's ire rose. "Are you saying Senator Seldortin won't stand up to Domataland?"

Jilly put her hands on her hips. "Bradley Seldortin is a coward. I bet he's in league with Bezgog."

"Or," Rebecca said, "Bezgog deceived Senator Seldortin. It's easy to be deceived if you don't follow God."

"Wait a minute," Leeha said, "I thought Senator Seldortin's religious."

Jilly was almost shouting. "He's Kettish!"

Rebecca pointed a finger in Leeha's direction. "Remember, Leeha, the Kettish Church worships a false god. Worshipping a false god has worse consequences than worshipping no god."

An image of a Kettish prayer medallion popped into Leeha's mind. The medallion was hers; it was sitting on a shelf in the family farmhouse. Cookie also had a medallion; when she wasn't wearing it, she kept in on her pillow. Leeha could take no more. This conversation must end. "Well, thanks for letting me know about the rocket."

"You're welcome," Jilly said. "Do you believe us now? The End of Time is upon us! The Last War is about to begin."

Leeha ignored the question. "Are you still planning to listen to Pastor Townly at the True Followers service tomorrow night?"

Jilly's eyes glowed. "Yes, we can't wait!"

"Leeha," Rebecca said, "have you changed your mind about going? Do you want to come with us?"

"You know, we've lots of stuff to get done by the end of the week. If we don't finish it, we'll be working late tomorrow. You wouldn't want to be late for the service, would you?"

"No way!" Jilly said. "We don't want to miss a single word! Pastor Townly is inspired by God."

Rebecca put her hand on Jilly's shoulder. "Leeha's right, we better get our work done."

Jilly and Rebecca hustled out of the cubicle. Thank goodness!

Ver-Nuvelin, Domataland
THURSDAY, APRIL 27, YEAR 1007 EE
7:00 P.M., CENTRAL FEWWOK TIME

President Demnar Tarish spread butter over a thick slice of dark, hearty bread. The Presidential Compound cafeteria, which was bustling at six o'clock, emptied by seven. An elderly ruzhman, who had worked for the Domataree government for decades, was the only other diner.

A waiter appeared as Demnar was about to raise a spoonful of stew to his lips. The young man's voice trembled with nervousness. "Honorable President, may I bring you anything else? More tea, perhaps?"

Demnar removed the teapot lid. The robust fragrance of Lowland Golden escaped in a puff of steam. "I have enough tea, thank you, but I'd like dessert after I finish the stew."

"We have yellowberry cobbler; I hope that will suffice, Honorable President."

"Yellowberry cobbler is perfect, thank you."

"Very good, Honorable President. I'll check back with you shortly." The waiter bowed and raced away.

In the silence of the dining room, Demnar's fast-paced thoughts slowed. Solutions to the world's complex problems, though, eluded him. He touched the wall next to his table. A window formed. He gazed at the garden view. Newborn leaves in vibrant shades of green glowed like a multitude of tiny lights in the evening sun. Early blooming flowers had faded, but a new round of blossoms hurried to show off their own splendor.

"Spring is here," a familiar voice said. Intelligence Chief Rozula Kolensha stood near the table. She wore dark exercise clothes. A Goodwill Ship memorial ribbon was pinned to the cloth.

"Yes, Rozula, spring has definitely arrived. I'm surprised to see you here. You've been putting in lots of hours. I thought you would've already left to enjoy the nice weather."

"I was afraid if I went home, I'd find an excuse to skip my workout."

"I know how that goes. Have you ordered anything, Rozula?"

"A lilac protein shake. I like to order flavors to match the season. Lilac fits the bill."

Demnar knew what Rozula was up to; she was trying to cheer him up. He gestured toward the chair on the other side of the table. "Would you care to join me?"

"Sure." She took a seat. Concern reflected in her blue eyes. "I told you my reason for being here late, Demnar. What's yours?"

"I have a few more briefs to read. I needed a break; I thought a meal might help me make sense of things."

"Is it helping?"

Demnar took a sip of tea. "No, not really."

The waiter brought Rozula her drink.

"That smells good," Demnar said. "I can smell lilac from here."

"Would you like a sip?" She handed him the cup.

The thick liquid tasted cold and fresh. "It's quite good," he said.

The waiter returned. "Honorable President, your yellowberry cobbler."

"Thank you, it looks delicious."

The waiter bowed and walked away.

Rozula leaned forward and eyed the dessert.

Demnar said, "Would you like to try it?"

"Sure, if you're willing to share."

"I am." He held a forkful of cobbler to her mouth. She shut her eyes as she chewed.

"So, Rozula, what's the verdict?"

"It is extraordinary!"

"Would you like another bite?"

"Yes, but the rest is yours. You have briefs to review, after all."

He noticed a tiny crumb sticking to the left corner of her lips. Demnar picked up her napkin and dabbed away the speck of crust. Her breath, moist and warm, brushed over his fingers.

Her voice lost its playful tone. "Honorable President, since you have many things on your mind, would you like to bounce thoughts off me? Sometimes talking things through helps."

Demnar wanted her carefree mood to continue, but work was work, and he was her boss. "Rozula, our problems keep growing. Cadona blamed us for turning the J2 virus into a biological warfare agent, and now they're blaming us for shooting Flight Ten Seventy out of the sky. Cadona isn't going to stop. They're itching to find other ways to discredit us, and if we face them head-on, we'll lose."

Rozula pushed a lock of pale blond hair away from her pretty face. "And a direct fight is what Cadona wants, Honorable President. They proved it when they gave Izvyona the go-ahead to sink the Goodwill Ship. The Freedom Party is obsessed with military power. When their Toxic

Sphere weapons system goes live, Cadona's advantage in open warfare will grow."

"Our only shot at protecting ourselves," Demnar said, "is with a different kind of weapon—a weapon that rips Cadona apart from within." Demnar took a bite of cobbler. "Do you have news on the Guiding Light document?"

"It has not yet been found, but three groups are making progress on identifying the brown Monarch sedan that the thief was driving when she stole the document. One group is General Douglass Willirman's military loyals. Another group consists of Cadonan government employees who oppose the Freedom Party. The third is Bob Fullerby's Andecco News Service team."

"What's the best-case scenario, Rozula?"

"Getting our hands on the actual manuscript is ideal; it's easier to authenticate the source and age of a document printed on paper than text stored in an electronic file. I have operatives planted inside Andecco and in Senator Sandra Pettock's staff. If one of those groups finds the Guiding Light, my agents will steal it. They'll take it to one of our embassies or consulates outside of Cadona. Antropka would be a good location. Once in our hands, we'd make the document public before General Willirman can fabricate a Back-to-Basics Club lie."

"Rozula, it sounds like a long shot."

"It is, Honorable President. In the meantime, my people are working on ways to confuse General Willirman. We want the Cadonan military to chase the wrong rabbit. Our goal is to buy our agents more time to find the document."

"Do you know what I'd like to do, Rozula?"

"What's that?"

"I'd like to hold the Guiding Light in my hands and speak in person with the lady in the brown Monarch."

SOLDIERS OF GOD
JUSTICE GROUP

Cadona City, Cadona
FRIDAY, APRIL 28, YEAR 1007 EE
5:30 P.M., EAST CADONA TIME

Leeha Ritsagin yawned as she opened her apartment door.

Cookie Davis was cutting vegetables in the kitchen. "Hi, Leeha. You worked another long day. You get paid for it, right?"

Leeha hung up her raincoat. "Nope, I'm a part-time employee. I get paid for thirty hours no matter how long I work."

"That sucks!"

"Yeah, I know, but if I complain, I'm afraid they'll fire me."

"I wish I could find a long-term gig," Cookie said. "I really want to help out with expenses. I feel bad that you work so hard, and it must be terrible to be stuck all day in an office with a bunch of nutty True Followers."

"You'll eventually get a good gig, Cookie. Anyway, you help out a lot, and you're a great cook."

"Speaking about cooking, Leeha, I was thinking about making a summer stew to go with sandwiches, but we're low on spices. Do you want to run to the store with me?"

"Do you mind going alone? You can take my car."

"I don't mind at all. I'll be back in a bit."

Cookie left.

Leeha settled into her old, comfy sofa, but disturbing thoughts popped into her mind. Her brother had joined the True Followers of God Church. Jeremy was once normal. What had happened to him?

She stood and stared out the raindrop-dotted living room window.

From the vantage point of her fourth-floor apartment, she saw Cookie climb into the brown Monarch. Leeha watched as the car drove away. She wished she had gone to the store; the trip might've taken her mind off her troubles.

Once again, the weird document called to her. Things written in it matched Jeremy's new beliefs about Domataland and women's rights. The existence of the Soldiers of God Justice Group proved the church supported the use of violence to meet their goals. Justice Group bad guys were behind the Agel Yungst shootings at the Hughes Medical Center. They'd also murdered Mary Kronvelt and planned to kill the other ninety-nine women on the justice execution list.

Another terrible thought came to her. She'd sent messages to Nancy Pitman and the other ninety-eight women on the list who were, hopefully anyway, still alive. If the Justice Group knew about the messages, she might be a target, too.

What if the wormy guy was a soldier of God? What if he was stalking her because he was waiting for an opportunity to strike? She'd been worried about police arresting her; maybe the police were the least of her worries.

Her stomach burned. She couldn't go on like this. Stress was making her sick.

Leeha went into her bedroom and slid open the closet door. She pulled a quilt off a tall, slender object leaning against a dark corner.

Even though she knew what the object was, it gave her chills.

She shimmied the man-shaped form out of the closet and dragged it across the bedroom floor. Now came the hard part. She clutched the rubbery man at the waist. It took all her strength to heave the mass off the ground.

One swing, two swings, three swings—at last, the ring at the head of the object latched on to a ceiling hook.

Leeha stared at the punching bag. His features were crude—but realistic enough. Rubberman had a nose, eyes, throat, groin, knees, and feet. She paced around the figure. *Panic will make you careless,* Grandpa Ritsagin had taught her. She told herself not to be scared. The wormy guy, unlike Rubberman, had weak points.

She hit Rubberman's nose. Her aim was off-center. Pain seared through her wrist and into her arm. She struck again. This blow was better. Her arm hurt less.

The wormy guy was in for it now! Leeha hit his throat. She kicked the backs of his knees. It felt good to strike him.

She fought like Grandpa Ritsagin had taught her long ago. She was tired of being afraid, sick of being a victim. She punched and punched the rubbery stomach. "Wormy guy! Wormy guy! How do you like *this,* wormy guy!"

"Leeha!" Cookie was standing in the doorway to the bedroom. Her eyes were wide.

"Oh, hi, Cookie. Sorry, I didn't hear you come in."

"Leeha, what on earth are you doing? I thought someone was killing you!"

"Sorry, I didn't mean to scare you. I haven't beat up on Rubberman for months. I decided it was time to get back into it."

"Rubberman?"

"Yeah, I've had him for a long time. Grandpa Ritsagin gave him to me. When I was little, Grandpa showed me how to defend myself. He told me it's best to get away or hide, but sometimes those things don't work. Then, you have no choice but to fight." She jabbed an elbow into the punching bag's spongy side.

"I've never seen you move so fast," Cookie said.

Leeha felt sweat roll off her nose. "Yeah, it's been a while. It feels good."

"Sometime, will you teach me what your Grandpa taught you?" Cookie asked.

"I didn't think you'd be interested in self-defense, Cookie. You go all over the place and never worry about bad stuff happening."

"Most of the time, I'm not afraid," she said. "Sometimes, though, I do get scared. I still worry about my ex or his buddies showing up. And, once in a while, I think about those awful murders we keep hearing about in the news. Remember that woman who was murdered in her own apartment?"

"Yeah, I remember." Images crept into Leeha's imagination. She and Cookie would be walking to the market. Members of the Soldiers of God Justice Group would drag them into an alley. The criminals would do to her and Cookie what they had done to Mary Kronvelt. Leeha imagined her own hands nailed to the ground while the wormy guy stuck unspeakable things inside her. In the distance, she would hear Cookie scream in agony.

Cookie's voice shattered her string of gruesome thoughts. "Hey, Leeha, are you okay?"

"Oh, sorry. I'm okay. I was … thinking about something. Sure, I'll teach you. Do you want to start now? It's a while until movie-time with Mrs. Furley."

"Are you looking for a neighborhood filled with trees, parks, and gardens, but you are not rich enough to live in the Sunset District? If this sounds like you, explore the Hillside District. You may just fall in love."

Hillside District Visitors Bureau

Cadona City, Cadona
FRIDAY, APRIL 28, YEAR 1007 EE
10:30 P.M., EAST CADONA TIME

Paula Arvish pulled herself upright in the seat as the CadTranS bus squealed to a stop. The vehicle's giant windshield wipers whisked away raindrops. Through streaky glass, she saw street signs for Apple Grove and Seventeenth. They'd reached the Hillside District! Soon, she'd be home.

She rested her head against the window and gazed at the nighttime view. Blossoms of lush apple trees were aglow in the soft, yellow-tinted light of a streetlamp. Her mother had loved those trees, especially in springtime.

Paula heard a familiar voice. "Hey, Paula, hello! May I join you?"

"Hi, Molly. Of course."

Paula moved her briefcase out of the way, and Molly settled into the seat.

The bus pulled away from the curb and lumbered down the road.

"How's Keith doing?" Paula asked.

"A little better. He has good days and not-so-good days, but at least he has a great doctor now."

"That's good."

"Well, Paula, I must say, I haven't seen you much since your mother's funeral."

"I've been spending a lot of time downtown looking for work. Today, I had three interviews. One, I think, went well. I hope so anyway."

Molly pushed a lock of gray-streaked brown hair away from her heavily made-up face. "You had interviews this late at night?"

"No, the interviews were during the day. I take classes in the evenings."

"A young girl alone at night! You should be more careful, Paula."

"You're alone, Molly, and all dressed up. Did you do something fun?"

"Well, I'm old. And I was out with friends. We went to a Thamm concert. The music was beautiful. Just beautiful! I wish your mother were here. She would've loved it."

"Yeah," Paula said, "Mom did love Thamm."

The bus drove by Hillside Central Square. Her mother also loved the apple, pear, cherry, walnut, and oak there. "Molly, how's the movement going to save the trees? I haven't been keeping track since Mom got sick."

Paula noticed a change in Molly's voice. It sounded impersonal—almost angry. "I don't participate in that cause any longer. The True Followers of God Church says such things don't matter. We need to worry about people, not trees or animals. Only human beings matter to God." Her voice softened. "How are you holding up? Your house must be lonely after your mom passed."

"It is," Paula said, "but I spend so much time looking for work and studying, I'm not home much." A wave of sorrow filled her soul. Tears gushed from her eyes.

"Oh, dear, dear," Molly said, "do you want to stop by my place for a nightcap?"

"Thanks, but I have to water Nancy's plants and make sure everything's okay in her house."

"That Nancy Pitman is never home," Molly said. "Where does she go?"

"I don't know, but she pays well for taking care of her place. Right now, it's the only income I have. If it wasn't for Nancy, I don't know what I'd do."

"Are you sure you don't want to come to a True Followers service with me? They can help with house payments, medical bills, food, all kinds of expenses. After the service, they have people there you can talk to."

Molly was trying to convert her again, but Paula was too tired to argue. "I'll … I'll think about it, Molly."

"You know, the True Followers can help deal with grief and guilt as well. They have great counselors. There's one lady there, *Cindy Coraway*, who is simply amazing. She overflows with God's Light. I bet Cindy can help you realize it's not your fault your mother died."

"It is my fault. If I had been there …." Paula wiped tears from her cheeks.

"You didn't kill your mother, Paula. Diabetes did. And you didn't kill your father either. Cancer did."

"It sure doesn't feel that way," Paula said.

Pity filled Molly's eyes. "Maybe tomorrow we can have biscuits and tea?"

"Sounds good, Molly. Thanks."

The bus pulled to the curb.

Molly stood. "I miss your mother, too, Paula. She was a good friend. We'll talk tomorrow. Try to get some rest."

"I will. Good night."

Paula watched apple and cherry trees pass by as the bus ambled along quiet streets. Guilt consumed her. Until she'd started spending time in dirty downtown Cadona City, she hadn't realized how fortunate she was to live in the Hillside District. Her parents had worked hard on their townhouse. Losing the family home would be a tragedy.

Guilt and sorrow weren't her only burdens. She was angry with herself, too. She'd let Molly get to her again—all that crazy True Followers nonsense!

Molly hadn't always been flippy. Her mother's longtime friend joined the church and the Back-to-Basics Club to get medical care for her ailing husband. Such a price Molly paid! After baptism, she was suspicious of every new person she met who didn't belong to the church, and she'd lost interest in things she once loved, like saving the neighborhood's cherished trees.

Paula dabbed tears from her eyes. There must be another way to keep her family home. She didn't want to sell her soul as Molly had done.

The bus slowed.

Paula looked out the window. She was almost there. Nancy Pitman's tall, slender townhouse stood on the corner like a graceful work of art. The home was the largest on the block. Perhaps it was the home's size and artistic flair that made Molly wary of Nancy. Molly was right about one thing, though; Nancy did spend a great deal of time away.

The bus stopped. Paula grabbed her belongings and climbed down the muddy, metallic stairs.

As she crossed the road, the big, rumbling vehicle disappeared around a bend. The world fell dark and silent. Not the slightest breeze stirred the warm, damp air. She wanted to go straight home, but Nancy's flowers needed tending.

Paula walked up the steep, flower-petal-covered stairs leading to Nancy's front porch. A tiny bulb hanging above the door cast only faint light, so she lit her personal device luminaire and checked the plants growing in front of the house. In a few days, she'd need to pluck some flowers, but, for now, the blossoms were still fresh.

She opened the door. Lights popped on, brightening a broad entryway and living room.

This was the first time she'd visited Nancy's house after dusk. The place had an eerie, heavy feeling even though the rooms were tidy and uncluttered.

Something told her to run away. Perhaps it would be better if she did her chores in the daytime. But what if the indoor plants died?

Maybe she was overreacting. She was in no danger. Her imagination was running wild because the hour was late, the world was dead silent, she worried about losing the family home, and her mother had passed away.

Paula wiped her feet and stepped inside Nancy's house.

Potted plants lining the counter seemed vibrant and healthy. The kitchen sink was clean and dry. None of the perishable groceries in the refrigerator had reached its expiration date. She sniffed an open milk container and a block of cheese just to be sure. No unusual odors.

Her last task for the night was watering plants. It shouldn't take long.

She picked up a pitcher from a tall end table.

Something moved!

For heaven's sake, she was behaving like a child. Her own reflection had startled her.

She looked into the gold-framed mirror and pushed wisps of dishwater blond hair away from her cheeks. Puffy, dark bags hung below her red-rimmed eyes. Worry lines creased her forehead. She was a mess.

A picture of Nancy Pitman sat on the end table. Nancy was a good decade older than she was, but anyone who didn't know better would think Nancy was younger. It was amusing how much she resembled Nancy, though. People in the neighborhood sometimes mistook her for Nancy—Nancy on her bad days.

Now, however, was not a good time to worry about her appearance. Plants needed tending.

She watered the plants on the counter.

The potted tree next to the patio door needed watering, too. She bent down and pushed aside a large leaf. Something unusual caught her eye. A few brown spots soiled the white tile in front of the sliding glass door.

Prickling fear returned. She had cleaned the floor just three days ago. No one was supposed to have been in the house since then. Paula examined the plate beneath the tree. She found no sign of water overflow.

Something else was odd. The vertical blinds covering the patio door weren't hanging straight. One of the strips was askew. Not long ago, she had dusted those blinds. She had taken care to ensure that all of the strips were straight.

Paula turned on the patio light and peeked outside. Nothing seemed out of place in the back yard or the common area beyond it.

Her hands trembled as she straightened the blinds and watered the tree. Although not a sound met her ears, her fear grew. She'd leave after taking care of the plants around the fireplace. The upstairs flowers would wait until morning.

A noise came from a hallway. The sound was a single, brief click.

Again, all fell quiet.

She poured water into a planter box.

Another noise came from behind her. This time, there was no mistaking it—footsteps.

Four men stood in the living room. They were dressed in black. Whatever covered their heads concealed all features; their faces appeared as black ovals.

One man, the one with broad shoulders, tapped a rusty rod against his left palm as he spoke. "Servant of Bezgog, this is your judgment day."

Another man clutched a knife.

Paula struggled to speak. "What are you doing here?"

"We are the wrath of God," the man with broad shoulders said. "Tonight, murderess, we send you home to Bezgog."

"What are you talking about? What do you want?"

"We want you to suffer at our hands. Then, you will suffer even greater at God's hands. Soon, you will wish you had never been born. Your lot will be everlasting pain and torment."

"Who are you?"

"Avenging angels," the man with the knife said. "In the name of God, we administer your judgment." He lunged forward with the blade.

She raised the pitcher. Metal struck metal with a squeal and screech. Water sprayed into the air.

The man with broad shoulders lifted the rusty rod. "You little witch!"

He swung the bar. It hit the pitcher.

Pain shot through her right arm. Her hand went numb. The crushed pitcher tumbled to the floor.

With her left hand, she grabbed the neck of a statuette.

The man swung the rod again. The figurine shattered.

Paula lost her balance. Her back slammed into the floor.

She needed a weapon. A thin leg of a golden book rack was within reach. She stretched out her left arm, but a blow to the chest forced air from her lungs.

The sole of a black boot hovered above her. The heel smacked into her stomach. Something struck the left side of her head. A piercing ring pealed in her ears.

The four men towered over her. They appeared as shadowy demons silhouetted against ceiling lights.

Paula tried to raise her head. A sharp pain stabbed her neck. Her vision blurred.

The screeching in her ears faded. The human shapes transformed into swaying trees. Where the ceiling lights had been, warm sunlight filtered down through evergreen limbs. Her body rocked to and fro, but no pain or fear came with it. She found herself floating on a wilderness lake and lying on a cushion as soft as a cloud.

⊕

Lars placed two fingers on the woman's neck. "We've got to make the suffering last longer. This one died in a couple of minutes."

Axle kicked the corpse's limp legs. "What's the difference? She can't tell anyone how long she suffered."

"But investigators can," Lars told him. "The longer the torture, the greater the public fear. Let's not forget our goal."

Zoff said, "Well, it's done. Lars, do your work."

"Yes, Boss." He squatted down and pressed the tip of his shiny knife into the supple skin of the woman's belly. With ease, the sharp blade sliced into layers of flesh.

The best part came next. He slid his right hand into the incision. Clumps of spongy tissue glided past his fingers.

He found the organ he was fishing for—intestines. The gooey coil gurgled as he pulled it from the body cavity.

The guts steamed in his hand. A rush of pride raced through him. The disembowelment of evil!

The wrinkled, slimy entrails unfurled as he rose to his feet. "Damn, this feels good. We've gotten rid of another piece of trash. God is avenged!" He let go of the mucus-covered thread of flesh. Like a giant, dead worm, the spindly organ flopped onto the white floor.

Rips stood nearby. He clutched fistfuls of kitchen napkins. "Look what I found! What pretty little birds and flowers!" He tossed some of the napkins. "Hey, Axle, catch!"

Lars stepped aside so Axle and Rips could soak the napkins in the woman's blood. Red drops dripped onto the white floor as they carried the cloths across the room. Rips wrote *fetus* on a pale wall. Axle spelled the word *revenge* on another.

"How does it look?" Rips asked.

"Not messy enough," Lars said. "This is a big place. Lots of wall space. Let's spruce it up, fellas!"

Axle and Rips wiped up more blood.

Lars didn't bother with a napkin. He collected a handful of red, tepid liquid in the palm of his left hand.

He chose a wall next to the patio door. Making broad strokes with his right hand, he wrote one word on the white surface. He stepped back and admired his artistic twist; instead of *revenge*, he spelled *avenged*.

Zoff said, "That's enough writin'. Let's not overstay our welcome."

"Hey, Boss," Lars said, "the hallway could use some paintin'."

Zoff shook his head. "No, we've made our point. Don't worry, Detective Brunish will show up soon enough, and Bob Fullerby will be right behind him. Let's clean up. We can't leave anything behind that can tie us to the scene."

Lars' stomach growled. Nancy Pitman's house was fancy. No doubt she had delicious food stashed somewhere. He went into the kitchen and yanked open the door of the sparkling clean refrigerator. He picked up a wedge of cheese. His teeth sank into the yellowy block.

Zoff's voice boomed from across the room. "Lars! What the heck are you doing?"

"Grabbin' a bite. Pitman may be a servant of Bezgog, but she knows how to pick a damned good cheese. Wanna try it?"

Rips said, "I'll try some."

"No!" Zoff said. "No one is trying anything. We're here on business, which does not include raiding refrigerators. Lars, you'll need to take that cheese with you. Your DNA is all over it. And, for heaven's sake, close your face-shield."

Lars stuffed the food into his pack. All in all, the cheese was worth the scolding. As he fastened the satchel, he noticed that an object was wedged between two of his teeth. A push with his tongue dislodged the clump.

Zoff said, "Lars, when you're done cleaning up, check out the purse and briefcase in the foyer. They weren't there when we got here. Pitman must've brought them in with her."

"Will do." Lars wandered into the entryway. A well-used purse and scuffed briefcase sat on a polished bench. He opened the briefcase. "Hey, Boss, I got something weird over here."

"What?"

"Printed résumés, a bunch of them."

"So?"

"They're not Pitman's."

Zoff, Axle, and Rips huddled around him.

"Whose are they?" Zoff asked.

"Paula Arvish."

Zoff grabbed the purse sitting next to the briefcase. He dug through the stuffed handbag. "Oh, shit."

"What's wrong?" Axle asked.

"The ID belongs to Paula Arvish, too. Damn it!" Zoff stomped into the living room. He held the facial identification display next to the dead woman's head. "Shit! This woman isn't Nancy Pitman. We whacked the wrong bitch."

"You sure?" Lars asked. "She sure looks like Pitman."

Zoff nodded. "Yeah, I'm sure. We hit an invalid target."

"So what?" Axle said. "We made our point. Whoever she is, she must know Pitman. This Paula woman deserves what she got for hanging out with trash."

"I may agree," Zoff said, "but I doubt others in the Justice Group will. Let's get out of here. We'll need to report this right away."

9

JUSTICE EXECUTIONS

"The golden age of cinema lives on in old classics such as 'Too Many Goodbyes.' Anka Vigaro's starring role in the film earned her an eternal place in the Movie Hall of Fame."

"Review of the Legends"
Year 1007 of the Enlightened Epoch

Cadona City, Cadona
FRIDAY, APRIL 28, YEAR 1007 EE
11:00 P.M., EAST CADONA TIME

Leeha Ritsagin scooted to the end of her old sofa. If she didn't grab a treat now, Toofy would eat it all. She reached into a bowl and gathered a big handful of spicy popcorn.

The classic movie, *Too Many Goodbyes*, entered its final scenes.

She recalled the last time she'd watched the film; an Andecco News Service alert had interrupted the show. Investigative journalist Bob Fullerby had delivered a grave report: the Izvyonsk Navy sank the Domataree Goodwill Ship in the faraway port city of D'nevtnya, Bakhadaland.

This time, *Too Many Goodbyes* ended without interruption.

Mrs. Furley clapped her hands. "I love this film! I just adore Anka Vigaro. It's too bad she died so young. She was a great actress and a stunning beauty to boot."

Toofy gazed at Cookie as he spoke. "She's a good actress, but there are better-looking women."

Leeha's mood sank. No one ever said flattering things about her. She distracted herself by staring at the viewplane.

Movie credits scrolled on top of a fuzzy image of Anka's face caught in the moment when the character she played pleaded with God to stop a destructive war.

"You know," Leeha said, "Anka Vigaro reminds me a lot of that widow we saw on the news the other day."

"What widow?" Cookie asked.

"You might not have seen her. Mrs. Furley and I were watching news about Bakhadaland while you were in the kitchen. There was this beautiful lady sitting outside. She had blond hair and blue eyes, just like Anka. Mrs. Furley told me the lady was a widow."

"I remember her," Mrs. Furley said. "We were watching a memorial service for the sailors who died on the Goodwill Ship. A lady in the crowd was wearing a purple mourning robe. Lotish widows do that."

Leeha recalled images of the widow. "You know, even the expressions on her face remind me of Anka's character. So much sorrow!"

Toofy said, "Lots of stuff in the movie are like things happening today. The bad guys in the film remind me of our own jerks: Fischer, Rineburg, and Willirman. Not to mention Pastor Leon Walls. He's as big a nutball as the religious wack jobs in the movie."

Three glasses of wine didn't keep Mrs. Furley from speaking her mind. "You know, things are actually worse today than in the film. The leaders in *Too Many Goodbyes* are bumbling idiots. They stumbled into war thinking that war is a game where you run around like a maniac, swinging your shiny sword. Our real-life leaders stir up trouble on purpose. They think it's part of some divine plan."

Leeha recalled the weird document hidden beneath her kitchen cabinets. If Freedom Party, Back-to-Basics Club, and True Followers of God Church leaders were really behind the text, then Cadona's rising rulers had despotic plans far worse than those portrayed in the film.

Cadona City, Cadona
FRIDAY, APRIL 28, YEAR 1007 EE
11:45 P.M., EAST CADONA TIME

Senator John Rineburg caressed the hips of the curvy girl sitting on his lap. The sequins of her sparkling dress tickled the palms of his hands. Her strawberry blond hair smelled of perfume. His nephew sure found a good-looking crop of women to entertain customers!

A waiter in coat and tails appeared. "Senator, may I bring you another drink?"

John shook his glass. A lemon slice and ice cubes swirled against the crystal sides. "Yes, I think it's time for a refill. Also, bring one for Liddy. She's had a busy day."

The waiter tapped an autopad. "Right away, Senator." The server strutted away.

John wiggled his legs. Liddy giggled as her shapely body swayed in his lap. He said, "Say, Beautiful, do you prefer satin sheets or silk?"

She wrapped her long, slender arms around his neck. Bracelets jingled. She ran her tongue over her glossy, red lips. "Fuzzy! I like fuzzy, fuzzy sheets."

"Okay, fuzzy it is, my angel."

Over her tanned shoulder, John saw a man he hadn't expected to see. Martin, his assistant, rushed up to him. "Senator, I have news."

"What is it?"

Martin whispered in his ear. "There's been a justice execution tonight."

"What!" John shoved Liddy off his lap. "Martin, are you sure?"

"Positive. General Willirman was unable to reach you, so he called me. He's on his way here."

John stood. "Someone may be eavesdropping. Let's talk in RR's den. It's as secure as anywhere can be these rotten days." John stomped into his nephew's nightclub office. He slammed the door the second Martin walked in.

"Martin, what exactly did Dougy say?"

"Not much, Senator. Only that there was a justice execution, and that he wants to discuss it with you in person."

Rage set John's heart pounding. "We called off all executions until further notice. How the hell did this happen?"

"I don't know, Senator. General Willirman didn't tell me anything else."

The office door opened. Martin drew his sidearm.

General Douglass Willirman stood in the doorway. "Whoa, there, partner. It's just me."

"Sorry, General." Martin holstered the pistol. "Senator, I'll guard the door. I'll be right outside if you need me."

After Martin left, John said, "Dougy, did Martin get it right? There's been another justice execution?"

"I'm afraid so, John."

"What the hell! We called off all executions until the Guiding Light issue was resolved. I gave the order myself."

The cushion of a leather chair groaned as Doug's wide body settled into it. "I know you did, John. The teams on the street misunderstood the order. They assumed the Pitman hit was still on. It gets even worse; there's been another ... mistake. They took out the wrong woman."

"Frick, frick, frick!" John's hand stung as his fist slammed against the top of RR's desk. "The wrong woman? How the hell did they frick that up?"

"They killed the housekeeper by accident. She looks like Pitman, they tell me."

"Just great! Just fricken great! They killed Mary Kronvelt when they weren't supposed to, and now they fricken killed Nancy Pitman's housekeeper. How do those imbeciles frick up so much?"

"We have several layers between the teams on the street and us," Doug said. "Word doesn't travel down the chain of command quickly—that's the downside. On the plus side, that distances us from the murders."

John slumped into a chair. "Do Mitch and Leon know?"

"Not yet," Doug said. "I wanted to talk to you about it first."

"Ah, frick, Dougy! Mitch is gonna piss. Leon will have a hissy fit. Where was this murder?"

"Inside Nancy Pitman's townhouse in the Hillside District. Pitman wasn't at home when it went down."

John rubbed his eyes. How did they hire so many screwups? "Who's the housekeeper? Is she on the list?"

"No, she's not. Her name's Paula Arvish. She's also Nancy Pitman's neighbor."

"Where's Pitman now?" John asked.

Doug poured himself a glass of bourbon. "Don't know yet. We're trying to locate her. But I have confirmed that Pitman received one of those warning messages sent from Hughes Medical Center. Maybe Pitman shit her pants and skipped town."

"Damn, Dougy! This is fricked up! Brunish is going to link the killing to the Mary Kronvelt murder in no time. That prick detective already tied Kronvelt to the Agel Yungst shootings at Hughes. Brunish can't prove it in court yet, but he will … eventually."

"Well, John, at least whoever has the Guiding Light won't find Paula Arvish's name in there. It may be a good thing they whacked the wrong bitch."

"Nonetheless, we need to throw up flak," John said. "Pitman's name is in the document, and Arvish was murdered in Pitman's house. We need to create an alternate story, one that points away from the Soldiers of God Justice Group."

"I already have loyals handling it, John. I just hope that Karther doesn't start nosing around. Brunish's snooping is bad enough. We don't need the defense secretary poking his nose in it, too."

John's pulse thumped in his temples. "Let's not forget about Fullerby. He's more on the ball than all of the others combined."

"Why do you say that, John?"

"The only reason Karther has the guts to stick his neck out is because President Meyfeld makes him do it. Brunish is a brave son-of-a-bitch, but he's by-the-book honest. He's predictable. His dedication to the law is his weakness. Bob Fullerby is different. He and his Andecco chums know how to play the game. More importantly, Fullerby's not *afraid* to play the game. That old fart is patient; he'll keep quiet until he feels the moment is right. When that moment comes, he'll swing the hammer hard."

Doug twirled the bronze-colored liquor in the crystal glass. "John, we need to move faster in cleaning up the press. Especially Andecco News."

"Do you have particular plans in mind, Dougy?"

"I do. Our press corps is crawlin' with Domataree agents. We can use it as cover to take out troublemakers. Fullerby's old boyfriend, Barry Kingle, has links to the Cadona Guardians defector group. Kingle would be a good place to start."

"I like your idea, Dougy. Let's run it by Mitch and Leon when we fill them in on the Paula Arvish fiasco."

10

THE MYSTERY WOMAN'S NAME

Cadona City, Cadona
SATURDAY, APRIL 29, YEAR 1007 EE
3:00 A.M., EAST CADONA TIME

Leeha Ritsagin awoke with a jolt. She looked around. Her body relaxed; she was in bed where she was supposed to be at three in the morning.

Loud raps shook her bedroom door. She heard Cookie's voice. "Leeha, are you okay? May I come in?"

"Yeah."

Cookie walked in. "What's wrong? I heard shouting."

"I had a nightmare."

"What about?"

"It's silly."

"Tell me."

"People who work for Senator John Rineburg were chasing me."

"You know, Leeha, you're probably having bad dreams because we watched *Too Many Goodbyes*, not to mention the discussions we had with Toofy and Mrs. Furley afterward."

"Yeah, I'm sure you're right, Cookie."

Leeha felt an odd sensation. She got up and looked out the bedroom window. Far below, three shadowy figures were huddled together on the sidewalk by the far end of the building.

"Is something wrong, Leeha?"

"I see guys out there."

Cookie joined her by the window. "You know, they just look like they're talking."

"At three in the morning? Nothing's open around here at this hour."

"Leeha, stop worrying. They can't get into the building without a code. Anyway, we're in the middle of the fourth floor. If they're thieves, the odds of them hitting our unit are slim. You're jumpy because of the nightmare. Do you want me to make you some avavarian tea?"

"No, I'm okay. Thanks."

"Do you want me to stay with you awhile?"

"No, I really am okay, but thanks for offering."

"Okay. Call me if you get scared."

"I will, thanks."

Cookie walked out of the bedroom and shut the door behind her.

Leeha peeked out the window. The men were still huddled in the same spot.

Something startled them. They turned in circles as if they were searching for unseen danger in the night. The men exchanged a few more words before scurrying off in different directions.

Leeha was about to call Cookie, but she stopped herself. She mustn't let paranoia get to her. The guys were probably petty thieves or drug dealers looking for a score. A noise unnerved them, so they ran away.

She lay down and closed her eyes, but her heart pounded. The weird document, not a movie, gave her bad dreams. She must get more sleep. The sun would rise soon; then, she and Cookie would go for a run. Running was hard enough when rested, let alone when exhausted.

It'll be okay, she told herself. It would happen; she'd get rid of the document. She'd found the strength to destroy it before, but the attempt failed because Cookie and Mrs. Furley came home.

She'd find the strength again. All she needed to do was find some time when Cookie would be away for an hour or two. That day would come, and the document would be out of her life forever.

Cadona City, Cadona
SATURDAY, APRIL 29, YEAR 1007 EE
5:00 A.M., EAST CADONA TIME

The parking lot grew dark when Rona Betler turned off the headlights, but the print shop's vast security system didn't find danger. She climbed out of her little car and waved at a camera hidden near the rear entrance of the aging building.

Rona opened the vault-like door. Angela was sitting at the old wooden table.

"Good morning, Ang."

"Morning, Row. Sorry to call so early."

"No problem. What's up?"

"Mr. Fullerby learned about another homicide. Detective Brunish thinks it's related to the Mary Kronvelt murder."

"Did it happen in the same area?"

"Nope, this one happened in the Hillside District."

"Hillside District, wow!" Rona hung up her raincoat. "That's a nice neighborhood. Mary Kronvelt was killed in a slum."

Rona poured herself a cup of coffee before settling into a chair. "So, Ang, who's the vic?"

"Paula Arvish. She worked as a housekeeper for her neighbor, Nancy Pitman. It happened in Pitman's house. Pitman herself wasn't home."

"When was she killed?"

"Late last night. Mr. Fullerby sent photos." Angela slid an autopad along the tabletop.

Rona studied an image. "Wow! How gross! They pulled her insides out." She flipped to another photo. "Get a load of this! The killers wrote on the walls just like they did in Kronvelt's apartment."

Angela said, "Mr. Fullerby thought you'd enjoy looking into it."

"Yeah, for sure!"

"Oh, Row, he said to use Detective Brunish's private line; crooked cops may intercept calls on police channels."

"Got it," Rona said.

Angela folded her computer.

"Are you off somewhere, Ang?"

"Yep, you're not going to believe who wants to talk to me in person."

"Who?"

"Rosie Stanton."

"You mean Rosie Stanton, as in the Stanton Weapon Research Facility?"

"Yep."

"Why does she want to talk to you? I thought all the Stantons hate Andecco News."

"She didn't want to tell me by PD," Angela said, "but she sounded desperate."

"Where are you meeting her?"

"Her downtown boutique, *Fashion Indulgence.*"

"Yikes! It's an expensive store."

"No kidding. It's a good thing I'm not into fancy clothes. Call me if you need me, Row."

"Will do, Ang."

Angela left through the back door.

In the silence of the print shop, Rona examined more of the gruesome pictures.

Her personal device vibrated. Degio Ellis from Jenton's Auto Body and Repair was calling. "Hi, Degio. You're up early."

"Hey, Row. I hope I didn't wake you. I was planning to leave a message."

"It's okay. I'm taking calls. I'm already at work."

"I'm working, too. We were up most of the night getting the computer running. I have news about the car you were asking about. I may have the answers you need."

Rona set the Paula Arvish murder photos aside. "Really? That's awesome!"

"Yep, I have the info right in front of me, but I suspect you don't want to talk about it over PD."

"Definitely not. I can come to you. Tell me where."

"There's a Caffeine Alley next to the garage. Is that okay?"

"It sounds great, Degio. I'm on my way."

"See you soon, Row."

Rona ended the call.

The smell of freshly brewed coffee rushed out as Rona opened the door to Caffeine Alley. Degio Ellis was sitting on a tall stool at a table for two.

"Hey, Row," Degio said, "good morning. I got your favorite: cappuccino, extra hot, no sweetener."

"Thanks, Degio, but I was supposed to buy this time."

"You know, for a chance to see your pretty face … it's worth the price of a cappuccino. Actually, it's worth much more. I'm getting off cheap."

His cliché lines were oddly charming. Rona said, "So, Jenton's computer is back up?"

"Some of the data's restored. I have a name for you. The person who dropped off and picked up the brown Monarch is *Leeha Ritsagin.* I have—"

"Hold on a sec, please." She sent a coded message to Bob Fullerby, Kever Carsen, and Angela Thirgal. If Degio's information proved true, the mystery woman now had a name. "Sorry, Degio. I got a little excited. You were saying …?"

He pulled a crinkled piece of notebook paper from his pocket. "Here's her name, contact info, and address … at least according to our records."

She unfolded the scrap of paper. "*Leeha Ritsagin* …. Degio, do you remember anything about her?"

"Nope. I figured you'd want to know, so I've been bashing my brain. She must have been unremarkable—unlike you. I would've remembered you." He flashed one of his flirtatious grins.

Rona stared at the neat, boxy, handwritten letters. After numerous dead ends and hours of searching, here was the information her team had sought.

Degio said, "So this must be big-time important, huh?"

"It may be. It could be huge!" Rona fought to control her emotions. The best investigative journalists knew how to remain stoic when the situation called for it. The greatest among them, like Bob Fullerby, conjured up emotions to present the face they wanted the public to see.

Degio's voice was apologetic. "Row, I'll need to give the government agents Ritsagin's name; I have no choice. But I'll hold off as long as I can so you have time to do whatever it is you need to do."

"Thanks, I really, really owe you one."

"I like the sound of that." He flashed another smile.

Rona stood. She had to get to the print shop and see if Leeha Ritsagin was the woman in their Hatchets Bar video.

"Leaving already?" Degio asked. "You didn't finish your coffee."

"You're welcome to it," she said.

He turned the cup. "Ah, your lipstick. I hope I someday get closer to the real thing." He licked the red marks from the rim of the mug. "Mmm! Mmm! Tastes good."

"Degio, you're plain weird. You might catch J2 doing things like that."

"If I catch it from you, it would be worth it. Talk to you later, sweetheart." He gave her a wink.

Rona rushed out the door.

Cadona City, Cadona
SATURDAY, APRIL 29, YEAR 1007 EE
6:20 A.M., EAST CADONA TIME

Kever Carsen watched as Police Officer Anson Dailey's foot slipped off an easy toehold. "Anson, are you okay?"

"Yeah, lower me down, please."

Kever eased up on the rope. Anson's muscular body hung like a heavy sack of bricks until his feet touched the climbing gym floor.

"You seem off today, buddy," Kever said. "What's up? Hope you're not coming down with the J2 thing."

"No, it's work. Weird shit going on."

"Like what?"

"Kever-o, you still work for Bob Fullerby, right?"

"Yeah, part time. Like always."

Anson didn't say anything, but he looked worried.

"Why do you ask?" Kever said. "Thinking of a career change?"

"The way things are going, maybe I should." Anson unfastened his harness and sat on the spongy mat below the man-made climbing wall. "Military intelligence special agents are investigating Cadonan citizens."

"Wait a minute," Kever said, "I thought the military isn't supposed to investigate our own people."

Anson released an audible sigh. "That's the problem. They're not, at least not on Cadonan soil."

"What happened?"

"Three agents showed up at my station in person and unannounced. They asked our clerk for information, but they wouldn't tell her why they needed it. They didn't bring paperwork, a case number ... nothing. The clerk reported it to Lieutenant Neese. He said she had to give the agents what they wanted or the whole department would be in trouble. From what I gathered, the report's going out this morning. This doesn't feel right, Kever-o, especially after I looked into the situation they were asking about."

"What were they asking about?"

"I ... I don't know if I should say."

Kever sat down next to him. "Police business. I get it."

"That's just it, Kever-o. It should be *police* business, not military business."

"Was that why you asked if I still work for Bob Fullerby?"

"Yeah, I ... I know Andecco News Service investigates things like this, like government bodies overstepping their boundaries. Look, Kever-o, if I gave you some info, could you keep it between us and Mr. Fullerby?"

"To be honest, Angela Thirgal and Rona Betler may also find out."

"Angela Thirgal? Yeah, she'd be cool. Who's Rona Betler? The name sounds familiar, but I can't place her."

"She's another reporter who works for Mr. Fullerby."

"Do you trust her?"

"Only with my life."

"So ... you can limit it to this group?"

"Yep," Kever said. "Ang, Row, and I all work directly with Mr. Fullerby."

"Okay. Okay. I'll tell you." Anson drew a deep breath. "These military intelligence agents are looking for the owner of a vehicle."

"What type of vehicle?"

"A seventeen-year-old, brown Monarch sedan."

Kever didn't expect to hear those words. The mystery woman's Monarch was seventeen years old, and it was brown. "Anson, are you sure they asked specifically about a seventeen-year-old model?"

"Positive. A brown one."

"Was such a car at your station?"

"Yeah, sure was."

"Why was it there?"

"The owner reported a crime. She was heading to Altage Enterprises; she had an interview coming up and wanted to make sure she knew the way so she wouldn't be late. There was a detour, and she got lost in the Helmsey District. A gang attacked her car while she was waiting at a red traffic signal."

"You said, *she*. The driver was a woman?"

"Yeah, she seemed like a good person."

"Why does the military want to find her?"

"They say she's a grave threat to national security. She's labeled an *enemy apparent*."

Kever hadn't expected those words either. "Enemy apparent! Wow! That's serious."

"No kidding. Kever-o, the agents' story isn't adding up. Her record is squeaky-clean. She's never even left the country."

"Anson, did the agents say what this woman did?"

"Nope, they wouldn't tell us anything; the guys didn't even give us their names."

Kever recalled the Drop Case bug-eye video. The footage showed a brown Monarch parked in front of Hatchets Bar. The geography made sense; major Helmsey District streets led to the Hatchets area, and the bar was close to Anson's satellite police office. "Say, Anson, do you remember when the Monarch was at your station?"

"Yeah, I spent some time looking over the report to make sense of things. It happened on March twenty-sixth. She arrived at my station at eight twenty in the morning."

Kever's heart pounded—a breakthrough in the Drop Case at last! "Anson, the driver's name; do you know it?"

"Yeah, I know it. It's *Leeha Ritsagin*. I got her address, too. I'll send it to you."

"No, write it down instead. That way, your lieutenant will be less likely to find out that you told me." He handed Anson a pen and paper.

Anson wrote down Ritsagin's name and address.

Kever knew he had to get to the print shop. He had research to do. "Okay, I'll pass this on to Mr. Fullerby. Why don't you take a break from climbing? You look like you can use some recoup time."

"That's probably a good idea, Kever-o. Are you free for climbing on Monday evening? Say, five or so?"

"Works for me."

They strolled to a long, narrow parking lot next to the gym. He tapped Anson on the shoulder. "Hey, take care of yourself, buddy," Kever said. "I'll tell Mr. Fullerby what happened."

Anson appeared burnt out, but relieved. "Thanks, Kever-o."

"Oh, Anson, one more thing; I think it's best if you don't tell anyone else about the Monarch or the agents, at least until Mr. Fullerby has a chance to give it some thought."

"Sure thing." Anson walked to his car. He squeezed his muscular body into the compact front seat.

Kever pretended to be in no particular hurry. The less Anson knew about the urgency of the Drop Case, the safer his friend would be.

The vehicle disappeared around a corner.

Kever sent an encrypted message to his team; they must know that the mystery woman might have been identified.

A message from Rona caught his eye. She, too, had news about the Drop Case.

Kever flipped up the hood of his rain jacket and jumped onto his bicycle. He had to learn more about Leeha Ritsagin. She was the last person known to be in possession of the Guiding Light. Very bad—and very powerful—people were looking for her and the document.

11

SOMEONE'S AT THE DOOR

Cadona City, Cadona
SATURDAY, APRIL 29, YEAR 1007 EE
8:00 A.M., EAST CADONA TIME

The soles of Leeha Ritsagin's feet stung as they slapped against the pavement. Her lungs ached as the slope of the hill steepened. Stinky industrial fumes didn't help matters.

At least the streets were empty. Cars weren't spewing exhaust, and she didn't have to dodge around people walking on the sidewalk.

She looked up.

Cookie was still running at lightning speed. Was she ever going to stop? Leeha gasped for air.

Up ahead, a sparsely leafed sapling clung to life along the roadside.

Tree—she would make it to the tree. Breathe, breathe, breathe. Step, step, step. One, two, three.

The plant lay behind her now.

A utility pole stuck up from the pavement.

Pole—her next target was the pole. She passed by it, but still Cookie was running.

The Happy Day Diner lay just ahead. An old-fashioned restaurant sign cast a faint shadow on the sidewalk.

Leeha passed by the restaurant.

At last Cookie stopped. Sweat glistened on her smiling face. "Leeha, you did great! I'm so proud of you! You made it the whole way."

Leeha thought her lungs might burst. She bent forward and rested her hands on her knees. "About ... ready ... to die." Perspiration dripped from her face.

Cookie was running in place. "But you're getting in shape fast!"

"Don't ... feel ... like it."

"You are! Go ahead and go home. I'm going to do some hill-work."

Leeha recovered enough strength to stand upright. "Hill-work?"

"Yeah, I'm going to run up and down the steep part a couple of times."

"Are you going to be okay out here by yourself?"

"You worry too much, Leeha. I'll be fine. I run this route lots of times by myself when you're at work. If something happens, I'll go inside the diner and get help. Go home. I'll be back around nine o'clockish."

Cadona City, Cadona
SATURDAY, APRIL 29, YEAR 1007 EE
8:05 A.M., EAST CADONA TIME

Investigative journalist Angela Thirgal parked her old, gray pickup in the rear lot of the Andecco hideaway office.

She opened the print shop's back door.

Kever and Rona looked up as she stepped inside the windowless room.

"Guys," Angela said, "there's something weird going on. Rosie Stanton's fiancé, Timothy Becker, is missing. Nobody will tell her where he is. I mean, he works at Stanton Weapon, and her family owns a controlling stake in the company. Don't you think it's odd she can't find out where he went?"

Neither Kever nor Rona spoke. They stared at her, their eyes wide.

"Kever-o, Row ... what's going on?"

"I take it you haven't read your messages," Kever said.

"Sorry, no. I've been preoccupied with the Becker thing. You have news?"

Rona's cheeks were flush with excitement. "Do we ever! We know who the mystery woman is."

"Excellent! Who is she?"

Rona pointed at a viewplane. "*Leeha Ritsagin*, twenty-five years old, single, lives alone in an apartment in the Warrenton District."

Angela took a seat. She studied the face displayed on the viewplane. "This does look like our girl. How did you identify her?"

"Kever and I both found out this morning," Rona said. "The computer at Jenton's Auto Body and Repair is back online. Degio got her name, contact info, and address for me. It's weird because Anson gave Kever-o the same name."

"Anson? The cop?" Angela asked.

"Yeah," Kever said. "He confided in me because he knows I work for Mr. Fullerby. Get this—military intelligence special agents came to his police station looking for the owner of a seventeen-year-old, brown Monarch. Turns out Leeha Ritsagin did take her Monarch to Anson's station on March twenty-sixth."

Angela poured herself a cup of coffee. "Kever-o, why did Ritsagin go to the police?"

"To report a crime. A gang attacked her car while she was stopped at a red light in the Helmsey District."

"The Helmsey District! Why was she in such a dangerous area?"

"She got lost," Kever said. "She was heading to Altage Enterprises and lost her way because of a detour."

"Does she work for Altage?"

"No, she told Anson that she had a job interview coming up. She wanted to make sure she knew the way so she wouldn't be late on the day of the interview. There's an unexpected twist; Anson checked Ritsagin's record; she's squeaky-clean. She's never even left the country. And get this, Ang, the military has labeled her an enemy apparent."

"An enemy apparent? Goodness! That means she's a serious threat to national security. What did she do?"

"Anson doesn't know. The agents wouldn't tell the cops anything."

"Kever-o," Angela said, "when were the agents at his station?"

"I'm not exactly sure, but Anson said Ritsagin's report was getting sent to the military this morning."

Rona looked worried. "Ang, what should we do? Kever-o and I thought about calling her, but we're not sure if it's a good idea."

Bob Fullerby wasn't there; Angela feared she lacked the strength to lead. "This is a tough decision. If we call, we may spook her, or spook whoever instructed her to steal the Guiding Light."

"Ang," Kever said, "where's Mr. Fullerby? Row and I have been trying to contact him all morning. He hasn't responded."

"He took a bus to the downtown Andecco office for some big meeting with Mr. Marantees. I suspect it's about Flight Ten Seventy."

Kever said, "Ang, I don't think it's a good idea to wait for Mr. Fullerby. The military is right on Ritsagin's tail."

"I agree. Kever-o, let's run over to her apartment. We can take Mr. Fullerby's car. He just had his underground tech buddies scan it for tracking devices."

"I'm with ya."

Angela stood. "Row, see what else you can dig up on Leeha Ritsagin. If Mr. Fullerby calls, let him know where we're going. But be careful what you say. We don't want to trigger the attention of eavesdroppers."

"Got it, Ang."

"Oh, Row, be sure to leave a channel open when you talk to Detective Brunish about the Paula Arvish murder. Something tells me we'll need his help with Ritsagin."

"Will do."

Angela took one more sip of coffee. "You ready, Kever-o?"

"Yep, let's go!"

Cadona City, Cadona
SATURDAY, APRIL 29, YEAR 1007 EE
8:35 A.M., EAST CADONA TIME

Leeha walked into her little, quiet apartment. She peeled her sweat-soaked shorts and exercise shirt away from her sticky skin.

Her personal device was as gross as her clothing. She gave the device a rinse. As she set it on the counter, a gold color caught her eye. Yet again, Cookie had forgotten her physical key. It was okay, though. Cookie had the passcode to get into the building, so she wouldn't be stuck outside.

Leeha checked the time. She could squeeze in a shower before Cookie got home.

The pulsating water felt good, but the bathroom got steamy and hot. She stepped out of the shower and wiped mist from the bathroom mirror.

She looked at her reflection.

What a terrible sight! The showerhead's hyper-spray setting had turned her acne blemishes a brilliant shade of red. She mustn't let Cookie see her like that.

Leeha patted herself dry and ran a concealer stick over her crimson pimples. She glanced in the mirror. The pimples were less noticeable, but fat circled her middle like a tire.

It was hopeless, no amount of makeup would hide her plump body. She dressed in a baggy shirt and wide jeans.

Just as she walked into the kitchen, the nodes in her left arm vibrated. She grabbed her personal device.

"Hi, sis," her brother said. "How ya doing?"

"Okay, but what are you doing up so early on a Saturday? It's not even six o'clock over there in Ramsten."

"Sonna, Skyla, and I are heading out to help with a Life March. A lot of planning goes into those events."

"Jeremy, you've got to get away from that crazy church. The True Followers are nuts. They're brainwashing you."

"They speak The Truth, Leeha. That's why I called. Tomorrow is Sunday; Pastor Walls' Sunday Sunrise Service is in the True Followers film studio. Sonna checked the CadTranS schedule; you can get there by train, no problem. Please, go tomorrow. Let Pastor Walls lead you to light and peace."

"Jeremy, I'm not going. One True Followers service was enough to last a lifetime. What they preach is not light and peace; they teach hate and war."

"They teach truth, Leeha. When you live apart from the True God, truth causes pain like vinegar in a wound. But when you accept The Truth in your heart, the world makes sense, and peace fills your soul."

"Jeremy, the True Followers hate just about everybody. They want to go to war."

"We don't want to go to war, Leeha. The people of Domataland are the children of Bezgog. It's Bezgog who wants to fight, not us. The Evil One is giving us no choice but to prepare for war. Our battle cries are, *Remember J2,* and, *Remember Flight Ten Seventy.* If we don't stop Domataland, Bezgog will win. Evil will rule over us all."

"Jeremy, listen to yourself. Can't you hear how crazy you sound? How on earth can you believe the Domats are the children of Bezgog?"

"Because God told us they are. It's written in the Holy Books; Bezgog sent his demons to mate with the Nastebyans. The modern-day Domats are descendants of the ancient tribe of Nastebya. They have demonic blood."

"Jeremy, you're smarter than this; I know you are."

"Leeha, it's painful to hear truth when you live in darkness, but that darkness is caused by separation from God. When God walks with you, the pain goes away."

"Do you know what hurts, Jeremy? Watching your brother turn away from reason as he becomes someone else, someone you can't recognize. Something's happening to you. Something awful."

"No, Leeha, I've found something wonderful. I spoke with Mom; she's agreed to go to a True Followers service. Leeha, I want you to join the True Followers, too. Will you please attend Pastor Walls' Sunday Sunrise Service tomorrow? Sonna, Skyla, and I are going to watch it on WorldLink. Maybe we'll spot you in the congregation."

"Jeremy, I'm not going."

"Leeha, I understand where you're coming from. I was like you in the beginning. I was full of doubt. But now, it all makes sense."

Enough was enough. "Jeremy, I'm hanging up now."

Leeha ended the call.

What was he thinking? He was dragging their mother into that awful church. How could he do such a thing?

Images haunted her. Jeremy would be at a True Followers of God Church service. Like the rest of the nutballs in the congregation, he'd make the Mark of the Compass, kick the chair in front of him, and shake his fists over his head like a crazy person.

How was it possible that her very own brother would volunteer for the Family First Initiative and participate in Life Marches? Who knew what dreadful things went on at those events? Why, oh why did he join that awful church? He once had been so normal. Her brother had ransomed his soul for better medical care and help with paying rent.

She must stop thinking about it; she'd make herself sick.

Beating up Rubberman seemed like a good way to distract herself, but her body needed rest after her hard run. She turned on the sound array instead.

An Andecco reporter was speaking.

> "The battle of words over what happened to Flight Ten Seventy—"

Not more war talk! She switched to a different Andecco program.

> "Senator Bradley Seldortin stressed that the government's first priority must be fighting the J2 epidemic—"

Politics, yuck! She again changed programs. Scott Walters' voice came through the sound array.

> "Last night, another young woman was brutally murdered. The victim has been identified as Paula Arvish.

Detective Carl Brunish has released a statement claiming that Ms. Arvish's murder appears to be connected to the Mary Kronvelt slaying and the Agel Yungst shootings at Hughes Medical Center. He declined to provide details, as the investigation is ongoing."

Not another murder! *Paula Arvish*—the name wasn't familiar.

Leeha reached into the hiding place beneath the kitchen cabinets and pulled out the weird document. She flipped to the page containing the justice execution list. Mary Kronvelt topped the list, but Paula Arvish wasn't on it.

The news report continued.

"Ms. Arvish was murdered in her neighbor's townhouse in the Hillside District. The owner of the home, Nancy Pitman, was out of town at the time of the crime."

Nancy Pitman? No way! Leeha stared at Nancy's name. It was second on the justice execution list.

Someone knocked on the apartment door. So much for reading more of the text; Cookie had returned.

Leeha rewrapped the document and hid it under the kitchen cabinets. "Coming!"

She opened the door, but it wasn't Cookie who stood in the hallway.

PART ◈ TWO
LOST

THEY TOOK HER!

Cadona City, Cadona
SATURDAY, APRIL 29, YEAR 1007 EE
8:55 A.M., EAST CADONA TIME

Cookie Davis trotted up the apartment building stairwell. Despite a great workout, she was glad to almost be home. A fun day awaited her. After a hot shower, she'd prepare a high-protein breakfast. After eating, she and Leeha would drive to the market. Next, they'd relax a bit. Maybe they'd listen to music or watch a movie.

She reached for her key, but her pocket was empty.

A grin crossed her face. Soon, she and Leeha would share a good laugh; forgetting the physical key was becoming a habit.

Cookie pushed open the door to the fourth-floor corridor.

Something wasn't right. A thin beam of light flowed across the hallway. The bright spot looked like natural daylight, but there weren't any windows. Where would the light be coming from?

She ran to their unit. The door was ajar. She didn't see Leeha, but theme music for Andecco News Service flowed through the doorway.

"Leeha, I'm back."

No one answered.

She walked inside and turned off the sound array.

"Leeha, are you here?"

Silence.

She looked in the bathroom. Leeha wasn't there, but she must've already washed because fresh drops of water dotted the shower curtain.

Cookie stuck her head into the bedroom; Leeha wasn't there, either. Where in the world had she gone?

Cleaning supplies! They were running low on cleaning supplies. Maybe Leeha went to the store and, by accident, left without locking up.

Cookie looked out the living room window. The Monarch was parked in its assigned place.

Something must be wrong. It wasn't like Leeha to walk alone to the store.

Cookie reached for her personal device, but before she could place a call, motion caught her eye. Down below and to the right, a man was walking on the weedy lawn. He was heading away from the building and toward the street. The guy looked suspicious; people in the area didn't wear tailored, black suits. The man stopped walking. He seemed to be waiting for someone.

Three more people—two men and a woman—came out through the emergency exit at the far end of the building. These men also wore crisp, black suits. The woman, though, wore casual clothing. Something was wrong with her. She dropped to her knees. As the men hoisted her to her feet, her head flopped backward.

Leeha! The woman was Leeha!

Cookie slapped the window. "Leeha! Leeha!"

None of the people on the lawn looked up.

A red van raced down the street and came to a stop in front of the building. The men shoved Leeha into the back of the vehicle.

Cookie ran into the hallway. "Mrs. Furley! Toofy! Help! Please! Help!"

The door to Mrs. Furley's unit swung open with just a touch.

Mrs. Furley and Toofy lay on the floor. Her friends looked dead. Blood covered their bodies.

"Somebody, help! Please, help!"

No one came to her aid.

The bad guys were getting away. She must hurry.

She ran to the emergency exit and lunged down a flight of stairs.

It was taking too long. She swung her legs over the handrail and slid down to the landing at the bottom of the staircase.

She pushed open the steel door leading outside.

The red van pulled away from the curb.

She chased after the automobile.

They were getting away, but her legs wouldn't move any faster.

The van stopped at a light. The vehicle then turned right.

Up ahead, it made a left turn.

She arrived at the corner, but it was too late. The van had disappeared.

The time had come to call the police.

She reached for her arm patch. It was empty! Her personal device was missing. How had she lost it?

"Help me! Somebody, help me!"

No one showed up. No faces appeared in the windows. Many of the nearby buildings were shuttered.

She must find her personal device.

Cookie wiped the perspiration from her face and scanned the asphalt roadway.

Her device was nowhere in sight. She had to do something! The van was getting farther away with each passing second, but she mustn't go into the apartment building. Bad guys might be inside.

She came up with a plan. She'd retrace her steps. If she found the device, she'd call the police. If she didn't find it, she'd drive the Monarch to the Happy Day Diner and ask for help.

Sweat burned her eyes as she ran, but she mustn't slow down. The sooner she got help, the sooner someone could save Leeha.

◎

Cadona City, Cadona
SATURDAY, APRIL 29, YEAR 1007 EE
9:20 A.M., EAST CADONA TIME

Angela Thirgal looked out the passenger side window of Bob Fullerby's old, maroon-colored car. "Kever-o, there's Pineland Apartments. If this is where Leeha Ritsagin really lives, her unit will be on the fourth floor, number four thirteen."

Kever Carsen steered the vehicle to the curb. "Interesting name for the apartments; I don't see a single tree, pine or otherwise. I wonder if anyone really lives here. The whole neighborhood's deserted."

"I don't think it's deserted, Kever-o. The parking lot's full."

"Well, Ang, let's see if we can get into the building. It looks like we may need a passcode." He stepped out of the vehicle.

Angela climbed out from the passenger side. She spotted a flicker. "At least one person is home. Window blinds on the second floor moved."

"That's not the only sign of life," Kever said.

Angela looked down the street. A woman with an hourglass figure, long legs, and vibrant hair was running toward them. "Wow! That lady's in a hurry. One thing's for sure, she's in great shape."

"You said it, not me," Kever said. "No holding it against me later. But since you brought it up, I will add everything that's supposed to bounce bounces just right."

"Kever-o, is your mind always in the gutter?"

"What did I do now, Ang? You started it."

She shook her head. Kever was such an idiot at times!

His voice turned serious. "Hey, Ang, she might be in trouble."

"I think you're right. It looks like she's flagging us down."

A look of panic covered the woman's sweaty face. "Help me! Please! Help!" She didn't stop until she was right in front of them.

"Ma'am," Kever said, "what's wrong?"

"They took her!"

"Took whom?" Kever asked.

"My roommate!"

Angela had a hunch; she hoped it was wrong. "Ma'am, is your roommate's name Leeha? Leeha Ritsagin?"

The woman's eyes widened. "Yes! How … how do you know?"

"Because we're looking for Leeha," Angela said. "She may be in trouble."

Suspicion filled the woman's voice. "Who are you?"

Angela pulled a press badge from her pocket. "I'm Angela Thirgal, a reporter for Andecco News Service. This is Kever Carsen. He works with me."

The woman appeared even more wary. "You're Angela Thirgal? *The* Angela Thirgal from Andecco News? Really?"

Angela was tired of the delays. "Yes, I am. Ma'am, when did they take Leeha?"

"A few minutes ago. Three guys, they threw her into a red van."

"Were you with Leeha when they grabbed her?" Angela asked.

"No, I'd just returned from a run. Leeha wasn't home. When I looked out the window, I saw guys dragging her across the lawn. They threw her into the van. I ran after them, but they got away."

"Can you identify the van?" Kever asked.

"I think so."

"Ma'am," Angela said, "will you come with us? And show us where the van went?"

"Yes! Let's go! We've got to find Leeha."

Angela climbed into the back seat. "Ma'am, ride in front."

Kever hopped into the driver seat and said, "Ma'am, what's your name?"

"Cookie … Cookie Davis."

"Cookie," Kever said, "which way did the van go?"

"Straight ahead."

The car took off. Angela's head pressed against the seatback. Kever was driving like a maniac again. They were in a hurry, though, so she didn't protest.

"Cookie," Angela said, "have you called the police?"

"No, I was going to after I lost sight of the van, but I dropped my PD while I was running. I was circling back to look for it when I saw you and Mr. Carsen."

Kever said, "What about Leeha? Did you try to call her?"

"No, there wasn't time. I'd just gotten home when I saw them throw her into the van."

"Hey, Ang," Kever said, "maybe Anson can help us."

"Good idea. I'll call him."

Cookie's voice sounded frantic. "Who's Anson?"

Kever said, "A police officer."

Angela had just sent Anson a message when Kever slammed on the brakes. He opened the door and leaned out.

"Kever-o, what the heck are you doing?"

"PD." He grabbed a personal device that was sitting on the road and tossed the device in Cookie's direction. "Cookie, see if it's yours."

"Yes, it's mine."

"Cookie, listen carefully," Kever said. "Disable it, and, whatever you do, don't call Leeha or the police. Her kidnappers will be able to find us. Do you understand?"

"Yes."

Angela clutched an armrest as the car sped away. It was a good thing there weren't traffic monitors in the area. The cops would write up a speeding citation for sure.

The cops! That's it! Rona Betler was meeting with Detective Carl Brunish about the Paula Arvish murder. Leeha Ritsagin had been abducted; the detective's sleuth skills might come in handy.

She sent Rona an encrypted message: *Tell the detective our person of interest was taken this morning.*

Angela heard Kever's voice. "Cookie, where to now?"

"The van stopped at that light and turned right. Then, it went left by the appliance repair sign. I lost them after that."

Kever followed her directions. He parked the car along the curb by the appliance repair shop and said, "From here, they either had to get on Interstate Eleven or go beneath the overpass."

Tears rattled Cookie's words. "I ... I don't know where they went. By the time I reached the corner, they were gone."

"Hey, Ang," Kever said, "how 'bout we check the interstate?"

"Let's do it. I-Eleven would give them jumping-off points to any part of the city."

The car leaned hard to the left as Kever drove onto the entrance ramp. He said, "The straightest shot is to go east. Keep an eye out for a red vehicle."

Somewhere in Cadona ...

Leeha Ritsagin wondered where she was. Hands grasped her shoulders and knees. Why would someone be touching her?

Her body rose. Seconds later, her back pressed against a hard surface. She opened her eyes, but she had a hard time keeping them from closing.

The world around her looked distorted, like peering through a fish-bowl. Several people hovered over her. Some wore black and others white. All of them had something covering their faces.

Above her was an unfamiliar, padded roof. To the left, she saw seams and trim, like the inside of an automobile.

Nothing made sense. Where was she, and how had she gotten there?

Her body felt as if it were floating. The padded roof glided away, re-placed by a high, gray ceiling. Industrial light fixtures hung from the ends of grimy cables that were attached to massive beams.

She rolled her head to the side. All she saw were stacks of old crates. She rolled her head in the other direction. Something glistened. The big, shiny, red object she saw seemed out of place in the dirty room.

Her body moved again.

Another shiny surface, this time white in color, lay to her left.

Nightmare—she must be having a nightmare. But if this was a dream, why didn't she wake up?

She felt one rough jerk. All motion stopped.

A different roof hovered above her. This one was smooth and gave off a faint glow.

Something pricked her left arm. Her eyelids shut.

13

TRAINED TO NOT TALK

"Economic decay, fueled by the fall of Cadona's industrial might, has left warehouses, office buildings, and exquisite examples of architecture in utter ruin. Elect Senator Mitch Fischer as President. He will restore Cadona's rightful place as the industrial hub of the world."

Senator John Rineburg
"Mitch Fischer for President"
Freedom Party Campaign Speech
Year 1007 of the Enlightened Epoch

Cadona City, Cadona
SATURDAY, APRIL 29, YEAR 1007 EE
9:35 A.M., EAST CADONA TIME

Angela Thirgal let Kever Carsen and Cookie Davis watch for the red van that had whisked Leeha Ritsagin away.

She had something else on her mind—just who was this woman claiming to be Leeha's roommate? Angela studied Cookie's reflection in the rearview mirror. Besides faint bruises on her face and neck, her skin, features, and raven hair were flawless. Her manicured appearance didn't fit with this lower-middle-class neighborhood.

Angela tapped her personal device. In seconds, she found a long string of life-bits on WorldLink. A few years back, Cookie was a regular on the chic Cadona City social scene. She'd earned a business degree from Rockwood University, a top-notch—and expensive—school. She had a fiancé, a handsome guy named Rodney Pinkerman. Image after image showed the couple at their lavish engagement party.

Not long ago, though, Cookie vanished from the in-crowd news.

Also scarce was information about her childhood. What did exist on WorldLink suggested a poor, working-class upbringing. Somehow, she'd climbed the social ladder. Then, like many other people in recent years, it appeared she'd lost her livelihood in the economic downturn.

While nothing in Cookie's public record revealed anything suspicious, just how was it that this cultured woman happened to be there to witness the kidnapping?

"Hey, Cookie," Angela said, "did you recognize the men who took Leeha?"

"No, I've never seen them before."

"Do you have any idea why someone would take her?"

"No! She's a good, decent person. She goes to work, watches movies ... she's good. I can't imagine why anyone would want to hurt her. We've got to find her, or she'll end up like Mrs. Furley and Toofy."

"*Mrs. Furley* and *Toofy*," Angela said, "who are they?"

"They were killed. It was awful! They were covered in blood. I ...."

Kever said, "Cookie, how do you know Mrs. Furley and Toofy?"

"They live ... lived a few doors down the hall from us. They were our friends."

"How do you know they're dead?" he asked.

"I ... I saw them. They were lying on the floor."

"Where did you see the bodies? In Leeha's apartment?"

"No, in Mrs. Furley's apartment. Toofy's a big guy. I thought he could help. When I knocked on their door, it just opened on its own. Both Toofy and his grandma were lying on the ground."

"How were they killed? Were they shot?"

"I think so. There was blood everywhere. They weren't moving."

Angela said, "Cookie, how long have you known Leeha?"

"Almost a month now."

"How long have you been Leeha's roommate?"

"It's coming up on three weeks. Leeha saved my life. She let me stay with her after my fiancé beat me up. I thought he'd kill me."

"How did you meet her?"

"We both interviewed at Altage Enterprises. We talked after the interview."

"When was the interview?"

"April third," Cookie said. "I remember it like it was yesterday. My interview totally sucked. Leeha was so nice to me!"

Angela recalled one of Bob Fullerby's lessons: look for signs someone is lying. Do the person's words match the tone of voice? Do facial expressions fit with the emotion the person wants to convey?

Again, she glanced at Cookie's reflection in the rearview mirror. Cookie seemed to be telling the truth.

"Hey, Cookie!" Kever said. "There's a red van."

"That's not it." Her wail was piercing. "It's my fault! It's all my fault! Leeha's going to die. Mrs. Furley and Toofy are dead, and it's my fault, too."

Angela said, "Why do you think it's your fault?"

"We went for a run, Leeha and I. She got tired, but I wanted to run some more. I told her to go home. When I got home, it was too late. They got her! They took her! And Mrs. Furley and Toofy were dead."

Kever said, "Cookie, listen to me. If you were with Leeha, they would've taken you, too. Or maybe killed you. If that happened, you wouldn't be able to help us find her or your friends' killers."

She wiped tears from her cheeks. "Some help I am! We've gone a long way. We haven't found the van."

Angela said, "Good point. Maybe it's time to turn around. They could've gone anywhere from here. What do you think, Kever-o?"

"Ang, did you figure out what's beyond the overpass?"

"I did. According to WorldLink, there are a bunch of warehouses and wrecking yards down there. It seems like a good place to hide a van. Let's check it out."

"Will do," Kever said. The car swung to the right as he steered onto a jughandle. The exit ramp led to a road near the Pineland Apartments.

Angela's personal device vibrated. "Hey, Kever-o, I got a message from Anson. He wants to meet at noon at the Nutty Squirrel. I suppose you know what he's talking about."

"Yeah, it's a pub we go to after climbing."

"Noon!" Cookie said. "You're kidding me! We can't wait that long. We've got to do something now."

"We are," Kever told her. "We're going to check beneath the overpass in case the guys in the red van are hiding down there."

"That's not enough! We've got to do more. These guys are killers! They have to be the ones who killed Mrs. Furley and Toofy. They have Leeha. She's with those monsters."

"Cookie," Angela said, "I've asked a coworker to contact a police detective. He'll have access to resources regular cops won't."

"I'm sorry, Ms. Thirgal, I really am. Thanks for helping. I feel so worthless. None of this makes sense. One second, everything's fine, then boom! This happens."

Angela decided it was time to pretend to be more friendly. "Please, call me *Ang.*"

Cookie wiped tears from her face. "Okay."

Angela said, "You must really care about Leeha."

"I do. I never had such a good friend. She's real. Not at all phony. So many people I know turn out to be ... not what they seem."

"Cookie, we'll do everything we can to find her."

The vehicle slowed. Angela looked out the windows. Businesses were closed. Many buildings seemed abandoned. The streets were narrow, and litter filled the gutters.

Cookie's voice sounded panicky. "It's icky! If they brought Leeha here, she'll be terrified. What are we going to do?"

Kever said something to Cookie. Angela didn't hear his words, but whatever he told her worked—Cookie calmed down.

Angela relaxed into her seat and pieced together information about the Drop Case. Cookie portrayed Leeha Ritsagin as a quiet-living, honest person. Leeha, though, had stolen the Guiding Light. Maybe Cookie was wrong about her roommate. Or perhaps Cookie was lying.

Kever pulled the car to the curb.

Angela said, "Kever-o, why are we stopping?"

"There's a guy. Maybe he knows something."

Angela saw a man staggering along a crumbling sidewalk. Grime covered his face and hair. He used a garbage bag as a rain poncho.

Kever rolled down his window. "Excuse me, sir."

The bum, stooped beneath the weight of a makeshift backpack, lumbered up to the vehicle. His dirty face loomed large in the open window. He was maybe forty years of age, but his crinkled skin made him appear much older. He stank of stale alcohol.

Kever said, "Sir, did you see a red van this morning?"

"Nope, no red vans. Only cars besides yours were a couple of trucks droppin' off junkers at the wreckin' yard."

"Where's the yard?" Kever asked.

Strings drooped from the man's sleeve as he pointed down the road. "Straight over there, off to the right."

Kever handed the guy a wad of paper bills. The bum swiped the money from Kever's hand and said, "Much obliged. You might want to talk to Reb and Ginger. They hang out on the far side of the yard. They built themselves a shelter along the fence where the railroad used to be."

"Thank you, sir," Kever said.

The man ambled away. Kever rolled up the window.

"Kever-o," Angela said, "I'm surprised you haven't gotten yourself killed by now. You let that guy get too close."

"Ang, you do realize that the men who kidnapped Leeha Ritsagin are a bigger threat to us than an old drunk, no?"

She hated it when Kever was right.

Cookie said, "Why are we still sitting here? Let's see if the guy's friends or the people at the wrecking yard saw a red van."

Angela slumped into the seat. Cookie was taking Kever's side. Why in the world did so many girls fall for him?

The car pulled away from the curb.

They hadn't ridden far when Angela spotted an earthen yard filled with junky automobiles. An aging, chain-link fence surrounded the facility.

Kever said, "That must be the wrecking yard."

"I think you're right, Mr. Carsen," Cookie said. "I see guys over there. Maybe they saw something."

Angela saw four men dressed in grease-stained overalls. "Be careful, Kever-o. If the red van did come this way, these guys may have been involved in hiding it."

"Ang," Kever said, "you're armed, right?"

She wasn't sure if Kever's question was serious or if he was picking on her. "I'm sort of armed, I guess. I'm carrying pepper spray."

The men in overalls looked up as Kever steered Bob Fullerby's car through an open gate. Kever rolled down the window.

One of the men approached. "Is there somethin' I can do for you folks?"

"Yeah," Kever said, "we're wondering if you saw a red van this morning."

"Nope, we didn't bring in a red van today."

Angela didn't notice any fear in Kever's voice. "What about driving up or down the street?"

The man called out to the three other guys. "Any of you fellas see a red van driving around this morning?"

Two of the workers shook their heads, but the third man said, "Yeah, I did. I think it was a Verim Wagon, a newer model. It was headin' toward the old rail station. Not sure why someone would go there; the trains don't use those lines any longer."

"Do you remember when you saw it?" Kever asked.

"Not exactly, but it wasn't all that long ago."

"Thank you, gentlemen." Kever rolled up the window.

"Mr. Carsen," Cookie said, "do you know where the old rail station is?"

Angela fought a wave of irritation as she spoke. "Contrary to popular belief, Kever-o doesn't know everything."

"Aw, come on, Ang," Kever said, "I know a few things ... but not that."

Angela said, "Well, I know. I checked it out on WorldLink. The road we were just on dead-ends at the station."

Kever looked over his shoulder and winked. "To the train station it is."

They drove by one dilapidated building after another.

"This whole area looks abandoned," Angela said, "but people must be around. All this garbage had to come from somewhere."

The pavement yielded to gravel. The road curved to the right. A huge, crumbling building stood nearby. The road dead-ended at a drooping, cable fence. Beyond the fence lay the remains of railroad tracks.

Kever pulled into what once must have been a loading yard. He stuck his head out the driver side window. "Someone was here recently."

"How can you tell?" Cookie asked.

"There are three sets of tire tracks in the gravel. Two of the vehicles must've been big and heavy."

"I'm glad you're helping, Mr. Carsen; you're smart."

Angela caught a groan before it escaped her lips. Cookie graduated with honors from Rockwood University, yet she didn't know that tires left tracks. Fancy schools must not teach common sense.

"Hey," Kever said, "I thought I saw someone slinking around over there."

Angela didn't see anyone. "Where?"

"Behind that junk pile by the fence." Kever climbed out of the car.

Angela clutched her pepper spray canister and got out, too. "Be careful, Kever-o."

"Don't worry. By looking at the tire tracks, whoever drove in here has already left. I'm betting Ginger or Reb is hiding over there."

Cookie opened the front passenger side door.

"Cookie," Angela said, "stay in the car."

"No way! I'm going with you. We've got to find Leeha."

"Okay, but stay behind me." Angela stared into the tangle of rubble and weeds. Cloistered in the mess were the ruins of a building. "Kever-o, you may be right; it may be a homeless person's shelter."

Kever didn't sound the least bit afraid as he spoke. "Hello, is anyone there?"

A scraggly male emerged from behind a sheet of discarded plastic. "Hold on there, dude. We mean no harm. We don't care what you're up to; we only wanna be left alone."

"Sir," Kever said, "it's okay. We're just looking for a red van. Have you seen one this morning?"

A woman with mussed hair crept out from the same squalid hole. "Reb, don't say nothing! We don't need no trouble."

"Ma'am," Angela said, "a woman is missing. We need to find this red van so we can help her. We're hoping you can tell us what happened here this morning."

Ginger shook her head.

Cookie sounded frantic. "Please! You must help us. Someone I care about is in danger. If you know something, please, please, tell us."

"You know, Ginger," Reb said, "I trust these folks."

"Well, I most decidedly do not!"

"Ginger, their friend is in danger. If I were in trouble, wouldn't you want someone to help you find me?"

Ginger didn't argue. Instead, she clung to a useless light post like an alley cat ready to dash for cover.

"Sir," Kever said, "what do you know about a red van?"

Reb scratched his strawberry blond beard. "No one ever comes back here, that is until this morning. We had lots of excitement."

Ginger let down her guard. "Yeah, we had oodles of excitement! We saw a red van all right. And a big, white truck, too."

Reb said, "We heard this awful noise. Everything's shakin'. I peeked out. A big, white truck drove into the warehouse."

Ginger stretched out her pencil-thin arms. "The truck was long. Big as a train car, I tell you!"

"It was like those driverless trucks," Reb said, "only clean and shiny white."

"This white truck went into the building?" Angela asked.

Animation filled Reb's voice. "It sure did. All got quiet for a while. Until we heard more noises. Then the red van showed up."

Cookie said, "Was there a woman with them? She's around my height. She has long, wavy hair. It's a light, reddish color."

Reb shook his head. "We didn't see no woman, only men. Not sure how many in total. Maybe ten or there-abouts."

"Sir," Kever said, "where did the red van go?"

Ginger spoke before Reb had a chance to answer. "It drove into the building, too. Right on in it went. Both the white truck and the red van were in there, side by side."

Reb said, "Then, they closed the warehouse door. We didn't hear or see anything else until—"

Ginger flung her arms again. "Until the door opened. The red van drove away normal."

"Normal?" Angela asked.

Reb said, "Yeah, it went back to the paved street and was gone."

Cookie had calmed down a bit. "What about the white truck?"

"This is the weirdest part," Reb said. "Another vehicle showed up. It parked right here where we're standin'."

Ginger's eyes grew wide. "It looked like a backhoe did the nasty with an army tank and had a kid. A long thing came out of the back of it. This thing went up and up!"

Reb waved his arms over his head. "It formed a bridge, a temporary one, mind you. The bridge stretched over the tracks."

"The white truck drove over the bridge," Ginger said. "Then, poof! The bridge folded up real fast. Clip, clap, clump, it folded up."

"Where did the white truck go?" Kever asked.

Reb pointed toward weed-covered railroad tracks. "An old road runs along the rails. The truck got on that road and kept goin' and goin' for as far as we could see."

"Thanks," Kever said. "What about the vehicle with the bridge in the back?"

Reb gestured toward the street. "It drove away normal. We ain't heard or seen nothin' else until you three showed up."

Ginger pulled something out of a pocket. "Want to look inside the building?"

Reb said, "Ginger! I told you never to let anyone know about the key."

"We won't tell anyone," Angela said. "We only want to find the woman."

Ginger opened a side door to the old warehouse.

Angela followed her into a run-down office. The place smelled musty. Cobwebs covered chairs, a rotting desk, and crooked filing cabinets. Two benches were the only furnishings that were free of dust.

Reb's voice was a whisper. "We come in here when it's really nasty outside. We never bother nothing."

"We believe you," Kever said.

Ginger led them down a long hallway.

The place was dark except for narrow beams of light coming through skinny, vent-like windows near the ceiling. Angela turned on her personal device luminaire. The amber beam spotlighted broken pipes and bundles of decaying wires.

At the end of the hall, a door, hanging askew on its hinges, opened into an enormous bay.

Reb pointed into the huge room. "This is where the white truck and red van were. Whatever they were up to, they didn't stay long."

Angela took pictures.

"Do you see something, Ang?" Kever asked.

"Not much. There are fresh footprints and tire tracks in the dust on the floor. Nothing else looks disturbed."

Ginger had a big grin on her face. She seemed happy to have helped. "See, all's quiet again, just like we told ya."

"I hope it stays quiet," Angela said.

The smile fell from Ginger's face. "What do you mean?"

Kever pulled paper money from his wallet. "The men who were here, they are very bad people. They may hurt you if they come back." He handed the cash to Reb. "Here, take this. Maybe you and Ginger can find somewhere else to stay, at least for a while."

"I don't wanna take your money," Reb said. "We didn't do that much for y'all. We didn't find your friend."

"You were a great help, sir," Kever told him. "Please, take it. We'd feel terrible if something happened to either of you."

Reb took the cash. "Thanks. Maybe Ginger and I will get a hot meal, too."

This was one of those times when Angela admired Kever. She pulled bills and coins from her pockets. "Ginger, here, take this, too."

"But you don't have any left for yourself," Ginger said.

"It's okay, I have more. This is money I keep for places where you can't pay by PD."

Ginger took the cash. "Thank you!"

Angela took one last look around before following the others out the office door. Once outside, she watched as Reb and Ginger crawled into their makeshift dwelling. She hoped they'd take Kever's advice and find safer shelter.

"Hey, Ang," Kever said, "let's go. We need to head out to meet Anson."

She climbed into the back seat of the big, old car.

They drove away.

Thoughts raced through her head. What were Leeha Ritsagin's kidnappers up to?

She pulled up a map on WorldLink Direction Finder. "Hey, Kever-o, I found something interesting."

"What?"

"I was trying to figure out why the kidnappers would go through all the trouble of using a temporary bridge. I'm looking at a map … the only place a big truck could get to by taking the old road is Trans-City Barge Port Number Two."

Kever said, "My guess is they went that way because there aren't security cameras between here and the port."

"I don't think it's the only reason, Kever-o. Guess who runs the barge facility?"

"Who?"

"Big shots in the Paxton gang."

"Ang," Cookie said, "who are they?"

"They're a nasty group of thugs, but very organized."

Cookie's voice quivered. "Are you saying these bad people have Leeha?"

Kever said, "Cookie, we don't know who has her. Whoever took her may have used the port because, for the right price, the Paxtons will keep their mouths shut."

Cookie burst into tears. "Everything's terrible! Leeha's gone! We looked for a red van, but she may have been in a white truck. Now, you tell me she's on some … some … barge."

"Cookie," Kever said, "whoever took Leeha went through a lot of trouble to kidnap her. They wouldn't have gone through so much effort if they didn't want something from her. We may still have time. Don't give up yet."

"That's … that's true. I mean, they killed Mrs. Furley and Toofy, but they took Leeha alive. What are we going to do next, Mr. Carsen?"

"Talk to my friend, Anson."

"The cop?"

"Yep. Oh, by the way, Cookie, call me *Kever-o*. Everyone else does."

Angela tuned out their conversation; they weren't talking about anything important.

She stared out the window. Perhaps it was her fault that bad guys had gotten to Leeha first. If Bob Fullerby had been there to make decisions, things might've turned out differently.

"Hey, Ang," Kever said, "you're quiet."

"I was sending Mr. Fullerby a message. I told him about our meeting at the Nutty Squirrel."

"Can he make it?"

"Don't know yet. He's still not accepting calls."

She leaned back and closed her eyes. Questions raced through her mind. Where were the kidnappers taking Leeha? Were the abductors military intelligence agents? National Police? Soldiers of God Justice Group mercenaries? So many unknowns! So few answers!

Some of her questions, though, did have answers: whoever took Leeha Ritsagin must be connected to the Freedom Party and the Back-to-Basics Club. Leeha stole the Guiding Light. Senator Mitch Fischer, Senator John Rineburg, General Douglass Willirman, and Pastor Leon Walls were desperate to find the document.

A depressing thought weighed on her. Senator Fischer and his buddies have been winning too many battles. Today, they won yet another—they got to Leeha first. The bad guys were everywhere; where were all the good guys hiding?

Cadona City, Cadona
SATURDAY, APRIL 29, YEAR 1007 EE
10:45 A.M., EAST CADONA TIME

Verona Vondelle leaned against the trunk of a long-dead, nearly limbless tree. Gravel, mixed with slimy mud, stuck to her militia-style tromping boots. It was hard to imagine that this dead patch of earth had once been an urban green space.

Besides a vagrant sleeping on a broken bench, no one was in sight.

She checked the time. At any moment, her contact would arrive. He'd better hurry; their window of opportunity was short.

A tall, fit man with a tote bag appeared. He walked at a brisk pace down a cracked footpath. If he wasn't her contact, she must destroy the contents of the envelope she carried.

The man drew closer.

She recognized him: Tracker, a Cadona Guardian compatriot.

As their team had planned, he stopped alongside a stuffed trash can sitting beneath the branches of another dead tree.

Verona walked up to him. "Hey, Tracker. Did you get all the stuff?"

He tapped the tote bag. "Yeah, got everything."

Tracker was a nice man; he seemed too compassionate for this type of work. He said, "Ms. V, listen, I'm really sorry about Becker. He was a good guy. I know you two were close."

"Yes, on both counts. He was a good person, and I shall miss him."

"Ms. V … you know … Becker and I, we talked …. The feeling was mutual. He cared for you. I wanted you to know how he felt in case he never told you."

"Thanks."

"Um, hey, Ms. V, are you sure you're up to this?"

"I'm sure. Timmy's mission failed, but he did his duty. Now, we need to do ours. Look, Tracker, I know you miss him, too, but this may be our single chance to go inside and clean house. Only local cops are investigating the homicides, but the Back-to-Basics goons will return."

"I agree, they'll come back. Whom did they kidnap?"

Verona pulled a sheet of paper from the envelope. Tracker handed her a cloth. She brushed the fabric over the printed image of a bouquet of flowers. The blossoms faded. Text and a woman's portrait appeared on the page. "This is Leeha Ritsagin, the one they took."

"Ms. V, why does the Back-to-Basics Club want her?"

"She has something they want—some kind of document. It's called the *Guiding Light*. The odd thing is, Ritsagin appears to be *a nobody*."

Tracker studied the image. "Well, she must be *a somebody* because the goons held nothing back to capture her."

Verona said, "You're right. I've heard they may use Mind-One on her to learn what she knows."

"Wow! They're serious for sure! So, who got killed?"

"Two witnesses to the abduction: an elderly woman by the name of Bercette Furley and her grandson, Toofelance Furley."

"We're erasing someone?" he asked.

Verona wiped the cloth over another flowery photo. "Yes, this woman. Her name is Cookie Davis. She's been secretly living with Ritsagin for a few weeks. She moved in after her fiancé beat the crap out of her."

"Who's Davis' replacement?"

Verona pulled another sheet of paper from the envelope. "This woman."

Tracker took the sheet from her. He squinted at the image. "It's blurry, but she does resemble Davis. Who is she?"

"That's the good part—for us anyway. Unidentified. She's listed as killed in the Mik-la-tah Tsunami."

"No body?" Tracker asked.

"Nope, no body was ever found. It was likely washed out to sea or buried under rubble. All the Sohn-Suran government has on her is a fuzzy photo and some DNA."

"Good work, Ms. V. It'll be nearly impossible for anyone to figure out who she was."

Verona stuffed the papers and cloth into the envelope and dropped them into the trash can. The envelope and its contents turned to powder.

"Tracker, do you have the stuff for our covers?"

"I do." He handed her a cord with a badge hanging from the end of it. He slipped a similar lanyard over his head. "So, what do you think, Ms. V? Do I look like a forensic nerd?"

If the man she loved hadn't been blown to pieces in Flight 1070, she might've given Tracker a smile. "Yeah, you'll blend in perfectly. Come on, let's get this over with."

She and Tracker headed down the street to Leeha Ritsagin's apartment.

A police van was parked in front of the building. Two Warrenton District officers were pushing a sealed evidence box into the back of the vehicle.

Verona lowered her head. "Tracker, be sure to avoid eye contact with the cops."

"Will do, Ms. V."

She and Tracker entered the lobby. "Let's take the stairs," she told him.

They didn't meet anyone in the stairwell, but officers were clustered at the far end of the fourth-floor corridor. She whispered in Tracker's ear. "Where the cops are—that's the Furley's unit. Ritsagin's unit is halfway down the hall. It's number four thirteen."

She checked door numbers as she and Tracker walked along the hallway. She stopped. "This is Ritsagin's apartment. Any sign of surveillance devices?"

"That is a negative," Tracker said.

"Good. Turn on your airshield."

"Airshield on."

She followed Tracker into the unit.

Tracker said, "I'm glad it's a small place without much furniture. We'll be in and out in no time. Where do you want me to start, Ms. V?"

"The kitchen and living room." She pulled open bi-fold doors. "And this laundry nook. I'll take the bathroom and bedroom."

"Sure thing, Ms. V."

Verona looked inside the cramped bathroom. A few faded, frayed towels were stacked on a set of shelves built into the wall. She fluffed up the towels. A cheap, two-drawer container rested beneath the sink. She opened the drawers to expose the contents.

Now for the bedroom. She opened the closet door. A strange shape hovered in the corner. "Oh, this is just creepy!"

Tracker appeared in the bedroom doorway. "What is?"

"This … thing. It looks kind of like a man."

"It's a punching bag, Ms. V. It's for self-defense training. This one's an old, simple model. You seem surprised to find it here."

"I am; nothing in Ritsagin's file suggests she'd own a fighting tool."

Verona separated clothes that were hanging in the closet and removed the lids from storage bins. Next, she fluffed up the covers on the bed. "I think I'm ready. Are you?"

"Ready."

The wave-deflector coating crinkled as it covered their bodies. Verona slipped goggles over her eyes and made sure the seal was snug. "All set, Tracker?"

"Yep, let's do it." He handed her an eraser element.

Verona inserted Cookie Davis' code into the silvery device. "Do your thing, little fellows." Glittery specks flew out of the eraser. The device and its sparkly children glided around each room, piece of furniture, and pile of clothing. The eraser element came to rest on the floor near her feet. The shiny flecks hurried back home to the canister.

"Done," Verona said. "Cookie Davis is erased. Your turn, Tracker." She handed him a tiny disk. "Here's our unidentified Tsunami victim."

Tracker inserted the slip disk into the DNA pattern scatter element. He guided the scattering device to places where DNA is typically found. "What do you think, Ms. V? Good?"

"Yep, good job. Let's clean up and put everything back like we found it."

"Tracker, are you ready to leave?"

"Yeah, let's get out of here."

Verona reached for the doorknob and said, "Remember to turn off your airshield the second you step out. Local cops probably won't detect it, but you never know."

"I'm ready, Ms. V. My finger's on the button."

She glanced down the hall as she stepped through the doorway. The commotion by the murder victims' unit had settled down a bit.

When all of the officers were facing the other way, she set a self-destructing eraser element above the doorframe. With luck, it would remove any remaining signs that Cookie Davis was ever there. "Okay, let's get out of here."

"I'm right behind you, Ms. V."

Verona breathed a sigh of relief when they made it out of the apartment building. She noticed the resident parking lot that lay across the street. "Tracker, did your people tow the brown Monarch?"

"We did. It might already be shredded and melted. I heard nothing of interest was found inside." He took a few steps and said, "Ms. V, just wondering, the woman we erased, Cookie Davis, where is she now?"

"Not sure. We lost her."

"Lost her?"

"Yeah, Rineburg, Willirman, and their Back-to-Basics Club goons are tightening their grip. It's making our job harder, but we'll find her. In any case, a trusted contact will make sure she doesn't return to the apartment."

"They'd better," Tracker said, "or she'll end up a prisoner like Leeha Ritsagin or dead like the Furleys."

Cadona City, Cadona
SATURDAY, APRIL 29, YEAR 1007 EE
11:45 A.M., EAST CADONA TIME

Pastor Leon Walls rushed into the True Followers of God Church headquarters.

Tammy Smith trotted up to him. "Good morning, Pastor Walls. General Douglass Willirman and Senator John Rineburg are in the lounge. I provided coffee and lemonade."

"Thank you, Tammy. Do you know what's going on?"

"No, the gentlemen didn't share news with me. Oh, and … Senator Mitch Fischer is on his way. He'll be here soon."

Leon hurried to the lounge. Doug and John had already made themselves comfortable.

Doug held a crystal glass in his hand. "Good morning, Leon."

"Good morning, Dougy. Hello, John. Do you fellows bring good news or bad?"

"It's a mix, Pastor," Doug said.

The lounge door opened. Senator Mitch Fischer walked in. "Good morning. Please pardon my tardiness. The fundraiser ran longer than expected." He took a seat. "So, gentlemen, what do you have to report?"

Doug cleared his throat before speaking. "Ritsagin is in custody."

"Excellent news, Dougy," Mitch said. "Any complications?"

"Just one. Neighbors tried to interfere with her arrest, but the Justice Group took care of them. Loyals on the police force will handle the cleanup."

Mitch poured himself a cup of coffee. "Did we find the Guiding Light?"

John said, "Nope."

"What about electronic copies?"

"Nope."

"What about Ritsagin's Monarch? Any clues in the onboard systems?"

Irritation filled John's voice. "Don't know, Mitch. The Monarch's missing."

Doug's voice, however, sounded hopeful. "We do have Ritsagin's computer, though. We have people studying the content. Automated files and links may provide clues."

Mitch toyed with the handle of his white cup as he spoke. "Do we have evidence linking Ritsagin to Timothy Becker or the Cadona Guardians?"

"Nope," John said.

Leon's shoulders tightened. Things were not going well. They'd caught the thief but hadn't found the Guiding Light. "What did we learn from her PD and nodes?"

"Nothing, Leon," John said. "The bitch opted out of tracking."

"I don't get it, John. What does that mean?"

"It means we have no records. We don't know whom Ritsagin called, or who called her."

Doug said, "But we do have her PD. If someone tries to contact her, we'll know who it is. What we don't have is her call history."

Leon's face flushed from worry. "Is there any chance Ritsagin is working for Domataland or Sohn-Sur?"

Doug's nose whistled as he drew a deep breath. "Anything's possible, but we've found nothing to link her to a foreign government."

"I'm concerned," Leon said. "We don't seem to know a heck of a lot about our document."

Mitch leaned back in his seat. "I was thinking the same thing. John, when will Ritsagin's interrogation begin?"

"Soon. They'll start prepping her later today."

Somewhere in Cadona ...

Leeha Ritsagin didn't know where she was. She was lying on her back. A headache pounded in her temples.

She heard a man speaking in the background. His voice was stern and deep. "What did you find on the bitch's computer?"

Another man spoke. His words were softer. "Nothing that points to our prize, but she must be a Bob Fullerby fan; she accesses Andecco News Service broadcasts on a regular basis. She also seems to have an interest in Bakhadaland."

"Bakhadaland? Why do you think that?"

"She's viewed WorldLink photos, lots of them."

"Photos of what? Facilities? Troop deployments?"

"No, her interest seems to be in scenery shots—the Bakhadaree coasts and forests. There is one more thing we're looking into. There's some kind of complex search routine on her computer."

"Search routine for what?"

"I'm not sure yet. It's … difficult to decipher. It'll take more digging."

Leeha felt a hand on her right arm. A different man spoke. "Hey, hey, bitch! Wake up." He sounded young—and angry.

She opened her eyes. A man stared down at her. She made out the shape of his head and shoulders, but everything looked blurry.

"Hey, bitch, I'm talking to you. For whom do you work?"

"I'm very thirsty. May I please have a drink of water?"

"Not until you answer my question."

"I work at Franklin Technologies in the Warrenton District."

"Wrong answer! Who's your *real* boss?"

"Mr. Manning, at Franklin Tech."

"Lying bitch! Are you a Cadona Guardian?"

"A what?"

"Who's paying you? Domataland's intelligence service? Sohn-Sur's?"

"What? No! The only pay I get is from Franklin Tech. Why don't you call them and find out?"

"Why, you little—"

The man with the deep voice said, "Let her be, Mr. Beller. She's an *enemy apparent*; she's trained to not talk. Don't worry, Doctor Millerman's people will get answers out of her."

Something soft covered her face. A strange odor filled her nose. All sensations faded.

NUTTY SQUIRREL BEER & EATS

"The Nutty Squirrel Beer & Eats Pub, serving Cadona since 927 EE."

*Nutty Squirrel Advertisement
Year 1007 of
the Enlightened Epoch*

Cadona City, Cadona
SATURDAY, APRIL 29, YEAR 1007 EE
11:55 A.M., EAST CADONA TIME

The lumbering, maroon-colored car slowed. Angela Thirgal checked the time. "Hey, Kever-o, how much farther? It's almost noon."

"We're just about there, Ang."

Angela studied the old neighborhood. Narrow buildings, few of which stood more than four floors tall, lined both sides of the skinny street.

Up ahead, a huge sign protruded from a brick building.

As they drew closer, she saw what was embossed on the sign. A vintage-style image of a cartoonish blonde held a giant mug of beer in one hand and a hamburger in the other. Her exaggerated bosom and smile could've been found on an ad from eighty years ago. Squirrel ears poked through her yellow hair, and whiskers stuck out alongside her pink, button nose. Next to her were the words, *Nutty Squirrel Beer & Eats.*

Leave it to Kever to frequent a weird spot like this.

Kever drove into an alley. The car bounced.

"Kever-o, where in the world are you taking us?"

"Sorry for the rough ride. The parking lot's not paved."

Angela heard Cookie Davis sigh. Just great—Cookie was waking up; now she'd resume her incessant whining and crying.

Kever parked and turned off the engine.

"Kever-o," Cookie said in a sleepy voice, "where's the policeman?"

"Probably inside the pub." He climbed out of the car and opened Cookie's door.

Angela waited for him to do the same for her. He didn't. She opened the door herself.

Damp gravel crunched beneath her feet as she and Cookie followed Kever to the front of the building.

A skinny, redheaded man looked up when they walked in. "Howdy, Kever-o! Your friend's in the back corner."

"Thanks, Suds." Kever gave the bartender a childish salute and said, "Come on, ladies, it's this way."

Angela rolled her eyes. "Hey, Kever-o, his name is Suds? You've got to be kidding."

"All the people who work here have an alias, Ang." Kever counted on his fingers. "There's Draft, Pitcher, Mugs, Brew." He pointed toward the rear wall. "And there's Anson. It's his real name, not an alias."

A man with chiseled features sat along the back wall. He stood as they approached. His massive muscles bulged beneath his worn T-shirt and faded jeans.

"Hey, Anson," Kever said, "glad you're here. We appreciate your help. This is Angela Thirgal."

Anson held out his hand. "Glad to meet you, Ms. Thirgal."

"It's good to meet you, Anson, but there's no reason to be so formal. Please, call me *Ang*."

"Then *Ang* it is."

Anson extended his hand in Cookie's direction. "And you must be Rona Betler?"

Kever said, "No, she's not. This is Cookie Davis, Leeha Ritsagin's roommate."

As everyone took a seat at the table, Angela scanned the room. Three couples danced in front of an old-fashioned jukebox. Four people played pool. A few customers were gathered at the bar. She saw two employees: Suds and a slender woman with cropped, purple hair.

No one looked like a Back-to-Basics Club spy.

Anson sipped iced coffee and then set the glass on a coaster with an image of the buxom squirrel-girl printed on it. "So, Kever-o, what's the emergency?"

Angela saw Kever's mouth open, but he didn't have a chance to speak. Cookie's voice blared. "They took her! They took Leeha!"

"Shh, Cookie," Angela said. "Not so loud! Keep your voice down."

"I'm sorry; I'm so worried!" She burst into tears as Suds approached. He looked like he'd rather be anywhere else. "Can ... um ... can I get you all something?"

"I'll have tea," Kever said. "Strongest you have. And one of those nut-mushroom-grain burgers. Bring it with sweet potato fries and a spinach salad, please."

Angela pretended to study the menu. "I'll have the same, but water instead of tea."

Cookie pulled a tear-soaked napkin away from her face. "I ... I'll do the same. With water." Out of nowhere, she wailed like a bawling child. Suds stared at her.

Angela said, "There's been ... it's a death situation."

Suds cleared his throat. "I'm, um, I'm very sorry to hear that. I'll be right back with your drinks." He scurried away.

Angela felt her personal device buzz. "It's Mr. Fullerby. He says he's almost here."

Anson squirmed in his seat. "Bob Fullerby's coming?"

"Yeah," Angela said, "I let him know where we are."

Anson's face brightened. "I can't believe it! I'm going to meet Bob Fullerby in person."

Cadona City, Cadona
SATURDAY, APRIL 29, YEAR 1007 EE
12:10 P.M., EAST CADONA TIME

Bob Fullerby looked out the big, streaked windows of the city bus. He saw a sign for his CadTranS stop. He was almost there.

He reread Angela Thirgal's latest message. She hadn't explained why she wanted to meet at the Nutty Squirrel Beer & Eats Pub instead of the print shop. One thing, though, was certain; Angela, Kever, and Rona identified the mystery woman in the brown Monarch, but something had gone wrong.

The bus squealed to a halt. The rough-looking but friendly driver said, "Watch your step, sir."

Bob climbed down the steep, mud-splattered stairs. The bus sputtered away, leaving smelly, gray smoke in its wake.

He spotted the Nutty Squirrel's low-hanging sign. It stuck out from a building that was a block and a half away.

Debris crackled beneath the soles of his shoes as he headed down the fissured sidewalk. Age had taken its toll on the neighborhood, yet the place still had life and character.

The sidewalk tilted at the entrance to a rutted, gravelly parking lot. One of the parked cars caught his eye.

The vehicle was his! Why had Angela borrowed his automobile? Something very interesting must've happened.

Bob walked up to the Nutty Squirrel's front door. The entranceway needed a new coat of green paint, and the brass handle and hinges hadn't been polished in some time. Somehow, however, this weathered appearance added to the pub's charm.

He opened the heavy door. The smells of beer, roasted cheese, and grilled butter hung in the air.

The place was dark, so it took his eyes a while to adjust to the low light.

He spotted Angela. Kever was with her, but Rona was not. They were seated at a corner table. Two other people were with them: a lovely, dark-haired woman and a muscular young man with a military-style haircut.

Bob now understood why Angela didn't want to meet at the print shop; she and Kever were with people not associated with Andecco News Service.

Angela waved.

Bob headed toward the table.

Kever said, "Glad you could make it, Mr. Fullerby."

The young man with the military haircut jumped to his feet and held out his hand. "I … I don't believe it! You're Bob Fullerby!"

"I am."

"Wow! I'm a big fan, sir. I never imagined I'd actually meet you."

"Believe me, there are far more exciting things in this world than making my acquaintance."

Kever said, "Mr. Fullerby, this is my friend, Anson Dailey."

"Ah, the police officer," Bob said. "Kever-o's mentioned you. Good to meet you, Anson."

"Thank you, sir."

Kever gestured toward the pretty woman. "Mr. Fullerby, this is Cookie Davis, the mystery woman's roommate."

Faint bruises marred the roommate's face and long, slender neck. Her eyes were swollen and red from crying. Despite it all, she was stunning. Bob shook her hand. Her skin was soft and her nails manicured. "Cookie, it's good to meet you."

Her voluptuous lips moved, as if she tried to speak; instead, tears rolled down her cheeks.

Bob said, "I can see something bad has happened. I sincerely hope I can help." He took a seat. "So, Ang, I take it our mystery woman now has a name?"

"She does, Mr. Fullerby. It's *Leeha Ritsagin*."

Leeha Ritsagin. The name was unfamiliar. "Okay, Ang, fill me in."

Somewhere in Cadona ...

Leeha Ritsagin opened her eyes. She was still lying on her back, but her surroundings had changed. A single, bright light seared her eyes. The bed was different as well. This one was narrow—only slightly wider than a gurney.

Acid churned in her stomach. A sickening taste filled her mouth.

She tried to sit up. Her head raised, but her shoulder blades remained pressed into the stiff mattress.

Paralyzed! Maybe she was paralyzed! She pulled and pulled, but her arms and legs stayed pinned to the bed. Something else seemed wrong. Her limbs hurt as if strong hands held her down, but no one was there.

She raised her head as far as she could. She saw a white sheet. It covered most of her body. She saw something else as well. Gray straps with tan padding fastened her upper arms and forearms to the bed rail. Her thighs and ankles were also strapped down.

"Help me! Please! Help!"

No one answered.

"Let me out of here! Let me out!"

Shouting made her throat hurt, but it didn't matter. "Can anyone hear me? Please! Untie me! I've got to get up! I've got to move! I can't take it anymore!"

She fought the restraints. The cuff on her left upper arm slid against her flesh. A shocking pain ran through her arm. She turned her head as far as she could. She noticed an incision covered with yellow ointment. The thin, red line lay above the place her nodes would be.

"What did you do to me? Where am I? Tell me!"

A chill raced through her left arm. Pink fluid gushed into a tube attached to the inner part of her elbow. Her body relaxed. All pain disappeared.

The bed rocked. It felt like riding in a vehicle. But what kind of vehicle could this be?

She looked around. Medical equipment hung from white walls. Maybe she was in an ambulance. An ambulance, though, didn't make sense; the room was much too large.

Another question came to her. How had she gotten ... wherever she was?

Last memory ... perhaps if she recalled her last memory, the whole thing would make sense. She remembered a man looming above her, but the images were fuzzy. Someone referred to him as *Mr. Beller.* He'd asked her where she worked. He didn't believe her answer; he got angry.

The memory, though, didn't explain how she ended up tied to a bed.

Maybe things would make sense if she recalled her last *clear* memory.

She remembered being at home. Andecco News was playing on the sound array. She was looking at the weird document, but Cookie knocked on the door. She hid the document so Cookie wouldn't see it. Her next memory didn't fit—she recalled three strangers dressed in dark suits. One of the men unfolded an odd gadget. Rows of lights blinked.

The sound of footsteps interrupted her recollections. She heard Mr. Beller's voice. "Doctor Anderson, you better get in here. Something's happening."

A male with a deep voice said, "Randy, what's wrong?"

"Doctor, I think she's awake."

A man's face hovered over her. He was dressed like a surgeon. A white mask covered his nose and mouth. Veins crisscrossed the whites of his blue eyes. Wrinkles lined his forehead. He said, "Randy, how far 'till we're on site?"

"I'll check."

Seconds later, Randy Beller spoke again. "They say an hour and a half."

Doctor Anderson said, "Put her back under. If we don't, she'll be fully lucid by the time we arrive. Then we'll have to prep her from the start. We can't waste more of the drug."

"Yes, Doctor."

The face of a different man peered down at her. No redness stained the whites of his brown eyes. He also wore a medical mask, but he appeared young. The skin on his forehead and around his eyes lacked wrinkles. He held a needle. She felt a sting in her right arm. A cold sensation flowed through her veins.

Her eyes would not stay open no matter how hard she tried.

Another man spoke. "We're getting more questions about the bitch's brown Monarch."

Dr. Anderson said, "Tell them we don't have it. Our job was to grab the thief, not her car. Altman's team was supposed to tow it."

"Altman said the Monarch wasn't there."

The voices faded. Leeha sensed nothing except the hypnotizing, rhythmic motion of the vehicle.

15

ROADSIDE INN

Cadona City, Cadona
SATURDAY, APRIL 29, YEAR 1007 EE
1:30 P.M., EAST CADONA TIME

Bob Fullerby almost spilled his iced tea; he caught the glass just in time.
He centered the drink on a thick, Nutty Squirrel coaster.

A headache pounded in his temples. Of the many questions about
the Drop Case, only one had an answer: Leeha Ritsagin was the mystery woman.

"Cookie," he said, "are you sure you've never seen an unusual document in Leeha's apartment? Are you sure she never mentioned a printed
text of great value?"

"Yes, I'm sure. Like I've told you already, she didn't have anything
unusual or expensive. Mostly, she read boring technical manuals."

"What about unusual people in her life? Did she have unorthodox
acquaintances?"

"No."

"What about electronic friends? Did she send automated messages to
groups of people that seemed ... out of the norm?"

"No."

"Did you notice surprising behavior? Like, did she disappear at odd times without giving a reason?"

"No! Leeha works at Franklin Technologies. She watches old movies; she takes computer classes at home through WorldLink."

"Where does she go besides the office?" Bob asked.

"Nowhere special: the grocery store, the gas station. Once, while I was living with her, we went to a theatre and saw a film. We went to a couple of cafés together, some diners and coffee shops."

Anson said, "Cookie, did Leeha ever mention being afraid of anyone? Were there times she behaved as if she was worried or anxious about something?"

"Who wouldn't be afraid sometimes? The economy sucks. She used to work full time, but to avoid layoffs, Franklin Technologies put most of their employees on part-time schedules. She's afraid she could lose her job any day."

Anson's voice sounded like a policeman's now, not Kever's buddy. "Cookie, was Leeha concerned about anything besides financial issues?"

"Just normal stuff. The crime rate is crazy, especially now with so many people out of work. You know, she's lived alone for a long time. A woman on her own must be cautious." Cookie fiddled with her napkin. "Leeha's worried about her brother, Jeremy, too. He lives in New Cadona, in Ramsten. She isn't afraid *of* him, though. She's afraid *for* him."

"Why is she afraid for him?" Anson asked.

Cookie pursed her lips as if to hold back a fresh round of tears. "He called her the other day and said he joined the True Followers of God Church."

"Okay," Anson said, "we've established that Leeha was concerned about money, crime, and her brother becoming a True Follower. Has she ever expressed being afraid of a specific individual?"

"She doesn't like some people at the office. A bunch of them are True Followers. Two girls especially are total fanatics. They're always preaching to her and trying to get her to go to their services, but these girls *bug* her; I wouldn't say she's afraid of them."

Bob's personal device buzzed. If the call had come from anyone else, he would've waited until Anson finished asking Cookie questions. The caller, however, was his Drop Case informant. Bob said, "Excuse me, folks. I have to take this call."

He walked outside and ducked beneath the eaves to avoid raindrops. "Pastor Walzelesskii, hello. What can I do for you?"

"Mr. Fullerby, something important must've happened. My dad received several new messages. Unfortunately, I only had time to read the most recent one. Zoff sent it. He wrote that a brown Monarch was missing. They expected it to be in a parking lot by an apartment building, but the car wasn't there."

"Do you know the name or address of the apartment building?"

"No, but I do remember the time of the message. Zoff sent it to my dad just a few minutes before ten this morning. Oh, and Zoff suspects a defector group hauled the Monarch away."

"*Defector group* …. Pastor, what does that mean?"

"It's a group of people the Freedom Party sees as an enemy and is powerful enough to be a threat. Most of the time, it refers to an internal adversary, not a foreign one. I wish I had time to read other messages, but I needed to be careful because my dad kept coming and going."

"Pastor, as I've always said, *don't take unnecessary chances.*"

"Thanks, Mr. Fullerby. Speaking about being careful, in a few minutes I'm catching a flight on a True Followers jet—my dad doesn't want me to fly with a regular airline after Flight Ten Seventy blew up. I'm pretty sure General Willirman is monitoring all activity on my dad's planes, so please don't call. When I get settled, I'll let you know when it's safe to contact me."

"Thank you for letting me know. Where are you off to?"

"New Cadona. I'm meeting with Senator Seldortin and officials in Ramsten about the J2 virus. I'm also going to say *hello* to Annetta Longstreet. I promised her a while back that I'd visit."

"Ah, so mixing business with pleasure," Bob said. "Good to hear it. You need to have fun while you're young."

"Yeah, it'll be nice to see her. She's a nice girl. Even my dad likes her. I'll talk to you as soon as I can, Mr. Fullerby. I'll pray for you, for good health and well-being."

"Thank you, Pastor. I appreciate it. I need all the help I can get."

"We all do, Mr. Fullerby. Talk to you soon."

The line grew silent. A breath of fear swirled in the air. Pastor Mark Walzelesskii was a man of integrity; Cadona City would be a little less safe without him in it.

Bob went back inside the Nutty Squirrel. Anson, Angela, Kever, and Cookie were all quiet. "What did I miss?" Bob asked.

"Not much, Mr. Fullerby," Angela told him. "We learned Leeha has some fighting skills."

Cookie appeared upset and weary. "You're exaggerating. When she was little, her grandpa taught her how to defend herself. It's not like she had formal training. She's pretty good at it, though. I wouldn't want her to get mad at me."

Bob sipped his now lukewarm iced tea. "Cookie, I've been pondering the sequence of events you laid out for us. Just before the men dragged Leeha to the red van, you said you looked out the living room window and saw her Monarch in the parking lot. Did I hear that right?"

"Yes."

"I just got word that the Monarch is missing. Are you absolutely sure the car was there?"

"Yes, I'm positive."

"What time was it when you looked out the window?"

Cookie twisted in her seat. "How the heck do I know? Mr. Fullerby, they took Leeha, and I'm supposed to worry about a stupid car?"

Angela said, "Um, Mr. Fullerby, excuse me; Kever-o and I arrived at Leeha's apartment at nine-twenty. At that time, Cookie was returning from chasing the van, so she would've looked out the window around nine o'clock."

"Thanks, Ang," Bob said. "That means someone ran off with the Monarch between nine and ten this morning. Cookie, are you sure you didn't see anyone around the apartment building or parking lot besides the three kidnappers and Leeha?"

"Yes, I'm positive. If someone had been around, I would've sought their help."

"Cookie, have you ever seen the inside of the Monarch?"

"Yes, lots of times. I've even driven it. I know your next question, Mr. Fullerby; you're going to ask if I'd seen something suspicious inside. No, nothing odd. No weird document, no secret compartments. It's a simple, old car."

"Do you know if anyone else had access to it?"

Cookie's voice echoed through the room. "Our neighbor, Toofy—who's now dead—"

"Cookie!" Angela said. "Lower your voice."

"Sorry …. Toofy put in a security system and fixed the air conditioner. Leeha also takes the car to Jenton's Auto Body and Repair for service. That's all I know. Why is everyone so worried about that dumb car? They took Leeha, and you're all worrying about the Monarch." She glared at Anson. "Tell me, how many cops are out there looking for Leeha? How many, huh? There should be hundreds trying to find her." She fidgeted in her seat. "I'm sick of hearing about that stupid Monarch."

Anson said, "Cookie, there's a reason we're interested in the car. People from the military—intelligence special agents—recently showed up at my station. They wanted information about the owner of a seventeen-year-old, brown Monarch sedan."

"So what? Lots of people have old Monarchs."

"Only one such Monarch showed up at my station during the period the agents asked about."

"How do you know it's Leeha's?"

Anson leaned back in his seat. "I know because I'm the officer who took her statement on March twenty-sixth."

Bob watched as the expression on Cookie's face turned from skepticism to shock.

Her lips trembled as she spoke. "Anson, why did Leeha go to your police station?"

"To report a crime. She got lost in the Helmsey District, and a gang attacked her while she was waiting at a traffic light."

Bob said, "Cookie, did Leeha mention an attack on March twenty-sixth?"

She slouched into the chair as if the last bit of energy was about to drip from her body. "I do remember her talking about an attack. It happened in a slum, but I don't remember where or when it happened. She … it really scared her. It gives her nightmares."

"Cookie," Bob said, "there's one more piece to the Monarch story. We've linked the Monarch to a very important printed text. We have every reason to believe the guys who abducted Leeha did so because of this document. Are you sure she never mentioned some kind of book? Are you sure you never saw her with some kind of binder?"

"No, you guys asked me about a document a bunch of times already. You can repeat the question a hundred more times, and I'm still not going to remember. There's nothing *to* remember."

Her expression again turned to one of suspicion. She stared at Anson for a moment. Next, she studied Kever's face, and then Angela's. Bob felt Cookie's hostile glare when her dark eyes met his. She said, "I realize I'm upset and not thinking clearly, but something is not right. Why are we sitting in a pub? Why am I not at a police station filing a formal report?"

Bob wanted to keep information internal to his Andecco News team, but Officer Anson Dailey and Cookie Davis knew things about Leeha Ritsagin that he didn't. "It's a fair question," Bob said. "My team and I have been investigating a story for quite some time. There's a group of vigilantes called the *Soldiers of God Justice Group*. This group is a secret fraternity made up of people from many walks of life, including policemen. The scary thing is, I'm not talking about a handful of cops. I'm talking about many."

Cookie shook her head. "This doesn't make sense, Mr. Fullerby. What does the Soldiers of God Justice Group have to do with Leeha?"

"This group reports to some of the most powerful, wealthy people in this country. These powerful people lost a very important document. These same people believe Leeha stole it."

Cookie's hands shook. "This is crazy! Leeha's not a thief. There's no way she stole a document or anything else." Her eyes turned to Anson. "You're a policeman; do you believe all this?"

"I don't know about the Soldiers of God Justice Group specifically, but I've been noticing odd stuff happening on the force. I know cops who don't show up for work weeks on end but draw full pay. Others suddenly are able to afford fancy cars and move into expensive apartments. At my satellite station, a good third of the cops moonlight at the True Followers of God Church or the Back-to-Basics Club."

Cookie's eyes grew wide. "Oh, my goodness! Mr. Fullerby, I get it now. You think the Club or the True Followers have Leeha."

"I don't know who has her," Bob said. "What I do know is that powerful people think Leeha stole a document, and now she's missing."

Cookie kneaded a paper napkin in her hands. "I can't believe this is happening. You know, Mr. Fullerby, if anyone else but you told me a story like this, I'd be convinced he's a nutball. Whoever has Leeha has the wrong person. That must be it."

Bob said, "Maybe they'll figure it out. Right now, though, they're convinced she's the thief."

Cookie dried her damp cheeks. "I feel so helpless; I don't know what to do or how I can help."

"You'll think better after you get some rest," Bob said. "After what you've been through, you must be exhausted."

"I can't ... how can I rest when I don't know if Leeha's okay? How can I rest knowing Mrs. Furley and Toofy were killed?"

Angela said, "Mr. Fullerby, we have another problem. Cookie doesn't have a place to stay. She can't go back to the Pineland Apartments. It's not safe. Who knows, the kidnappers may come back to take her, too."

"Good point, Ang. We'll need to keep her safe. Cookie, I know a place. It's a motel about ten minutes from here called the *Roadside Inn*. The owner is a friend. I can get good deals, and he's prior military. Did lots of security work, too. How about we run over there and see what he can do for us?"

Cookie seemed on the edge of panic. "I need to go back to the apartment and get my belongings."

Anson said, "Cookie, it's too dangerous. The people who took Leeha may be watching the place. Ang is right; the kidnappers may be looking for you, too."

This time, Cookie didn't wipe away tears. They dripped off her chin. "But I have to get my stuff. Except for what I'm wearing, everything I own is in there."

"Give me your sizes, Cookie," Angela said, "and I'll get you something to wear."

"Almost all of my money's in the apartment. I'm hiding from my ex-fiancé, so I haven't been paying by PD. I'm afraid he'll track me down. And ... and my Kettish prayer medallion, it's in there, too."

"I'll pick up a medallion for you. No problem," Angela said.

Bob had many questions, but he'd ask them later. "Cookie, don't worry about money right now. We'll cover the costs."

"Why are you helping me?"

"Because it's the right thing to do," Bob said, "and because you lived with Leeha Ritsagin. You know things about her other people don't."

"Okay, I'll go to the motel if it'll help find her."

"Good," Bob said. "Anson, do you mind coming along? I'd like to get your opinion about the young lady's security."

"Sure, I'd be glad to, Mr. Fullerby."

"Kever-o, Ang," Bob said, "are you okay taking the bus? We'll need the car to drive Cookie to the motel."

Kever gave him a mock salute. "Roger, that. I'm good with the bus."

"Me, too," Angela said.

Bob paid the bill, and they walked outside. Patches of orangey-blue sky peeked through the grayish-brown overcast.

"See you later, alligators," Kever said. He and Angela headed for a bus stop.

Bob led Anson and Cookie to his car. "Say, Anson, do you mind driving? I'm pretty beat. I might be a road hazard."

"Sure, but I thought an important person like you would have a self-driving car."

"I used to. The technology aged out, and the new equipment is too expensive for my blood."

They arrived at the Roadside Inn Motel. Anson parked in the back to stay out of sight.

"You two stay here," Bob said. He climbed out of the car and walked into the lobby. A woman in a glossy, white blouse was helping a customer.

The customer grabbed his suitcase and walked away.

Bob strolled up to the counter.

The woman in the white blouse said, "May I help you, sir?"

"I hope so. I'm looking for Mr. Dremmer. Is he here?"

"Your name?"

"Tell him an old friend from Kamchandom, Sohn-Sur, is looking for him."

The lady gave him an odd look and typed on a touchpad.

Moments later, Ralph Dremmer emerged through a door behind the counter. He looked as fit as ever. His thick mat of gray hair was mussed, as if he had been exercising. "Bob! Good to see you!"

"Ralph, good to see you as well. It's been a while."

"It has, we haven't talked since poker night. Had to be two months ago by now. What can I do for you?"

"May we speak in private?"

"Sure. This way."

Ralph led him to a private room next to the lobby. "What's the problem, Bob?"

"A young woman is helping me on a case. She needs a safe place to stay. This lady, she knows things that could put her in danger. It's best not to use her real name."

"I see," Ralph said. He walked to the counter. "Teresa, put a lady by the name of Donna Miller in room two oh one."

Teresa tapped on a touchpad. "For how many nights?"

Bob said, "Ralph, can you swing two weeks?"

"We can. With the J2 virus, Flight Ten Seventy, and the economy, not many people are traveling. Will Ms. Miller be needing a physical key?"

"Yes, please."

Teresa unlocked a drawer and dug out a brass-colored key.

Ralph said, "Come on, Bob, I'll show you the room. By the way, you can trust Teresa. She's my nephew's wife. She's former army. A damned good shot, too; darned better than I ever was."

Bob followed Ralph out the back door. Ralph pointed toward the building. "The room's up there, right over the office. I'll let you know if anything unusual happens."

"Thanks, my friend. I appreciate it."

"Bob, if not for you, I would've been dead ages ago. I wouldn't have had thirty years of marriage with the best woman in the world. I wouldn't have my three beautiful children and five grandchildren. Helping you out with things like this … why, it's nothing. Come on, let's get this young lady settled."

Somewhere in Cadona ...

Leeha Ritsagin opened her eyes. She was still in the same room and strapped to the same bed. This time, though, she felt groggier, and her stomach gurgled and churned. An awful chemical taste filled her mouth.

She heard a booming, unfamiliar voice. "Randy, I'm telling you, you gave her too much."

"You're wrong. I followed the instructions exactly."

The loud man said, "No, you didn't. You screwed up. She's not responding like she's supposed to."

Leeha heard a door open and close. She heard Doctor Anderson's words. "How's it going?"

"Not good," the loud man said. "She's totally unresponsive. Randy gave her too much."

"That's not true! I followed the instructions to a T."

The doctor said, "Everyone responds differently. Let the drug settle in a bit and try again."

Leeha felt like she was floating. All sounds faded.

16

STRAWBERRY MILKSHAKES

Cadona City, Cadona
SATURDAY, APRIL 29, YEAR 1007 EE
6:00 P.M., EAST CADONA TIME

Bob Fullerby turned his old car onto Lexler Street. He spotted someone sprinting down the sidewalk.

As he drew closer, he realized why the man looked familiar. The runner was Kever Carsen. Sweat glued his workout shirt to his lean body, but a broad smile stretched across his youthful face.

Bob recalled the days when he enjoyed working out. Middle age and too many years of high-stress work had stolen the pleasure that vigorous physical activity once gave him.

He drove down an alley and parked in the lot behind Ben's and Bertha's shops.

At least he'd get a little exercise—it was about thirty paces to the edge of the neighbors' property.

He climbed out of the car, took his thirty steps, and squeezed through a broken spot in the plank fence that ran along the property line.

Kever was waiting for him in the print shop parking lot.

"Kever-o, thanks for coming back. I know you've already worked a long day."

"I did, but so did you, Mr. Fullerby."

"That's true." Bob pictured his cramped, eighty-sixth-floor apartment. "I spend more time here than at home these days."

"Is Ang coming back to work, too?" Kever asked.

"Yep, after she finishes picking up supplies for Cookie."

Kever wiped the sweat from his brow. "Speaking of Cookie, did she get settled okay?"

"As best she can under the circumstances. Anson's going to spend a few nights in the room next to her to keep an eye on things."

"Good idea," Kever said. "Lots of weird crap going down."

Motion caught Bob's eye. Angela Thirgal was walking down the driveway. She joined them in the parking lot.

"Done shopping already?" Bob asked.

"Yeah, there's an All-in-One Mart near the Roadside Inn. They even sell Kettish prayer medallions."

Kever used his jester's voice. "Do I detect frustration, Ang?"

She rolled her eyes. "I couldn't wait to leave the motel. Cookie drives me nuts with all that wailing, screeching, and arm flailing. I'd rather shovel rocks all day than babysit her."

"I don't know about that," Kever said. "She's eye sugar."

Angela said, "Kever-o, what is it with you and those goofy sayings? You're so weird." A few raindrops fell. "Just great, it's raining again." She yanked open the rear door of the print shop.

Bob followed her and Kever inside.

Specks of light coming from electronic equipment glowed in the otherwise dark room.

The faint outline of a human form took shape in the dim illumination.

"Hi, guys," Rona said.

"Why are you here in the dark?" Bob asked.

"I was just heading out. I'll get the lights."

Old-fashioned bulbs popped on.

"Wow!" Kever said. "Row, look at you! You must have a date."

"I do. Degio wants to get together, and I want to thank him for helping us identify Leeha Ritsagin."

Kever let out a teasing chuckle. "Is that the only reason you're meeting him? You're dressed to kill."

Rona brushed a curled lock of copper-tinted hair over her delicate shoulder. "I'm sure. Degio's fun, but he's not the type of guy I'm looking for."

Angela said, "Are you sure about that, Row? This is the first time I've seen you so fancy. Where did you get that shiny skirt? I don't remember seeing it before."

Rona swung her waiflike hips. "Do you like it? I made it. Craft World had a big sale on material. I fell in love with the rose pattern and the gold background. And check it out! The ribbing is so swift!"

"It looks great on you, Row," Angela said, "but it doesn't seem like a casual outfit. Where's he taking you?"

"Pickerings."

"Pickerings!" Kever said. "Ritzy place."

Youthful joy sparkled in Rona's eyes. "Yeah, I heard it's nice. I should get going. Oh, Mr. Fullerby, I briefed Kever-o on all the stuff I dug up on Cookie Davis, Leeha Ritsagin, Bercette Furley, and Toofelance Furley. Oh … and the Paula Arvish murder, too. It's all on my computer in stand-alone files."

"Get going, Row," Bob said. "You don't want to keep Degio waiting."

Red lipstick glistened as she flashed a big smile. She snatched her raincoat and sparkly handbag. "See you guys later!" She hurried out the door.

Kever whistled. "Wow! Row is lookin' for some fun tonight. Miniskirt, high heels, wicked makeup—she's certainly decked out. So, Ang, when are you going to dress up and hit the town?"

"Never … that you'll ever see, anyway."

Kever placed a hand over his heart. "Ouch, Ang, that hurts!"

Bob sat down by the old wooden table. "Okay, kids, I'm also jealous that Row has a hot date and I don't, but we have work to do. Kever-o, fill Ang and me in on what Row learned."

Angela and Kever joined him at the table.

Kever tapped on Rona's touchpad. "Detective Brunish, like Anson, found nothing suspicious in Leeha's background. The worst blemish on her record is a parking ticket from two years ago. Other than that, she grew up near Oakwood. The family had a rough patch while she was in secondary school. They lost the family farm and her dad died. Besides Oakwood, the only places she's ever lived were near her university and in the Pineland Apartments. There's no record of her ever leaving the country. She is a tech-head, though. She graduated second in her class from Cadona Technical."

"What about the Monarch?" Bob asked.

"Two things. The first is mundane. When she was in college, her mom bought the car for her."

Bob said, "I take it Carl's other Monarch discovery is not so mundane?"

"Bizarre describes it better," Kever said. "A couple of days before military agents visited Anson's station, the National Police put out a search order to find a brown Monarch sedan. And guess what? Detective Brunish traced the original requester to the echelon-above-corps military intelligence branch of the Combined Armed Forces. Mr. Fullerby, I bet General Douglass Willirman's fingerprints are all over that order."

"I bet you're right, Kever-o, seeing that General Willirman is the commander of the Combined Armed Forces and a Back-to-Basics Club leader. It's a good thing their photo of the car and Ritsagin was so blurry. If Willirman's people had a clear image, they would've found her much sooner."

"It gets even more interesting, Mr. Fullerby. Leeha's abduction hasn't been recorded. As far as official records go, she's not missing."

Bob said, "Besides Cookie, did anyone else witness the abduction?"

"Yeah, at least two people in the apartment building. A woman on the second floor told police that she saw three men in dark clothing shoving something shaped like a human body into a red van. Another tenant saw two men dragging a woman down a staircase. His description of the woman fits Leeha. He assumed the woman had fallen ill and the men were taking her to a hospital."

A sense of unease crept up Bob's back. The police were hiding information again. "What are the cops saying about the Furley murders?"

"That Toofelance Furley killed his grandmother, Bercette Furley. People who know them don't believe it. They say he took good care of her."

"People don't always act the same in front of others," Bob said. "Maybe he wasn't so nice to her in private."

"Actually, Mr. Fullerby, it does smell like a cover-up."

"Why?"

"Around the time Leeha was kidnapped, neighbors heard men fighting in the hallway. A couple of the witnesses are former military. They swore they heard three muffled gunshots. No one heard a woman's voice until several minutes later, when a woman screamed for help. What do you want to bet those screams were Cookie's when she found the Furleys lying on the floor? Detective Brunish said none of this info made it into the official police record. And it's not only the Furley murders that the cops are lying about. They're covering up the Paula Arvish murder, too."

Angela asked, "What's the storyline for that cover-up?"

"They're trying to make the murder look like a burglary gone wrong," Kever said. "Simple street thugs broke into Nancy Pitman's townhouse. The housekeeper surprised them; they killed her. The report doesn't mention Arvish's ritualistic execution or the blood-writing on the walls."

"What did Carl have to say about Cookie Davis?" Bob asked.

Kever said, "His info matches what Ang found. She was a rising socialite. She was engaged to a man with a super-high income, but they both lost their jobs, ate through their savings, and were forced to give up their fancy apartment in the Sunset District. Her fiancé turned into a drunk and beat the crap out of her. She filed an abuse report against him, but the cops never took any action, as is typical these days. One thing in her record that's a bit unusual is how she was able to afford Rockwood University since she's from a lower-middle-class background. Detective Brunish suspects she had some kind of … arrangement. She had three different male roommates, all from upper-class families. She eventually proved herself. In her junior year, she got a full scholarship and graduated with honors."

A growl tainted Angela's voice. "Cookie shacked up with rich guys … figures. Besides being a gold digger, did Detective Brunish find anything suspicious about her?"

"Nope," Kever said.

Bob scratched a rough fingernail against a bump on the nicked tabletop. "We're missing big puzzle pieces in the Drop Case."

"What do you mean, Mr. Fullerby?" Angela asked.

"I was sure that once we identified the mystery woman, we'd learn why the Guiding Light is important and why someone would want to steal it. Now, we know the mystery woman is Leeha Ritsagin. Nothing in her background explains why she'd be involved with the Guiding Light's disappearance. And Cookie Davis doesn't know anything about the document even though she's been living in Ritsagin's apartment for nearly three weeks. Ang, Kever-o, any thoughts?"

Angela said, "Maybe Cookie Davis isn't who she says she is. She shows up in Leeha's life shortly after the Guiding Light disappears. What if it's not a coincidence?"

"Ang, are you thinking we have a case of identity theft?"

"Maybe, or perhaps General Willirman recruited her to get close to Leeha Ritsagin to find the document. Cookie and her fiancé are in financial straits. Maybe she's on the Back-to-Basics payroll. Identity theft works as a theory, too, though."

"Ang," Bob said, "next time you check in on Cookie, see if you can collect DNA and fingerprints. I know people who can analyze the samples outside of the system. Make sure the samples are hers; it's obvious that our adversaries are not averse to planting evidence."

"Will do, Mr. Fullerby. Shall we involve Anson?"

"Not yet. Let's keep it internal to our team."

Kever shut his eyes. He opened them and said, "Mr. Fullerby, we're heading down a slippery slope. Is it ethical to take samples without the person's knowledge?"

"You're right, Kever-o. It is a slippery slope. It's not a step I take lightly. But what choice do we have? We can't go to the police. Evidence is mounting that large swaths of the force have aligned themselves with the Freedom Party, the Back-to-Basics Club, and the True Followers of God Church. For better or worse, Cookie is close to us now, and, at the moment, we're protecting her from Ritsagin's kidnappers. For our own safety, we need to know with whom we're dealing."

Angela said, "Mr. Fullerby, even if we confirm the roommate is Cookie Davis, we still won't know if she's working with General Willirman."

"You're right about that. We'll need to see if anyone contacts her at the motel."

Warning lights flashed.

Bob studied the security monitor. "It's Row! That was a short date. Maybe Degio had more news about the Monarch."

Rona walked in. Rain had stripped curls from her hair. The typical spring in her step had abandoned her, too, as did her smile.

"Row," Kever said, "is everything okay? We weren't expecting you back so soon."

She removed her raincoat. "I ... I hope everything's okay. Degio never came. I left a message but haven't heard back."

Kever pursed his lips. "That son-of-a ..., the jerk stood you up?"

Rona lowered herself into a chair. "I hope that's what happened. He called me around one o'clock to make sure I was going to make it. It seems weird that he'd call to confirm and then not show."

Angela said, "Sorry, Row, that's a bummer."

Bob recalled what it was like when he was young and having his heart broken. So different it was from a marriage that fell apart bit by bit over the years. "Row, all I can say is that young man better have a good reason for not showing up. If he doesn't, the loss is his."

Her calm compassion reflected a maturity beyond her nineteen years. "Thanks, guys, but I'm okay. It's Degio I'm worried about. I mean, look what's happened—someone threw Leeha into a van, and two people in her apartment building were murdered. Degio worked on the Monarch ... I hope he's not in trouble, too!" She grabbed a carrot stick from a snack bowl. "I'll call Jenton's tomorrow if I don't hear from him before then."

Angela said, "Mr. Fullerby, speaking of missing people, is there any word on Barry Kingle?"

"No, nothing. I'm getting concerned. The boss thinks Barry got himself in hot water with *News, News, News* managers."

"For what?" Kever asked.

"For blowing open General Willirman's schemes. Just before the National Police summoned him, Barry interviewed sources who told him that our military is secretly sending units and equipment to Izvyona."

Kever said, "Mr. Fullerby, I don't get it. The military's been illegally arming Izvyona for a long time. Why would they go after a reporter now?"

"My guess is that General Willirman and company want to know who Barry's sources are. According to the boss, bigwigs in the defense establishment told Barry why they're sending the illegal shipments, and it's not good. The goal is to throw off the balance of power at the border, giving Izvyonsk forces the advantage."

Angela said, "Mr. Fullerby, if Barry's right, Domataland's leaders are not going to be happy."

"No, they're not. Rumor has it, Tarish is planning to move tactical strike troops to the Izvyonsk border."

"Doesn't that break the ceasefire agreement?" Angela asked.

"It does."

Angela shook her head. "Bad move; Tarish is playing right into Willirman's hands."

Ver-Nuvelin, Domataland
MONDAY, MAY 1, YEAR 1007 EE
6:00 A.M., CENTRAL FEWWOK TIME

A situation globe hovered above President Demnar Tarish's office desk.

He spoke to the translucent map of the Earth. "Expand Izvyona."

A map of Izvyona separated from the sphere and grew large. Green dots marked the locations of confirmed Cadonan military assets while red dots showed suspected ones. Both green and red dots clustered near the shared borders of Izvyona, Bakhadaland, and Domataland.

A knot twisted in his stomach. Cadona's military leaders were liars. Proof of a massive armed presence in Izvyona lay right before his eyes, yet the Cadonan ambassador denied they were sending new military units and supplies into Izvyonsk territory.

Presidential Assistant Druzha Timkensha's voice came through the sound array. "Honorable President, Chief Kolensha wishes to see you."

"Send her in, Druzha."

Rozula walked into his office. She bowed. "Good morning, Honorable President. I see you're reviewing Rivar's latest report."

"I am. It looks like our worst fears are coming to fruition. Cadona is readying Izvyona for a full-scale assault on Bakhadaland. Rozula, is there any sign that President Meyfeld will regain control of the military?"

"I doubt it. The Freedom Party's hold on Cadona's armed forces keeps growing."

Demnar studied the situation globe, searching for a ray of hope. He saw none. "Rozula, if Mitch Fischer is elected president in October, all of this will be legal—then imagine how bad it will get."

"We may have a way to discredit the Freedom Party, Honorable President, but it's risky."

"I'm listening, Rozula."

"My agents in Cadona learned that the Hansen Hills Federal Facility has reopened as a secret prison. Freedom Party and Back-to-Basics Club leaders are behind it."

"What evidence do your contacts have?"

"Senator Bradley Seldortin has uncovered funding requests that are inconsistent with the facility's only legitimate function: urban warfare training. Senator John Rineburg and General Douglass Willirman signed off on those requests."

"What kind of funding are we talking about?"

"Expenditures consistent with holding and interrogating prisoners, Honorable President. Also, money is going to the facility for the manufacture of drugs. One of my agents reported that Mind-One is being created there."

"You mean the truth serum?"

"Yes. I believe Cadona has used, or will soon be using, Mind-One on prisoners."

"Does Bob Fullerby know about the facility and Mind-One?"

"He does, Honorable President. He hasn't made the news public yet."

Demnar sank into his seat. "Ruzhmen Seldortin and Fullerby are sitting on the Hansen Hills and Mind-One stories. I wonder why?"

"We suspect it's because they're searching for more proof, Honorable President."

"Rozula, how can we use this information to discredit the Freedom Party?"

"We can slip news about Hansen Hills and Mind-One into Cadona's rumor mill."

"And the risk, Rozula?"

"Ruzhman Seldortin and Ruzhman Fullerby may have a plan. If we inject reports into news streams, we may ruin those plans."

Demnar enlarged the ethereal map. The Izvyonsk military, augmented by Cadonan reinforcements, were poised to storm Bakhadaland's western border. "We're in a bad situation. General Willirman and his Freedom Party allies are making their move in Izvyona. President Meyfeld and Defense Secretary Karther are unable to stop them. Ruzhmen Seldortin and Fullerby may be good men, but they're concerned about Cadona, not Domataland. Unless you have another idea, Rozula, let's take the chance. Let's pump Hansen Hills and Mind-One stories into Cadonan media."

"I have no other ideas, Honorable President. We'll start pumping stories tomorrow."

"This is it, Rozula, we've committed the Sin of Deception. *With lies and slithers, our war with mighty Cadona begins against our will.*"

"Honorable President, you quote Thomas Fillimore, the Cadonan freedom fighter from the Awakening Epoch."

"I do. Thomas Fillimore was a good man."

"Yes, he was."

Demnar expected Rozula to leave. She didn't. "Rozula, is there something else on your mind?"

"There is, Honorable President."

"Okay, Rozula, what is it?"

"I have failed."

"What happened?"

"My operatives learned the name of the woman who stole the Guiding Light: *Leeha Ritsagin.*"

"Isn't that a good thing?"

Rozula drew a deep breath. "I was unable to find her in time, Honorable President. The Back-to-Basics Club has her."

"We always knew the odds were against us finding her first, Rozula."

"I know, but one of my agents inside Andecco News Service told me Ruzhman Fullerby's people arrived just a little too late. They barely lost the race."

"Do you think Lady Ritsagin is alive?"

"Yes, for the moment. The Guiding Light hasn't been found. The Club needs to keep her alive until they find it, along with any copies."

"Where is the Club holding her?"

"We don't know, Honorable President. We have another mystery as well; nothing in her background explains why someone would recruit her to steal the document. She doesn't have an intelligence, military, or policing background. She doesn't have a criminal record."

"Is she linked to politics or politicians?"

"No, Honorable President. She's registered with the Allegiance Party, but beyond voting records, she's not active in politics."

"Is she a Cadonan citizen?"

"She is. She has zero foreign connections."

Demnar knew time was against them. "If the Club has her, she'll eventually give up the location of the document."

"Your assumption is reasonable, Honorable President. We also have a new twist. She has a roommate, a woman named *Cookie Davis*. If there's a bright spot, this is it: Ruzhman Fullerby is hiding Lady Davis in a motel. If anyone tries to contact her, his people will know."

Demnar closed his eyes. From deep in the quiet of his mind, a flicker of hope lit the darkness. When he raised his eyelids, he saw concern etched on Rozula's face. "Don't worry, Rozula, I'm okay. Something occurred to me—hope still lives. The Back-to-Basics Club may have found Leeha Ritsagin first, but maybe someone less vile will win the race to the Guiding Light."

◈

Somewhere in Cadona ...

Leeha Ritsagin awoke. Strong hands grasped her shoulders and knees.

A man said, "Ready, one ... two ... three."

Leeha's body rose. A moment later, cold sheets touched the backs of her arms and calves. Someone strapped bands around her ankles and wrists.

Her back ached. She wanted to stop the pain.

She tried to roll onto her side.

Her body wouldn't turn.

She twisted and twisted. The narrow bed clanked, yet she couldn't roll over.

Trapped! She was trapped!

"Cham pune rog puja!"

Something was wrong. She shouted for help, but the words came out as gibberish. Even stranger, the sounds came from across the room, not from her own mouth.

"What's wrong with the crazy bitch?" a man said.

She recognized his voice. It was loud and mean. She hated him, but how did she know him? *When* did she know him? Time, past and present, stretched out and grew close at the same time. It didn't make sense. She'd first heard his voice long ago, when the sun was forming, but she'd also heard it for the first time just now.

Place and time had fallen out of balance. Lights hovered over her face, but so did the sun. The sun, though, wasn't the one she expected. It was coalescing and churning in the rage of its birth. Solar wind flogged her. How did she survive in its wake?

Wait! Her body was not with her. That's how she survived.

But what was she? Whatever she was, the angry sun flung her into cold, dark space. A void, profound and infinite, consumed every part of her being. No one and nothing traveled with her as her consciousness tumbled farther and farther away.

Maybe swimming would work. She'd swim back to the sun. But how? She had no body, only mind. How might she swim?

A man's hideous face formed in the star-speckled expanse. He was dressed like a doctor, but he was no real practitioner of medicine. This man was evil. He took her far from the sun.

"Randy," the man said, "you'll need to tranquilize her again. If she keeps thrashing about, she'll kill herself."

She felt a prick on her arm even though her body was far away.

The sun returned, as did her body and solid earth. She recognized her surroundings. She was at home on the farm where she'd lived as a child. But this place was better than home. Soft grass cushioned her feet, and dainty flowers grew in neat rows. Her dad was alive. Her mother, young and happy, stood on the porch. Her brother, flush with the joy of childhood, kicked a ball around the yard. "Come on, Leeha," Jeremy said, "let's play!" He picked up the ball and ran to her. She saw deception in his eyes. He lied; Jeremy didn't want to play a game. He wanted to lead her to evil. Past and present merged in the little-boy body of her brother. How had he fallen into wickedness with an immoral god?

The doctor's evil face appeared in the vast wasteland beyond Jeremy's eyes. "Randy, give her a little more."

A third voice said, "Doctor, Altman's unit just arrived."

Leeha felt her body move. Then, all fell silent once again.

When she opened her eyes, she found herself in a different place. The mattress below her was soft. She felt no pain. Above her, hazy lights blinked off and on.

A shadowy form appeared. It loomed over her. It looked like a man's head and shoulders, but the face had no features except for bulges where the ears would be. He spoke. "Can you hear me?"

"Yes."

"Tell me your name."

"Leeha."

"Sorry, I couldn't hear you. Tell me again. What's your name?"

"Leeha."

"Ah, good, I heard you that time. Your name is Leeha."

"It is."

"What's your last name?"

"Ritsagin."

"Leeha Ritsagin, I need you to remember something for me. Do you understand?"

"I understand."

"Good. Leeha, I need you to remember a document, a very important one. You stole it."

Oh, no! They knew! How did they know? It was a long time ago, wasn't it? The memories were faint.

"Leeha, do you remember a document? The one you stole?"

"Kind of ...."

"Take your time, Leeha, and retrieve your memories. Concentrate on the document."

Images came and went. Randy Altholder sat across from her. Where was it? Secondary school! They were in secondary school; she remembered that.

The shadowy figure said, "Leeha, do you remember?"

"Bits and pieces. Like scattered pictures."

"But you're remembering?"

"Yes."

"Good. Here's what I want you to do. Put the images that you remember in order. I'll come back later, and you'll tell me everything you remembered. Do you understand?"

"Yes."

The shadowy man disappeared.

The overhead lights changed colors and blinked at a different pace. She heard a rhythmic hum.

Memories of secondary school no longer seemed like events from the past. She was really there. She felt the hard chair beneath her bottom. Her arms rested on a cold tabletop. Randy Altholder sat across from her. He wore a short-sleeved T-shirt. She saw blond hairs on his muscular arms. Randy was smiling. He seemed happy to be with her, but where were they? She looked around. Beakers sat on the table. Some sort of chart filled a giant viewplane. What was printed on the chart? The periodic table! She and Randy were in the chemistry lab! Why was he at her table? He always sat with the popular kids: the athletes and cheerleaders. Something else was out of place. They were the only people in the classroom. Where was everyone else? Why would Randy want to be with her? He was a sports star. He was gorgeous … wait! She was helping him with something, but what?

Vivid memories of an earlier day returned. The chemistry teacher had just embarrassed her again. *Congratulations, Leeha! Excellent work on your science project.* Leeha cringed; now, she'd get picked on the entire week. She got picked on enough. Ms. Carlyle didn't have to give the popular kids more fodder.

It took forever, but the class ended. Leeha slinked toward the door, wishing she could make herself invisible.

Then, something amazing happened. She heard Randy Altholder's sexy voice. He was calling her name, but he wasn't making fun of her. She turned around. He stood right there. He was tall, broad-shouldered, and so, so splashy. "Leeha, can I talk to you for a minute?"

"Sure." Her face flushed. What if blushing made her zits stick out? She mustn't get wet armpits. He'd totally get grossed out.

His gorgeous, blue eyes made her swoon. "Leeha, my coach isn't happy with my grades, especially in this class. I was wondering if you'd help me study. I know how smart you are."

"Um, sure, I'd be glad to help you … um … study."

"Beautiful! Thank you. When can we start?"

"Well, um, well, whenever. Whenever you want." With luck, her pounding heart wouldn't flutter her sweatshirt.

Randy appeared as calm as a cucumber. "When does your last class end, Leeha?"

She feared he'd hear the quiver in her voice. "Three thirty."

He stepped closer. "Want to get together then?"

She struggled to swallow. "Okay, but we'll only have an hour. The bus leaves at four thirty."

"I can drive you home if you'd like. Then we can study longer."

Was this for real? Randy would drive her home in his new sports car? Her mother would be so happy! Someone finally noticed her—Randy Altholder, nonetheless.

She was starting to sweat. She had to get away before she grossed him out. Thank goodness she had deodorant and makeup in her backpack. Oh, no! She'd need to freshen her breath. Did she have gum? Yes, she did have gum.

A voice from the other time line interrupted her thoughts. "Something's wrong. Her heart's racing."

Images of Randy Altholder from chemistry class dimmed like a fading movie scene.

The shadowy figure's voice sounded annoyed. "She's reacting to her memories. Don't disturb her recall process."

"Sorry," the other man said.

The shadowy man leaned over her. "Leeha, can you hear me?"

"Yes."

"Leeha, your memories … what were you thinking?"

"He's gorgeous. I want him. I love him."

"Whom?"

The memories slipped away. What was she supposed to remember? She felt weak. "I don't know."

"Leeha, you were going to tell me about a document you'd stolen. Did it have to do with this man you love?"

"Yes. I'm so tired. Please, let me rest."

"Okay, you may rest awhile, but I need you to keep remembering things about the stolen document. Will you do that for me?"

"Yes."

Another man said, "We don't have time for this. Make her tell you."

"Recall with Mind-One doesn't work that way. If she's exhausted, she won't remember. In rest, her mind will continue to reconstruct events."

A warm hand touched her forehead. "Rest now, Leeha. Let your mind wander to the document and why you stole it. Do you understand?"

"Yes, I understand."

All sounds ended except for a background hum. Sensations of her body sinking into the mattress retreated. She was in chemistry class again. Ms. Carlyle set a test paper face down on the table. "Great job, Leeha. Congratulations!"

Leeha turned the paper over. A big *A+* was circled in red at the top of the page. She yearned to glance in Randy's direction to see the expression on his face; if he looked happy, it would mean he did well on the test, too. Glancing his way, though, might seem too ... presumptuous ... too much like she was flirting. She didn't look.

Class ended. She headed out the door.

As she walked down the hallway, she heard Randy's voice. "Hey, Leeha! Wait up."

He met her in the middle of the busy corridor, in full view of everyone. "Leeha, check out this grade." He held up his test paper. "*B-plus*! I can't believe it! Ms. Carlyle told me I'll get a *B-minus* in the class. My coach will be happy with me. I can stay in sports."

"You worked really hard for it, Randy. Congrats."

"Thanks, but I couldn't have done it without you, Leeha. You saved my life."

He set a hand on her shoulder. She thought she'd faint. Passing students stared at them.

Once again, Leeha felt the bed against her back. She hadn't done what she was supposed to do—she hadn't recalled how she'd stolen the document for Randy Altholder.

The memories were ethereal, like specks of dust floating in rays of sunshine streaming through a window.

Then, she remembered something else. The school year had ended. She hadn't seen Randy for a long time ... until a hot summer day.

She found herself in the farming town of Oakwood. She was waiting to cross a street. Her mother stood next to her.

Leeha felt someone touch her shoulder. It was Randy. "Hey, Leeha, haven't seen you in a while."

His skin was tanned to gold. His hair was sun-bleached to almost white. He wore dark sunglasses, a sleeveless T-shirt, and shorts.

"Randy, hi. This is my mom."

He held out his hand. "Mrs. Ritsagin, good to meet you."

"Ah, you're the boy who drove Leeha home from school a few times."

"Yeah, I don't know what I would've done without her. Say, ma'am, if Leeha wants, may I take her out for a treat?"

"Well, that's up to Leeha."

Leeha's heart raced. Was this a dream? They stood on the busiest street in town. It was broad daylight, yet Randy was talking to her in full view of everyone. "Yeah, okay, I'd like to go."

"Do you like milkshakes?" he asked.

"Love 'em."

Leeha wandered off with him. She hadn't the slightest idea what to say as they strolled down the hot, bright sidewalk.

"So, Leeha, how's your dad?"

"Hanging on."

"I heard your family sold most of your farmland."

"Yeah, we didn't have much choice …." What was she doing? She sounded so negative! "But we got a reasonable price for it."

They stopped in front of a little café named *Bubbles*. He said, "Have you ever eaten here?"

"No."

"They make killer shakes. Would you like to try one?"

"Sure."

They went inside. The place was bright and cheery. She walked—with Randy by her side—up to the counter.

He said, "So what flavor would you like?"

"I'll try strawberry."

A pretty waitress with huge, green eyes appeared. Her blond ponytail bounced with each step. "Randy, hello! What can I get you?"

"Two strawberry milkshakes." Randy paid for the drinks.

Leeha said, "You didn't have to pay for mine."

"I want to. Seriously, Leeha, I would've been kicked off the team if not for you. I have colleges looking at me for sports scholarships. If I failed chemistry, it would've been all over for me before it ever started."

Leeha realized she was blushing. She must distract herself and calm down. "You passed on your own. You worked hard."

"I passed because you're a good teacher. You know how to explain things."

Leeha heard noises from the other time, from the time of weird drugs, gurneys, and shadowy figures.

A man said, "Sir, I think she's waking up."

She was aware of someone hovering over her. The shadowy man said, "She's not fully lucid yet. Let her wake up on her own."

COOKIE IS LOOKING FOR YOU

Cadona City, Cadona
MONDAY, MAY I, YEAR 1007 EE
4:00 P.M., EAST CADONA TIME

Cookie Davis paced the floor of her room in the Roadside Inn Motel.

Where was Leeha right now? Was she still alive? Cookie pushed aside a curtain and stared outside.

Rain was falling. Drops formed dimples in parking lot puddles.

With no warning, a fierce gust hurled raindrops against the window. Wind whistled. It shook the branches and leaves of plants growing along the back edge of the parking area. Beyond the greenery, a tall, windowless wall blocked the view. A strip of gray sky peeked above cracked, dirty bricks.

She gazed toward the heavens and fingered her Kettish prayer medallion. Maybe God would hear her pleas and help Leeha.

A buzzing sound interrupted her prayers. The noise was a personal device alarm. She didn't remember setting it. The words, *match found*, displayed on the viewplane. A picture of a man appeared. She recognized his face. It belonged to the wormy guy. Leeha's programming routine had worked!

The man appeared younger in the image than he did in the photo that Toofy took when the guy was snooping around Leeha's Monarch.

The man did, though, have the same scraggly mustache and stringy, red hair. Text beneath the picture gave his name as *Allen Bosswell*. According to the article, he worked as a private investigator at Fassel and Howell, and he was once an army special forces reconnaissance officer.

Fassel and Howell ... the name wasn't familiar. Cookie searched for it on WorldLink. It seemed the agency was a well-thought-of, private investigative firm. Bosswell, however, wasn't mentioned in recent company news. His current whereabouts didn't appear in any WorldLink file.

None of this made sense. Why would Allen Bosswell, a private eye and former military man, stalk Leeha?

Cookie wiped tears from her cheeks. Enough was enough! She had to do something.

She dug through the cheap purse that Angela had bought for her. Yes! Her CadTranS pass was still valid.

Angela had also purchased a rain poncho. Cookie pulled the rain gear over her head. It was the perfect thing to wear; many people wore this type of garment, so she'd blend in with the crowds. Also, she'd be unrecognizable beneath the baggy, rubbery fabric.

She slid the motel room key into a pocket and slipped out the door.

Wind howled and twirled around her. Rain slapped the waterproof, yellow material of the poncho. The air, although sopping, brushed lukewarm against her face and hands.

She followed a gaggle of guests down the outdoor stairs and into the parking lot. As others jumped into a vehicle, she walked down a gritty alley that ran along the side of the building.

WorldLink Direction Finder pointed the way to a bus stop on the next block.

She didn't have to wait long. A bus belched black smoke as it squealed to a stop. She climbed on board and found an empty seat.

It would take three buses for her to get to Leeha's apartment building in the Warrenton District.

◈

Somewhere in Cadona ...

Leeha Ritsagin awoke to flickering lights. With each pulse, her muscles stiffened.

The blinking pattern changed to a soothing rhythm. Her body relaxed.

She was supposed to remember something. What was it?

A document! The shadowy guy had asked about a document.

Another world appeared. She was standing in a bright, noisy hall in Oakwood Secondary School. Graduation was just weeks away. Sadness weighed on her. Death had claimed her father. He wouldn't see her get her diploma. He would've been proud; she'd been accepted to Cadona Technical University.

Fear also tormented her. She must leave the only home she'd ever known. Unlike her brother, who was attending a nearby trade school, she'd be moving far away. What would happen in college? Would she pass the classes? Would she make friends?

Back to business—the shadowy man hadn't asked about her emotions. She was supposed to be thinking about a document. This school-day memory came to her for a reason. Why was she standing in the hall? Ah, yes, she was looking at pictures on a bulletin board.

Her connection to the real world dimmed.

The image on the school bulletin board came into focus. Randy Altholder was in the photo. He wore a tuxedo. A crown sat on his head, and a medal hung around his neck. A caption below the picture read, *Prince Randy*.

Leeha's heart ached. Jessica, from the cheerleading squad, was his date to the graduation ball.

The next pictures captured the lives and times of the senior class. A few images showed girls running track. Others were of boys playing ball games. The theme switched to students raising their glasses and soda cans in the cafeteria while doing a senior toast. Then came pictures of students horsing around in the school hallways.

Her face didn't appear in any of the photos. She didn't even see herself standing somewhere in the background.

The slideshow started over, showing the king, queen, princes, and princesses from the ball. What a terrible night that was! While she sat at a table, Randy and Jessica lived it up on the dance floor. The only good things about that evening were the cake and punch.

Thank goodness the stupid ball was over! She'd never have to attend another.

Knowing this, however, didn't dampen the pain. She had to get control of herself. Finals were coming up. She must study for them.

Leeha headed down the hall toward the school library.

She heard Randy Altholder's voice. "Leeha, can I talk to you a minute?"

Just great, him again! She was trying to forget him. After the milkshake at Bubbles Café, the only attention he'd given her was an occasional *hello*, but even those greetings dropped off as the months passed. She didn't have a prayer. His heart would never be hers.

She turned around. There he stood, more gorgeous than ever. So much for getting over him. "Um, hi, Randy."

He focused on her and her alone. "Leeha, I heard about your dad's death. I'm sorry, I know he was looking forward to seeing you graduate."

"Thanks."

"Hey, Leeha, do you remember last year when you helped me out in chemistry?"

"Yeah, I remember. You did really well. You got a *B* in the class."

"I did well because of you. I need your help again, Leeha."

"What do you need?"

"I'm getting a *D* in BIM. If I don't get a *C* or better on the final, I'll lose my sports scholarship. Bellmore is too expensive; my family won't be able to send me there without financial aid."

"Bellmore University? Randy, you have a scholarship to Bellmore? Really?" How unfair it seemed! She studied like a fiend and got good grades, but she hadn't a prayer of getting accepted to Bellmore.

"Yeah, I got a sports scholarship. Pretty awesome, huh? But it'll be all over for me if I don't ace the BIM final. Will you help me?"

"I ... I don't know if there's time. The final is in three days."

He leaned close to her. She almost tasted his luscious lips. "Leeha, I have some intel. Ms. Jenton has a printed answer key in her office."

"How do you know?"

"A couple of friends saw a paper booklet on her desk."

"How … how will that help you?"

"Leeha, please, will you get the answer key for me?"

Was this guy crazy? If she got caught, her own future would be over.

"Leeha, I know this is asking a lot, but I don't know what else to do. You're smart. Ms. Jenton will never suspect you. You can take the booklet from her office, I'll copy it, and then you can put it back. She might think she'd misplaced it. Her desk is buried under papers."

This was not a good idea.

He rested his hands on her shoulders. "Please, Leeha, if you do this for me, I'll take you to a nice dinner, and we'll go dancing. We'll go anywhere you want. It'll be a graduation gift."

Her heart was pounding because of the crazy request and the warmth of his touch. "Okay, Randy, I'll see if I can figure something out. No guarantees, though."

"Awesome, Leeha. You're the greatest."

He winked at her before walking away. His backside did look great in those jeans! He disappeared around a corner.

She missed his company and his touch, yet she wondered what she had done. She agreed to steal an answer key from a teacher's office. How dare he ask such a thing of her? On the other hand, this might be her chance. Randy was entering the real world; maybe he'd find value in a loyal, hard-working girl over a pretty, sexy one.

Stealing the booklet, though, would make her a thief ….

Did it matter? After all, where had being good gotten her? Nowhere! It wasn't the studious, honest, plain-Jane girls who had dates to the ball. How different her memories of secondary school would be if she'd look back on graduation as the time when she sat in a romantic restaurant with Randy Altholder.

She'd do it; she'd steal the document.

Leeha's heart raced as she headed down the hallway. She needed a plan. A thought came to her. She could tell Ms. Jenton that she might be a few minutes late for the Business Interlink Management final because she had another exam right before it. A lame alibi, but it would do.

The faculty offices were just ahead. Students were everywhere. Perhaps many seniors, like Randy, feared they'd fail a class and miss a once-in-a-lifetime opportunity.

As Leeha walked along, she felt—for the first time—like part of the student body; she was one of them.

Ms. Jenton's office was across the hall. The door opened.

Leeha bent down and sipped from a drinking fountain. Out of the corner of her eye, she watched as Ms. Jenton rushed down the hall and entered the faculty restroom.

The door to the office was ajar. What a golden opportunity!

Leeha tapped on the door. No one responded. She peeked into the office. She didn't see anyone, so she poked her head inside. "Hello?" No one was there. She tiptoed into the cluttered room and shut the door behind her.

Randy's reconnaissance was accurate. Ms. Jenton did seem to have a thing for paper. Printed documents and individual sheets filled the small room. Some pages lay on the floor.

No surveillance devices were in sight, so she approached the desk.

Something stank.

Leeha peeked into a garbage can.

Gross! Puke! Ms. Jenton must've fallen ill, which was probably why she went to the restroom without locking her office door.

Where in this mess might Ms. Jenton hide an answer key?

Then she saw it; a thin document lay partially covered by other papers. The stack rested on the floor in front of Ms. Jenton's desk. Below the booklet lay a sheet with a list of test dates and times.

Leeha bent down and flipped open the answer key. The booklet was only a few pages long. The print was tiny. Perhaps she didn't need to steal the document. With luck, snapshots of the pages would be clear enough to read.

Just in case a hidden camera was spying, she pretended to review the final-exam calendar while she photographed pages containing answers to the Business Interlink Management test.

The doorknob turned. She grabbed the fallen papers and jumped to her feet.

Thank goodness! Marci from drill team, not an instructor, stood in the doorway.

Marci seemed nervous. Despite the poised way she tossed a lock of shiny, red hair over the shoulder of her chic, silk blouse, her voice quivered. "Oh, Ms. Jenton isn't here?"

Leeha fought to calm her own nerves. "No, she went to the restroom. I don't think she's feeling well."

Marci glanced into the wastebasket. "She's throwing up a lot. It must suck being PG."

"Ms. Jenton's pregnant?" Leeha asked.

Sarcasm tainted Marci's words. "Well, yeah. Gee, I thought every-one knew."

"Well, I didn't, but now I do," Leeha said. It was time to leave. She had what she came for. She handed Marci the calendar. "If you're looking for test times, here's the list."

"Thanks, yes, that's exactly what I'm looking for."

Leeha knew it was a lie, but she didn't care. She had more important things to think about: a romantic dinner and a night of slow dancing with the most incredible guy who walked the planet.

She set the answer key and other papers on a guest chair by Ms. Jenton's desk. "Good luck with finals, Marci."

"Yeah, thanks." Marci's thoughts were easy to read. She wanted the office to herself so she could snoop around.

Leeha left the room and strolled down the hall. She wanted to run, but she forced herself to amble. Drawing attention to herself could lead to disaster.

A tall, skinny boy walked up to her. She recognized him but didn't recall his name. He wore the baggy clothes of the grunge clique.

He said, "Hey, did you just come out of Ms. Jenton's office?"

"Yeah."

"She in there?"

"No, she wasn't feeling well and went to the bathroom. She's PG, you know."

"Yeah, I heard. It creeps me out. Some schmuck is willing to rage that bitch."

Leeha made a disgusted face. It seemed the thing to do at the moment. "Yeah, gross, isn't it?"

"Is her door unlocked?" he asked.

"Yeah."

"Thanks."

"No problem." Leeha swaggered away. She was a rebel now. If fate was kind, the text in the images would be legible, and Randy would have his prize.

The lights darkened. The school hallway faded. She felt a hand on her forehead. The shadowy man said, "Leeha Ritsagin, can you hear me?"

"Yes."

"Do you remember the document you stole?"

"Yes."

"For whom did you steal it?"

"Randy Altholder."

"Why did you steal it?"

"Because I love him. He promised me things."

"Money?"

"No, dinner and dancing." A burning sensation churned in her stomach.

"Did you give him the printed document?"

"No, I sent him pictures."

"What did you use to take the pictures?"

"My PD."

"The PD you used, where is it now?"

"I recycled it."

"Why?"

"I was afraid I'd get caught."

"What did you do with the printed document?"

"I left it on a guest chair."

"Where is this chair?"

"In Ms. Jenton's office."

"What happened to the printed document after that?"

"I have no idea. I left. I didn't want to get in trouble." Pain shot up from her belly and into her chest. "I don't feel good."

"Leeha, why did Randy Altholder want the document?"

She tried to speak, but her chest hurt too much.

The man called out to someone. "Get Doctor Millerman! Something's wrong."

Burning fluid filled her mouth. Breath would not fill her lungs.

A different male spoke. "Did you get everything you need out of her?"

"No," the shadowy man said. "We got some intel, but not everything."

"Then get out of my way. We can't lose her until we're done with her."

The sounds of the real world drifted away. Leeha was back in secondary school. She boarded a bus. The temptation to peek at the answer-key pictures gnawed at her, but she didn't dare look at the photos until she returned home.

The house was empty when she arrived. A note sat on the kitchen table; her mother and Jeremy had gone out.

Her heart pounded as she enlarged the pictures of the answer key.

Yes! Legible words appeared. My, the questions were easy! Why would anyone cheat? Much was at stake, however. If Randy didn't get a *C* or better, he'd lose his athletic scholarship to one of the best universities in the nation.

She sent him the images.

A message arrived in seconds. *Leeha, you're the greatest!*

Her feet barely touched the floor as she made her way to the refrigerator. She poured herself a glass of milk and sat at the table. There were many things to do. Her date with Randy must be perfect. She needed a dress—a slinky one, but not too much so. *Classy* was the correct word. And new shoes! They must be made for dancing but still pretty.

The planning finished, she took a sip of milk and relaxed into her seat.

She was alone, yet she sensed a presence. It was her father. His spirit floated across the kitchen. He sat down in his favorite chair. He'd come to comfort her as he'd done so many times when he was alive.

But why was he visiting now? She didn't need comforting. She was happy! For once, she felt like she belonged. And, best of all, she'd soon be dancing and dining with Randy Altholder.

Her father made the purpose of his visit clear; he didn't approve of what she'd done. She'd risked her own future for a man who didn't love her … for a man who was willing to cheat on an exam.

Leeha rested her head in her hands. Her father was right.

She sent Randy another message.

He replied. He had copied the images and deleted the messages she'd sent. No one would ever know what transpired.

Electronic footprints, however, never disappeared; they faded. To protect herself, she needed to get rid of as much evidence as possible. She came up with a plan. In a few days, she'd recycle her personal device and buy a new one. The purchase wouldn't look suspicious; students often started college with a new device.

Tears fell from her eyes. How could she be so stupid? Randy didn't care about her; he used her.

Like a faint echo, she heard her father say, *You are not alone, Leeha. You have friends. Cookie is looking for you.*

Cookie? She didn't know anyone from secondary school named Cookie.

Leeha's thoughts drifted away from the old farmhouse. She returned to the other time line.

Her surroundings had changed. She was still laying on her back, but some sort of device covered her nose. Squishing and beating sounds gurgled and pulsed around her. The memories from secondary school had lost their freshness.

One recollection, though, hadn't dimmed as much as the others, as if it straddled both past and present. Her father had mentioned someone named Cookie. Leeha didn't know a *Cookie* in her hometown, but she did know someone with that name in Cadona City: Cookie Davis, the beautiful, raven-haired woman who was staying in her apartment.

Where was her roommate now? Had she also been kidnapped?

Leeha prayed. She begged God to keep her friend safe.

A man spoke. "She's stabilized."

The shadowy man said, "Doctor Millerman, can we give her another round of Mind-One?"

"No, she wouldn't survive. We'll need to use old-fashioned methods to make her talk."

18

PINELAND APARTMENTS

Cadona City, Cadona
MONDAY, MAY 1, YEAR 1007 EE
5:00 P.M., EAST CADONA TIME

Cookie Davis stepped off the CadTranS city bus.

People waiting at the stop and on the nearby commuter train platform ducked against whipping wind and lashing rain. No one paid attention to her.

She pulled the poncho hood low over her face and headed down a pitted sidewalk.

What would she find at the Pineland Apartments? Would danger be waiting for her? In her heart, she wished the kidnappers realized they'd made a mistake and had set Leeha free. If that was the case, though, why wouldn't Leeha have called?

Cookie stopped walking and pushed the hood away from her face.

The apartment building lay across the street. As usual, the neighborhood was quiet. She glanced into the parking lot. The brown Monarch wasn't there. Bob Fullerby was right; the car had vanished.

Wind hurled rain against her as she dashed across the road.

Nothing seemed amiss at the entryway to the building, yet her fingers trembled as she typed the access code.

Cookie rushed into the lobby. It appeared exactly as it always did.

She took the stairs to the fourth floor.

As she made her way down the deserted hallway, a chill came over her; the last time she'd walked down this hall, Leeha was about to be thrown into a red van.

Cookie stopped by unit 413. The moment of truth had arrived.

The door was closed. She turned the doorknob. It was locked. She knocked. Nothing happened. Tears misted her eyes. She recalled what it was like to return home and find Leeha waiting inside. Now, haunting emptiness hung in the air. She missed her so much!

A voice came out of nowhere. "Lock yourself out?"

An old man stood behind her. She recognized him. He lived across the hall. She didn't know what to say.

"Don't try to deny it," he said. "I know what you two girls are up to."

"Excuse me, sir, what … do you mean?"

"I know there are two of you livin' in there. Just because the wife and I are hard of hearin', doesn't mean we don't know what's going on."

Her lips quivered.

He said, "Now, now, don't fret, young lady. I ain't gonna tattle on you. I take it the other gal is at work?"

"No … well, sort of. She's … traveling."

"Hold on, miss. I'll get a key."

"Sir, you have a key to four thirteen?"

"I have a physical key for all the units on the floor. I help out the managers. Not sure if you know this, but they don't get over this way much."

He went into his apartment but left the door open.

Cookie saw an old lady sitting on a chair. A quilt was draped over the woman's hunched shoulders. Her gaze was fixed on a giant viewplane showing image after image of beautiful scenes of nature.

The old guy returned with a key.

A crackly woman's voice flowed through the old man's doorway. "Arny, what's going on?"

"Just helpin' someone out."

"What?"

"Stop shoutin', woman! I'm helping a tenant."

Arny shook his head and pointed to his left ear. "Sorry, miss. The wife needs a new hearing aid." Arny unlocked the door to Leeha's unit. "There ya go, miss." He hobbled into his own unit and shut the door behind him.

Cookie stepped into her apartment and froze. Someone had torn the place apart. The kitchen cupboards and drawers were open. Cups, plates, and silverware were scattered around the room. Someone had stolen all the food, even the ice cubes. Her physical key, however, sat just where she'd left it—on the kitchen counter. She stuffed the key into her pocket.

The living room was also a mess. Her belongings, which she'd kept neatly stacked, were tossed about as if a tornado had blown through. Her designer purse had been ripped open. Its contents, even the paper money that she'd gotten from pawning her Taysar wristwatch, lay spread out on the floor. Odd. Why would a burglar steal food but not take a wad of cash?

She heard footsteps in the hallway.

Whoever was out there stopped by her door. Two men spoke. Their words were too low to understand, but neither voice belonged to Arny.

The doorknob jiggled. Someone was coming in!

The nearest hiding place was inside the laundry nook. The bi-fold door rattled as she pulled it open. She squeezed into the gap between the machines and the wall.

Cookie pushed the divider shut just in time; someone entered the apartment. Through spaces separating slats in the bi-fold door, she saw two males. They looked fit. One had dark hair, the other blond.

The dark-haired man said, "I don't get why we were sent back. We've already torn the place apart. We even dug through the food. We're wasting time."

"Zoff was adamant," the light-haired man said. "He wants us to search this rathole again. Let's give the closet another go-over."

The men went into Leeha's bedroom. Cookie lost sight of them, but it sounded like they were ripping the place apart. She knew she had to escape. If they didn't find what they sought in the bedroom, they'd search the rest of the unit.

Careful not to make noise, she pushed open the laundry nook door and tiptoed across the living room.

Now came the risky part; she had to pass by the bedroom doorway to get to the exit.

She peeked into the bedroom. She didn't see the dark-haired man. The blond man had his back to her. He was swinging some kind of long, bright tool. With each blow of the shiny weapon, Leeha's Rubberman punching bag hopped about on the bedroom floor.

Luck held. She crept by the open door unseen. She was almost free.

One of the men said, "It's not here. Like I told Zoff and Hands, the bitch must've stashed it somewhere else."

Cookie's heart raced as she slipped out of the unit and into the hallway. Coming here was not a good idea. She must get out of the building.

"Psst," someone said. It was Arny. His head was poking around his apartment door. "Come on in until they leave."

She darted into the old man's unit. It smelled of baked bread and cinnamon.

He said, "I could tell you were sneakin' out. How did you get away without them catching you?"

"I hid in the laundry nook until they went into the bedroom."

"I bet they gave you quite a scare. Sometimes they knock. Sometimes they just barge on in. I don't know what's going on around here lately, but somethin' just ain't right."

"Sir, what do you mean? What's going on?"

"All kinds of oddball stuff. I heard that Bercette, the gal in the unit at the end of the hall, died. Rumors are flying that she was murdered. Some say Toofy, her grandson, did it. But I don't buy it. Far as I know, Toofy took good care of her. Tenants are tellin' me strangers have been lurking around the grounds. Some folks think these outsiders killed her. Heck, I even heard that both Bercette and Toofy are dead. The cops were crawlin' around the place awhile. Then, poof, they vanished without a word 'bout what really happened. Now, we're havin' serious-looking young fellows rummaging all over the building."

"What are these guys doing?" Cookie asked.

"All kinds of stuff," Arny said. "They spent a good hour this morning snooping around the mechanical room. When I asked if they needed help, they told me to keep my mouth shut if I didn't want trouble. I don't know how many units they hit. Honestly, I think they roughed up old George. They ransacked his place late last night, but George wasn't gonna tell me what they did to him. He was scared. I saw it in his eyes. They came to our place yesterday looking for keys and building schematics, but they didn't break anything—not yet anyway. Now, they're in your place. Count your blessings you got out and the gal you live with isn't home."

She considered telling Arny about Leeha's abduction, but she decided it was best to reveal as few details as possible. Instead, she said, "These guys who are nosing around, are they cops?"

"To tell ya the truth, I don't know who they are. One of them showed me some sort of badge, but it didn't look like any identification I've ever seen."

"Sir, do you know what they're looking—"

"Shh." Arny held up a crooked, wrinkled finger.

She heard footsteps in the hallway. The sounds faded.

"There," Arny said, "sounds like they're gone. To answer your question, nope, I have no idea what they're after. Since they went through your stuff, maybe they won't bother you again."

She had little hope of that, but she said, "Yeah, that would be good. It was kind of scary having guys waltz into our place."

Clanking noises came from another room.

"Zelda!" Arny said. "What are you doin' in there?"

"Garbage tipped over. It's stuffed full."

He said, "I get the hint, hon. I'll run it down."

"You know what, sir?" Cookie said. "I'm heading out. I'll drop off the garbage for you."

"That would be mighty nice of ya."

Zelda waddled into the room and handed her a plump bag of trash. "Thank you, miss. It's rare to find young people willin' to help old folks nowadays."

"No problem at all. Glad to help," Cookie said. She felt a wave of guilt. The reason she volunteered to take out the garbage was because she needed an excuse to leave the building through the rear exit.

Arny stuck his head out his apartment door. "It's all clear. The hall's empty." He opened the door all the way. "Young lady, let me know if anything else out of the ordinary happens. We like to live in peace and quiet here at Pineland."

"Okay. Thanks, sir, for helping me." She headed for the emergency stairwell at the far end of the hall. She paused in front of Mrs. Furley's unit. Images of bloody bodies popped into her mind. The memories made her stomach hurt. It was time to go.

She trotted down the dimly lit staircase.

An exit sign glowed red at the bottom of the last flight of steps.

She stopped walking when she reached the landing. What if someone was waiting outside?

Hinges squeaked as she pushed open a stained, dented, metal door.

Outside, bursts of wind blew waterlogged rubbish along crumbling asphalt. The gusts threatened to tear pieces of trash from the stubby branches of long-dead trees. Nothing else moved.

Even though she didn't see surveillance devices, hidden cameras might be watching. She mustn't do anything that would arouse suspicion. Thank goodness for the wet, blustery weather! It provided the perfect excuse to conceal her face beneath the hood of her rain poncho.

Ducking against the wind, she stepped around squashed bottles, mangled cardboard, and plastic bags as she made her way to a dumpster. The huge, smelly garbage bin was overflowing with trash. She flung Zelda's bag onto the top of the heap.

So far, so good. She saw no sign of danger.

Cookie followed the tall, rickety fence that ran behind the apartment building. At the end of the fence, a muddy path meandered across a weedy patch of ground. She followed the path to a sidewalk. From there, it was a straight shot to the CadTranS stop.

When she arrived at the platform, a commuter train was waiting. Two transit buses sat nearby.

Her heart pounded. Might someone be following her? Maybe she should call Kever or Anson for help. But if she did, they would know she had left the motel. She'd never hear the end of it! Besides, no one waiting at the stop looked suspicious.

Cookie tapped her personal device. WorldLink Direction Finder listed CadTranS train and bus stops. She chose a route that, with luck, would confuse anyone who might be tailing her.

She hopped onto the train. Most of the passengers looked like tired factory workers. Some wore coveralls stained with grease or paint. Others had splotches of flour or mud on their clothes.

Cookie mimicked the passengers' blue-collar mannerisms as she plopped into a seat.

Then, she pretended to be asleep, all the while listening for signs of trouble.

An automated announcement broadcasted the train's location: *southwest fifteen-A, Lower Shanna Road.*

The train screeched to a stop. She joined a stream of passengers leaving the coach.

The rain and wind had subsided, but moisture filled the air. Patches of fog hung over the rooftops of old, dingy buildings. Vehicles drove by, spitting up water from the rutted roads. People ambled along the sidewalk. Nothing suspicious caught her eye.

She peeked at the map displayed on her personal device. Her bus stop was just a few blocks away. She strolled along, pretending to not be in a hurry.

Tires squealed. The noise overwhelmed the droning hum of the city. Horns honked, followed by more tire squeals.

She heard a woman say, "What's going on? What's that blue car doing?"

Cookie saw a long, old automobile with faded, blue paint. Two men sat in the front seat. The vehicle zigzagged through traffic.

The car slowed.

Was she imagining things? The passenger in the blue car seemed to be glaring at her.

He stuck a dark, long object out the passenger side window. The object looked like some sort of weapon. It vanished. Did she imagine that, too?

Then, she saw the weapon again, but only faintly. It was as if it had taken on the dull blue color of the car.

A piercing whine echoed down the street. A self-driving autopod barreled around a corner.

A woman said, "Why is that autopod going so fast?"

The blue car swung to the right. Tires screeched. The passenger leaned out the window.

Cookie saw a bright flash. A beam of light hit the autopod. Sparks flew. A whistle shrieked. A chunk of the pod broke away. Smoke rose, but the pod didn't stop. It rammed into the blue car. Shrapnel burst into the air. People screamed.

An old man grabbed Cookie's arm. He spoke with an accent. "Lady, hide! Hide!" He pulled her into a parking garage. "Lady, get down!" They crouched behind a concrete wall.

She recognized the messy-haired fellow squatting beside her. She'd walked past his vendor stand on her way to the bus stop. The man appeared concerned but unafraid. "Lady, who are you? Before the autopod showed up, that guy in the blue car was aiming dead at you."

"I'm … I'm no one."

Sirens wailed. The police were coming. Bob Fullerby had told her that the police and military had worked together to kidnap Leeha.

Cookie stood. She had to get away.

The old man said, "Hey! Where are you going? The cavalry's here!"

"I've got to go." She sprinted toward the Hoode Street exit of the garage. With luck, no cops or bad guys with weird guns would be waiting for her.

◈

Somewhere in Cadona ...

Leeha Ritsagin opened her eyes. Her head throbbed. It felt as if a spear gored her stomach. Her chest rose and fell, but she wasn't breathing on her own. A machine was pumping oxygen into her lungs.

She heard a series of raps. A man said, "Come in."

Another male spoke. His voice sounded like Randy Beller's. "Excuse me, Doctor Millerman, Senator Rineburg wants to know how she's doing."

"Tell John she's improving, but she'll need time to recover before we deliver her."

All fell silent.

Dr. Millerman spoke again. "Randy, is there something else?"

"Senator Rineburg asked about the brown Monarch again."

"Remind John that he's asking the wrong people. I don't know anything about the car. He'll need to ask someone from Altman's team."

"I'll send Rineburg's people a reminder, Doctor."

Leeha didn't hear anything else.

19

THE WORMY GUY

Cadona City, Cadona
MONDAY, MAY 1, YEAR 1007 EE
6:45 P.M., EAST CADONA TIME

Assistant investigative journalist Rona Betler hurried out of the downtown Cadona City Police Department office building. She jumped into her car and spoke into her personal device—encrypted line. "Hi, Mr. Fullerby, I'm finished with my assignment. I'm going to check on Degio. I haven't heard from him."

She started the engine and headed toward Jenton's Auto Body and Repair.

When Rona arrived at the repair shop, she parked in the customer lot.

She saw Degio's Dynamo Roadster. It sat in the employee parking area. A good sign! Maybe he was okay. Perhaps he decided he didn't want to see her again. His vanishing act might have been as simple as that. The thought didn't upset her; going out with him was fun, but she'd never expected—or wanted—her relationship with him to last.

Large windows in the front of the building gave her a good view of the lobby. A few people milled about, but Degio wasn't among them.

She went inside. No sign of him.

His friend, Ray, stood behind the counter. "Hi, Ray, is Degio here?"

Ray shook his head. "He hasn't been to work since Saturday. To be honest, I was hoping he went off somewhere with you."

"No, I haven't heard from him since Saturday afternoon. He called around one o'clock to make sure we were still *on* for a date."

"Wow!" Ray said. "That's about the time he left for lunch."

"Ray, did he seem okay?"

"Yeah, he was stoked about taking you to dinner."

A wave of guilt ran through her. She'd gotten Degio mixed up in the Drop Case investigation. If something happened to him, it was her fault. "Ray, his Roadster's parked out front."

"I know. It's been sitting in the same spot since Saturday."

"That doesn't make sense," Rona said. "He loves that car. He'd never leave it behind."

Ray leaned forward on the counter. His voice lowered to a whisper. "Row, I'm going to tell you something I shouldn't. Another employee is missing."

"Who?"

"Candy Fellerman."

"Degio mentioned her," Rona said. "He told me they worked together. Were Candy and Degio ... maybe ... involved?"

"I doubt it. She recently met a lady. I think it's getting serious."

"Ray, how do you know she's missing? Degio told me she was out of town."

"She was. She was visiting her grandpa in Banderville. Her mom called us. She was frantic. From what I gathered, Candy left her grandpa's house to grab some stuff at a grocery store but never returned."

"Did her mom say when this happened?"

Ray's eyes grew wide. "Saturday, midafternoon. Row, is something going on?"

"What do you mean?"

"I know you work for Bob Fullerby at Andecco News Service. I also know that you and Degio met around the time people from the military showed up asking about a brown Monarch. Is there a connection?"

Rona decided to feign ignorance. "Why would there be a connection?"

"Because both Candy and Degio worked on a brown Monarch."

"Did anyone else work on it?"

"I checked the vehicle in when the driver dropped it off. A couple of people probably assisted with repairs here and there, but Degio and Candy did most of the work. Row, I'm not supposed to do this, but I like Bob Fullerby, and I'm worried about Degio and Candy. Do you want me to pull up our files? Maybe I can find something that'll help."

"Nah, that's okay. I don't want you to get in trouble, but if you hear from Degio, would you mind giving me a call?"

"Sure thing. Will you do the same, Row?"

"Of course."

Apprehension haunted her as she walked to her car. Terrible things happened to anyone connected to that brown Monarch sedan. Leeha was kidnapped. Bercette Furley and her grandson, Toofelance Furley, were murdered. Now, Degio Ellis and Candy Fellerman had vanished.

Rona hoped Cookie Davis was still safely locked away in the Roadside Inn Motel.

Cadona City, Cadona
MONDAY, MAY 1, YEAR 1007 EE
9:15 P.M., EAST CADONA TIME

Cookie Davis hurried down the sidewalk. The sun had set. Thick clouds added to the murk. A big sign for the Roadside Inn Motel glowed like a lighthouse in a raging storm.

She should've listened to Bob Fullerby and stayed put in her room. She glanced over her shoulder. Pedestrians were going about their business. Automobiles rolled down wet roads; wheels sprayed sludgy water in their wake. The world around her seemed normal. If someone had been tailing her, she must've given them the slip.

Grit stuck to her shoes as she walked along the alley next to the motel. Faint light from two lamps outlined vehicles parked in the rear lot. Anson Dailey's car was not there. Good. No one would know she'd sneaked out.

Cookie bounded up the outdoor stairs and rushed down the walkway to her room. She opened the door just enough to reach inside and switch on the lights.

Nothing in the room had been disturbed, but a feeling of being watched hung over her.

She yanked open the closet door. No one was hiding inside the narrow compartment.

Her heart pounded as she tiptoed into the bathroom. She shoved aside the shower curtain. No one was hiding in the tub either.

The weight of fear lifted from her shoulders. Now, all she wanted to do was rest. She pulled off her rain poncho and threw her body onto the bed. The old mattress bounced and squeaked, but it didn't matter. For the moment, she was safe.

The situation, though, was every bit as grave as Bob Fullerby had warned. The guys in the blue car might've been trying to shoot her with a weapon that could change colors. Leeha was still missing. Scary men ripped up the apartment where she and Leeha once lived. Bad guys were hunting for some sort of document, and, somehow, this book was linked to Leeha.

Tears trickled from her eyes. The world was a bitter place. No pair of rose-colored glasses would make it better. Her ex-fiancé's meltdown and beatings were bad, but he was one person. These latest events were part of something much larger, much more insidious. They stole from her the most honest, sincere person she'd ever known. Would she ever see Leeha again?

Someone knocked.

Cookie sprang to her feet. She crept to the window. Through a gap at the end of a thick curtain, she saw a shadow on the outside walkway. She pushed the drapes a tad farther to the side. It was Anson!

She opened the door.

Rainwater trickled down the blue fabric of his police overcoat and dripped onto his exercise pants and athletic shoes. He held a plastic bag. "I brought some takeout. I figured you'd be hungry."

"Thanks, I'm starved. Please, come in. I have important news."

Anson sat down and set the bag on a table. "What kind of news?"

"I know who the wormy guy is."

"Wormy guy? Cookie, what are you talking about?"

"I haven't told you about him?"

"Not that I remember. Who is he?"

"A weird guy. Leeha swears he's been following her."

"Cookie, someone was following Leeha, and you didn't tell us?"

"I thought I had. I must be mistaken."

"Cookie, tell me about this man."

"A while back, Mrs. Furley pounded on our door in the middle of the night. She told us that she and Toofy had just gotten home from a casino. They saw a guy snooping around the Monarch. Toofy took a picture of him and chased him off. He gave us the photo. Leeha started calling the man in the pic the *wormy guy*. After that, she swears he was following her. Sometimes, she told me he was driving an old, white car. Other times she said he was skulking around on foot."

"Were you ever with Leeha when he was following her?"

"A couple of times, but I never actually saw him, except in Toofy's picture. After Mrs. Furley and Toofy told us about the guy, Leeha got scared, so Toofy put a security system in her car. She felt better after that. The system never caught the wormy guy, but she was convinced he was still hanging around. Now, I feel really bad."

"Why?"

"I thought maybe Leeha was imagining things. But after what happened to her, he might have really been there, but I didn't believe her. What's really weird is that Toofy thought the wormy guy was a private eye or bounty hunter looking for Monarchs to steal. Turns out the guy *is* a private eye who used to work at Fassel and Howell. What's even weirder is he used to be in the special forces."

"Cookie, I'm confused. How did you figure out the wormy guy is a private investigator?"

"Leeha had written a program to search for him. The code was some kind of face recognition routine, I think. If it found a match, it would alert us."

"May I see the photo?"

"Sure. This is the guy."

Anson stared at the picture. "*Allen Bosswell.* Cookie, do you know anyone who works at Fassel and Howell? Did Leeha ever mention it?"

"No, I never even heard of it until now. Does it ring a bell with you?"

"It does. They hire top-notch investigators. Police sometimes use them to assist in cases. I'll see what I can find out about this guy."

He pulled a box of food from the plastic sack. "You should eat before it gets cold." He stood and headed toward the door.

"Anson, please stay, I'd like some company."

"All right. I'll be right back. I need to tell Kever-o about Leeha's wormy guy."

In a few minutes, he returned. Without saying a word, he sat down and opened a food container.

"Anson, did you reach Kever-o?"

"Yep."

"Well, what did he say?"

"He's going to tell Mr. Fullerby about it."

"That's good." She sat down and opened a box of food. "So ... how is Kever-o doing? Did you guys have fun climbing at the gym?"

"We did. Kever-o's a darn good climber, and the girls love him. It's kind of funny to watch."

"Ang said the same thing; girls throw themselves at him. He certainly is charming."

A noise came from outside. Her heart raced.

Anson twirled spaghetti around a plastic fork. "Don't worry, someone just closed a car door."

She felt his eyes on her; did he suspect she'd left the motel?

"Cookie, besides figuring out the wormy guy is Allen Bosswell, is there something else you want to tell me?"

"Um, no. Nothing."

"You sure? You seem jumpy tonight."

"I guess the storm kind of spooked me. Anson, do you mind if we watch the news?"

"Sure, as long as it's Andecco. I can't wait to hear what Senator Fischer and Senator Rineburg lied about today."

Somewhere in Cadona ...

Leeha Ritsagin opened her eyes. She was lying on a bed. A canopy arched over her. It gave off a weird glow.

Her mind had cleared. A tad of strength had returned to her limbs. Bonds no longer strapped her arms and legs to the bedframe. She bent her knees. Nothing in the universe was better than being able to move.

She listened for sounds, but all she heard were the rhythmic squishes and hums of medical equipment.

Where was she? Had she been rescued?

She raised her head. The world spun. She clutched the sheets and prayed the dizziness would stop. At last, the whirling calmed to a slow twirl.

A man appeared. Leeha saw anger in his squinting eyes as they glared from above a surgical mask. His voice was gruff. "Ah, I see you're awake."

A chair screeched as he dragged it to the bedside. "You have one more chance; tell me why Randy Altholder wants the document you stole."

Leeha tried to speak. Only raspy sounds emerged.

The man clenched the bed railing. The bed shook. "Damn you, witch! Where is the document?"

"I don't know."

"That's not good enough. Where is it? Why does your lover boy want it?"

She kept quiet.

A big hand reached for her face. Her head bounced as he ripped the breathing apparatus away. The room spun. Acid lurched up from her stomach.

She heard another voice. "What's going on in here?"

"Doctor Millerman, the bitch is awake. She started thrashing around."

A different pair of eyeballs peered down at her. The man placed the breathing apparatus over her nose. Air filled her lungs. He shined a light in her eyes and then set something on her chest. The burning sensation subsided. Several moments passed before he spoke. "Lucky for us, she's not harmed."

"Doctor Millerman," the man with the gruff voice said, "so what if she croaks. She's an enemy apparent. The world's better off without her."

Doctor Millerman said, "If she dies, you'll be answering to Senator John Rineburg. I don't think you'd like that."

Leeha's left arm felt cold. Her eyes shut.

THE SOHN-SURAN WOMAN

"THREAT LEVEL 1—<u>Target:</u> Unknown woman, blurry photo only visual ID. <u>Nationality:</u> Sohn-Suran. <u>Wanted For:</u> Grave national security threat. <u>Last Known Location:</u> Pineland Apartments, Warrenton District, Cadona City. <u>Directions:</u> Apprehend alive, consider suspect armed and dangerous."

National Security Alert
Year 1007 of the Enlightened Epoch

Cadona City, Cadona
MONDAY, MAY 1, YEAR 1007 EE
9:30 P.M., EAST CADONA TIME

Pastor Leon Walls sat at his office desk in the True Followers of God Church headquarters. He rested his head in his palms. Worry consumed him. Bezgog the Deceiver was attacking his church, the Back-to-Basics

Club, and the Freedom Party. As prophecy predicted, the Evil One was arming his children, the Domats, in preparation for the Last War.

Now, Bezgog was sowing divisions among God's people.

Leon rubbed his tired eyes. His own son, Mark, was being led astray. Mark long held beliefs contrary to God's Word, but his heresy was deepening. He came up with the crazy notion that God cherished animals and plants as well as people.

More recently, Mark had come to the conclusion that human abortion wasn't a mortal sin because a woman might face physical and financial hardship while dealing with pregnancy, delivery, and postpartum recovery. He was starting to sound like a crazy Lotish priest or a Shinchik powslor.

Even worse, he failed to understand the danger. Senator John Rineburg and General Douglass Willirman found evidence suggesting that Mark was collaborating with a leader of Cadona's unrighteous: Andecco News Service Investigative Journalist Bob Fullerby.

Leon heard a knock on his office door. He glanced at the security monitor. Tammy Smith's radiant smile stretched between her rosy cheeks. John stood close to her. Behind them stood Doug and Senator Mitch Fischer.

"Come in," Leon said.

Tammy opened the door. "Pastor, your guests are here."

"Thank you, Tammy, for escorting them. Good evening, gentlemen. Please make yourselves comfortable."

John strutted into the office. Mitch and Doug followed him through the doorway. They took seats.

"Pastor," Tammy said, "is there anything else I can do for you?"

"No, thank you. That'll be all."

With a wide grin still etched on her face, she left the room.

Mitch said, "Leon, thank you for letting us use your office. Dougy and John tell me this is the safest place to discuss sensitive matters."

John slumped into his chair. "It's campaign season; too many people are hanging around the senatorial offices. No telling who's who."

"As for me," Doug said, "I have Richard Karther's spies snooping around. That jackass still has allies in the Defense Department."

202 ◈ C. N. SKY

Leon's shoulders relaxed. Perhaps this meeting was a routine gathering rather than a fresh crisis or new complaints about Mark. "I'm always glad to help in every way I can."

"Your assistance is very important to us, Pastor," Mitch said. "We have a lot going on. The four of us need to stay on the same page. Dougy, tell us what you've learned about Randy Altholder."

Leon didn't recognize the name. "Wait a second; who's he?"

Doug said, "Leeha Ritsagin stole the Guiding Light for him."

John sounded annoyed. "Pastor, haven't you been reading your messages?"

"I'm afraid I'm behind, John."

"Not to worry, Pastor," Mitch said. "I'm a bit behind myself. Please fill us in, Dougy."

"At what point do you want me to start?"

"Tell us how Leeha Ritsagin and Randy Altholder know each other."

"They grew up in the same town. They both went to Oakwood Secondary School."

"Dougy," Leon said, "where's Oakwood?"

"It's a town due west of here. Not much is left of it. Agri-Growers owns most of the land there that's worth a crap."

"*Agri-Growers*," Leon said. "John, isn't that one of your companies?"

"Yes, sirree! The Oakwood area's washed up. It's a polluted dust bowl. Agri-Growers will need to move on."

Mitch said, "Gentlemen, let's stay on topic, please. Dougy, you were telling us about Randy Altholder and Leeha Ritsagin. Please continue."

"Altholder and Ritsagin graduated the same year. Strange thing is, we haven't found a single contact between them since then."

"Did they go to college together?" Leon asked.

Doug shook his head. "Nope. Ritsagin went to Cadona Technical and Altholder went to Bellmore. He had a sports scholarship but couldn't keep up his grades. He never graduated. Ritsagin did. She graduated with honors."

Mitch poured himself a cup of coffee. "Dougy, where's Altholder today? Back in Oakwood?"

"No, the kid skipped the country after he dropped out of college. We traced him to Antropka. We have reason to believe he's hiding out in the ungovernable part of Tahagaruza. The real kicker: Randy Altholder's a Rustlers gang member. Given what's written in the Guiding Light ... the gang could make a big score if they got their hands on the document. Domataland, Sohn-Sur, or even our own homegrown defector groups would pay a fortune for such information."

"Is Ritsagin associated with the Rustlers gang, Dougy?" Mitch asked.

"Not that we can tell."

Leon shivered at the thought of the Guiding Light in enemy hands. "How much did she get paid for the heist?"

"That's a good question, Pastor," Doug said. "Nothin'. She was supposed to get a dinner-and-dance date out of the deal."

"That's it?" Leon asked.

John said, "It's a classic story, isn't it? Ugly girl meets handsome man. Desperate bitches are easy to control. They'll do anything for a little romance, for an escape from a boring, worthless life. Altholder must've wanted our document shit bad. I can't get the image out of my head: a greasy, pimply blob lying willingly on a bed with her flabby legs spread. It's enough to make me puke."

"Dougy," Mitch said, "the Guiding Light, do we know where it is?"

"Ritsagin sent Altholder a copy by PD. From what we know, it's the only copy in existence. She recycled the PD afterwards to keep from getting caught."

"And the printed version of the document?" Mitch asked.

Doug's stubby thumbs slapped together as if they were locked in a to-the-death battle. "Ritsagin worried about getting in trouble, so she left the document on a guest chair in Jenton's office. We suspect *Jenton's* refers to Jenton's Auto Body and Repair. She dropped off her Monarch there shortly after the Guiding Light vanished."

Sweat formed on Leon's temples. "I'm not seeing how the pieces fit together. We haven't found recent links between Ritsagin and Altholder. He's hiding in Antropka, and she's never left the country. She claims to have sent the Guiding Light to him by PD, but we found no such record of any of it. Dougy, how is Ritsagin communicating with him?"

"Another excellent question, Leon. We may have identified a go-between. We found DNA in Ritsagin's Warrenton District apartment. The DNA belongs to a Sohn-Suran woman who is supposed to be dead—killed in the one-thousand-three Mik-la-tah Tsunami. Our best explanation is the woman was recruited as an agent, her death was faked, and then she was assigned to help steal our document."

Mitch placed his cup on a saucer. "Assigned by whom, Dougy?"

"Could be anybody: the Rustlers, Sohn-Sur, Domataland. But I'm beginning to suspect the Cadona Guardians. Our tech folks found something on Ritsagin's computer—a face-recognition search routine. It was set up to find the face of one man: Allen Bosswell, a suspected Cadona Guardian member."

Leon dabbed perspiration from his face. "I'm confused. I thought we didn't find a link between Ritsagin and the Guardians."

"We hadn't," Doug said. "Until this."

John twitched in his chair. "Hold on a second, Dougy. If Ritsagin's a Guardian herself, why would she need to run a routine to find another fricken Guardian member?"

Doug shrugged his shoulders. "At this point, John, we don't know."

"So, Dougy, do we know anything useful about this routine?"

"It was written to broadcast when a facial match was found. We have Ritsagin's PD, so we got the match notice."

"Who else was notified?" John asked.

"Don't know," Doug said.

"Why the hell not?"

"The broadcast itself went out to WorldLink Heavens. The program to pick it up needs to be on a PD. Whoever wrote the routine went out of their way to make it hard to track. We may find residue traces, but with so many people opting out of PD call tracking these days, our odds of finding the bread crumbs aren't great."

Mitch said, "Thanks for the update, Dougy. What are the next steps?"

"Loyals are checking out employees at Jenton's Auto Body and Repair. If Ritsagin left the document in an office there, someone must know about it. Someone may even be involved in the theft. We haven't found Randy Altholder yet, but our people in Tahagaruza know finding him is a priority.

As for the Sohn-Suran woman, clearly, she's not dead. A ghost doesn't leave DNA. She was in Leeha Ritsagin's home, and we've gotten reports that a lady fitting the woman's description was seen near the Pineland Apartments. The woman will make a mistake. We'll find her."

"How's Ritsagin's interrogation going?" Mitch asked.

John said, "It was going well, but Mind-One made her sick. Doctor Millerman says another round would kill the bitch. Doctor Palchero's people will wring out the rest of her secrets using good, old-fashioned techniques."

Leon's stomach gurgled. Stress was getting to him. His body trembled as he stood. "Excuse me a moment. I need the lavatory."

Mitch also rose to his feet. "Gentlemen, I think we can all use some rest. Plans are in place. Orders have been issued. There's not much more the four of us can do tonight."

Cadona City, Cadona
MONDAY, MAY 1, YEAR 1007 EE
9:45 P.M., EAST CADONA TIME

The breeze shifted. Bob Fullerby smelled the noxious fumes escaping from the Holbline Factory.

The protesters had a right to be mad. The odors alone were bad enough, but the chemicals were also deadly. Not even weeds grew in the yard around the huge, crumbling buildings.

"Mr. Fullerby!"

Bob recognized the elderly fellow shouting his name. He'd met Charlie in the Sunshine Diner a while back.

"Mr. Fullerby, thank you for coming. You're the only one who pays attention to us. You've got to tell the world what's happening here. Workers are getting sick from the fumes. Kids playin' in the neighborhood are getting burns in their lungs. Several people around here are havin' seizures."

"And it's not only the fumes," a middle-aged woman with rotting teeth said. "Stuff's leakin' out. There's poison in the ground. When it rains, it washes into our gutters and yards. We get gunk on our shoes and track it into our homes. Some college kids ran tests. They told us the toxins are seeping into the water system. We're drinkin' and washin' in this stuff."

Bob said, "I'll do what I can to get the word out."

Charlie looked hopeful. "We can't thank you enough. Not too many honest men rise to the top of the food chain in this country of ours, but a few do—fellows like you, Mr. Fullerby."

Bob fought a surge of shame. He didn't decide to cover the Holbline Factory protest because the site was spewing out toxins. He chose it because it was a few blocks away from Book Nostalgia. Defense Secretary Richard Karther had left secrets in the chimney dead drop again.

"Well, Charlie," Bob said, "I don't have much clout, but Senator Bradley Seldortin does, and he's a good man with integrity. He wants to clean up messes like this."

Charlie said, "Lots of us here will be votin' for Senator Seldortin in October, that I can tell ya."

"Good to hear. Bradley can use the support." Bob checked the time. "I've got to run, but I want you to know that Andecco News will make a report on Holbline tomorrow. I hope it does some good."

"We can't thank you enough for helpin' us," Charlie said.

Bob hurried down the pitted sidewalks to Book Nostalgia.

Yellow-glazed light poured out when he opened the doors to what had once been the main entrance to a Kettish church. The tall, bulky, gray-stone building had also once served as a library and a porn shop before it was converted into a bookstore.

Myrtle stood behind a counter. She adjusted her glasses as she looked his way. "Back again?" she said.

"I am. I decided to buy *The Voyages of Renn*. I found a place that can restore delicate, old texts."

Myrtle's aged hands smoothed tufts of white hair that had slipped away from her matronly bun. "I'll get the book for you."

Given her bird-thin legs and support hose, Bob wondered how she managed to work in this sprawling shop with its four stories and winding, bell-tower staircase. "That's okay, ma'am. I need the exercise."

He climbed to the third floor.

Old books, many with tattered pages hanging from worn bindings, filled the musty room.

Bob found *The Voyages of Renn*. He pulled it from a haphazard stack of other forgotten works of written art. A wave of melancholy fell over him as he brushed his hand over the battered, leather cover. They just didn't create grand legends like *Renn* anymore.

He must stop wallowing in things long lost. The time had come to collect what Richard Karther had left for him.

Bob pretended to search through mounds of other old novels as he made his way to the clandestine hiding place by the far wall.

He pushed on the side of the chimney. Loose bricks turned, revealing a small, dark hole. He stuck his hand inside. His fingers found a folded sheet of paper. He concealed the paper in his palm as he scooted the bricks back into place.

He now possessed what he'd traveled to the Langlire District to retrieve: important secrets from the secretary of defense.

Bob slipped the modern-day paper into a pocket, secured the antique novel under his arm, and headed down the stairs.

Myrtle tenderly wrapped the old book. "Tell me, do you really plan to restore her?"

"I most certainly do, ma'am."

The old woman gave him a grateful smile. "I'm glad *Renn* is in your hands. Good night, Mr. Fullerby."

As he stepped out the door of the shop, he turned up the collar of his raincoat.

On the street, a gaggle of drunks and bums mingled with poor factory workers and low-wage people from the service industry. To blend in, he walked in the hunched fashion of the late-night pedestrians as he made his way along gritty sidewalks. His next stop: the Sunshine Diner.

A bell tinkled as he opened the glass door of the restaurant.

Patrons, mostly men in worn work clothes, filled half of the tables.

A bony waitress, her face haggard from lack of sleep, said, "Take a seat wherever you like, sir."

Bob chose a corner booth.

A waitress hurried to his table. She raised a pitcher. "Coffee?"

"Decaf, if you have it."

"Ah, getting off work, I see. Be right back." She scurried away but soon returned with decaffeinated coffee. "You havin' something to eat?"

"A bowl of soup, please."

"We just ran out. How 'bout chili?"

"That'll do."

In minutes, the waitress returned. She dropped a bowl on the table and hustled away to wait on other guests.

He took a few bites of chili before pulling the square-shaped paper from his pocket. No one paid attention to him as he unfolded Richard's sheet. The defense secretary's tiny, boxy letters lay in neat rows. Each sentence was bullet-short, but the content spoke volumes. General Douglass Willirman's loyals linked a Sohn-Suran woman—who was supposed to be dead—to Leeha Ritsagin and a fellow named Randy Altholder. At the end of the last sentence, Bob noticed a tiny capsule. Richard had left him an important biological sample.

Bob stuffed the paper into his pocket. As he ate his meal, he pondered what he'd just read.

He needed help from forensics experts. He knew where to start; Detective Carl Brunish knew trustworthy people with such skills. He wouldn't have to wait long to seek Carl's help; he already had a meeting scheduled with him for the next day.

Somewhere in Cadona ...

Leeha Ritsagin's own squealing breath roused her from sleep. Air would not fill her lungs.

A man without a mask towered over her. His gloveless, hairy fingers squeezed shut a breathing tube.

She batted the man's hand. It did no good. Her vision narrowed.

He said, "I'm going to ask you a question. If you answer honestly, you live."

His hold on the tube slackened.

Air filled her chest.

She recognized the man's growling voice and tiny, glaring eyes, but this was the first time she'd seen his face. He was an older guy with a long head and a jaw as wide as the crown. A thin beam of light accentuated the deep pockmarks on his cheeks and bulbous nose. Stubbles of gray hair protruded from his scalp. His thin mouth, little more than a short slit, arched into a grin.

He bent forward. His face was close to hers. "Who is the Sohn-Suran woman?"

Her throat hurt as she spoke. "Who?"

Once more, he clamped shut the tube.

"The Sohn-Suran woman who was in your apartment. The one who knows Randy Altholder." He released the tube.

His questions weren't making sense. "I don't know whom you're talking about."

He blocked the flow of air again. "You're lying! We know she was in your place. How does she contact Randy Altholder? When will she next contact him?"

He let go of the tube.

This time, air entered her lungs in a trickle instead of a flood. "I have no idea what you're talking about."

He clamped the tube.

Pain stabbed her chest. An alarm blared. A red light flashed.

She heard footsteps and then Dr. Millerman's voice. "What's going on in here?"

The man with the gruff voice said, "Doctor, I respect you and your work, but we need answers. I'm tired of delays!"

Dr. Millerman sounded angry. "Get him out of here."

Two pairs of black-gloved hands grabbed the stubble-headed man by the arms.

"Listen very carefully," Dr. Millerman said, "if you disobey me again, I will give your name to Senator Rineburg. This is your last warning."

WRONG DOCUMENT

Cadona City, Cadona
TUESDAY, MAY 2, YEAR 1007 EE
1:30 P.M., EAST CADONA TIME

Bob Fullerby opened the door of the Nutty Squirrel Beer & Eats Pub. The aroma of freshly baked bread drifted by as he walked in.

He spotted Angela Thirgal and Kever Carsen. They sat at a corner table. He didn't see Rona Betler, but a small rain jacket was draped over the back of a chair. The coat was dusty tan in color, but glittery specks sparkled in the pub's dim lighting. No doubt the jacket was Rona's, as she tended to wear understated styles with touches of pizazz.

Bob joined his team at the table. "Howdy, folks."

Kever said, "Hi, Mr. Fullerby."

Suds the waiter appeared. He set a basket of crispy vegetables on the tabletop. "Good afternoon, sir. May I bring you something?"

"Just coffee, please."

"Oh, Suds," Angela said, "when you get a chance, I'd like more hot water."

"Sure thing. I'll be right back."

Bob noticed a grumpy look on Angela's face. "Ang, did something happen? You don't look happy."

"I got DNA and fingerprint samples from Cookie like you asked, but please, please, send Kever-o next time. That woman drives me nuts. She's so emotional. I never thought I'd escape."

"She's been through a lot, Ang," Bob said.

"I know, but all that wailing and moaning doesn't solve anything."

Suds returned. He filled their cups and walked away.

The thick fragrance of coffee filled the air. So did the scent of flowery perfume. Bob heard Rona's voice. "Hi, Mr. Fullerby." She scooted a chair up to the table. "Detective Brunish says he's running a few minutes late."

"Thanks, Row. Have you heard from Degio?"

"Nope, not a word."

Bob glanced around the room. None of the patrons seemed to be eavesdropping. "While we're waiting for Carl, I have an interesting update. Richard Karther shared some news that matches what the Drop Case informant told me earlier. Ritsagin and the brown Monarch caught the attention of a defector group called the *Cadona Guardians*."

"Let me guess, Mr. Fullerby," Kever said, "the Cadona Guardians are interested in her because of the Guiding Light."

"Sure enough. The Guardians somehow figured out she has the document. They searched for it in her apartment but didn't find the printed copy or any electronic versions. They did manage to haul away the Monarch, but nothing of value turned up inside it. Richard also told me the Soldiers of God Justice Group has gone back to the apartment a number of times, but they haven't found hide nor hair of the Guiding Light."

Angela's brow furrowed in thought. "This is weird. I wonder what Ritsagin did with it? We can't find it, neither can the military, the Soldiers of God Justice Group, nor the Cadona Guardians."

"Richard had other surprising news as well," Bob said. "One of his well-placed informants learned that General Willirman thinks a Sohn-Suran woman is connected to the theft. They know very little about her, not even her name. The only thing they do know is that she's listed as a victim of the Mik-la-tah Tsunami."

"Wait a minute," Kever said. "Mr. Fullerby, didn't the tsunami happen a long time ago?"

"Yeah, four years back."

Angela said, "Mr. Fullerby, how can a woman who died in one thousand three be involved with the theft of a document that was stolen a month ago?"

"She's presumed dead because her DNA was recovered from a crushed homeless shelter. No body was ever found."

Kever took a long sip of beer and stared into space.

"Kever-o," Bob said, "did you figure something out?"

"Maybe. What if someone planted evidence to make it look like a new, mysterious player is involved in the Drop Case, when, in fact, no new player exists? I mean, think about it; an unknown, dead woman has no history—what a perfect way to throw investigators off track."

Rona said, "Mr. Fullerby, how is the Sohn-Suran woman supposed to be tied to the Guiding Light?"

"The Back-to-Basics Club suspects she's a go-between for Ritsagin and a fellow named *Randy Altholder.*"

Angela let out a sigh. "Oh, no! Another new Drop Case player? Mr. Fullerby, is this Altholder guy real and undead?"

"Apparently. Ritsagin and Altholder went to secondary school together. The Back-to-Basics Club thinks she stole the Guiding Light for him because she loves him."

Rona held up her personal device. "Check it out! I found old pics of Altholder. He's a hunk! I wouldn't blame Leeha if she fell for him." Rona's glittery fingernails tapped a touchpad. "Mr. Fullerby, this is weird. It's like he vanished. I can't find any recent news."

"I'm not surprised, Row. Altholder's a Rustlers gang member somewhere in Tahagaruza. General Willirman doesn't know his exact whereabouts."

Angela said, "Mr. Fullerby, I hate to admit it, but I agree with Kever-o. Parts of the Drop Case story feel fabricated. All of a sudden, we have a Sohn-Suran woman and a gang member involved. One's long dead and the other's missing."

"Well, Ang, if you think Richard's news is weird so far, wait 'till you hear the rest. I don't know how he did it, but he managed to give me something very interesting." Bob set a red vial on the table. "Inside this tube is a tiny capsule containing the Sohn-Suran woman's DNA."

Angela picked up the vial and ran her fingers over its smooth, rounded surface. "Our defense secretary comes off as a coward at times, but he's certainly resourceful. I must give him credit."

"Well, folks," Bob said, "here's the crowning glory of Richard's secrets … Captain Timothy Becker's a Cadona Guardian and so are others who work at the Stanton Weapon Research Facility. Becker knows parts of Toxic Sphere's design, and, get this: some details about Toxic Sphere are in the Guiding Light."

Angela's eyes shot wide open. "Frick! All this time, we thought the document was about a justice execution list and crazy politicians, not apocalyptic weapons. No wonder people want the document. Foreign militaries will pay a fortune to get their hands on it."

Bob felt creeping fear.

Kever said, "Mr. Fullerby, is something wrong?"

"I'm trying to decide what's worse: Toxic Sphere in Freedom Party hands or an enemy nation learning about the most powerful weapon ever created. It comes down to who's the most dangerous: Mitch Fischer and his Freedom Party, Rashu Tapabanu and Sohn-Sur, or Demnar Tarish and Domataland."

"Excuse me, everybody," Rona said. "Detective Brunish is almost here. He's minutes away."

Angela jumped to her feet. "I better run to the restroom. That tea ran right through me. I'll be back in a sec."

Ver-Nuvelin, Domataland
TUESDAY, MAY 2, YEAR 1007 EE
4:45 A.M., CENTRAL FEWWOK TIME

Domataree President Demnar Tarish poured himself a cup of strong tea.

He heard his wife's sweet voice. "You're up early, Demnar."

"Yeah, unfortunately. Work is waiting for me."

"Why didn't you tell me, my love? I could've made you breakfast."

"I didn't want to wake you. You looked so beautiful sleeping. Anyway, I found food in the fridge."

Itena pulled a chair up to the kitchen table and touched a wall. A window formed. Dim lamps cast soft highlights over lush, spring grounds. Stars diminished as a dawn sun brightened the sky to velvet blue from navy. "It's too bad you must work. It's a beautiful morning. It would be a great day for a walk."

Demnar studied the soft curves of his wife's pretty face. He pushed a lock of gray-streaked dark hair away from her ebony eyes. The love he felt warmed his soul even as the troubles of the world pressed down like a crushing yoke. "Itena, how I wish we could stroll in the garden. A long hike in a forest sounds even better."

She gave him a soft smile. "Like we used to, before you were president."

"I do miss those days, Itena, believe me."

"Yet we have our duties," she said.

"True, we have our duties." He took her hand. "Well, perhaps tomorrow morning we can enjoy a garden walk."

Her tender fingers wrapped around his.

A doorbell's ring broke the spell of the moment.

"Demnar, are you expecting someone?"

"No."

A synthesized voice said, "Intelligence Chief Rozula Kolensha is at the front door."

Demnar checked the security monitor. Rozula stood outside. A sheer, floral scarf covered most of her pale hair. She wore a purple coat. The color brought to mind the sinking of the Goodwill Ship and the patriotic Domataree sailors who died when the flagship went down.

Itena said, "Rozula looks worried."

He kissed Itena's hand as he stood. "She does. Excuse me, my love."

The warmth of the kitchen abandoned him as he crossed the wide foyer. He opened the front door.

Rozula bowed. "Honorable President, I'm sorry to bother you at this hour. May we speak in your briefing room?"

"Of course. Please, come in." Demnar led the way to his home office. "Have a seat, Rozula."

She sat down and pushed the scarf off her head. The silky fabric came to rest around her shoulders. "I've received priority news, Honorable President. It's about the Guiding Light. We have reason to believe the document contains specifications about Cadona's Toxic Sphere weapons system."

"Wow!" Demnar said. "What kind of specifications?"

"We don't know for sure, but since the Freedom Party is putting so much effort into finding the document, there's a chance it might help us figure out how Toxic Sphere works."

"What about Leeha Ritsagin? Have your agents learned anything else about her?"

"We still don't know where Lady Ritsagin is, but we did learn an interesting piece of news. The Back-to-Basics Club believes they found the person who hired her to steal the Guiding Light. His name is Randy Altholder. He belongs to the *Rustlers*, a criminal gang in Tahagaruza, Antropka. Some of my agents doubt this man is involved, but, because of the source of the information, we're following up on the lead."

"Who's the source, Rozula?"

"Defense Secretary Richard Karther."

"The Cadonan defense secretary himself! That is impressive. Your network is well connected."

"We have good agents on our team," she said.

"Rozula, I've never doubted it for a minute."

"I have more news, Honorable President. A while back, my people injected a player into the rumor mill. It worked better than expected. The Club not only believes that our plant is involved, they also believe she's passing messages between Leeha Ritsagin and Randy Altholder."

"Is this player a real person?"

"She was. She was killed in the Mik-la-tah Tsunami. We created a story and fed it to Cadona. Now, General Willirman is wasting resources to find a fake adversary."

"Good work, Rozula. You may have bought us precious time. How is it going with the Hansen Hills and Mind-One stories?"

"We'll be injecting them into the Cadonan rumor mill in a few hours, Honorable President."

Cadona City, Cadona
TUESDAY, MAY 2, YEAR 1007 EE
1:50 P.M., EAST CADONA TIME

Bob Fullerby leaned on the Nutty Squirrel's thick bar. "Hey, Suds, can I get a bowl of spicy nuts?"

"Sure thing, sir."

Bob tossed a handful of nuts into his mouth the moment he sat down at the table.

Rona Betler gave him a scolding look. "Mr. Fullerby, you shouldn't eat so much salt."

Kever Carsen tapped a glass of beer. "Don't worry, Mr. Fullerby, Row's been lecturing me about alcohol. She never bugs Ang, though."

"Oh, I get it from her, too," Angela said. "She tells me I'm too serious, and I need to lighten up."

"You do, Ang," Rona said. "People who take time to relax live longer."

"Row, who wants to hang out in this crappy world any longer than we have to?"

"See, Ang, that's exactly what I mean!"

"Lesson learned, kids," Bob said. "We all have our vices."

The door to the Nutty Squirrel opened. Daylight poured in. The silhouette of a tall male appeared.

The door shut. Dim pub lighting outlined Detective Carl Brunish's dated, brown suit. Besides his style of dress, he had other identifiable traits. He took big steps with long, rubbery legs. His wide shoulders, though, were rigid and hunched. He strode to the table. Smile lines formed on his salt-and-pepper-stubbled cheeks. "Good to see you all."

Bob said, "Thank you for coming. Please have a seat."

Carl straddled his legs over a chair. "How may I help the good people of Andecco News Service?"

"We have a favor to ask," Bob said. "We have fingerprints and DNA. We'd like to know to whom they belong."

Angela slid a plastic bag and two vials—one red and one blue—across the tabletop. "Detective, the samples are in these. Would you like to leave it incognito, or would you like details?"

"I'd prefer to let the samples speak for themselves, Ms. Thirgal." Carl put the containers into a scuffed briefcase. "I should be able to get you the results in a couple of days."

"Thank you, my friend," Bob said. "I know we've been asking a lot from you lately."

"Well, Bob, I'm willing to bet you have your reasons. I trust you, and finding people to trust these days isn't easy. We're dealing with a lot of unscrupulous types. Speaking of bad folk, I have fresh updates on the thugs who murdered Paula Arvish. Do you have a moment for me to fill you in?"

"We do, Carl. Whatcha got?"

"Bob, I'm pretty sure I've identified a member of the Soldiers of God Justice Group."

"That is good news. Who is he?"

"Anthony Larson."

Bob didn't recognize the name. "How did you figure it out?"

"We've found various leads. Among the most recent, Larson's DNA was inside Nancy Pitman's townhouse. There's no apparent connection between Larson and either Pitman or Paula Arvish, so there's no reason to explain why he would've been there."

"Where was the DNA?" Bob asked.

"The clearest sample was on a piece of plastic wrap and cheese lying on the floor near the refrigerator. The forensic lab thinks the cheese had fallen there about the time Arvish was murdered."

Kever picked up a cheese stick and twirled it between his fingers. "I never thought about the perils of eating cheese."

Angela rolled her eyes. "Sorry about him, detective. Any guess as to why a housekeeper would be on the Justice Group's hit list?"

"I don't think Paula Arvish was the intended target, Ms. Thirgal. They were after Nancy Pitman. The two women look a lot alike."

Kever gave Angela a wink. "I have a pertinent comment this time, Ang. Similar question, detective, why Pitman?"

"By day, she works for a financial investment firm. By night, she volunteers to help the poor find medical care. Sometimes, that work involves linking women up with abortion providers."

"Detective," Angela said, "does Pitman volunteer with Health-Connect, by chance?"

"That's the place."

Kever said, "That explains why the Justice Group would target her. Senator Fischer, Senator Rineburg, and Pastor Walls have been harassing Health-Connect for a long time."

"Detective Brunish," Rona said, "do you think Anthony Larson had anything to do with the Mary Kronvelt murder or the Agel Yungst shootings at Hughes Medical Center?"

"Funny you should ask, Ms. Betler. Handwriting experts have matched blood-writing at both the Pitman and Kronvelt murder scenes to Larson. I suspect he helped Agel Yungst on his shooting spree at Hughes as well. We found a partial boot print next to Yungst's getaway car. The foot size, print depth, and distribution pattern all point to Larson."

Bob's mood brightened. At last, progress had been made in a years-long investigation into the Soldiers of God Justice Group. "What's next, Carl? Are you going to bring Larson in for questioning?"

"Not right now. I want to watch him first. Larson is a lackey. We need to bring down the ringleaders. I'm hoping he'll lead us to the big shots who deal directly with the Back-to-Basics Club." Carl checked the time. "Do you folks need anything else from me?"

"Not at the moment," Bob said, "but you're welcome to stay awhile."

Carl stood. "I wish I could; I've been on my feet all day. I'll let you know when I get the results on your samples." He strolled out of the pub.

The detective hadn't been gone long when Kever said, "Mr. Fullerby, when do you expect to hear from your Drop Case informant again?"

"Hopefully soon. He returns from New Cadona tomorrow." Bob was tired of keeping secrets. Only Angela knew the identity of the Drop Case informant. He'd withheld the truth from the rest of his team for so long that a revelation felt like a breach of confidence, but the time had come to share the knowledge. "Kever-o, Row, there's something I need to tell you. Ang figured it out a while back, but I swore her to secrecy."

Rona said, "What is it, Mr. Fullerby?"

"The Drop Case informant is Pastor Mark Walzelesskii."

Kever's eyes widened. "Walzelesskii! I'd guessed it was someone close to Senator Sandra Pettock because Fischer and Rineburg can't stand her. Boy, did I ever guess wrong! But Pastor Walzelesskii ... what a surprise! Mr. Fullerby, do you trust him?"

"He hasn't given me a reason not to. Every piece of info he's given me has been spot-on."

Angela's eyes squinted in anger. "You may trust him, Mr. Fullerby, but I don't. He's such an idiot! Did you see him at the Life March in New Cadona? He was right there on that hilltop—Compass Point, or whatever they call it these days—watching those awful True Followers rituals."

"Yeah, I saw it. It was disturbing. I admit that I had my own wave of doubt." Bob recalled watching Mark standing passively in the crowd as True Followers performed mock hangings and beheadings of people involved with abortion. "We need to remember that Pastor Walzelesskii is on *the inside*. If he doesn't pretend to go along with True Followers practices, his father will shut him out. Then, he won't be able to tell us anything. Or worse, he may find himself in mortal trouble. Mark is playing a daring game with savages, Ang."

"But ... but ... Walzelesskii just stood there with a drink in his hand when some ... some ... lunatic in a goofy robe cut open the stomach of a live cow. Then he ... he just watched as those thugs ripped a calf from her belly and slit the calf's throat. Someone should slit Walzelesskii's throat."

"Ang, under the circumstances, what could he have done?"

"What! Mr. Fullerby, his dad is Leon Walls, the fricken leader of the True Followers of God Church. Walzelesskii's a pastor himself. He should've gotten up on the altar and put a stop to it. Yet he did nothing!"

Kever said, "Mr. Fullerby, have you heard from Walzelesskii since he went to New Cadona?"

"Only to tell me where he's staying. I know he's been meeting with Senator Seldortin and local officials in Ramsten about launching a program to fight the spread of the J2 virus. Since he left town, he hasn't provided much in the way of intel. I hope when he gets back, he'll be able to find out where Leeha Ritsagin is."

Somewhere in Cadona ...

Leeha Ritsagin heard a male's voice. "Doctor Millerman, how's our thieving bitch doing?"

"Stabilizing."

"When can we deliver her? Senator Rineburg's growing impatient."

"We need to monitor her condition day-to-day. If Senator Rineburg or General Willirman gives you heat, let me know. I'll explain the situation to them; if we push her too hard, it'll kill her, and anything she knows will die, too."

"Thanks, Doctor."

Leeha heard footsteps and the closing of a door. The world fell silent. She opened her eyes. Overhead, a glossy cover gave off a dim glow. She rolled her head to the right. Tiny lights shone through the darkness of the small room. She tried to sit up, but straps anchored her arms and legs to the bed. This was the real world—a brutal world.

She focused on her time in secondary school, but the vividness of the images would not return.

For so long, she'd fought to forget her school days. Many terrible things had happened during those years. Her parents lost the family farm.

Her brokenhearted father got sick and died. Classmates picked on her. And Randy Altholder never took her on the date that he'd promised. Yet, good things had happened back then, too. Her family was close. She knew the beauty of growing things, the feel of fresh air, and the scent of wholesome earth. Most of all, she had hope that the future held wonderful things for her. It didn't. She lived in a dirty city. She got part-time pay for a full-time job. Her brother and his wife adored Pastor Leon Walls. Worst of all—a weird document had found her, and now she lay strapped to a bed. Illness racked her body. How could things get worse?

An itch danced on the front of her left thigh. Soon, the prickling faded.

It didn't stay away. The itch burst forth again like a million stabbing needles.

Move! Move! She must scratch the itch. She must get up.

She yanked on every bond. All stayed affixed. She pulled harder. It hurt, but she didn't care. Only breaking free mattered.

"I can't take it anymore! Do you hear me? Let me go! God! God! Help me! I can't stand it! Get me out of here! Why are you doing this to me?"

A thought came to her. She needed to calm down and make a plan. There had to be a way out. What about her arms? If she could free a hand, she'd be able to bend her elbow. Maybe then she could find a way to untie the straps.

Her right arm felt stronger than the left, so she twisted and turned her right wrist and fingers. If she could just pull her hand free ….

Nothing worked.

She jerked her right shoulder as hard as she could. The bed rattled. But still, she was held down.

"You can't do this to me! You can't! Where are you? Let me go! I'll do whatever you want. Just let me go!"

The room spun. It was hard to breathe.

To her left, a little light popped on. Pink fluid gushed into a hose hanging alongside the bed.

Her body relaxed. Images popped in and out of her mind. The thoughts were hers, but it seemed like someone else put them there, as if someone was trying to tell her something important. Scenes snapped together like watching a movie on fast-forward.

She saw herself in her apartment. There was a knock on the door. Three men stood there. They took her away. She woke up in a strange place. Other men asked about a document that she had stolen. In her entire life, she'd stolen only one document: a Business Interlink Management class answer key for Randy Altholder. But bad guys wouldn't have strapped her to a bed and pumped her full of drugs for something she'd done in secondary school.

Only one scenario made sense. The document they were looking for was hidden under her kitchen cabinets. The bad guys were torturing her to make her tell them where the document was, but she remembered the wrong one—she remembered the answer key. The bad guys hadn't yet realized their mistake.

No matter what happened next, she mustn't tell them where to find the weird document. It was obvious they were desperate to find it. She mustn't let them get their grubby hands on it.

Another glob of pink fluid dripped down the tube. Her eyelids slid closed.

HANSEN HILLS
FEDERAL FACILITY

Cadona City, Cadona
WEDNESDAY, MAY 3, YEAR 1007 EE
11:50 P.M., EAST CADONA TIME

Investigative journalist Bob Fullerby stepped off the CadTranS commuter train. Every manner of downtown debauchery was represented on the platform and sidewalks. His contacts had the habit of meeting in the most unpleasant places. Defense Secretary Richard Karther's place du jour was filthy Stratten Park. Now, Detective Carl Brunish requested a midnight meeting in one of the slimiest areas of Cadona City's Central District.

Bob picked out Carl's broad-shouldered, stooped form against the faint lighting that surrounded the smelly Ring Fountain. Carl was not alone; a tall, lanky figure lurked in the shadows.

Carl stepped forward. "Bob, good evening."

"Good evening, Carl. I see you have company."

"I do. I'll let the young fellow fill you in."

The other man emerged from the shadows. Bob recognized him. "Pastor Walzelesskii! I wasn't expecting to see you today. I'm glad you made it home from New Cadona in one piece."

Mark pushed locks of straight, dark hair away from his pale cheeks. "Thank you, Mr. Fullerby. I'm sorry I haven't called lately. I have news; it's important."

Carl said, "Excuse me, fellas, I'll stay out of earshot. There are things I don't need to know." He wandered to the end of the fountain and took a seat on the concrete wall surrounding the mucky pool.

Bob studied Mark's face. He looked exhausted. "I hope you're feeling well, Pastor. I heard the heat in New Cadona got to you."

"It wasn't the temperature, Mr. Fullerby. I can't believe the stuff that's going on in my church. Then, after I got home, I had the strangest thing happen. That's how I ended up with Detective Brunish. I'm glad you had told me how much you trust him. Anyway, Mr. Fullerby, that's not what I came to tell you."

"Okay, Pastor, whatcha got?"

"Does the name *Leeha Ritsagin* mean anything to you?"

Bob's heart thumped. Mark did indeed have news. "Why do you ask, Pastor?"

"After my plane landed, I stopped by the True Followers headquarters and snooped in my father's office. I found a message from Zoff on the computer. He wrote about Leeha Ritsagin. I think she may be the mystery woman in the brown Monarch—the woman who stole the Guiding Light document."

Bob pretended to be less interested than he really was. "She is. My team recently figured it out. What did Zoff say about her?"

"The news is bad, Mr. Fullerby. Back-to-Basics people have her."

"Do you know where Ritsagin is?"

"No, but I know where they're going to take her: the Hansen Hills Federal Facility."

"My! That is news. Do you know when she'll get there?"

"Not exactly, but I have the impression it's soon. Zoff's note said they will transport her to the Hills when she's well enough."

"She's ill? Injured?"

"They'd given her the Mind-One drug. It made her sick. They're going to take her to the Hills so they can interrogate her *the old-fashioned way,* as Zoff worded it."

"Any info on the Guiding Light?"

"I didn't have much time to go through the files, but I remember she stole the document for someone by the name of *Randy Altholder*. He's a member of some criminal gang in Tahagaruza. The gang had an unusual name ... darn! What was it? Oh, it was the *Rustlers*."

"Pastor, does Randy Altholder have the document?"

"According to Zoff's message, Leeha Ritsagin sent an electronic copy to him."

"What about the printed version?"

"She left it on a chair in an office. I don't remember exactly, but the name, *Jenton*, comes to mind. In any case, the Club thinks Ritsagin knows more about the Guiding Light than she's revealed. They also believe she knows why Randy Altholder wants it. That's why they want to interrogate her further."

Motion caught Bob's eye. Carl was ambling toward them. He appeared at ease in the crime-infested night.

Mark's voice was almost a whisper. "Mr. Fullerby, there's something else. Zoff's worried Detective Brunish is getting close to proving the Mary Kronvelt and Paula Arvish murders are related to the Agel Yungst shooting at Hughes Medical Center. And it gets worse; he thinks Detective Brunish is close to proving the Soldiers of God Justice Group is working for the Back-to-Basics Club."

"Pastor, have you warned Carl?"

"Yeah, I did."

"Excuse me," Carl said. "Pastor, you should be getting back to your signal home. No need to risk detection on your new PD's maiden flight."

Bob found the words strange. "Carl, what's going on?"

Carl rested a hand on Mark's back. "Pastor Walzelesskii can fill you in later, Bob. Right now, this young man needs to skedaddle."

Mark and Carl walked away. The dark, littered, urban streets swallowed them.

Bob rubbed his face. The lines on his forehead grew deeper every day. This late-night trip was worth the effort, though. He'd learned that Leeha Ritsagin was on her way to the Hansen Hills Federal Facility for interrogation.

His personal device buzzed. He'd received a delayed message; Carl wanted to meet at the High Wheelers Saloon after Mark was safely on a train headed for home. So much for getting more than a few hours of sleep tonight.

Sleep tugged at Bob Fullerby's eyelids as he sat at a tall table for two that was squeezed into a secluded corner of the High Wheelers Saloon.

A barmaid dressed in a bustier, fishnet stockings, pleated skirt, and front-laced boots walked to the table. "What can I getcha?"

"Milk, please."

She gave him an odd look. "With what liquor, sir?"

"None. Just plain, old milk."

"Okay, whatever, farm boy." Stiff eyelashes flittered like spider legs as she gave him a wink. Her derrière swung like a pendulum as she strutted away.

Bob spotted a man walking toward him. Rows of tiny lights hanging above the bar illuminated the man's antiquated, plaid suit. Detective Carl Brunish had arrived. His appearance served him well. Anyone who didn't know him would see an inner-city drunkard who tipped a few too many bottles. No one would suspect him to be a sharp-witted police detective.

Carl swung a leg over a stool. "Bob, thanks for hanging around."

"Not a problem. Did Mark get off okay?"

Carl shoved a few greasy string chips into his mouth. "Got him on a train, anyway. Interesting young man. I've been wondering if he and his father saw eye to eye. They do seem to have major philosophical differences."

"Mark's coming of age," Bob said. "He's thinking for himself now."

"Look, Bob, I know that you and the young pastor are communicating. What about, I don't need to know, but Back-to-Basics Club thugs are watching him. I wanted to let you know ... he may be in danger."

"Thanks, Carl. I always tell Mark to play it safe."

The barmaid returned. She set a cup of milk on the table.

Carl peered into the cup. "What's that you're drinking?"

"That would be a thing called milk," Bob said.

The waitress leaned against Carl's shoulder. "So, do you want moo-juice, too, handsome?"

"Heck no, that stuff will kill ya. I'm taking the bus home, so bring me whiskey, straight up."

"You are my kind of man," she said. In seconds, she returned with the hard alcohol.

The tawny booze was tempting, but the burning stomach and head-ache that would follow … Bob was glad he stuck with milk. "How's the wife, Carl?"

"Lynn's good; she's still working with the county."

"Is Cassidy still in school?"

"Yep, she's in her last year." Carl jiggled the glass and watched the waves settle. "I wish she'd chosen another career. Cass could've been an artist, but my girl's too much like me, only smarter. I'm worried about her."

"Why?"

"She got an internship as a forensic pathologist at VitalTech Labs. The new management doesn't take kindly to Cass' lifestyle. She has to keep her relationship with Lorainne a secret."

Bob said, "It's a shame we must hold so many secrets these days."

"To be honest, Bob, I never thought something like this would hap-pen in our country. For so long, we thought we were special. We thought we were above the political and theological tyranny infecting most of the world, yet here we are."

Bob took a sip of milk. "Here we are, indeed."

Carl drew a deep breath. "Well, I got good news for ya. Cass and Doctor Platcher got answers on the DNA and fingerprints you gave us."

"The verdict?"

"The DNA in the blue vial and the fingerprints belong to someone Ms. Betler asked me about before: Ms. Cookie Davis. The sample in the red vial turned out to be quite a surprise. The DNA matches that of a woman assumed killed in the Mik-la-tah Tsunami in Sohn-Sur."

"Is the Sohn-Suran woman related to Cookie Davis?"

"Beyond both being human and having partial Visstellin ancestry, no. I'm tempted to ask why you care about the DNA of a long-dead woman, but it's better if I don't know. I do, however, have additional information about Ms. Davis' ex, Rodney Pinkerman. His record was clean until a few years ago … until he lost his job. Not only did he beat Ms. Davis, but he also got involved with a petty crime ring."

"Carl, if I remember right, Ms. Davis filed an abuse report against her ex."

"That's right."

"Do you know when she filed the report?"

"Early in the morning on April tenth, a Monday."

Bob remembered something that Cookie Davis had told him—she moved in with Leeha Ritsagin on April tenth. Carl's information seemed to corroborate Cookie's story.

"Carl, on another topic, does the name Randy Altholder mean anything to you?"

"Not sounding familiar. Should it?"

"I understand he's involved with a gang down in Tahagaruza, Antropka. They call themselves the *Rustlers*."

Carl rubbed his unshaven chin. "The *Rustlers* I've heard of. They have branches in several countries, but *Randy Altholder* doesn't ring a bell."

"Might Davis' fiancé, the Pinkerman fellow, be connected to the Rustlers?"

"I doubt it. The Rustlers are big-time. They're a nasty bunch, but they're organized and high-tech. I'd be surprised to find a link between Cookie's ex and a gang like that."

"Thanks, Carl, I appreciate your help." Bob chugged down the remainder of his now lukewarm milk. "I better head home and get some sleep. My workdays don't get shorter when I work late into the night."

Carl chuckled and swallowed the last of his whiskey. "Mine neither."

◉

Somewhere in Cadona ...

Leeha Ritsagin awoke to find a settled stomach. Breath glided in and out of her lungs without the aid of a breathing machine. Restraints, though, anchored her arms and legs to the bed railing.

Panic snaked over her. She stared at the tube attached to her left arm. If only the pink fluid would squirt down the hose and quiet her mind!

The liquid didn't come.

Muscles cramped, but she couldn't do anything about it. Being ill was better than this torture.

A tall man with dark hair walked into the room. This was the first time she'd seen him without a mask, but she recognized his eyes: Dr. Millerman. Two other maskless men followed him.

"Good morning, Leeha," Dr. Millerman said. "Do you know who I am?"

Leeha pretended not to; she shook her head.

Dr. Millerman examined a monitor before shining a light into her eyes. "I'm a doctor. You're looking much better today, Leeha. How are you feeling?"

Could he have asked a more stupid question? She was tied to a bed. She'd been given drugs that made her sick. "I've been better, sir."

Dr. Millerman gave a hearty laugh. "I bet you have!" Like a miracle, he removed the restraints. "Can you sit up for me?"

Her back ached, but she managed to push herself into a sitting position.

The room spun. Dr. Millerman took hold of her arm. "Don't worry, some dizziness is normal."

The spinning stopped.

He lowered the bed rail. "Can you swing your legs over the side, Leeha?"

Her body swayed, but dangling her legs felt incredible.

"You're doing very well, Leeha. Can you stand for me?"

Her feet hit the floor. Her knees buckled.

Dr. Millerman caught her.

One of the men drew a weapon.

"Frank," Dr. Millerman said, "there's no need for that. She won't hurt me."

Leeha struggled to pull herself upright. Several seconds passed before she was able to stand on her own.

A smile crossed Dr. Millerman's face. "Very good, Leeha! Here's what I want you to do; walk across the room and sit down in that chair by the wall. Can you do that for me?"

She took one shuffling step and then another and another. Feeling returned to her legs. Only then did she realize how numb they had been.

The toes of her right foot smacked into the back of her left ankle. Her body tipped forward. She clutched the edge of a counter.

"Doctor, step away!" Frank said.

"Why?"

"Those instruments would make good weapons. Remember, she's an enemy apparent."

"I know who she is, Frank. She's a young lady who's going to cooperate with us. Isn't that right, Leeha?"

She nodded.

Dr. Millerman took hold of her arms. "Find your balance, Leeha. Look how close the chair is! Just take a few more steps."

Her body swayed. The bottoms of her feet slid along the cold floor.

Finally, the back of the chair was within reach. She grabbed the metal frame.

"Excellent, Leeha! Now sit and rest."

What had once been a simple task took every drop of energy.

She turned to the left. Her body plopped onto the seat.

Dr. Millerman sounded more like a coach than a villain. "Excellent, Leeha! Great job."

Her vision darkened as if the sun had slipped behind a skyscraper. A faint memory awakened. Had it really happened? Yes! It had. Cookie Davis was smiling as she spoke. *You did great, Leeha!* Why was Cookie happy? Running! That was it! They had jogged up a steep hill; Cookie was proud of her.

Light returned to Leeha's eyes. She fought to hold on to the image of Cookie's pretty face, but the vision disappeared. Were these awful people hurting Cookie, too?

"So, Leeha," Dr. Millerman said, "would you like to have longer restraints? You'd be able to move around and stretch."

She nodded.

Frank said, "It's not a good idea, Doctor."

"Your concerns are noted. If she violates our trust, we'll tie her back up. Randy, bring the e-bands."

She recognized the third man in the room: Randy Beller. He was the guy who shoved needles in her arms and administered the Mind-One drug that made her sick.

Frank held a weapon at ready as Randy fastened black bands to her ankles and wrists.

Dr. Millerman once again had the voice of a coach. "There you go, Leeha. You'll be more comfortable. Now get up and walk back to the bed."

Leeha pushed herself up from the chair. Fatigue pressed down like a yoke, but her legs moved more easily now. She crawled onto the mattress.

"Excellent, Leeha," Dr. Millerman said. "Try to get some exercise, but don't overdo it."

His demeanor changed. It was as if a second personality pushed the first one aside. "You have access to the bed and the chair, no more. If you feel an electrical shock, you'll know you have reached a boundary. Let me make this clear: if you tamper with the bands or try anything sneaky, we'll know. We will make you sorry. Do you understand?"

She nodded.

All three men left the room.

Leeha sat upright until her muscles gave out. She lay down, but not on her back; she'd spent too much time in that position. Instead, she lay on her side. She closed her eyes. Scenes of her little apartment floated through her mind like glimpses of heaven. Cookie was there. Mrs. Furley and Toofy had stopped by for a delicious dinner. How she missed that life!

23

THIS SITE IS COMPROMISED

Cadona City, Cadona
THURSDAY, MAY 4, YEAR 1007 EE
10:00 P.M., EAST CADONA TIME

Cookie Davis woke up. Her heart pounded. Where was she?

She looked around.

Everything was okay; she was laying in her bed in the Roadside Inn Motel. The men in the blue car were not there. No one was trying to shoot her. It was just a nightmare.

The bed was cozy. She snuggled into the soft bedding.

Her body relaxed, but noises echoed through the darkness.

She uncovered her head and listened.

The world fell quiet. She was being silly; a guest was likely coming or going. Her eyes closed.

More noises. Shadows flickered against the sheer curtain liner at the edge of the window.

The doorknob jiggled. Someone was at her door!

She reached across the nightstand and pressed the button for the front desk. No one answered. She grabbed her personal device. Music and laughter came through the ear-piece. She heard Anson's voice. "Hey, Cookie, what's up?"

"Anson, some … someone's out there! And the office isn't answering."

"Are you in your room?"

"Yes, but I think someone's trying to break in."

"Kever and I are at the Nutty Squirrel. We'll be right there."

Through the personal device, Cookie heard chairs scooting. Anson and Kever were on the way.

"Cookie," Anson said, "go into the bathroom and jam the door."

"With what?"

"Whatever you can find, like a chair. I'll stay on the line with you."

"Okay."

She dragged a chair into the bathroom and crammed the seatback against the doorknob. It wasn't enough. What else might she use? There wasn't much furniture in the room, and she had few possessions. She opened the closet door. An ironing board hung on a side panel. She yanked the ironing board from its hangers and wedged the board between the chair and the wall. It worked! "Anson, I've blocked the bathroom door."

"Good. Hang on; we're almost there."

Outside, a man shouted. "Hey! Hey! What are you doing up there?"

"Anson, people are fighting. They're right in front of my room." Her personal device fell silent. "Anson, are you there? Anson? Can you hear me? Kever-o, are you there?" No one spoke.

Sounds of a fight filled the night. People were running.

A whistle rang out.

"Anson, if you can hear me, I … I think someone shot a gun."

Silence rang in her ears.

Someone pounded on the outside door.

Words came through her personal device. "Cookie, this is Kever-o. Are you okay?"

"Yes, but someone's knocking."

"Cookie, it's me. You can come out now."

"You're here?"

"Yes, I'm at your front door."

She tugged at the ironing board and chair until they broke free. She dashed across the motel room. Her fingers fumbled with the bolt. She opened the door.

Kever stood in the doorway.

She swung her arms around him. "Kever-o, oh my God! It's so good to see you. You have no idea."

He looked worried. "Let's go inside." He rushed to shut the door. Without saying a word, he pulled a small, electronic gadget from a pocket.

"Kever-o, what are you doing?"

Several seconds passed before he answered. "Looking for surveillance devices. Don't worry, the room's clean."

"Kever-o, you're a reporter; why would you have a gadget like that?"

He slipped it back into his pocket. "Um ... Anson gave it to me."

"Anson! Oh, my God, Kever-o, where is he?"

"He's fine."

"But where is he?"

"Cookie, he's fine."

Kever was hiding something. "Tell me, where's Anson? Is he hurt?"

"No, he's fine. He's taking pictures of the scene."

"What scene?"

"Some people were killed. He's watching over the bodies until Detective Brunish gets here. Mr. Fullerby's on his way, too."

"Anson, he ... did he kill someone?"

Kever shook his head.

"You? Did you kill someone?"

"No, we're not sure who killed whom."

"Oh, my goodness, Kever-o, Mr. Dremmer, and his—"

"Cookie, listen to me; they're fine. Bad guys blocked signals coming and going from the office. That's why you couldn't reach the front desk."

"Thank God!" With the danger over, she trembled. "So ... who was killed, exactly?"

Kever rested his hands on her shoulders. "I don't know. I'm sure Anson and Detective Brunish will figure it out."

Cookie said, "Kever-o, that thick bolt that Mr. Dremmer installed ... he knew someone was after me, didn't he?"

"Probably. Mr. Dremmer and Mr. Fullerby are old friends. Cookie, how about tea?"

"Please." She sat on the edge of the bed. Kever put two cups into the warmer.

His personal device buzzed. He spoke into it. "Yeah, she's okay." He put the device back into his arm patch.

"Kever-o, who called?"

"Mr. Fullerby. He just arrived. He asked how you're doing."

Cadona City, Cadona
THURSDAY, MAY 4, YEAR 1007 EE
10:45 P.M., EAST CADONA TIME

Bob Fullerby drove down the alley next to the Roadside Inn Motel. Spotlights shone on the far corner of the parking lot. Yellow police tape fluttered in gusts of wind. Human-shaped silhouettes loitered in the stark lighting. The rest of the parking area lay shrouded in darkness.

A policeman stepped away from the spotlights and raised a hand.

Bob stopped the car and rolled down the driver side window.

The policeman shined a flashlight beam into the front seat. "Sir, this area is closed."

Bob held up his Andecco News Service badge. "Good evening, officer, I'm from the press. I heard there was a rumpus. Is Detective Carl Brunish here?"

The policeman scanned the press badge. "Yeah, he's at the scene. Please leave your vehicle here."

Bob parked and walked toward the lights. As he neared the police tape, he spotted Anson. He was dressed in his gym clothes. "Hi, Mr. Fullerby."

"Evening, Anson. Where's Kever-o?"

"He's with Cookie in her room."

Detective Brunish walked away from a group of officers. "Good eve-
ning, Bob. Once again, we meet under less-than-ideal circumstances.
So you know, I asked Officer Dailey to fill me in on a few things about
Cookie Davis and Leeha Ritsagin. Hope that's okay."

"Given the circumstances, Carl, you need the info. Yeah, it's okay.
What went down here?"

"If full analysis confirms our preliminaries, we have three dead
Soldiers of God Justice Group members." He pointed a foot in the direction of one of four bodies. "That one's Rigger Zofferman. We think
he's a team leader. And that one's Robert Pomero. The one on the end is
Ronald Millhands."

"Wait a minute," Bob said, "one is *Zofferman* and another is *Millhands*?"

"Yeah, why? Does it mean something to you?"

"Maybe. I have a source who gave me what I assume are code names:
Zoff and *Hands*. Pretty unimaginative, though."

Carl rubbed his chin. "When a person thinks he has divine protection,
he thinks he can get away with being careless. Of course, these fellas really
did have protection—of the political variety."

Bob gestured toward the fourth body. "So, Carl, who's the last vic?"

"I'll let Officer Dailey tell you."

Anson lifted a corner of the tarpaulin to reveal a broken, swollen
face. "You're not going to believe it. It's Allen Bosswell, Leeha Ritsagin's
wormy guy."

"Any theories about what went down here?" Bob asked.

Anson covered Bosswell's bloody head. "When Kever-o and I first got
here, we saw three men in front of Cookie's door. When we got closer, we
saw the damnedest thing: a man shimmying up the edge of the building.
Turns out the man was Bosswell. He climbed onto the walkway and took
on all three goons himself. The thugs took off down the stairs. Bosswell
jumped them. The fight took them to this spot."

"Okay, Anson," Bob said, "let me see if I got this straight. Rigger
Zofferman, Ronald Millhands, and Robert Pomero were trying to break
into Cookie's room. Allen Bosswell, the wormy guy, stopped them."

"Right."

"I'm confused, if Bosswell had been stalking Leeha Ritsagin, why would he protect Cookie?"

Carl said, "I can shed some light on that, Bob. I'm pretty sure the Cadona Guardians recruited him."

"Interesting! That means Allen Bosswell—the wormy guy—was a good guy. Not what I expected. How was he killed?"

"Shot by a fifth man hiding in the shrubs," Carl told him.

"Do we know anything about this fifth man?" Bob asked.

"Quite a bit. He got wounded somewhere along the way." Carl pointed toward the rear corner of the parking lot. "Looks like he escaped over that broken section of wall. He left some blood on the bricks. His DNA is a perfect match for Anthony Larson, our cheese eater from Nancy Pitman's townhouse."

"Small world," Bob said. "Do we know where Larson is now?"

"Unfortunately, no, but we think we have images of his getaway vehicle. The security cam at Olex Pharmaceuticals caught scratchy pics of a man staggering into a city utility van that was parked by the old Glesen Hotel. The man was probably Larson."

Anson said, "Mr. Fullerby, there's something we haven't figured out. Do you know how the Justice Group found Cookie?"

"No idea, but we'll need to come up with a cover story for what happened here."

Carl said, "Officer Dailey and I already did. The official yarn will be that drunks in a car struck folks walking across the parking lot. That resulted in a brawl and shots being fired."

"You know," Bob said, "we're getting as good at lying as the bad guys. It makes you wonder what we're all becoming." He felt a chill creep up his spine. "Something just occurred to me, Carl. This site is compromised. Cookie can't stay here."

"You're right. The Justice Group will be sending more goons. Don't worry, Bob. I'll help you get her away from here."

"Thanks, Carl."

◈

Somewhere in Cadona ...

A buzzing sound roused Leeha Ritsagin from sleep.

The room was dark. She was alone, but footsteps and shuffling noises clicked and thumped beyond the walls.

Men spoke in whispers. The murmurs grew louder and more urgent. She made out a handful of words. Randy Beller was speaking to Dr. Millerman. She heard Randy say *several* and *dead*.

Dr. Millerman's voice boomed. "Tell them I'll call back in a minute. I'm busy!"

Her captors sounded worried. Perhaps something bad happened to the creeps. Good!

THE PRINT SHOP

*"Mr. Marantees, per your request, we've updated security at
our hideaway office in the old print shop building."*

Investigative Journalist Bob Fullerby
Encrypted Message to Andecco
News Service Managers
Year 1003 of the Enlightened Epoch

Cadona City, Cadona
THURSDAY, MAY 4, YEAR 1007 EE
11:30 P.M., EAST CADONA TIME

Cookie Davis heard a knock on the motel room door. She heard Bob
Fullerby's voice. "Kever-o, open up. It's me."

Kever opened the door.

Behind Bob stood a man with gray-flecked, dark hair and a heavy afternoon shadow. In the background, stood another man, this one in a cop's uniform.

Bob said, "Cookie, I'm glad to see you're okay."

"I am, thanks to Anson and Kever-o."

Bob's words sounded grave. "Kever-o, we need to talk. Let's go. Carl will handle things from here."

"Sure thing, Mr. Fullerby."

Cookie grasped Kever's arm. "Kever-o, please! Take me with you."

He put his hands on her shoulders. His palms felt warm. "It's okay; the guy next to Mr. Fullerby is Detective Carl Brunish. You can trust him."

Her heart sank as Bob and Kever walked away.

Detective Brunish stepped into the room. He tossed a satchel onto the bed. "Ms. Davis, pack your belongings. You're coming with us."

Her heart pounded. "Why?"

"You need to make a statement. We're taking you to the precinct."

"I will give you my statement here."

"That won't do, Ms. Davis."

"Where's Anson?" she asked.

"Officer Dailey went home. He's off duty. He helped us out because he happened to be in the vicinity. Come on, get packed. We've got to go."

"No! I'm not going anywhere until I see Anson."

"Ma'am, pack your things," Detective Brunish said. "This is not a request."

"I want an attorney."

"You really don't want to do that, ma'am."

"Oh, yes, I do."

Detective Brunish turned to the man wearing the uniform. "Officer Reynolds, secure Ms. Davis."

"Yes, sir." Officer Reynolds stomped through the doorway. He pulled out handcuffs. "Turn around, ma'am, and put your hands behind your head."

"No! Like I told you, I'm not going with you."

Officer Reynolds walked toward her. "Ma'am, you can make this hard, or you can make this easy."

"I am not going with you!" A primal force took control. She leapt onto the mattress. On hands-and-knees, she scrambled across the bed. The door leading outside was just a few steps away, but Officer Reynolds and Detective Brunish stood between her and the exit. She must not let them take her. "Mr. Fullerby! Help me!" He didn't answer. "Kever-o! Can you hear me?" He didn't respond.

Detective Brunish leaned against the doorframe. "They can't help you, Ms. Davis. Mr. Fullerby and his friend are long gone."

Officer Reynolds stepped closer.

Cookie grabbed a desk lamp from the nightstand. "Get out of my way."

"Really, ma'am?" Officer Reynolds said. "You want to do it this way? You want to make it hard on yourself?"

He took a few steps forward. She swung the lamp. It distracted him— it was a trick Leeha had taught her.

She kicked him with all her might. Officer Reynolds crashed into a wall.

The officer shook off the pain as if he had stubbed a toe. Yet escape was her only hope. She lunged at him again.

A crackling sound came and went.

Sheets pressed against the right side of her face. Her head and torso lay prostrate on the bed. Her knees rested on the floor. She didn't know what had happened. She tried to push herself up, but a cold band bound her wrists together behind her back. She recalled images of men in black suits dragging Leeha across the Pineland Apartments lawn. They had taken Leeha; they must not take her.

She tried to scream. No sound came out of her mouth. They must've done something to her.

"On your feet," Officer Reynolds said. He yanked her upright.

Detective Brunish's dark eyes glared at her. "Sorry about this. You'll be okay." He slipped a gray sack over her head.

She couldn't see. Her breath dampened the inside of the hood. She heard Detective Brunish say, "Officer Reynolds, get her out of here."

"Yes, sir."

Someone grabbed her right arm. Someone else took hold of her left. The unseen persons guided her along the walkway.

She heard a woman's voice. "We're going down a set of stairs now."

After several steps, the woman said, "Okay, we're on flat ground. Take four paces, then you'll get into a van."

A van? Did she say a *van*? Leeha had been thrown into a van. Cookie struggled, but she couldn't break free. In minutes, she was strapped into a seat.

Her ability to speak returned. "I can't get enough air! There's not enough air!"

"Yes, there is," the woman said. "Regulate your breathing—in and out, in and out."

Cookie battled the restraints pinning her to the seat, but to no avail. "Please, get the hood off. I can't stand it! It's scratching my face."

"It must stay on," the woman said. "Don't worry, it's a short trip."

A short trip to where?

Cookie heard the van doors slam shut. The vehicle moved forward, turned left, stopped, and then turned right. She knew the path; they had just driven out of the motel parking lot.

She recalled an old movie that she'd watched with Leeha. A man was kidnapped. He memorized each turn the vehicle made and counted the seconds between turns. The plan seemed pointless, but she must do something, or else she'd lose her mind.

The van came to a stop.

The woman said, "Okay, time to get out."

Cookie slid off the seat.

Her feet hit solid ground. Damp wind brushed against her hands. The rough cloth of the hood fluttered against her skin. She heard many sounds: distant voices, automobile engines, and the clunking and clanging of factories. "Where am I? Why are you doing this to me? What do you want?"

She heard Officer Reynolds' voice. "We need to get you someplace safe."

"Why? I didn't do anything wrong."

"There are those who think otherwise. Start walking."

Two people guided her over a smooth, hard surface. She was pretty sure at least one other person loitered behind them.

"Stop here," the woman said.

The handcuffs came off. Someone took the bag off her head.

People stood in front of her whom she didn't expect to see. "Mr. Fullerby! Anson! Kever-o! What are you guys doing here?"

"She's all yours, Mr. Fullerby," Officer Reynolds said. "The coast is clear. You'd better leave while the area is secure."

Officer Reynolds and three other Cadona City police officers disappeared into the night.

Cookie looked around. In all directions, arch-like structures and dead trees cast faint shadows in dim light. "Mr. Fullerby, where ... where are we?"

"Arches City Park. We're standing under Todderlane Arch." Sadness laced his words. "It's hard to imagine this place had once been the pride of Cadona City. Now, it's a shantytown. In any case, it's a temporary protected zone, but we may be compromised at any moment, so let's go."

"Where?"

"The only place we can think of that's safe: the print shop."

"The print shop? Mr. Fullerby, what's that?"

Kever stepped toward her. "It's where we work. We have a nice setup. You'll love it there." He reached out a hand. She took it. His palm and fingers felt warm. "Come on, Cookie."

She clung close to him as they walked from one huge sculpture to the next.

Here and there, tiny flames flickered in the darkness. In the scant light, she made out the shapes of tents and makeshift shelters. Whiffs of smoke drifted on currents of air.

They reached an enormous parking lot with only a handful of vehicles parked in it. "Hey, I know that car."

Kever's breath tickled her ear as he spoke. "You should, it's Mr. Fullerby's. You rode in it when we were driving around looking for Leeha."

"Yes, that's right, I remember."

Bob stopped walking when they reached the remains of a massive arch. "Kever-o," he said, "wait here. Keep an eye on her. Anson and I will check out the car."

Anson and Bob circled the vehicle several times. They even looked beneath it.

Cookie pressed into Kever's side. His sturdy, warm body comforted her. "Kever-o, they're taking a long time. Do you think something's wrong?"

"I don't think so. They're just being thorough."

"What are they looking for?"

"Explosives, tracking devices, surveillance equipment. Investigative journalism is a risky profession these days."

Kever slipped an arm around her waist. "You okay, Cookie?"

"I'm terrified."

"That surprises me; Detective Brunish told Mr. Fullerby that you put up quite a fight at the motel."

"It wasn't because I was brave. I was scared to the bone. I thought they were coming for me like they came for Leeha."

"Sorry, Cookie, we had to be careful. The people who tried to break into your room were members of the Soldiers of God Justice Group. They work for the Back-to-Basics Club and the Freedom Party. We had to get you out of there, and the best plan we could come up with was to make it look like an arrest."

Something caught his attention.

"Kever-o, what is it?"

"Mr. Fullerby's waving at us. We're good to go."

Kever hurried to the car. She trotted to keep up with him. Anson opened the right, rear door. Cookie ducked inside and slid across the seat. Kever scooted in next to her.

Anson jumped into the front seat after Bob started the engine.

Cookie had no idea where they were going. Their journey took them on major expressways and skinny, neighborhood streets. "Kever-o, how far is this place?"

"We should be there soon."

Darkness, stress, and lack of sleep had taken a toll. She forced herself to stay awake. Who knew what might happen next?

At last, they pulled into a narrow parking lot alongside an old building.

"Here we are," Bob said. "Sorry for the long trip. I wanted to make sure we didn't have a tail." He and Anson stepped out of the car.

Cookie followed Kever through the rear passenger side door.

Dim lighting revealed a building made of stained cement and faded bricks. A door, which looked like an entrance to a bank vault, added to the gloom.

Kever opened the vault-like door. Faint, red-tinged light spilled out. "Don't worry, Cookie, it's homier than it seems at first."

She walked inside. Angela Thirgal and a pretty, petite woman sat at a wooden table.

"Hi, Ang," Cookie said.

Angela had a frown on her face. "Cookie, this is Rona Betler. She'll get you settled."

"Hello, Rona."

Rona's shiny, copper-colored hair bounced about as she stood. "Howdy, Cookie, it's good to meet you. Come on, I'll show you to your bunk. It's not as nice as a motel room, but it's comfy."

Cookie followed her across the windowless room.

Rona pushed open a sliding panel. The bedroom was little more than a closet. A lamp rested on a slender table. A single clothing rod ran along the wall at the foot of the bed.

Kever appeared in the doorway. He held a satchel. "Cookie, here's your stuff from the motel. Detective Brunish had it sent over."

She took hold of the strap. The room spun.

"Hey, are you okay?" Kever asked.

"Yeah, I just felt a little dizzy for a second."

"How long has it been since you had a meal?"

"I'm not sure. It's been a while, I guess."

"I'll fix you something. I'm starved myself anyway." Kever walked away.

"Excuse me, Rona," Cookie said, "where's the restroom?"

"Are you getting sick?"

"No, I'm all right. I'm on my period."

Rona pointed toward the opposite wall. "It's over there. All the towels are clean."

"Thanks." Cookie grabbed the satchel and headed toward the bathroom.

Like the bedroom, the bathroom must've once been a storage closet. A coffin-sized shower filled the space to the right. The toilet was to the left. The sink's long, deep trough reminded her of a fixture that might be found in a communal bathhouse at a labor camp. While utilitarian in design, the entire room was sparkling clean.

She sat on the narrow toilet seat and dug through the satchel. Thank goodness! Detective Brunish had packed her amenities bag that contained her sanitary supplies.

After cleaning herself, she slid open the bathroom door and peeked out. Bob, Angela, Rona, Kever, and Anson were gathered around the wooden table.

Kever called out to her. "Cookie, have a seat. I made you a snack."

She stashed her satchel in the bedroom and joined them at the table.

A sandwich, stuffed with cheese and vegetables, rested atop a chipped plate. A scratched drinking glass filled with water sat next to the dish.

The sandwich tasted delicious. She was hungrier than she realized.

"Cookie," Bob said, "how are you feeling?"

"Better, thank you, but I'm still a little shaken up. I'm not used to … all this. I don't know how you guys do the kind of work you do. You're always somebody's target." A shiver ran up her back as she recalled hiding in the motel bathroom. "It just freaks me out … if it hadn't been for Kever-o and Anson, I'd probably be dead now. Those people almost broke in!"

Kever said, "Anson and I can't take the credit, Cookie. Allen Bosswell is the one who chased them off."

"Allen Bosswell, the wormy guy? He helped me?"

"He did," Kever said.

"Wow! Leeha and I thought he was stalking us."

Bob said, "We think Allen Bosswell belongs to a group that's opposed to the Back-to-Basics Club and the Freedom Party. The Freedom Party refers to people like him as *defectors*."

Cookie fought back tears. "I feel awful! All this time, I thought he was bad. Where is he? I'd like to thank him."

No one spoke.

"What's wrong?" she asked.

Anson poured himself a cup of tea before speaking. "You can't thank him."

"Why not?"

Once again no one answered.

"Anson, what's going on?"

"Allen Bosswell is dead, Cookie."

"Oh, my God! How?"

"Kever and I got to the motel too late to help. Bosswell got rid of the three men who were trying to break into your room, but another guy was hiding in the parking lot. That guy took Bosswell by surprise."

Cookie trembled. "This is all my fault! He's dead because of me."

Bob said, "No, it's not your fault. The Soldiers of God Justice Group is responsible, not you."

"You don't understand, Mr. Fullerby. You don't know!"

"Cookie, what don't I know?"

"I thought I … I … thought I'd lost them."

Bob leaned forward. "Cookie, what are you talking about?"

"Mr. Fullerby, I'm so sorry! I did something I shouldn't have. I didn't listen to you. On Monday, I … I went to Leeha's apartment."

"What! Why would you do such a stupid thing? Do you have any idea how dangerous it is?"

"I know! Mr. Fullerby, I know it was stupid."

"Then why did you do it? Why didn't you stay put like I told you?"

"I kept having these dreams. In them, Leeha was set free and went home. I imagined going to the apartment, and she'd be there. But she wasn't. I'm so sorry, Mr. Fullerby! I know it was wrong, but it got so hard sitting in that motel room doing nothing."

"Cookie," Kever said, "do you think someone spotted you while you were at the apartment building? Someone involved with Leeha's kidnapping?"

"I'm not sure. I think it's possible. Something weird happened."

"Tell us," Bob said.

"Just in case someone saw me, I took a long way home. I rode the train to Lower Shanna Road. While I was walking to a bus stop, a blue car showed up. It was moving funny, like weaving through traffic, then slowing down, then speeding up. Two men were in the front seat. The passenger had some kind of weapon. I'd never seen anything like it; it's like it changed colors to match the background. It was almost invisible. Then an autopod came zooming around a corner. The guy in the car shot at the pod. Things started exploding. Everybody on the sidewalk ran for cover. I hid in a parking garage. When the police came, I took off. I didn't know if they were the good cops or the bad cops."

Rona displayed a map on the wall monitor. "Cookie, here's a map with the CadTranS stops on Lower Shanna Road. Can you show us where you were?"

"Yeah, when I was in secondary school, I worked at a bakery there, so I know the neighborhood. The stop I got off at was Southwest 15 A. And see that flat, gray building straight down the street? That's the parking garage I hid in."

Anson said, "Cookie, do you think the guys in the blue car were after you?"

"It seemed like it. The passenger, the guy with the gun, I swear he was staring right at me. And an old, foreign guy hid next to me in the parking garage. He told me the guy in the car was aiming the weird weapon in my direction."

"Cookie, this happened *after* you left Leeha's apartment, right?" Anson asked.

"Yes."

"What happened while you were in the apartment?"

"Leeha wasn't there, but someone had been. The place was trashed, like people were searching for something."

Anson said, "Was the door open? Smashed in?"

"No, it was locked. A neighbor, Arny, let me in. He's like an assistant manager."

"Don't you have an access code?"

"No, I'm not officially living there, so I don't have a code. When I moved in, Leeha gave me a physical key. I'd forgotten the key when we went on our run, and I forgot it again when I chased after the red van."

"Was anything stolen from your apartment?" Anson asked.

"Yeah, they took all the food. But they left paper money behind. Then ... I ... I can't ... I don't want to ...."

Kever touched her arm. "Cookie, what is it?"

"Please, I don't want to talk about it."

"It's okay," Kever said, "you're safe. Take a deep breath and tell us what happened."

"I was standing in the kitchen. I was shocked. The place was trashed. I heard people walking in the hall. They stopped by the door. I heard men's voices, but I couldn't make out the words. They started opening the door. I knew I needed to hide; the only place I could think of was the laundry nook."

Her body trembled. Kever pulled her close. "Cookie, did the guys come in?"

"Yes, I saw two men."

Anson said, "Cookie, did you recognize them? Had you seen them around the apartment building or in the neighborhood?"

"No, they didn't look familiar at all."

"Describe what they looked like."

"They were about my age. Both had short hair, but not really short—not crew cuts. One had blond hair, the other brown. They looked like they were in good shape. The one with dark hair was slender and tall. The blond guy was shorter; he had big muscles, kind of like you, Anson."

"What were they wearing?"

"Casual pants and shirts."

"What did the men do after they came inside?"

"They went into Leeha's bedroom. They were searching for something, like *really* searching."

"These men, did they speak to one another?" Anson asked.

"Yeah, one guy complained that they'd already searched the place. He said it was a waste of time to come back, but someone had ordered them to." She gritted her teeth. "He called Leeha a bitch. Can you believe it? Leeha, a bitch? He said *the bitch* hid it somewhere else."

"Cookie," Anson said, "did these men refer to each other by name?"

"No, but they did mention other names, really short ones. I think these names belong to the people who told them to search the place again."

"Do you remember the names?" Anson asked.

"They were weird. Wait, I remember one. It was *Hands*. Gosh, the other name is on the end of my tongue. It was something like Zid, Ziff ... Zoff! It was Zoff. That was it."

"Cookie," Bob said, "did they give any clues about what they were looking for?"

"No."

"How did you get away?" Bob asked.

"I sneaked out when they were in Leeha's bedroom. Arny was waiting in the hallway. He told me to hide in his place until the guys left. He also told me strangers were nosing around the apartment building, but he didn't know who they were or what they were looking for. Some people who live in the building think these outsiders killed Mrs. Furley and Toofy. My God! I can't believe they're dead. I can't believe Leeha's gone."

Bob said, "Cookie, why don't you get some rest."

"I don't want to rest. Leeha's out there somewhere, but I don't know how to help her. I feel so worthless."

"Cookie," Kever said, "Mr. Fullerby's right. You need to rest. Come on, I'll help you to your room."

◉

Cadona City, Cadona
FRIDAY, MAY 5, YEAR 1007 EE
2:00 A.M., EAST CADONA TIME

Bob Fullerby heard a chair squeak against the floor.

Rona stood and said, "I'll clear the table."

Anson yawned and got up. "I'll help you, Row. If I sit much longer, I'll fall asleep."

Rona and Anson stacked dinnerware and headed toward the counter.

Angela was slumping in her seat. Bob saw the grumpy look on her face. "Something on your mind, Ang?"

"Mr. Fullerby, do you think it's wise bringing Cookie here?"

"I couldn't think of another plan. As far as we know, she's clean. Carl and Anson didn't find a single sign of suspicious activity in her records."

"Speaking of Anson," Angela said, "is he moving in, too?"

Bob looked across the room. Rona was helping Anson stretch a mattress pad over a bench. "Well, it does look like he's crashing here tonight."

Angela scowled. "Allowing strangers in our building is not a good idea, Mr. Fullerby."

"We have to trust someone, Ang. You, Kever-o, Row, and I can't take on the world by ourselves."

"I agree, Mr. Fullerby, but we don't know much about either Cookie or Anson. For all we know, they're Back-to-Basics Club spies. And let's not forget Pastor Mark Walzelesskii; logic says he's an enemy, yet you accept him as an informant. We're taking many risks."

"We are, but if Cookie is on our side, then her life is in danger. And Anson took a huge risk telling Kever-o about Leeha Ritsagin; he can get into serious trouble over it. As for Pastor Walzelesskii, I worry more for him every day. I fear Senator Fischer, Senator Rineburg, and General Willirman are figuring out Mark's been talking to me. There's no way around it, Ang; we all need allies. The Freedom Party and the Back-to-Basics Club are organized. We must be, too."

⊕

Somewhere in Cadona ...

Leeha Ritsagin awoke. Someone was squeezing her right arm. She pried open her eyes. A stranger hovered over her. He removed the e-bands from her wrists and ankles. His voice was gruff. "Stand up."

She slid off the edge of the bed.

"Turn around and put your hands behind your back," the man said.

He cinched her wrists together with handcuffs.

Another man stood nearby. She recognized him. His name was *Frank*. He held a weapon.

"What's ... what's happening?" she asked.

Neither man spoke.

A door opened. Dr. Millerman walked in. "Is she ready, Buzz?"

"She is, Doctor." Buzz gave her a shove. "Start walkin'."

A wide door glided open. Beyond it lay a night sky and a few portable lamps, like the kind she'd seen at construction sites.

Buzz said, "Go down the stairs."

The metal grates of the steep steps poked into the soles of her bare feet. She spotted tires. At last, she knew where she'd been held for so long: a huge, long vehicle. Its shiny, white exterior glowed in the artificial illumination.

Cool air brushed her cheeks. Wherever she was, it wasn't Cadona City. The air was far too dry.

She stepped onto solid earth. The ground beneath her naked feet felt like a rock slab covered with sand. Smoke filled the air. The smell reminded her of autumn-leaf bonfires from her childhood hometown. "Where are we?"

Buzz ignored her question. "You're getting in that van."

She saw a gray vehicle with bars covering the back windows. "Where are you taking me?"

"Shut your trap, bitch, and get moving."

They made it to the van.

"Get in," he said.

Leeha put a foot on a step, but her leg lacked the strength to lift her body.

"What the frick are you waiting for?" Buzz said.

"It's too high, and my hands are tied."

He heaved her upward. "Get in, you worthless slob."

She wriggled her way inside. He fastened her into the seat.

"Where are we going?" she asked.

"If you speak again, I'll rip out your tongue."

Dr. Millerman was standing outside on the dusty earth. The evil side of his personality had control. "Knock her out."

Buzz held a gadget in front of her face. The shiny object resembled the one the guys in suits used when they took her from her apartment. Rows of lights flashed. She felt sleepy.

PART ⊕ THREE
FOUND

WHAT THOSE RAGS PUBLISH

Cadona City, Cadona
FRIDAY, MAY 5, YEAR 1007 EE
4:00 A.M., EAST CADONA TIME

Bob Fullerby's personal device roused him from sleep. Bill Marantees was calling. Bob glanced around the windowless, back room of the old print shop building. Anson Dailey, Kever Carsen, Rona Betler, and Angela Thirgal lay motionless on makeshift beds.

He kept his voice low. "Hey, Boss, what's up?"

"Sorry to call so early," Bill said, "but something big is going down. Senator Seldortin canceled campaign appearances in New Cadona. He's on his way back to Cadona City."

"Why? What's happened?"

"He's not sayin'. He's going to make an announcement at seven a.m. our time."

"I hope he's not pulling out of the race," Bob said.

"I don't think that's it. I'm not sure what he's going to say, but I have a theory; our night shift crew found interesting reports on the National Fortress and Real Conspiracy newsfeeds."

"Why would Bradley care what those rags publish?"

"Bob, take a look at the articles and see what you make of them. I'd like to talk to Bradley myself, but I'm already scheduled to chat with President Meyfeld and Richard Karther. I'll deal with the president and the defense secretary. You see what Bradley's up to."

"Will do, Boss." Bob ended the call and turned on his computer. The Real Conspiracy News Network had indeed published a string of interesting stories, and the faux-journalists at the National Fortress Press laid out fact after fact in their typically evidence-free reports.

Bob checked the time. If he didn't dawdle, he'd be able to squeeze in coffee as well as a shower before heading to Capital Plaza.

He tip-toed to the counter, grabbed a brewing pitcher, and turned on the faucet.

Creaking noises came from across the room. Kever was tossing and turning on an old cot. Bob slowed the flow of water, but it was too late; Kever was awake. "Mr. Fullerby, why are you up so early?"

"Sorry I woke you, Kever-o. You usually sleep like a baby."

"I was having weird dreams. What's going on?"

"I got a call from the boss. He says Bradley's halting his campaign activities in New Cadona and flying back to Cadona City."

"Why?"

"To give a news conference."

Kever said, "Why couldn't he do it from Ramsten?"

"Good question. I don't know."

"What's this news conference about?"

"We're not sure, Kever-o, but the boss has a guess. The National Fortress and Real Conspiracy have published interesting articles about Hansen Hills and Mind-One."

"Interesting in what way, Mr. Fullerby?"

"Somehow those rags got wind of Bradley's research. One report claims that at least twelve prisoners are being illegally held at Hansen Hills. They even reported that the Mind-One drug is being produced there."

"Senator Seldortin wouldn't tell the National Fortress or Real Conspiracy about his findings, would he?"

"I doubt it, Kever-o. Not so long ago, Bradley agreed with Bill and me ... it's better to wait until we have rock-hard evidence about the Hills before going public."

Kever rose to his feet. He pulled a mug from the cupboard.

"Kever-o, you can go back to bed. I'm heading out soon to attend Bradley's briefing. If I get there early enough, I may be able to catch him before he gets behind the podium."

"I don't think I'll be able to sleep, Mr. Fullerby. It's spooky knowing there may be a snitch in Senator Seldortin's inner circle. Can I help? Do you need a lift?"

"Thanks, but I already called a taxi. Anyway, I want you to keep an eye on Cookie Davis today. She seems to trust you. Maybe you can get more info out of her. And, who knows, she may try to sneak out again, like she did when she pulled that dumb stunt and went to Leeha Ritsagin's apartment."

"What about our assignments?" Kever asked.

"Ang will handle the J2 virus and Flight Ten Seventy stories. Row will cover the Soldiers of God Justice Group and the Paula Arvish murder."

Bob heard shuffling sounds. The door to Cookie's room slid open. She wore a baggy T-shirt over a flowing nightgown. She walked toward them. Her graceful steps and long sleepwear made her look like a floating angel.

Kever had a grin on his face. "Thanks for the assignment, Mr. Fullerby. I got the good job. She's easy on the eyes."

"Minding Cookie isn't your only task, Kever-o. I need you to study those Hansen Hills and Mind-One stories on the rag sites. I want to know who the leaker is. You can do that from the print shop."

"Will do."

Concern filled Cookie's big eyes. "Mr. Fullerby, why are you and Kever-o up so early? Is it about Leeha?"

"Unfortunately, no. The boss called. I have an assignment in Capital Plaza. If you'll excuse me, I'd better jump in the shower."

Steam covered the mirror the second Bob stepped out of the shower. He dried himself with a paper-thin towel and yanked clothes from a hanger.

He dressed and then glanced in the foggy mirror. The bathroom lighting wasn't the best, but the colors of the shirt matched—close enough anyway—with the slacks.

Cool air rushed in when he opened the bathroom door.

While he'd been washing, everyone had gotten up. Kever, Anson, and Angela were sitting at the wooden table. Cookie and Rona stood by the stove. Food sizzled.

Rona set a platter laden with delectables on the tabletop. "Have a seat, Mr. Fullerby. Breakfast is ready."

Cookie said, "I used to make this dish for Leeha, Mr. Fullerby; she loved it. I bet you will, too."

"I'm sure I would, but I need to get going." His personal device chimed. "In fact, Maatus just arrived. I've got to run, but, boy, would I ever love to join you all. I'm starved."

Rona darted to a cupboard and pulled a to-go container from a shelf. "No problem, Mr. Fullerby. I'll pack some for you." She piled food into the box. Cookie poured steaming coffee into a travel mug. Rona handed him the food and drink. "Here, you go, Mr. Fullerby. You can eat on the way."

Hansen Hills, Cadona ...

Leeha Ritsagin heard Buzz's voice. "Wake up, bitch."

A bright light turned the black behind her eyelids red. "Leave me alone. Let me sleep."

He slapped her cheek. "Uh-uh, you're done sleeping. Time to rise and shine."

"Please, I'm very tired."

"Too bad, you're ... home."

"Home?" Leeha opened her eyes.

Buzz dragged her out of the gray van.

Wherever they'd taken her, it wasn't her apartment in the Warrenton District. Dusty concrete cooled the soles of her bare feet. A few round lights pierced the darkness.

Before she had a chance to look around, someone put something soft over her eyes. Except for a thin sliver of faint light peeping in from the bottom of the blindfold, all she saw was black.

Buzz grabbed her arm and said, "Start walking."

With each step, her grogginess faded. She heard a grinding noise. The sound reminded her of a storefront grate sliding open. "Where am I?"

"Don't worry, you'll find out soon enough."

After a few more steps, the light seeping in beneath the blindfold brightened. The ground under her feet changed; it felt smooth, like a floor. Clicking footsteps and the hum of a fan or vent were the only sounds.

Chill from the floor raced up her legs. She feared her bladder would empty at any moment.

Buzz jerked her arm. "Stop here."

The blindfold disappeared. Bright lights hurt her eyes.

The big, bare room was painted white. Three men, two of them in military camouflage uniforms, stood near a shiny door. The third man, the one wearing civilian clothes, approached. "Is this the thief?" he asked.

"She is, Colonel Strickland," Buzz said.

A smirk twisted Colonel Strickland's lips as he studied her face. "So, this is the bitch who's caused so much trouble. I'm surprised; I expected a more formidable figure. This one's a piece of rotten shit. What a disappointment!"

"Colonel, may we leave her with you?" Buzz asked. "Doctor Millerman is waiting for us at the transfer point."

"You'll be able to leave soon, Buzz. We're waiting for word from Doctor Palchero."

Leeha felt pressure in her belly. She clenched her pelvic muscles, but drops of urine escaped. "I need a bathroom, please."

Colonel Strickland's deadpan, blue eyes glared at her. "You'll have to hold it."

"I don't know if I can." Another trickle of warm liquid slid down her thighs. "Please, I really need to go."

"Why is she speaking?" Colonel Strickland said.

Buzz smacked her cheek. "You heard the man! Shut your trap."

"But, I ... I really need to use a restroom."

Buzz squeezed her arm. "You don't get it, do you? We don't give a damn if you piss or shit yourself. So, pig, shut the frick up."

The shiny door opened. A broad-chested man appeared. His uniform looked like a security guard's. "Colonel, sir, Doctor Palchero said to take her to the examination room."

Colonel Strickland said, "Buzz, you're getting your wish; we'll take her from here. You and your men are free to go."

"Good, I'm sick of this thing." Buzz gave her a push.

Her body tipped forward. Her right knee slammed into the floor. Urine gushed from her bladder. She hoped the men wouldn't notice.

Colonel Strickland pointed at her. "Will you look at this! What a useless excuse for a human being. She pissed up our clean floor."

The men snickered.

"Get her up," Colonel Strickland said. "Let's not keep Doctor Palchero waiting; she's a busy lady."

Leeha felt a strong hand grasp her arm. She looked up. The security guard towered over her. "Let's go."

He pulled her through the doorway and down a stark, white hall. He opened one of several doors lining the corridor. "In you go, bitch."

A shove to the back sent her flailing into the small room.

The guard removed her handcuffs. He said, "Doctor Palchero wants you to get dressed."

The guard left, slamming the door behind him.

Leeha dashed for the door and turned the handle. It was locked.

She looked around.

Another door! It was on the opposite wall. She ran to the door, but it was also locked.

Nothing else offered an obvious way to escape. The room was empty except for a slab-like table, one folding chair, and a protruding cabinet.

Everything in the room was white except for a plump, brown bag on the tabletop.

She peeked inside the sack.

Her clothes!

The bag contained the clothing that she was wearing when the three men stole her from her apartment. Only shoes and socks were missing.

Leeha pulled the hospital robe over her head. She found a dry spot on the medical garment and wiped places on her body that were still damp with urine. She dressed, relishing the feeling of her own clothes against her skin.

Fatigue took hold. She sat on the folding chair. Her eyes shut.

Her body twitched as her chin fell to her chest. She must stay alert and find a way out. The doors were locked, but perhaps there was another way to escape.

She got up and took a few steps toward the cabinet.

Her legs shook. She'd never make it. Her body crumpled back into the chair.

Her head felt heavy, but she mustn't fall asleep.

One, two, three. She counted, focusing on each syllable.

One thousand eight hundred!

Thirty minutes had passed. No one had checked in on her. Had she been forgotten? Was anyone looking for her? Did anyone miss her?

Exhaustion pulled her eyelids down.

HERE IS HOW BEGINS A WAR

"Thomas Fillimore left us many extraordinary works of art. His most enduring contributions, however, were his written works aimed at protecting our freedoms and the environment. He lived and died long ago, but his words still resonate with us today."

Chairman, Cadonan Literary Freedom Society Year 1007 of the Enlightened Epoch

Cadona City, Cadona
FRIDAY, MAY 5, YEAR 1007 EE
6:00 A.M., EAST CADONA TIME

Bob Fullerby swallowed his last bite of breakfast and took his final sip of strong coffee. He glanced out the taxi window. Colossal government buildings loomed against a smoggy, morning sky.

Maatus' eyes reflected in the rearview mirror. "Mr. Fullerby, Capital Plaza close now, but my dispatcher say many protesters there."

"Then take the west entrance, please. I can use my press credentials to get inside."

"As you wish, sir."

At the next intersection, traffic had ground to a stop. Bob studied the mass of people assembled in the streets. The scene reflected the great divide tearing his country apart. Rows of riot police, each donning a helmet and shield, stood shoulder to shoulder along the middle of Government Avenue. Shapeless, fluid crowds dwarfed the orderly columns of policemen. On one side of the road, Freedom Party supporters chanted for Senator Mitch Fischer. On the other side, people carried signs backing Senator Bradley Seldortin of the Allegiance Party.

"Noisy here," Maatus said. "Not good."

Angry demonstrators from both camps skirted the police barrier. A fight broke out. Punches flew. A tangle of brawling men weaved toward the taxi. A kick to the stomach sent one man sailing through the air. The man's back slammed into the rear passenger side door.

Maatus sounded frightened. "Mr. Fullerby! You okay?"

"Yeah, I'm fine. You?"

"I ... I good, too."

Traffic moved again, but at a snail's pace.

Up ahead, Bob saw a security barricade. Armed National Police officers in face-shields and thick vests manned the post.

"Maatus, head to that checkpoint, please."

"Yes, sir, Mr. Fullerby."

Bob called Senator Bradley Seldortin's private line. "Good morning, Senator."

"Hello, Bob, I was hoping Bill would send you. I left instructions for the guards to let you in. Please come to my chambers."

"Will do, Senator. We're at the west checkpoint now."

Bob walked into the lobby of Bradley's senatorial chamber. Lydia stood and slipped her reading glasses off her nose. "Mr. Fullerby, good morning. The senator is expecting you." Despite her advancing age, Bradley's longtime assistant appeared as professional as ever—in an old-lady sort of way. She opened the door to Bradley's chamber. He was staring out a tall, arched window.

"Senator Seldortin," Lydia said, "Mr. Fullerby has arrived."

Bradley took his time turning away from the view. "Thank you, Lydia."

Bob heard the door close as Lydia left the room.

Bradley gestured toward a chair. "Bob, good to see you. Please, have a seat. We can speak freely. People I trust secured the room."

Bob noticed a hint of fatigue on Bradley's long, narrow face. "Senator, what brings you back to Cadona City? As I recall, you had a few more weeks of campaign stops scheduled in Ramsten."

"That was our plan, indeed." Bradley sat on an unadorned, faux-leather sofa. "Things have changed, Bob. Have you read the National Fortress and Real Conspiracy newsfeeds?"

"I have, sir."

"Well, that's the reason for my hasty return. The cat's out of the bag about the Hills and Mind-One. We need to react to the news before the Freedom Party does."

"Senator, do you know how amateur reporters got wind of your senatorial investigation into the Hills?"

"No, Bob, no idea at all."

"How much of what's written in those stories matches your findings?"

"How much is true? Well, Bob, all of it. Every bit of it is true."

"Do you know who might have leaked it to the press?"

"You know, Bob, I was careful about who knew what. Only a few trusted souls had access to the whole body of work. Heck, I tell you a lot, but there were details in those articles that even you didn't know. I told your boss even less. Whoever got wind of my work knew what he was doing. He knew what he was looking for. Most of all, he could understand the implications of my findings. Here's what eludes me, Bob; why would someone with in-depth financial knowledge and investigative talent slip reports like these through B-rated media agencies? Why not release it to legitimate press?"

"I have a hunch, Senator. Agencies like the National Fortress and Real Conspiracy don't demand credentials; they don't demand proof. They get themselves a story, and they ask no questions."

"So, what you're saying, Bob, is whoever got their hands on my research wants to stay incognito."

"That would be my guess, Senator."

"Interesting, very interesting. Unknown persons uncover the story of a decade right before legislative and presidential elections, but they choose to remain hidden. Whoever did this isn't after glory or fame." Bradley stopped talking and stared into space.

"Senator, it looks like you have something else on your mind."

"I do, Bob, I most certainly do. On the surface, this looks like the work of a friend, an ally who wants the world to know prisoners are being held illegally at Hansen Hills and subjected to dangerous truth serums. This *friend* dares to expose the lies of the Freedom Party. However, when I examine the leaker's goal through a different lens, I don't know if the leaker is trying to bring down an illegal prison ... or bring down Cadona."

"You make a good point, Senator. Let's hope this leaker is benevolent."

Bradley rose from the sofa. "Well, Bob, you better get out there and grab a good spot in the briefing room. Lydia told me reporters are arriving in droves."

Bob stood. He'd forgotten how tall Bradley was. The bony, big-footed lawmaker towered over him. "Senator, I'll let you know if we find the source of the leak."

Bob joined a gaggle of people streaming down a bright, ornate hall.

Like water flowing to a drain, the multitude of human bodies flocked toward an open door. As Senator Seldortin had warned, journalists had arrived in throngs.

Sounds of voices, footsteps, scooting chairs, and humming equipment filled the briefing room. Bob recognized many faces, but only one friendly one; Scott Walters waved at him from the front row.

Bob pushed his way through the crowd.

"Good morning, Mr. Fullerby," Scott said. "I got here early and grabbed a great seat for you."

"Thanks, Scott, but I don't mind standing."

"Mr. Fullerby, please, take my seat. That way, you'll be right in front. No one will be allowed to get between you and the stage. Senator Seldortin will be able to call on you without getting charged with favoritism."

"What about you?" Bob asked.

Scott's face glowed with youthful enthusiasm. "I'll cover the mood in the room."

"Mood? Look around. We're the only ones here who don't work for an agency owned by the Freedom Party, or, more specifically, the Back-to-Basics Club."

"Mr. Fullerby, since when have a bunch of fanatics scared you?"

"The Freedom Party and the Club may be violent and crazy, Scott, but they're not inept. They've taken control of the media and succeeded in wooing half the nation."

"Have faith in the other half, Mr. Fullerby. And not everyone here is a reporter. All sorts of people are watching."

Noises dwindled. The briefing would soon begin.

Bradley appeared. He took his time crossing the stage and settling in behind the podium.

Scott said, "Have fun, Mr. Fullerby, because I'm going to. We're on the cusp of discrediting the Freedom Party and the Back-to-Basics Club." Scott disappeared into the crowd.

Bob hoped his colleague was right, but the Freedom Party had done many terrible things in recent years. Yet, today, the party wielded more power rather than less.

From behind the speaker's stand, Bradley spoke in a deep voice. He enunciated each syllable. "My fellow citizens, members of the press, and fellow lawmakers, it is with a heavy heart that I stand before you on this fine morning. I have grave news to share. What I'm about to tell you threatens the foundations of our illustrious democracy. As a leader of the Legislative Financial Committee, dedicated civil servants brought to my attention what appeared, on the surface, to be careless errors. With sorrow, I'm here to tell you these questionable financial requisitions were not mistakes, but something far worse. We have proof that our military, intelligence agencies, and the National Police are, once again, using the Hansen Hills Federal Facility as an illegal prison. In addition to this treachery, banned drugs, including the Mind-One truth serum, are being manufactured at the Hills."

"Lies!" someone in the audience shouted.

"Seldortin will say anything to get elected!" a woman shrieked.

If the outcry shocked Bradley, he didn't let it show. He continued to speak as a chant spread across the room. "Boo on Seldortin! Boo on Seldortin!"

A few voices called for silence. "Quiet! Let him finish."

Bob heard thumps. When he looked over his shoulder, he saw black-clad Capital Guard officers. They pulled rowdy people out of the room.

Unfazed, Bradley presented his evidence.

Ver-Nuvelin, Domataland
THURSDAY, MAY 4, YEAR 1007 EE
10:15 P.M., CENTRAL FEWWOK TIME

President Demnar Tarish's full attention focused on a wall monitor. A Cadonan news alert neared its end. Video showed Senator Bradley Seldortin striding away from a podium. A camera followed the tall fellow as he walked off the stage.

Demnar leaned back in his conference room chair. "Your plan worked like a charm, Rozula. Senator Seldortin responded to our leaked articles exactly as we had hoped. Excellent work."

Defense Minister Rivar Henik removed an interpreter ear-piece. "I couldn't agree more; this is a brilliant example of offensive intelligence, Rozula. Now, the world will know about Hansen Hills and Freedom Party lies. I must say, however, I don't know how the two of you understand Cadonan. If not for translation, I'd be at a loss."

"It takes a while to get used to the foreign sounds and syntax," Demnar said. "Stick with it, Rivar, it'll eventually sink in."

"I may be too old, Honorable President."

Rozula let out a laugh. "Don't give up so soon, Rivar. You've mastered the Cadonan alphabet."

"I sort of got used to the letters, I suppose. I still feel like I want to turn the text sideways and then read it in a mirror. I can't understand why that language uses all those extra words."

Demnar said, "Despite its complexity, there's a beauty to it, but it takes time to see it."

Rivar's dark, bushy eyebrows nearly hid his eyes as he squinted in thought. "The Cadonans may have an overly complex language, but they aren't stupid. General Willirman's analysts will figure out that we created those news articles. We have an opportunity to exploit that channel, but the window may close at any time. Are we planning to feed other stories?"

"My people did some brainstorming," Rozula said. "We're thinking of stirring up a protest at the gates of Hansen Hills."

Rivar fluttered his fingers against the tabletop as if he were striking piano keys. "To what end, Rozula?"

"We hope it'll turn Hansen Hills into a rallying cry for Freedom Party opponents."

Doubt deepened frown lines on Rivar's weathered face. "Rozula, do you have enough agents on the ground in Cadona to pull off a mission of that scale?"

"We would only sow the idea of a protest, Rivar. The goal is for Cadonans who oppose the Freedom Party to take care of the rest on their own."

"I think I get it, Rozula; we'd throw the snowball that launches an avalanche."

"Exactly, Rivar. What do you think, Honorable President?"

"It makes sense, Rozula," Demnar said. "My only concern is we are deceiving those Cadonans who should be our natural allies—those who don't like Senator Fischer, Senator Rineburg, General Willirman, and Pastor Walls."

"We can scrap the idea, Honorable President," Rozula said.

"No, let's move forward. We have no choice but to take atypical action against Cadona; they're too strong to face head-on. But every decision we make comes at a cost … such actions always do. *Subterfuge begets mistrust. Mistrust begets fear. Fear begets hate. Here is how begins a war.*"

"Who said that, Honorable President?" Rivar asked.

Rozula answered for him. "Thomas Fillimore, in his work, *The Origins of Conflict*. He wrote it a long time ago, in the Awakening Epoch."

Rivar's eyes widened. "Honorable President, you quote Thomas Fillimore? He was Cadonan!"

"Yes," Demnar said, "he was Cadonan, and he was a great and wise man, rather like Senator Bradley Seldortin and investigative journalist Bob Fullerby. Let's hope and pray our actions don't bring them trouble."

Hansen Hills, Cadona
FRIDAY, MAY 5, YEAR 1007 EE
6:30 A.M., CENTRAL EAST CADONA TIME

Restlessness crept through Senator John Rineburg's long legs as he watched a viewing monitor. Cameras were capturing events happening in a small, white-walled room.

Dr. Palchero leaned close to him. "John, is something troubling you?"

"I don't know where to start, Ellen. Senator Seldortin knows what we're doing here at the Hills. I have no idea how the frick he figured it out."

His anger deepened. He pointed at the monitor. "And what about her? That bitch stole our Guiding Light. Why are we gawking at the fat slob? Nothing's happening."

"Be patient, John. She'll do it."

"I don't think so. She's going to fall asleep in the chair."

Electronic eyes watched as Leeha Ritsagin rose to her feet.

Ellen patted his arm. "See, John, here she goes!"

"She's not going to do it, Ellen."

"I bet she will."

The prisoner walked to the examination room's lone cabinet and opened the door.

Ellen's voice had a teasing ring to it. "I told you so, Senator."

"Yes, you did. Now, let's see what the bitch does."

The thief seemed excited as she fiddled with various pieces of equipment and cables. Excitement turned to frustration. She stuffed the electronics back into the cabinet. The woman appeared tired now. She dragged her feet on the floor as if she carried a great weight. Her flabby body flopped onto the room's sole chair.

Ellen laughed. "See, John, I told you so."

"She didn't do anything but pull stuff out and shove it back in. So what?"

"Actually, John, what happened tells us a great deal about Ms. Leeha Ritsagin."

"Like what?"

"The equipment in that cabinet is used for comm-nodes. She realized it right away. This was her chance to call for help."

"But she didn't do anything."

"Yes, because she knew components were missing. She could never assemble an apparatus to contact anyone."

"Explain to me, Ellen, how this knowledge helps us?"

"First, it tells me she knows enough about comm-nodes to have sent those hidden messages to the ninety-nine women on the justice execution list. It also tells me that she may have been able to find sneaky ways to communicate with Randy Altholder and the Sohn-Suran woman. If she sent electronic copies of the Guiding Light to anyone, she'd have the skills needed to hide her tracks." Heat from Ellen's hand warmed his thigh.

"John, my advice to you: have our intelligence people look long and hard for surreptitious electronic activity."

"I'm impressed, Ellen. You planned your test well."

"Why, thank you, Senator. I am an excellent judge of … enhanced abilities." Ellen guided her long, slender fingers along the edge of his suit jacket. Red nail polish glistened. Her moist tongue licked her glossy lips. "Tell me, Senator, how's the wife?"

"Madalin is the boring, frumpy bitch she always was."

Ellen's gentle fingertips fondled his ears. "She's also still the *rich*, frumpy, boring bitch, right?"

"She is."

"Is something else troubling you, John?"

"We have another brewing crisis."

"Concerning Madalin?"

"No, it's about Pastor Leon Walls, or, more specifically, Leon's son, Mark Walzelesskii."

"Ah, what's up with Leon's scrumptious boy?"

"Scrumptious? That little prick? He's a pussy, homomaniac traitor. He's up to something. Dougy and I haven't caught him red-handed yet, but we're pretty sure he's consorting with the enemy."

"Domataland? Sohn-Sur?"

"No, with Senator Seldortin and Bob Fullerby."

"I see; we're talking about internal enemies. Sounds like you have your hands full."

"Too much so."

"Well, then, John, would you like a little rest and relaxation before going home to your wealthy, loving spouse and your traitorous, young pastor?"

"Is that an order, Doctor?"

Her laugh tickled his ear. "It is, Senator. It's the medicine you need."

ALL LIGHT VANISHED

"The way to utterly break a prisoner is not only to remove all hope, but also to remove all means for a person to distract himself from his plight. Some prisoners crack with exposure to bright light and noise; others fall apart more quickly with sensory deprivation, which includes a lack of comforts, light, and warmth."

Dr. Ellen Palchero
Cadonan Interrogation Service

Cadona City, Cadona
FRIDAY, MAY 5, YEAR 1007 EE
7:50 A.M., EAST CADONA TIME

The only sounds echoing in the hallway of the True Followers of God Church headquarters were those made by his own shoes striking polished stone. Still, Pastor Mark Walzelesskii's heart pounded.

He reached his father's office.

Mark drew a deep breath before knocking on the pale, smooth wood of the door. No one answered.

He stuck his head through the doorway. Pastor Leon Walls' office looked like it always did. The marble floor glistened, as did the chocolate-colored wood of the oversized desk.

"Dad, are you here?"

The room was quiet. Mark stepped inside and shut the door behind him.

A red light caught his eye. A caller had left a message on the desk phone. The call must've been important—so important that the caller wanted to make sure the message couldn't be hacked. Security was the only reason to use the old-fashioned device.

He stared at the phone. Should he listen to the message? All he needed to do was type in the code and hold the receiver to his ear.

Using a desk phone, though, would be out of character for him. It was best to stick to his original plan and read auto-mails on the computer.

He was steps away from his father's designer chair when he heard noises.

Mark hid in the bathroom and listened.

Someone was walking across the office.

His dad spoke. "Hello, John, you were trying to reach me? … No, John, I haven't read my mail. … How did that son-of-a-bitch Seldortin learn about Hansen Hills and Mind-One? … When did Ritsagin arrive at the Hills? … What about those screwballs from Jenton's garage: Ellis and Fellerman? Did we get anything out of them? … Nothing at all? That's terrible. … Yes, yes, I can meet. I'll head over to Dougy's office at the Defense Department. I'll call you when I get there."

Footsteps tapped against the floor. The office door slammed shut. Mark peeked out of the bathroom.

The office was empty.

He sat at his dad's desk and turned on the computer. His father had received a barrage of private messages. Mark noticed one auto-mail with attached images. The first picture loomed large when viewed through an eye-piece. At first, the photo appeared to be a black rectangle, but, as

software adjusted the lighting, details came into focus—frightening details. The image was of a cave-like room. The walls and floor were made
of unfinished stone or concrete. The bleak room was empty except for a
toilet, a steel door, and a thin mattress pad covered with ragged blankets.

Why would such a photo be among his father's messages? Mark viewed
the next image. It left no doubt; the photograph was of a torture chamber.

He copied the images and text onto a slip disk. He must get the disk
to Bob Fullerby right away.

Mark stood. He pretended to smooth creases from his shirt as he
dropped the disk into a pocket.

Other photographs—of a very different type—caught his eye. Family
pictures scrolled by on a viewplane sitting on top of his father's desk.
Everyone looked happy in the images. How different these photos were
from those taken at Hansen Hills!

Mark trembled. Should he ... could he ... go through with giving the
Hansen Hills photos to Bob Fullerby? Maybe this betrayal was too big.

He left his father's office and headed down the hall. The tiny slip disk
in his pocket felt like it weighed as much as a podsentian stone.

Tammy Smith appeared from around a corner. She walked toward
him. A broad smile widened her already round face. "Good morning,
Pastor Walzelesskii. May I bring you anything?"

"No, thank you, Tammy."

She continued down the hallway. If she spotted his distress, she didn't
let it show.

Mark went into his own office. The room's soft colors and lush plants
often comforted him, but not today. Maybe a stroll in the yard would help.
He stepped outside and ambled down a path. His nose caught the scent of
flowers and his ears the sound of rustling leaves. Yet he found no solace.

He sat on a bench and prayed.

Silent words didn't ease his pain, so he spoke in a whisper. "God, why
have you cursed me with this knowledge? You order us to love our fathers.
What will you have me do? Betray him completely? Please, God, don't
put me in this position. These photos, they tell too much. My father's
crimes, these things he's involved with, the depth of his involvement, the

inhumanity of his actions … it's too much. My dad and his partners are going to torture a young woman. She'll sleep on a dirty mat on a cold floor while I'll sleep in the comfortable bed my dad bought for me. Tomorrow, I'll wake up to light coming through a window in the house my dad gave me. Will Leeha Ritsagin live to see another sunrise? God, you want me to give these files to Mr. Fullerby … I feel in my heart you do. Well, I won't do it. I will not! Do you hear me?"

A ray of sun burst through a break in the clouds. Mark saw his reflection in an office window. He saw other things mirrored as well: his beloved plants and a True Followers of God Church Compass flag. The purple and yellow symbol of his father's faith fluttered atop a tall pole.

Something else, something unwelcome, appeared in the reflection. It presented itself more as a sensation than an actual apparition.

He'd seen it before. The churning, putrid, gray smoke had a habit of haunting him. It had visited when Senator Mitch Fischer agreed to run for Cadonan president on the Freedom Party ticket. Now, here it was again; the sinister vapor had returned. It emerged from the flagpole and spread in swirling currents.

In the mirrored image, the caustic mist wilted flowers and trees. Birds flopped about on the ground and choked. Mark's skin prickled as wickedness neared.

A second energy drifted into the yard. The strange power compelled him to look at his own reflected face. His expression proved that anger consumed him. He knew something else as well; the poison vapor rejoiced in his decision to acquiesce to evil.

He reached his hands toward heaven. "All right, God, I get it. I understand what I must do." In the reflection, the gray smoke retreated by the same route it had arrived. Trees, flowers, and birds returned to their living luster.

Mark stood. Dizzying anxiety had faded, but sorrow pressed on him. The world should've never come to this.

◎

Cadona City, Cadona
FRIDAY, MAY 5, YEAR 1007 EE
8:55 A.M., EAST CADONA TIME

Bob Fullerby leaned his head against the taxi's soft but worn backseat headrest.

The car slowed. Maatus glanced in the rearview mirror. "Mr. Fullerby, we here. Where I stop?"

"Anywhere is fine, thanks."

Maatus parked along a crumbling sidewalk. "Mr. Fullerby, Stratten Park bad place. Dirty. You sure I not wait?"

"No, I don't know how long I'll be. I'll take a bus home."

"Be careful," Maatus said.

Bob climbed out of the vehicle.

The taxi drove away.

The stench of garbage and overused, portable latrines met Bob's nose as he walked into the makeshift shantytown. An expanse of stained tents, crooked roofs, and amorphous lean-tos stretched out before him.

He headed for the rendezvous point beneath the trestle. It was a good location for a secret meeting. A while back, he and Defense Secretary Richard Karther had met there. Now, he was about to meet with his Drop Case informant, Pastor Mark Walzelesskii, in that same grimy spot.

The trestle ran through the middle of the park, so a long trek lay before him.

His heart ached at the memory of how this park once was. Long ago, people would sit under trees and read. Children would play. Families would gather for picnics. Now, the park was filled with desperate souls who had little access to clean water and decent food. Many lived in whatever shelters they could build from materials that others had discarded. No one knew how many people had died in the park. No one knew how many were whisked away for dangerous labor or prostitution.

As he made his way over trampled earth, a few people threw angry glances in his direction. Did they think he was there to exploit them? On the other hand, maybe they saw him as an easy target. Might they attack him for his shirt or shoes? People had died for less in such places. Most people, though, ignored him, as survival required their full attention.

Smelly mud stuck to his shoes as he weaved through a gaggle of skinny children playing ball. Beyond the litter-strewn playground, women, taking advantage of rain-free weather, hung laundry on the railings of a spiral walkway. The walkway once meandered through what, long ago, had been a city flower garden. Gone were the kaleidoscopic colors of blossoms, flowering shrubs, and exotic trees. In their places, ragged clothing fluttered in the wind.

On one railing, a scavenger bird, looking gaunt and its feathers in tatters, kept an eye out for a morsel of food. Vanished were fluttering songbirds, scampering squirrels, feeding fishes, waddling ducks, and crystal-clear ponds.

In the distance, he spotted desperate-looking people standing in crooked lines that ended at long, foldable tables. Stacks of food, clothing, and blankets covered the tabletops. Volunteers waited behind the tables. Bob watched the process. A volunteer in a green vest handed a person an aid package. After the person took his package, a charity worker in a white lab coat held a shiny medical device close to the person's forehead. Burly security guards loitered nearby, trying, without success, to blend into the crowd.

A tall, slender man appeared to be in charge of the event. Bob recognized the dark-haired, young fellow: his Drop Case informant, Pastor Mark Walzelesskii. Mark gave him a nod.

Bob turned away; officially, he was there to report on the tragedy of the ever-growing, makeshift slums.

He continued toward the trestle.

When he reached the lip of the structure's heavy shadow, he peeked over his shoulder. Mark was following at a safe distance.

A gust of air flowed beneath the broad overpass. The reek of human waste found Bob's nose. With reluctant steps, he entered the tunnel formed by the concrete-and-steel bridge. He glanced around. The number of homeless seeking shelter there had ballooned since his last visit. Rows of destitute people reclined on blankets, cardboard remnants, or ripped garbage bags. At the foot of a pier, two little boys crouched next to a man who was cooking something on a crumpled slice of aluminum foil. The man was almost a child himself.

Bob heard Mark's voice. "Mr. Fullerby, thank you for meeting me."

"Pastor Walzelesskii, good morning."

"I know this isn't the most pleasant spot, Mr. Fullerby, but I had plans to come here anyway, and I know you've been writing articles about Stratten Park, so I figured it's a good place for us to meet."

"You're right, it's a good choice, Pastor." Bob studied Mark's youthful, pale face. "You look stressed, Son."

Mark nodded. "I am. J2 is spreading. It's only a matter of time before it reaches the park."

"Yes, I've read your press releases on your J2 findings. Is that what you want to talk to me about, Pastor?"

"No, I have news on a different topic. Leeha Ritsagin has arrived at Hansen Hills." Mark reached into his pants pocket. A slip disk rested in his palm. "I have pictures of rooms in the facility. They don't only mean to interrogate her; they mean to torture her."

Bob copied files from Mark's slip disk onto a memory stick.

"Mr. Fullerby, Ritsagin isn't the only prisoner. There are at least twelve. And another thing, a new person has started sending auto-mails to my dad. He signs his name as *Axle*. I didn't see any recent messages from Zoff or Hands."

Bob decided not to tell Mark that Zoff and Hands had died in a parking lot behind the Roadside Inn Motel. Such details were better left secret. "Have you learned more about the Guiding Light, Pastor?"

"No, except they still haven't found it. The Freedom Party has agents in Tahagaruza looking for Randy Altholder, but the Antropkan government isn't cooperating. One more thing, two people who work at Jenton's garage are also prisoners at Hansen Hills. Their last names are *Ellis* and *Fellerman*. It turns out they have no knowledge of the Guiding Light, but interrogators think someone at Jenton's does." Mark swung his head in all directions as if he sensed danger.

"Pastor, is something wrong?"

"I think General Willirman is keeping tabs on me, Mr. Fullerby. I'm worried; he may suspect I've been talking to you."

"Pastor, whatever you do, keep a low profile. If you need to stay away from me for your safety, by all means, do so."

"I'll be careful, Mr. Fullerby. I promise." Mark handed care packages to a few people and then wandered away from the shadow of the trestle.

Hansen Hills, Cadona ...

Leeha Ritsagin opened her eyes. She squinted against bright light. Her back hurt as she peeled her left shoulder away from the wall that had kept her from tumbling off the folding chair.

Despite aches and pains, her circumstances had improved; she was no longer tethered to a bed.

A door opened. A security guard walked toward her. He didn't stop until his legs pressed against her knees. The man held an orange tray in wide, hairy hands. "Your name is Leeha Ritsagin, right?"

"Yes."

"I'm glad to see you're awake. Are you hungry?"

She nodded.

He set the tray on the table. Leeha eyed a sandwich and a glass of water.

"If you're hungry, Ritsagin, then eat."

She guzzled water and devoured the sandwich.

The guard said, "Doctor Palchero will be happy to hear you have an appetite. I have a few questions for you. If you cooperate, I'll bring you something soft to lie on, maybe even a pillow and blanket. Would you like that?"

She nodded again.

The man pulled an autopad from his pocket and unfolded the device on the tabletop. "Tell me who this woman is and where I can find her."

Leeha saw a fuzzy image. Panic struck; the woman in the photo resembled Cookie Davis. Leeha took a closer look. The cheekbones and chin weren't quite the same. Cookie was prettier. "I'm sorry, I don't know who she is."

The guard slammed a giant fist against the table. "You're lying! Tell me the truth."

"I am telling you the truth."

The man's mean-looking, wide face neared hers. His breath stank. "This woman was in your apartment."

"If she was, she was there when I wasn't home."

This time, both of his fists punched the table. "I want the truth. I want it now. No more games, understand?"

"The truth is, I don't know this lady."

He spoke into a tiny, cylinder-shaped gadget attached to his collar. "Come get her. She's not cooperating."

Two men burst into the room. Each man grabbed one of her arms. They forced her to her feet.

"But I am cooperating!" she said. "It's the honest truth. I don't know the lady in the photo. I swear!"

The guard glowered. "We don't tolerate liars. Gentlemen, follow me." He walked out of the room.

The men holding her arms dragged her down a long corridor. Dark, vault-like doors lined both white walls. The guard opened one of the doors. Cold, damp air belched out from a pitch-black room. The guard said, "Now, you'll understand what we do to liars. Get her inside."

The men shoved her into the gloomy room. Her knees smashed into the ground. The door clanged shut. All light vanished. She pounded on the steel door. "Please! Let me out! Let me out of here!" Her hands stung, but no one responded. "I didn't lie. I swear! I told you the truth. I don't know the woman. I don't!"

She searched for any trace of light. None existed. "You can't do this to me. Let me out! Let me out! I can't see. I can't see anything. Please don't leave me in here. Please! God, no!"

ENEMIES

Bob Fullerby opened the back door of the print shop.

Angela, Rona, and Kever were sitting at the old wooden table, their faces staring at their computer viewplanes. Anson and Cookie were standing by the counter.

Kever looked up. "Mr. Fullerby, I have good news and bad news."

Bob took a seat. "The bad news first, please."

"I hit a dead end on the National Fortress and Real Conspiracy stories. I got nowhere on tracking down the source of the leak. If there's information out there, it's not available to the public."

"Bummer! It's what I expected, but I was hoping otherwise. What's the good news?"

"You've arrived at the perfect time. Cookie and Anson are making lunch."

Anson set a bowl overflowing with leafy greens on the table. "Cookie and I are almost done, Mr. Fullerby."

"Thanks, I can use a break."

Angela pushed her computer aside. "What did Senator Seldortin have to say beyond his bombshell announcements?"

"It wasn't Bradley who dropped the bombshell. The Drop Case informant did. I have files to share, but first I have to fill you in on a few things."

Cookie placed a tray of dipping sauces and gourmet sandwiches on the tabletop. "It's about Leeha, isn't it, Mr. Fullerby?"

"It is."

"Is ... is she all right?"

"She's alive, but she's just arrived at Hansen Hills."

"Leeha's a prisoner?"

"I'm afraid so."

Cookie slumped into a chair. "Mr. Fullerby, can we visit her?"

"No, we can't. Despite Bradley's announcement, the Hills is still an illegal prison."

Anson brought tea and took a seat. "Mr. Fullerby, who's in charge at the Hills? General Willirman?"

"Actually, Senator Rineburg is calling the shots." Bob poured himself a cup of tea and said, "Row, there's something you need to know as well. Degio Ellis is also at the Hills. So is Candy Fellerman."

"Are they okay?"

"I don't know. The only thing I learned is that Degio and Candy don't know anything about the Guiding Light."

Tears brewed in Rona's eyes. "They don't know anything, but they haven't been released …. That's a bad sign, isn't it, Mr. Fullerby?"

"Probably. The only good news in all this is the bad guys still don't have the document. Willirman has people in Tahagaruza searching for Randy Altholder, but, so far, they haven't found him or the Guiding Light. We do—"

"Wait, wait!" Cookie said. "Mr. Fullerby, who's Randy Altholder?"

"Oh, that's right. We haven't shared everything with you. General Willirman thinks Leeha stole the document for a fellow with that name."

"Leeha's never mentioned him," Cookie said. "Mr. Fullerby, how does she know this guy?"

"They went to secondary school together."

"Hmm, Leeha went to school in Oakwood. What's he doing in Tahagaruza?"

"Hiding out in places where the police don't go. He's involved with a gang called the *Rustlers*. Cookie, did Leeha ever mention that gang?"

"No, of that, I'm certain."

Bob handed Rona a memory stick. "Here are the files the Drop Case informant gave me. I must warn you; the news is disturbing."

Rona linked the memory stick to her computer.

An image of a dark room appeared on the wall monitor. Except for an old toilet and a pile of bedding, the room was empty. Rough concrete served as the walls and floor.

Rona stared at the image. "Mr. Fullerby, what is this place?"

"It's a cell at the Hills. If Leeha doesn't cooperate with Rineburg's interrogators, this will be where they'll put her."

Cookie's whole body trembled. "They're putting Leeha in that awful place? Where are the windows? Look how dirty and dark it is! It's like a cave. She'll be terrified. We've got to do something! Mr. Fullerby, we've got to get her out."

"People are on it. I've told Bradley and Richard what's going on."

"Mr. Fullerby, that's not enough! We have to do more."

"Listen, Cookie, I know how difficult this is for you, but Bradley Seldortin and Richard Karther are the two people best equipped to deal with this situation."

Ver-Nuvelin, Domataland
FRIDAY, MAY 5, YEAR 1007 EE
8:00 A.M., CENTRAL FEWWOK TIME

President Demnar Tarish walked into the Ministry of Defense war room.

Defense Minister Rivar Henik rushed to greet him. He bowed. "Honorable President, we have a situation."

"What happened?"

"A Cadonan X-class submersible is sending unusual signals. I'll show you on the sit-globe."

Demnar followed Rivar to the huge situation globe that floated in the room.

Rivar said, "Display the Warm Sea, grids alpha-five-niner through oscar-seven-niner."

An ethereal map of the central Warm Sea area appeared in front of them. Rivar pointed at a blue, triangular-shaped blip. It hovered in the lower reaches of the Warm Sea, due south of the Port of Naltuk. "This is the X-class that sent the signals."

"What do you know about the signals?" Demnar asked.

"Not much, Honorable President. They're faint. The sender took advantage of ocean currents and undersea landforms to channel the signals to Naltuk."

"What type of signals?"

"Nonsensical. Just noise, but even without Whisper, we would've been able to detect them, but only from Naltuk."

"Rivar, how many times has this happened?"

"This is the third, Honorable President."

"Might the submersible be in trouble? An accident or malfunction due to the storms around the Djoyouzdolom continent, perhaps?"

"Maybe," Rivar said, "but it doesn't explain why they'd focus a signal toward our base instead of one of their own ships or an allied port in Visstel."

Demnar put himself in the shoes of the vessel's commander. His boat floated like a ghost beneath the waves. Why would he direct a signal to an enemy naval base? "Rivar, could the X-class crew be trying to communicate with us?"

"That exact thought has occurred to me, Honorable President, but I have no idea why they'd do it."

A young officer said, "Excuse me, Honorable President ... Minister Henik ... Intelligence Chief Kolensha is here."

Rozula looked like a model strutting down a runway at a fashion show. Shiny, pale curls bounced about her shoulders. She bowed. "Good morning, Honorable President. Rivar, have you learned more about the signals?"

"No, except that it happened a third time."

Rozula's pastel, opal blue eyes fixed on the triangle. "I'll put feelers out with my contacts in Cadona. Let's see if the Cadonan Navy has a rogue submersible crew. Not everyone in Undersea Command is thrilled with General Willirman and the Freedom Party."

"We need to be careful, Rozula," Demnar said. "We still haven't figured out who leaked Silver Star capabilities. Cadona could be playing with us to learn about Whisper."

"Understood, Honorable President."

"Rivar," Demnar said, "could you show me a sit-map of Cadona's strategic deployments?"

Rivar tapped a virtual display panel. A two-dimensional, situation map appeared. "Honorable President, green marks are known Cadonan assets and red, suspected."

Demnar studied the patterns of green and red blips. "It looks like Cadona's posturing is offensive against us ... but defensive against the rest of the world."

Rivar highlighted a spot on the map. "Except for some offensive posturing here, around northeastern Sohn-Sur, you're correct," Rivar said. "We're Cadona's prime enemy." He expanded the image of the Warm Sea area. "Honorable President, another shift is growing. Not only is Cadona tightening its grip on Izvyona, but also on Ostollia and separatists in northern Fletchia. Cadonan forces are targeting our southwestern flank."

"And Toxic Sphere?" Demnar asked. "What's the status, Rivar?"

"They're making incremental progress, but the Allegiance Party is blocking funding due to their economic crisis."

Rozula said, "But it's likely the weapon will eventually get funding, Honorable President. If the Freedom Party takes control of the legislature in July, and if Mitch Fischer is elected president in October, Toxic Sphere will get its money."

"Rozula," Demnar said, "every day, asymmetric warfare becomes more important. Any word on the Guiding Light?"

"Yes. The document hasn't been found, but Leeha Ritsagin is now a prisoner in Hansen Hills. All indications—she'll be tortured. We're putting together a plan to break her out."

"What's the plan, Rozula?"

"The call's gone out for a protest at the Hills. If the crowd gets big enough, it may give us the cover we need to get people inside and break Lady Ritsagin out."

"Rozula," Rivar said, "how can someone get inside undetected?"

"The Cadonan military is trying to hide what they're doing at the Hills, so perimeter security isn't advanced. A fancy system would draw suspicion."

"What are the chances your plan will work?" Demnar asked.

"Below thirty percent, Honorable President, but it may be our only opportunity."

Demnar nodded. "Do it, Rozula."

Hansen Hills, Cadona ...

A shiver roused Leeha Ritsagin from sleep. Why was she freezing?

She sat up.

What was wrong? She couldn't see!

She rubbed her eyes but still couldn't see.

Blind! She'd gone blind! How did it happen?

Wait! Something about a dark room .... That was it! Men in uniforms had locked her in a dark room. She remembered a door. It was big and made of steel. She must find it.

She reached into the blackness. Only air met her fingers.

Leeha jumped to her feet. She swung her arms in all directions but felt nothing.

At last, her hands touched a hard, cold surface.

An awful realization struck. The surface felt like stone, not metal. What she'd found wasn't the door.

She searched and searched.

It took a while, but her fingers found a straight, smooth frame and then a handle.

The door! She'd found it.

She rested her cheek against the cold steel.

A different kind of chill ran through her—the scary kind. A muffled noise echoed through the darkness. Tick … tick … tick tick tick.

Was someone there? She held her breath and listened.

The rhythm didn't change. Tick … tick. Water! It sounded like dripping water.

Out of nowhere, the need to urinate struck. She must find a toilet. If she peed herself, she'd freeze for sure.

Memories of a movie she'd seen years ago came to her. A boy had witnessed a crime. The criminals dumped him in a cave. The boy decided to search for a way out. In case he needed to circle back, he kept a hand on a wall and counted his steps.

She'd do the same thing as the boy.

Leeha put her hand on the wall. She counted each step as her palm slid along the rough stone.

One. Two. Three. Four. Five.

She reached another wall.

No sign of a toilet.

She followed the second wall.

At step number six, her right toes kicked something soft. She bent down and felt a pile of cloth. Something thin and spongy lay beneath it. Whatever the spongy thing was, it had square edges.

Bedding! It was bedding! She picked up a blanket to ward off the cold.

The blanket stank of mildew. She dropped the cloth—freezing was better than the stink.

Eight more paces took her to another corner. She followed the third wall.

At step thirteen, her toes hit something hard. With a foot, she traced the outline of the object.

It might be a toilet!

Her hands confirmed it; a toilet it was!

She fumbled with the button and zipper of her jeans. She pulled her pants down just in time.

Her bladder released its contents.

Something didn't sound right as urine sprayed into the bowl. It reminded her of outhouses she'd used when she went camping with her grandparents.

Toilet paper! What if there wasn't toilet paper?

Her hands groped the wall and floor. She found something soft.

Thank goodness! She'd found a roll of paper. It felt damp. She took a whiff. No funny odors.

Leeha peeled off only a few squares; her abductors, no doubt, wouldn't be inclined to bring more tissue.

She pushed down on the toilet handle to flush. Nothing happened. She pushed up, pulled out, and pressed in. Nothing. Disgusting!

Now, it was time to find a sink.

One more long step took her to another corner.

So far, no sink, but she did hear dripping water.

At step seven along wall number four, she found the source of the sound. Water seeped out from a chest-high spot in the wall. The water didn't flow in a stream, or even a trickle. Rather, an occasional drop managed to make its way out from the wall and plop onto the floor.

Seven more steps took her to another corner. If the room was four-sided, this should be the wall with the door. What if it wasn't? What if she never found the door again?

Her heart pounded. Step seven, step eight, step nine.

She reached the door!

Leeha rested her head against it. Comfort came from knowing light and warmth lay on the other side. Her quest to find a sink, however, had failed.

She crouched down and wrapped her arms around her knees. Her stomach growled from hunger. She shivered. Mildew-infested blankets no longer seemed as gross. She made her way to the spongy mattress and draped a ragged quilt over her.

The black behind her eyelids turned red. She opened her eyes. A streak of brilliant light poured through the doorway.

Three people approached. They appeared as ghostly silhouettes.

They stopped walking. A sharp, female voice said, "Get her up."

A man spoke. "Will do, Doctor."

Leeha watched as two men walked toward her. As they drew near, she saw their guard uniforms.

The men hoisted her to her feet and dragged her out of the cell. The bright lights in the hallway pierced her eyes, but the warm, dry air felt good on her chilled skin.

She tripped over her own feet as the guards towed her down the hall.

The doctor led the way. The formfitting, white suit she wore had a medical appearance, yet the cut of the clothing revealed a tall, slender, shapely body. Her shiny, black hair, pulled severely into a bun, glistened in the stark lighting.

"Where are you taking me?" Leeha asked.

No one answered.

She looked around. She recognized the dark doors and white walls; she'd seen them when the guards first took her to the dank cell. How much time had passed since then? She'd no idea.

The doctor-in-white stopped walking. She opened a door, this one normal looking.

Beyond the doorway lay a stark, bright room. Medical-like beds and odd devices lined the walls.

"Put her on the table," the doctor-in-white said.

The room had a sinister look. "What is this place?" Leeha asked.

No one spoke.

She struggled to free herself, but the guards were too strong. They dragged her to a narrow table. Her body rose and turned. Moments later, her back pressed into a cold, unpadded surface.

"Tie her down," the doctor-in-white said.

Leeha watched as one of the men stretched a thick band across her chest.

"Don't! Please don't tie me up. I beg you."

Without saying a word, the guards next strapped her legs and arms to the railings.

Leeha saw the doctor's face for the first time. At once, she was both beautiful and horrifying. High cheekbones, a straight nose, and a symmetric jawline all had a sharpness to them, like drawings of demons from religion class. The doctor's dark eyes, though large and striking, unmasked a heartless soul. Patches of pockmarks dimpled her tight skin. "Leeha Ritsagin, where is the Guiding Light?"

"The what?"

"Don't play games with me! The Guiding Light document, where is it?"

That's it! The Guiding Light must be the name of the weird document! She mustn't give up its location. "I don't know."

"Where can we find Randy Altholder?"

"I don't know."

"What's the name of the Sohn-Suran woman who's helping you?"

"There's no Sohn-Suran woman helping me."

A sharp pain burned in her right arm.

The doctor-in-white glared at her. "Do you want me to do that again?"

"No! It hurt."

"Then you'd better start talking. Let's try again. Where is the Guiding Light?"

Leeha knew she must say something, something that didn't contradict the story she'd told the people who'd used Mind-One on her. "I left it in an office."

"Whose office?"

"Someone named Jenton."

"Do you mean Jenton's Auto Body and Repair?"

Leeha knew she must lie. "Yes."

"Who at Jenton's is working with you?"

"No one."

"You're lying!"

Another shock raced up her arm. "I'm not! I'm not lying. I swear!"

"Then why did you leave the Guiding Light at Jenton's?"

"I was scared. I didn't want to get in trouble. I just wanted to get rid of the document. I saw an office. The door was open. No one was in the room. I put the document on a guest chair."

"What happened to the document after that?"

"I don't know. I left. I didn't want to get caught."

"How do you contact Randy Altholder?"

Her mind raced. She must be careful. She mustn't contradict herself. "I don't contact him. He contacts me."

"When will he contact you next?"

"I don't know. He may never contact me again."

"Why not?"

"I gave him what he wanted. I gave him a copy of the document."

"Why did he want it?"

"For a better life; a chance for a better future."

"How would the document give him a better life?"

"I don't know."

Another burst of pain ran up her arm.

"You're lying, Ritsagin."

"I'm not. I swear."

"Understand this, Ritsagin. I have two gifts. One—I know how to make people talk. Two—I know when someone's fibbing, and you're fibbing." The doctor-in-white spoke to the guards. "We'll need to take this to the next level."

One of the guards grabbed her head.

"What ... what are you going to do?" Leeha asked.

No one answered.

The second guard pulled a thick strap across her forehead.

Leeha tried to turn her head. She couldn't. "Please! Please don't do this. I can't move. Please, stop!"

The doctor-in-white said, "You leave me no choice, Ritsagin. You lied."

Leeha watched as a white towel neared her face. Soon, she saw nothing but the woven threads of the cloth. "Oh, God! Please! Please don't do this. Take it off. Please!"

Plop, plop, plop. Something was striking the towel. The cloth grew wet. "What's going on? What are you doing?"

The doctor-in-white said, "We'll leave her alone awhile."

Leeha heard footsteps and then the sound of a door shutting.

Drip. Drip. Drip. The water kept coming. The wet towel clung to her nose, then her mouth, then her eyes. "Please! I can't breathe. Please, make it stop."

She heard nothing except the tapping of the drops.

A memory returned—an awful one. In the memory, her body tossed about. Lapping water distorted her view of a swimming pool's blue wall. She struggled to grab the side; it remained out of reach. Up above, light rippled through the waves, but her body wouldn't rise. Water poured down her throat.

Recollections of that grueling day kept coming. It was her first year of secondary school. She had pleaded with teachers to excuse her from swim lessons. The pleas went unanswered.

The memories sharpened.

A physical education instructor forced her into a pool.

Deep water threatened to pull her feet away from the bottom.

Leeha felt the teacher's hands on her calves.

Her feet went up. Water gushed over her face and roared in her ears. Her nose burned.

Leeha stretched out her arms. She grasped the edge of the pool.

The teacher dragged her away from the side.

Again, her feet left the bottom. Her head fell into the water.

Like a miracle, a bell rang. Class had ended.

The teacher pulled her upright.

Leeha scrambled out of the pool.

A poolside shower was free. She darted straight for it.

The showerhead was spraying water on her face when hands clutched her arms.

Whoever the people were, they dragged her out of the shower.

Then she saw them: four girls from the cheerleading squad. Two of the girls pulled her forward while two others pushed from behind.

They forced her onto the diving board.

The world seemed a blur. Far below, students standing by the poolside howled in delight. Beneath the skinny diving board, ripples of blue water sparkled.

The cheerleaders dived into the pool. Their jumps made the board quiver.

Something went wrong. Leeha fell. Down and down, she tumbled.

Her body smashed into the water. She couldn't breathe. Her vision dimmed.

Leeha felt an arm around her. Her chest hurt, but air rushed into her lungs. A woman's voice commanded others to stop laughing.

When Leeha opened her eyes, she saw a white-haired lady in a nurse's cap.

A shudder roused Leeha from unconsciousness. Once again, she experienced the real world. The white cloth still covered her face. No nurse would save her now.

She heard voices.

Someone pulled the wet towel off her face. The doctor-in-white glared down at her. "Let's see if you'll be more cooperative this time. Tell me what you know about the Guiding Light."

"I ... I read parts of it, but not the whole thing."

The doctor's face disappeared from view. She said, "Gentlemen, please wait outside."

"Doctor," a male's voice said, "I don't think it's a good idea. She's an enemy apparent. She's dangerous."

"She's secured. Ritsagin won't be able to hurt me." The doctor's face reappeared. "But I'll be able to hurt her."

A man said, "We'll be right outside, Doctor."

Leeha heard footsteps and the sound of a slamming door.

The doctor's nostrils flared. "It's just you and me now, Ritsagin. Tell me what you read in the Guiding Light."

"I … I remember a list of women's names and addresses. This list is called the justice execution list. I didn't think too much about it at first, but then I heard on the news that a woman named Mary Kronvelt was murdered. Mary's name was the first one on the list. That's when I started to believe the document was real and not just something someone made up."

"Do you know what, Ritsagin? I believe you. You're telling the truth. What else did you read?"

"Whoever wrote the document doesn't like Bob Fullerby, the reporter guy. They want to silence him."

"Do you know Bob Fullerby?"

"Not in person, but I like him. He's a good reporter."

"You've never met him? Not even in passing?"

"No."

"Has he ever contacted you?"

"Never."

"Have you ever contacted him?"

"No."

"Ritsagin, do you know Detective Carl Brunish or Senator Sandra Pettock?"

"I know who they are, but only from the news."

A slight smile curled the doctor's red lips. "I'm pleased with you, Ritsagin. You're telling me the truth. What else did you read?"

Leeha feared saying too much. "I don't remember anything else."

"You're lying again, Ritsagin."

"I'm not! I'm not lying."

The doctor's voice was piercing. "Guards!"

Footsteps tapped against the floor.

"Take her back to her cell," the doctor-in-white said.

The men unfastened the straps and yanked her off the table.

"I'm dizzy!"

The doctor-in-white said, "Too bad, Ritsagin. Guards, get her out of here."

"Please don't take me back to that dark place. Please!"

They dragged her down the hall. The door to her cell was open. They pushed her inside. The door closed. All light vanished.

She pounded on the cold steel. "Please! Can I have a light? Please!"

Dripping water made the only sounds.

IZVYONSK-BAKHADAREE CONFLICT

"Brave sailors of Domataland, never shall the people
of Bakhadaland forget you or your sacrifice."

Goodwill Ship Memorial
Year 1007 of the
Enlightened Epoch

Cadona City, Cadona
SATURDAY, MAY 6, YEAR 1007 EE
11:00 A.M., EAST CADONA TIME

Bob Fullerby parked his old, long, maroon-colored car behind Ben's and
Bertha's shops.

After climbing out of the vehicle, he spotted his neighbor. Ben held a stuffed garbage bag in his left hand. The wrinkled skin of his bony right arm jiggled as he waved. "Mornin', Bob. How you feelin'?"

"Not bad. I slept in my own bed last night for a change. I crash at work too often."

Ben pointed toward the roof of his three-story building. "Bertha and I always sleep at work."

"At least you have a short commute," Bob said.

Ben let out a cheery laugh. "We sure do—a walk down the stairs. Well, good to see you, Bob. Have a good one." He stuffed the plump garbage bag into a dumpster and disappeared through the back door of the hardware store.

Bob squeezed through a gap in the fence that separated Ben's and Bertha's property from the print shop's parking lot.

Kever Carsen's bicycle, Angela Thirgal's old pickup truck, Anson Dailey's compact automobile, and Rona Betler's tiny car were parked near the back door of the hideaway office. With luck, his team cooked another yummy meal. His smidgeon of a breakfast had already worn off.

He pulled open the vault-like back door of the building. Bags of chips, fruit bars, and pretzels rested on the table. Coffee aroma filled the air, but he saw no sign of a big lunch.

Kever, Anson, Angela, and Rona were huddled around the wall monitor. A topographic map displayed on the viewplane. Cookie was nowhere in sight.

Anson seemed excited. "Mr. Fullerby, you're just in time. We've come up with a plan."

Bob recognized the map. It showed the area around the Hansen Hills Federal Facility. "What plan?"

Kever said, "When we heard Leeha Ritsagin was taken to Hansen Hills, Anson and I got an idea. The cliffs around the Hills have great rock-climbing routes. We're planning to do some climbing and have a look at the compound."

"Why would you do that, Kever-o?" Bob asked.

"From what we can tell, the defenses around the Hills aren't too robust. Maybe we can find a way to get inside and spring Leeha."

Had his team members lost their minds? "Kever-o, that's out of the question."

"But, Mr. Fullerby—"

Bob raised his hand. "No! Kever-o, it's madness. It's too dangerous. Ang, talk to these young men. Explain to them how risky it is."

"I can't do that, Mr. Fullerby," Angela said.

"Why not?"

"Because it's actually not a bad idea. A call's gone out on WorldLink. People from all over the country are organizing a protest at the gates of Hansen Hills."

Rona spoke with the blind enthusiasm of youth. "We've been doing exciting stuff, Mr. Fullerby. Ang and I wrote articles for the Andecco newsfeed to inspire more people to get involved in the demonstration."

Bob shook his head. "What's going on here? Group-think insanity?"

Anson said, "Not at all, Mr. Fullerby. Think about it; big crowds may give Kever-o and me the cover we need to slip inside and get Leeha out."

Cookie joined them. She looked sleepy, as if she'd just woken from a nap. "How awesome! I'm in."

Bob wagged his finger. "No, you're not *in*. That goes for all of you. I forbid it."

"Mr. Fullerby," Angela said, "Anson's right. If there's a huge protest, Andecco News Service reporters have a perfectly valid reason to be there. We couldn't ask for a better opportunity."

"No! Let Senator Seldortin handle it."

"Pardon me, Mr. Fullerby," Kever said, "but that might take too long. Leeha's in danger."

This was one of those moments when Kever felt like his son. "Kever-o, I can't let you do this. It's out of the question."

A serious expression covered Kever's face. "You don't understand, Mr. Fullerby. I'm going to Hansen Hills, and I am going to break Leeha Ritsagin out."

"And I'm going with him," Anson said.

Even Angela succumbed to madness. "So am I."

Rona said, "I'm in, too."

"You better believe I'm in," Cookie said. "We need to get Leeha out of that awful place."

Kever leaned over the tabletop. "Mr. Fullerby, we could really use your help. In your thirty-plus years as an investigative journalist, you've been in a lot of sticky situations."

"I will have no part of this. I will not participate in something that will likely get you all killed. We're dealing with ruthless people here, folks."

Angela said, "'*The role of an investigative journalist is to protect citizens from their leaders.*' Do you remember those words, Mr. Fullerby?"

"I remember. I was young and foolish back then. Listen to what I'm telling you now, not some garbage I uttered over twenty years ago."

Kever said, "So, you won't help us, Mr. Fullerby?"

"Absolutely not, Kever-o."

"Then we'll do it ourselves."

Cadona City, Cadona
SATURDAY, MAY 6, YEAR 1007 EE
8:30 P.M., EAST CADONA TIME

Raymond Corder straightened a pile of crinkled papers and peered out the big windows of Jenton's Auto Body and Repair. The same two suspicious vans were parked along the street. The vehicles had been coming and going all day.

"You still here, Ray?" Clyde Jenton said.

"Yes, sir. I finished entering the last stack of info into the system."

"Thanks, Ray. I hope the computers don't go on the fritz again. That was quite a mess."

"It sure was. Keeping paper records is no fun. Hey, Mr. Jenton, has there been any word on Degio or Candy?"

"Nope, nothing. Something's fishy; neither one of them would run off and vanish like that. I'm going to bug the cops again tomorrow." Mr.

Jenton's wide-knuckled fingers rested on Ray's shoulder. "Come on, Ray, get out of here. You worked another long day."

"On my way, sir; I'm shutting down the system, and then I'm gone."

Mr. Jenton ambled into his office. Soon, the sound of a news report about the Izvyonsk-Bakhadaree conflict flowed through the office doorway.

Ray laughed. What was it about old guys and listening to the news?

The last computer lights flickered out. "Good night, Mr. Jenton!" Ray grabbed his satchel and headed toward the exit.

He heard a whine. Shards of glass struck his body.

Mr. Jenton bolted into the lobby. "What's that racket?"

"The glass, it just shattered."

"Did someone throw a brick?"

"Not that I saw."

"Call the cops."

Ray tapped his personal device. "There's no signal, sir."

"No signal? That doesn't make sense. Stay back. Some of these frag-ments are sharp." Glass crunched beneath the soles of Mr. Jenton's shoes as he crept to the door. He inspected the doorframe and window edges. "What the heck did this?"

Ray saw shadowy forms moving along the edge of the building. Their bodies appeared transparent, like fluttering cellophane. "Mr. Jenton, be careful, I think someone's out—"

One of the shapes transformed. A man in combat gear stood there. A gloved hand grabbed Mr. Jenton's throat. The attacker was strong; a shove sent Mr. Jenton sailing across the lobby. His body slumped onto a couch.

Three other men materialized. All of them wore camouflage and weird masks.

Ray froze as one of the assailants approached. A voice came through a featureless face cover. "Are you Raymond Corder?"

"Y ... yes."

"Mr. Corder, you go by *Ray*, correct?"

"Yeah."

"Ray, were you involved in the theft?"

"Theft of what?"

The man said, "Are you acquainted with Degio Ellis and Candy Fellerman?"

"Yeah, they work here. They've been missing. Do you know where they are?"

"Ray, what do you know about the document?"

"What document? Is that why Degio and Candy are missing? Did they do something with a document?"

The man didn't respond. Instead, he walked up to Mr. Jenton. "What about you, old man?"

Mr. Jenton tried to act tough, but his voice trembled. "I don't know what you're talking about. Have you done something to Degio and Candy?"

"Look, Clyde, we know you're involved. Where is it?"

"Where's what?"

The intruder swung his arm. The back of his hand smacked Mr. Jenton's head. "You're lying, old man. I know the bitch left the document on a guest chair in your office. What did you do with it?"

Mr. Jenton pulled himself upright. "Both of my guest chairs are in my office. I haven't done anything with either of them."

The man grabbed hold of Mr. Jenton's overalls suspenders. "I'm not talking about the damned chairs, idiot. I'm talking about the document the bitch left in your office."

"What bitch? What document? I haven't the slightest idea what you're talking about."

"The bitch in the brown Monarch. She left the document in your office. It's no use lying."

"Look, I don't know what Degio and Candy did. The only thing I know is the two of them went missing."

The attacker pressed Mr. Jenton against the seatback of the sofa. The man made a fist.

Ray's shock turned to anger. "Stop it! Stop hurting him!" Ray didn't see the kick coming until it was too late; his body crashed onto the floor. The toe of a combat boot struck his left temple. Light faded. A ring pealed in his ears.

"Ray," the man said, "do you wish to live?"

"Yes."

"Then tell me, Ray; what do you know about the brown Monarch and its owner?"

"I know federal agents had questioned Degio Ellis and Mr. Jenton about a brown Monarch sedan. I never knew why the car was important. After Degio and Candy disappeared, I got curious. I found information about the owner in our restored computer files. The owner is a woman. She often brings her car here for service. The only reason I know this is because she's listed as a *valued customer*, but I don't remember anything about her—not her name, her age, what she looks like, where she lives, nothing."

"When she'd bring the Monarch in for service, did she come alone? With a girlfriend? A boyfriend?"

"I don't know. Like I told you, I don't remember anything about her."

Ray felt a blow to his neck. He struggled to breathe. His body weakened. He heard thumps and bangs. Mr. Jenton shouted in agony.

After more racket, all grew quiet except the voice of a newsman describing international upheaval because of the sinking of the Domataree Goodwill Ship in D'nevtnya, Bakhadaland.

D'nevtnya, Bakhadaland
SATURDAY, MAY 6, YEAR 1007 EE
2:00 P.M., WARM SEA TIME

Ina Ruzh-Venkina wished her sister and mother would let her walk on her own. Entwined arms complicated what should be a simple task of placing one foot in front of the other.

A gust of wind blew her purple headscarf over her face. The lightweight slippers she wore provided little protection when she stubbed her toe on a bump in the sidewalk.

Culasa's grip tightened. "Ina, are you okay?"

"Yes."

"Are you sure? Do you need to rest?"

"No, Culasa, I'm fine. Stop being so big-sisterly."

Tinsa said, "Inalenta, if you need to stop, let us know. We've plenty of time; we won't miss the ceremony."

"Momma, I'm okay, really."

"All right, Inalenta, but be sure to tell us if you need a break."

Their pace slowed. Other people making their way to the Goodwill Ship Memorial weaved around them like a river swirling around a stone.

"Momma, we don't have to walk so slowly."

"Yes, we do. You almost fell."

"I tripped because my scarf blew over my face, and I couldn't see where I was going. Besides, everyone was already staring at us. Plodding along makes us stand out even more."

"I thought you wanted to wear the mourning robe, Inalenta," Tinsa said.

"I do. I want to honor Rosik, and the tradition shows my respect for him—I know that. But I remember staring at widows myself. Women look so old wearing the purple. They all look like babbagurdies. Then there are all the questions—how did their husbands die? Did the Izvyon kill them? Did they get hurt and couldn't get medicine because of the blockade? I just don't want people to look at me and think all those things."

A murmur flowed through the crowd on the street.

"What's going on?" Culasa asked.

Ina saw the familiar shapes of warships on the horizon. "The Izvyonsk Navy is here, Culasa."

"Are those them, Ina? Are they Sea Ghosts?"

"The long, low ones are."

"Ina," Culasa said, "wasn't it a Sea Ghost that sank the Goodwill Ship and killed Rosik?"

"Yeah, Sea Ghosts are Cadonan made, so they're the most dangerous."

Culasa looked worried. "Ina, are they close enough to hit the Memorial?"

"Yes, easily."

The mood of the crowd changed.

Tinsa said, "Why are people cheering?"

Ina squinted as she raised her face skyward. Tiny, ethereal globes spun against the blue heavens. "The Domataree Air Force is here, Momma. They call the aircraft *Silver Star*."

Tinsa shielded her pale eyes with a delicate, gold-toned hand. "I ... I thought the new Domataree warplanes were shaped like sickles. Those things in the sky, they look like spinning waterdrops."

"They can change shape. Rosik told me it's a type of weapon Domataland has that Cadona doesn't."

Hopeful tones rang in Culasa's words. "Ina, can Silver Star stop Sea Ghosts?"

"Yes."

Tinsa said, "Then why didn't Silver Star protect the Goodwill Ship?"

Ina's heart ached. "Because the Izvyon learned secrets about Silver Star."

"What kind of secrets?"

"If a Sea Ghost gets close enough, Silver Star can't stop a light-strike. If the secrets hadn't been leaked, Rosik and Garrett might not have died. I doubt the Domats will make the same mistake again."

"I certainly hope not," Tinsa said, "or we'll be having more funerals. Our men and Tarmalenta are at the Memorial."

"Not to fear, Momma," Culasa said. "The three of us will be there soon. Then we can all die together."

Tinsa's voice was almost a whisper. "Together ... yes, I like the sound of that."

The thought of dying with her family gave Ina a wave of comfort, too. At the same time, she considered things yet to be done. "Some of us have stuff to finish, Momma. Zerin and Tarma are in love. They should get a chance to enjoy each other's company, at least for a little while." She then recalled a scene of her niece and nephews playing in a yard. "Culasa, you and Temlin have kids to raise. As for me, I want to avenge Rosik's death before I die."

Tinsa pulled her close. "My daughter, the philosopher."

They arrived at the Goodwill Ship Memorial. The shadow beneath the roof cast an aura of gloom. Ina said, "Can we sit in the sun? The shade feels so … depressing."

Tinsa's voice was that of a mother doting over a suffering child. "We can sit anywhere you'd like, Inalenta."

They found seats in the bleachers.

Culasa pointed toward the stage. "Look! I see Tarma. And there's Zerin."

"And I see our men folk," Tinsa said. "They must've finished giving their advice." She waved her arms over her head.

Ina looked into the crowd. She spotted Maktar, Temlin, and Solomor. Her father and brother-in-law wore the dress uniforms of Civil Defense officers. Her big brother wore the striking regalia of a National Defender commander.

Tinsa waved again. This time, Maktar waved back. The three men headed toward the bleachers.

"Momma," Ina said, "you could've also been down there giving advice. And you, too, Culasa. You didn't need to miss out to stay with me."

Tinsa said, "Culaslenta and I chose to stay with you. Besides, you're my daughter, and your husband was a hero. He died protecting us."

"Yes, my Rosik was a hero, but I missed out on hearing advice, and you missed out on giving it."

"Your time will come, Ina," Culasa said. "Your widow status will end, and you will be sworn in as a full-time National Defender, just like Tarma. Then you'll hear our advice."

Music played—military music. Those taking oaths walked onto the stage.

Ina said, "Zerin played those songs so many times when he was in the Youth Corps. It's hard to believe that this time he's on stage to be sworn in."

Tinsa said, "It is hard to believe. I'm told it's been five years since a seventeen-year-old was commissioned as a Civil Defense fourth lieutenant."

As Maktar, Temlin, and Solomor took seats in the bleachers, Tinsa said, "Look, Inalenta! Your friends Pada, Sulana, and Benid are here."

"Yes, I see them," Ina said.

They sat in the row behind her.

Tinsa said, "Sulana Ruzh-Tomavina, is your daughter okay?"

"She's well, thank you for asking, Lady Ruzh-Tovaleta. She had night-mares again last night, though. She's anxious to return home to Lestnya."

"It's a shame our children are exposed to such fear," Tinsa said, "but I'm relieved to hear your little Adela is healthy. Ruzhman Tomavin, will you be put on active duty?"

"I'm sure I will," Benid said. "I don't have an activation date yet, but I'm ready. I don't like the idea of leaving Sulana and Adelalenta, though."

Ina felt a small hand on her shoulder. Pada Rammak said, "It's a lovely tribute, don't you think, Ina, that they've chosen to have the swearing-in ceremony at the Memorial instead of the parade field?"

"Yes, it's a beautiful tribute to Rosik, Garrett, and all the sailors who died on the Goodwill Ship." Ina wished to say more. Pada had given her a Shinchik-style robe to wear as a wedding dress; she'd never told Pada how much Rosik loved the outfit. Then there was the time Rosik and Garrett had hidden in the Shinchik restaurant while performing a clandestine mission for the Domataree government; she'd never thanked Pada for sending her the secret message. If not for that message, she would've missed out on marrying the great love of her life. Ina wished to say many things, but if she spoke even one more word, tears would flow. She mustn't cry. This moment was for Tarma, Zerin, and all the Bakhadaree patriots about to be sworn in. Ina clenched her hands into fists. Her fingernails dug into her palms. The pain distracted her from waves of grief. This moment mustn't be about her. No matter what, she had to conceal her sorrow.

The music grew louder. Commander Samar took his place in the cen-ter of the stage. Tarma, Zerin, and all the others who were about to take an oath to defend Bakhadaland snapped to attention.

The Bakhadaree National Anthem began to play. Ina rose to her feet.

✧

Cadona City, Cadona
SUNDAY, MAY 7, YEAR 1007 EE
7:30 A.M., EAST CADONA TIME

Rona Betler peeked over Anson Dailey's shoulder. He was eating breakfast while staring at a computer. "What are you reading, Anson?"

"Catching up on what's going on in Bakhadaland."

"Anything interesting?"

"The situation looks like it's getting worse, like it's about ready to explode."

"What's going on over there?" she asked.

"They had a military ceremony at the Goodwill Ship Memorial. Izvyona has ships floating off the coast, and Domataland has aircraft circling overhead."

"You better watch out, Anson. We're going to convert you; you're going to become a reporter like us."

"Yeah, the print shop's starting to feel like a second home."

Kever Carsen walked out of the bathroom. His wet, dishwater blond hair twisted this way and that.

"Good morning, Kever-o," Rona said. "You're in luck; Ang isn't here yet."

He rubbed his head with a towel. "Why does that make me lucky?"

"Your messy hair would drive her nuts."

"My days are incomplete without her complaints."

Rona noticed the confused look on Anson's face. "Anson, you should know ... Kever-o and Ang have this ... thing. He does stuff that bugs her, Ang goes off, and he does stuff to make her even more annoyed. Honestly, I don't know what one would do without the other. They're like bookends, but you better squeeze lots of books between them to avoid fireworks."

"Fireworks?" Anson said. "Kever-o, is this relationship serious?"

Kever grinned as he poured himself a cup of coffee. "It better not be. The fire would be way too hot."

Rona felt her personal device buzz. The caller wasn't Detective Carl Brunish, as she expected. The voice sounded familiar, but the words were slurred.

"Ray, is that you?" she asked.

"Yeah. Did you hear what happened at the car shop last night?"

"No, what's going on?"

"Men in combat gear broke in just as we were closing for the day."

"Ray, where are you? Are you okay?"

"I will be. I'm at Salvation Hospital. Mr. Jenton is still in intensive care. Could you please come visit me? It kind of hurts to talk by PD."

"Sure, of course! I'll be right there."

Rona ended the call.

Anson said, "Hey, Row, what's up?"

"That guy, Ray, from Jenton's, is in the hospital. I'm going to visit him. His boss is in intensive care."

Kever said, "What happened?"

"Men in combat gear broke into the car shop last night. I have a feeling it has to do with Leeha Ritsagin and the brown Monarch. I'll see you guys later."

"Hold on one sec, Row," Anson said. "Someone should go with you. Kever-o needs to babysit Cookie, so that leaves me. I'm almost done with breakfast." He shoveled food into his mouth.

"This is all my fault!" Rona said. "I dragged Ray and Mr. Jenton into this. Degio and Candy, too."

"Row," Kever said, "you didn't drag anyone into this. The people at Jenton's got tied up in this mess because Leeha took her Monarch there for service."

Anson chewed his last bite of breakfast. "Kever-o's right, Row. Don't blame yourself."

Cookie leaned out of her bedroom doorway and said, "What's going on? Is Leeha okay?"

Kever said, "Some goons broke into Jenton's Auto Body and Repair last night. Row's friend, Ray, and his boss are in the hospital."

Cookie's eyes grew wide. "Oh, my! That's terrible! Row, are they going to be okay?"

"Mr. Jenton is still in intensive care, but Ray will be all right. Anson and I are running over to the hospital to see him."

Hansen Hills, Cadona ...

Leeha Ritsagin heard the cell door open.

Phlegm gurgled in her chest as she sat upright on the thin, spongy pad.

The doctor-in-white and two guards walked toward her.

They'd left the door open. This might be her chance to escape.

Leeha stood up. Her legs wobbled. She could hardly stand, let alone dash out the door. "What are you going to do to me this time?"

No one spoke. The guards grabbed her arms and towed her down the hall. The door to the bright torture room opened. "Please don't tie me on the table again. Please!"

The doctor-in-white said, "You're getting your wish. We're not going to put you on the table. Let's see how you like the spinner."

The spinner was a big contraption made of shiny wires bent to form a sphere. "What is that thing?"

"You're about to find out," the doctor-in-white said. "Strap her in."

One guard stretched her right arm over her head. He fastened a clamp to her right wrist. The other guard forced her left wrist into a different clamp.

The metal dug into her skin. "It's too tight. It hurts!"

"It's supposed to hurt," the doctor-in-white said. "That's the idea."

The guards took hold of her calves and put each ankle into a clamp.

"Make sure she's strapped in nice and tight," the doctor-in-white said.

Rods on the spinner pulled her limbs away from her body. "It hurts! Please, make it stop."

The doctor-in-white glared at her. "You want it to stop, Ritsagin?"

"Yes! Please! It hurts so bad."

"We'll release you when you tell us the truth. Who at Jenton's Auto Body and Repair conspired with you to steal the Guiding Light?"

"No one. I already told you the truth."

"No, Ritsagin, you didn't. You're holding something back."

"No, I'm not!"

"Did Randy Altholder or the Sohn-Suran woman pick up the document after you dropped it off?"

"I have no idea."

"Wrong answer," the doctor-in-white said. "Give her a spin."

One of the guards pushed on the sphere.

Leeha felt her body sway. Then the world whizzed by in a blur.

Bit by bit, the spinning slowed.

At last, the giant sphere came to a stop. Her neck hurt. She figured out why. She was hanging upside down. Her head angled to the left and her feet to the right.

"Let her hang awhile," the doctor-in-white said. "Maybe if she has time to think about her predicament, she'll be more cooperative."

The doctor and guards left the room.

Pain burned in Leeha's left shoulder. Her right arm went numb. Maybe if she moved a little to the left, the pain wouldn't be so bad. The wheel swayed. Her stomach churned. The wheel swayed again. Clumps of vomit poured into her mouth.

Her will to fight was nearing its end. She was almost broken, but she mustn't give up. Perhaps if she told her tormentors a true detail, she might live another day. Yet, she must be careful; she must keep the document away from those awful people.

She heard one set of footsteps. The doctor-in-white had returned. "So, Ritsagin, have you had a change of heart?"

Leeha tried to nod, but her neck hurt too much. "Yes."

"Good. What else did you read in the Guiding Light?"

"I read about Bakhadaland and Izvyona."

"What did the document say about them?"

"Someone in Cadona—someone involved with the document—wants to start a new war between the two countries."

"Why would Cadona want to do such a thing?"

"Because people in Cadona want to start a bigger war with Domataland."

"How would starting a new war between Bakhadaland and Izvyona start a war with Domataland?"

"Cadona is friends with Izvyona. Domataland is friends with Bakhadaland. The people who wrote the document want to force Domataland to help Bakhadaland, then we'd jump in to help Izvyona." Vomit burst into her mouth.

The doctor's voice was shrill. "Guards!"

Leeha's vision darkened. She was aware of hands on her shoulders and legs. Every time her body moved, she'd heave.

She heard the doctor-in-white say, "Wipe her up, give her fluids, and put her back in her cell. Give her a warm blanket. We have to keep her alive. She knows more than she's tellin'."

Leeha awoke in total darkness. The odor of mildew drifted on damp air. She realized where she was—in her prison cell.

Something had changed; an extra quilt covered her. The new blanket didn't stink as much as the others. She wrapped the fresh cloth over her head and shoulders.

As she settled into the bedding, something warm oozed between her legs. A twinge ran through her lower belly. She spoke into the darkness. "You've got to be joking!" Her period had started.

She dared not use toilet paper; there wasn't much left. Yet she needed to find something to soak up the blood. Leeha found the most tattered blanket and pulled as hard as she could, but a piece of fabric wouldn't rip away.

Her bra! She removed the undergarment. It was old; she knew where the little tears were. She yanked on the soft cloth.

It worked! A cup tore free. She shoved it between her legs. She hid the rest of the bra in the bedding to keep for later use.

Fatigue crept through her. She mustn't fall asleep; she needed to for-
mulate a plan to get out of this horrid place.

Leeha's body slumped into the cushion. Try as she might, she couldn't
keep her eyes open.

30

GOOD PEOPLE IN CADONA

Cadona City, Cadona
TUESDAY, MAY 9, YEAR 1007 EE
8:00 A.M., EAST CADONA TIME

Pastor Leon Walls checked the time. He was running late.

At last, the gilded, mirrored elevator came to a stop on level one thousand. He dashed out as soon as the doors glided open. A huge portrait of Beatrice Rineburg, John Rineburg's grandmother, scowled at him. Far in the distance, through enormous windows, he saw the gray-walled government buildings that stood on the west end of Capital Plaza.

A hostess in a black skirt and white blouse appeared. "Good morning, Pastor Walls, welcome to Beatrice Thousand. Senator John Rineburg, Senator Mitch Fischer, and General Douglass Willirman are waiting for you. This way, please."

Leon followed her across a pale, granite floor.

All of the tables in the northeast wing of the restaurant were empty except for one by a window. John, Mitch, and Doug were already seated. Breakfast food sat upon a white tablecloth.

The hostess said, "Senator Rineburg, Pastor Walls has arrived." She poured ice water into a glass and walked away.

Leon took a seat. "Good morning, gentlemen. What are we going to do about this mess?"

John took a bite of buttered toast. "Which one? We have several messes, Leon."

"I thought we were meeting again about the latest one; the one where Senator Bradley-the-snitch Seldortin told the whole world about Hansen Hills and the Mind-One drug."

Doug appeared more exhausted every day. "There's more going on than you know, Leon. Those crazy pro-liberty groups are planning mass protests, including at Hansen Hills itself."

A twinge raced through Leon's belly. "Just great! That slime, Bob Fullerby, is going to park himself at the gates of the Hills, and Andecco News drones will be zooming around all over the place."

"We can handle press drones, Leon," Doug told him, "but having a gob of cockamamie protesters out there is another matter. It'll be hard for us to get people and supplies in and out of the facility. The underground tunnels haven't been reopened yet. The first one won't be usable for another two months, at the earliest."

John said, "And let's not forget about Detective Brunish. He's been ordered to drop his investigation into the Soldiers of God Justice Group, but he's not listening. Every day, he's getting closer to tying the Group to the Back-to-Basics Club."

Doug gulped pink grapefruit juice. He burped as he set the glass on a coaster. "Seldortin, Fullerby, and Brunish aren't our only pains-in-the-arse. Richard-the-schmuck Karther still has friends in the Defense Department. People risked their lives—hell, even died—to give him info about what really happened to Flight Ten Seventy."

John said, "The nutballs will have a field day with that one. They'll drop a shit-bomb if they figure out that we blew up Ten Seventy, not the Domats. Those pro-lib numbskulls have no idea what's at stake."

Leon picked up a glass of orange juice. He set it down without taking a drink; his stomach burned enough. "Mitch, what are we going to do? Bezgog is attacking us on every front. He's stirring each pot and opening every lid."

Mitch dabbed his lips with a silk napkin. "Well, Leon, we'll need to put the lids back on."

"How do we do that?"

Mitch leaned back in his chair and crossed his legs. The troubles of the world failed to sour his calm mood. "By creating a distraction, Leon."

"What kind of distraction?"

"An international incident works best. It's time to stir up some of our overseas friends. Let's tell Izvyona to take a swipe at the Bakhadaree separatists. Not a major incident, just enough to push Domataland's buttons."

Despite fatigue, Doug's eyes twinkled. "So, Mitch, does this mean I get to unleash my Izvyonsk war dogs?"

"Yes, Dougy, it does, but remember, we want a noisy incident, not a major assault. We have more pieces to put in place before Izvyona launches its final attack on Bakhadaland."

"I get it, Mitch," Doug said, "a nice little border skirmish that we can blame on the Bakhads."

"You've got the idea, Dougy."

The plan didn't make sense to Leon. "How will that help us?"

John said, "Domataland scares the hell out of people, Leon. If President Tarish growls, our people at home will worry about the Domataree devils instead of us."

"Hmm," Doug said, "this may solve another problem as well. Karther keeps complaining about us slipping military assets into Izvyona. If we ensure Demnar Tarish is viewed as our top enemy, voters will be more likely to support our troop buildup in the Warm Sea area."

Mitch took a sip of coffee and chewed a piece of melon. "Karther's name comes up a lot, and not in a good way. Dougy, just how much does he know about Flight Ten Seventy?"

"Too much. He has the original files from Benson Air Traffic Control and Stroyger Air Command."

"What does that tell him?" Mitch asked.

"The files show our WK-One-Forty-One fighters forcing Ten Seventy into Domataree airspace. On top of that, Karther also figured out that Captain Timothy-the-traitor Becker was on the plane."

John said, "What! Dougy, how the hell did he figure it out?"

"Don't know yet. But someone in the Defense Department had to spill the beans."

Beads of sweat rolled down Leon's temples. "Dougy, who has Karther told about Ten Seventy?"

"We're still trying to figure it out, but he's keeping his info close to his chest. We don't think he's gotten the intel to Seldortin yet."

Mitch refilled his coffee cup. "But he will. It's a matter of time. Dougy, have you threatened Karther?"

Doug nodded. "Yes, sir, more than once. This time, Karther's not cowering."

"Mitch," John said, "maybe it's time to launch Operation Top Soldier."

By the calmness in Mitch's voice, one would think he was pondering what flowers to plant along a driveway. "Dougy, do your people have a plan in place for Top Soldier?"

"We do, sir."

The twinge in Leon's belly worsened. "Excuse me, but are we saying it's time to eliminate Richard Karther?"

Mitch showed not the slightest hint of trepidation. "Yes, Leon. That's what we're saying. Are you gentlemen in agreement?"

John and Doug nodded.

Mitch said, "Leon, do you agree?"

Leon's heart pounded. He wished he wasn't part of such decisions. "If the three of you think it's necessary, then, yes, I agree."

"Okay," Mitch said, "Operation Top Soldier is *a go*." He spooned more food onto his plate. "Leon, you should try the fruit. It's quite good, and it's good for the immune system. You need to take care of yourself. You've been under a great deal of stress."

"Yes, I have."

"Leon, may I offer you a piece of advice?"

"Of course, Mitch."

"Try concentrating on the good things. Leeha Ritsagin is at Hansen Hills. Her days of causing trouble are over. We haven't found the Guiding Light, but we have learned quite a bit, and we'll learn more. Doctor

Palchero will wring details out of the thief. Let's also remember our agents in Antropka. They're working night and day to find Randy Altholder."

"And don't forget, Leon," John said, "Richard Karther will be out of our hair for good, and we'll galvanize Demnar Tarish of Domataland as the world's top villain."

D'nevtnya, Bakhadaland
WEDNESDAY, MAY 10, YEAR 1007 EE
9:30 P.M., WARM SEA TIME

Ina Ruzh-Venkina awoke. Someone's hand jiggled her shoulder.

She pried open her eyes. Light coming from the hallway cast heavy shadows on Tarma Nedola's slender form.

Tarma's voice sounded distant, as if her words were from a faded memory. "Ina! Ina! Wake up!" Her voice grew urgent; the tones lost their dreamlike quality. "Ina, you must wake up! Something terrible has happened. Solomor has to leave."

Ina sat up on the narrow bed that Pada Rammak had prepared for her. "Leave? Tarma, I don't understand. He's supposed to be here three more days."

Tarma handed her the mourning cloak. "I know, Ina, but he needs to return to his post. He's packing right now. He's asking for you."

She followed Tarma to a room at the end of the hall.

Solomor, dressed in a combat uniform, was crouching on the floor. He was stuffing gear into a military duffel bag.

Ina joined the ring of family members encircling him. Her parents, Maktar and Tinsa, held each other. Her sister and brother-in-law, Culasa and Temlin, stood nearby, their bodies drooped with worry and pressing sorrow.

Zerin's mannerisms were different from the rest. He spoke in a serious tone. "Solomor, how far have the Izvyon penetrated?"

"I'm not sure. I only know they've struck targets inside our territory."

Ina's heart pounded; the Izvyon were up to no good. "Solomor, what's happening?"

"The Izvyon crossed our western border."

"What kind of forces? Where are they?"

"Special forces troops dropped into the Tratrebulin Valley. Strafers crossed the Strait of Tears."

Ina trembled. Even though the Izvyon had always been sneaking paramilitary troops over the border, the use of strafer aircraft was a major escalation; the tactical jets contained advanced air-to-ground Cadonan technology. "Solomor, has Satur been hit?"

"I don't know yet, Ina. I only know the Izvyon accused us of provoking the attack."

"What are they saying we did?"

"That we sent reconnaissance and sabotage units into their territory."

Temlin sounded angry. "The problem is, we didn't. Izvyona is lying … again."

Zerin pulled an ear-piece away from his head. "I just heard some news. Domataland is saying that the Cadonan military gave Izvyona a green light to cross the border, just like they gave the Izvyon permission to sink the Goodwill Ship."

Maktar said, "Son, what about the Cadonan press?"

"Senator Fischer is blaming us, as usual."

"What about President Meyfeld? What's he saying?"

Zerin shook his head. "Nothing of importance, Poppa. Both President Meyfeld and Senator Seldortin say they're evaluating the situation."

Temlin said, "Which, of course, means they'll do nothing. They don't care about the truth. Bakhadaland isn't important to them. They'll side with the Izvyon no matter what stunts the Izvyonsk government pulls."

Ina's heart ached. She agreed with Temlin's assessment even though Rosik had spoken well of Senator Bradley Seldortin. Rosik also had considered President Meyfeld a good man who'd lost control of the Cadonan military to the Freedom Party. Ina hoped to honor her late husband. "You know, Ruzhman Seldortin did challenge Senator Fischer on the illegal prison at Hansen Hills."

Culasa's cheeks flushed from anger. "The Hansen Hills prison doesn't have anything to do with us, Ina. Ruzhman Seldortin may fight for his own people, but not Bakhads."

A door opened. Pada Rammak stood in the entranceway. A lantern-shaped night-light swayed beneath her tiny hand. "I heard voices. Has something happened?"

Benid and Sulana appeared in the hallway behind her. "We were wondering the same thing," Benid said.

Maktar spoke as a father worried for his son. "Solomor must return to his unit. There's fresh trouble with the Izvyon."

Pada gasped. "Oh, no! Is it beginning? The new war we've been expecting?"

Solomor stood. He swung his duffel bag over his broad shoulders. "We don't know yet, Lady Rammak." He glanced at his military-issue personal device. "I have to go; they've sent a car for me. A helicopter is on the way. I'll stay in touch as best I can. Ina, will you come with me to the launch pad?"

"Of course."

Pada, Benid, and Sulana stepped aside as Solomor walked through the doorway. He bowed. "Thank you, Lady Rammak, for letting us stay here with you."

"Bakhadaree patriots are always welcome. May God protect you, Commander Tovalet."

"You as well, Lady Rammak; the Izvyon don't distinguish civilians from soldiers. No one is safe."

Before heading down the hall, Solomor bowed again. "Benid ... Sulana ... it was a pleasure to meet you. May God watch over you and your daughter."

Ina followed Solomor out of the restaurant. An auto was waiting. A woman in a National Defender uniform opened a door to the back seat. Ina slid across the cold, firm cushion. Solomor sat next to her. The car pulled onto the street.

"Ina," Solomor said, "I have something I'm compelled to tell you."

"What's that?"

A sad look covered his masculine face. "I remember what it was like when I lost Vinsa. It's coming up on fourteen years since the Izvyon killed her, yet I think about her every day. For a long time after she died, I was consumed by thoughts of revenge. What the Izvyon did to her …." He cringed as if he still felt the pain. "What I'm trying to say, Ina, is your time of revenge for Rosik will come, but you need to be fit to fight, which means clearing your mind and acting in a logical fashion. In rage, you may kill an Izvyon or two. With a good plan, you may kill thousands, maybe tens of thousands. *That's* revenge."

The vehicle came to a stop. The door next to Solomor opened. "In the meantime, Ina, I'll get revenge for Rosik as well as Vinsa, Uncle Motek, Aunt Tisha, and all the others the Izvyon have slaughtered."

Solomor stepped out into the night. Lights from a helicopter and the car's headlights provided the only illumination. He spoke to a woman in uniform. "Take my sister back to the Shinchik restaurant."

The woman saluted. "Yes, Commander Tovalet."

Solomor bent over and looked into the automobile. "Ina, remember what I told you. Don't strike until the right moment."

He trotted to the aircraft. As he climbed into the helicopter, the car pulled away. Ina prayed as she watched the chopper become tiny lights in the night sky.

An image of Solomor's National Defenders base popped into her mind. Long ago, she'd visited the site. It sat nestled among rocks and trees on the eastern shore of the Satur River.

A chill ran through her. How far were Izvyonsk forces from her brother's post?

Ina whispered another prayer; she longed for Rosik's opinion of Senator Bradley Seldortin and President Louis Meyfeld to prove true. She prayed that good people did reside in Cadona; she prayed those good people would take power and send criminals like Senator Mitch Fischer, Senator John Rineburg, General Douglass Willirman, and Pastor Leon Walls to jail where they belonged.

◈

Hansen Hills, Cadona ...

A sliver of light blazed into the dark cell. A sandwich and miniature cup slid through a gap in the steel door. Leeha Ritsagin pushed herself up from the mattress pad. She scrambled toward the bright spot.

"Please, leave it open. Please! I want light."

The hatch closed. Darkness returned.

She squatted down and grabbed the sandwich. It was too small. She devoured it in a few bites. She reached for the flimsy paper cup. It collapsed in her grip. Water gushed out. "No! No! No! I'm thirsty!" She licked up some of the water, but much of it soaked into the concrete. She pounded on the door. "More water! Please! I'm thirsty."

No sounds came from the hallway.

She tried to stand. Her legs buckled. On hands and knees, she crawled back to the mattress.

As she lay down, her head missed the cushion and smacked against the bare floor. A noise echoed through the hard surface. Tick, tick, tick.

Water! Water was dripping from the opposite wall.

An idea came to her. She patted the quilts until she found the clean bra cup hidden in the bedding. Next, she retrieved the paper cup and found her way to the drippy spot.

It took a while, but water soaked into the remains of the undergarment. She squeezed water into her mouth. Her thirst quenched, she sponged water into the paper cup. Now, whenever she wanted, she could take a drink.

Her quest for water succeeded, but the effort sapped what little energy remained. She made her way back to the bedding and curled up in the quilts.

With each breath, phlegm gurgled in her lungs. An odd, floating feeling came over her. Perhaps they'd given her another round of Mind-One. That didn't seem right, though; this wasn't what it was like on the drug.

Maybe she was dead! A childhood memory returned. She and Grandpa Ritsagin had watched an olden-day, spooky movie. The plot involved a man who had died after falling asleep while driving a car. The guy didn't realize he'd been killed. Somehow, he wound up in a strange hostel. All manner of terrible things happened in the lodging. During the last five minutes of the show, he realized he had gone to Hell.

Might she be in Hell? This place sure fit the bill.

Leeha sniffed the stinky blankets. She rubbed a hand against the floor. The surface scraped rough and hard against her palm. The floor was real; the quilts were real; she wasn't dead.

How long had it been since the men took her from the apartment? It seemed years, but it couldn't have been. She had menstruated only once since being kidnapped.

What were her captors up to anyway? Many questions remained. Had they found Randy Altholder? He should be easy to find; surely, he'd made it big in sports by now. If they did find him, what did they do to him? Was he locked in a cell, too? And who was the mysterious Sohn-Suran woman her abductors kept asking about? The woman in the picture resembled Cookie Davis, yet the lady wasn't Cookie.

Then there was the Guiding Light. So far, she'd kept the location of the printed document a secret, but her phony story wouldn't hold up much longer. The bad guys would learn that Randy hasn't spoken to her since secondary school. Worse still, she was on the verge of breaking. The time would come; she'd tell the interrogators that the Guiding Light lay hidden beneath her kitchen cabinets. The bad guys would have their prize, and she'd be dead for real.

Whatever was going on, she had to do two things. One, she had to break out of this awful prison. Second, she had to figure out where on the planet it was. It couldn't be in Cadona City. When she first arrived at the facility, she had noticed dry air and the smell of burning plants. In contrast, Cadona City was humid and stank of industrial fumes.

Perhaps she was in another country. Cadona, after all, had laws. The Back-to-Basics Club leaders were bad, but they were Cadonan citizens. They couldn't be so bad that they'd run a horrid prison like this one, could they?

31

ASSASSINATION AND MURDER

"Book lovers must visit! The new store is a treasure trove of classics. Also of note is its home. The building began its life as a Kettish church. As attendance waned, a museum moved in. When funds dried up, a porn shop took ownership. When the porn shop closed its doors, Book Nostalgia took up residence in a building as historic as its novels."

Investigative Journalist Bob Fullerby
"A Reader's Delight," Andecco News Service
Year 1002 of the Enlightened Epoch

Cadona City, Cadona
FRIDAY, MAY 12, YEAR 1007 EE
8:30 A.M., EAST CADONA TIME

Beams of sunlight and streaks of blue peeked through an otherwise orange-gray sky as Bob Fullerby made his way to Book Nostalgia. Richard

Karther had left another message in the unused chimney. Bob worried about him. Richard was playing a high-stakes game against ruthless enemies: the Freedom Party and its social arm, the Back-to-Basics Club.

Myrtle looked up when he walked in. She gave him a smile. "Mr. Fullerby, you're here early."

"I was going to say the same about you. Do you live behind that counter? Every time I visit, there you are."

She giggled as she adjusted the floral-printed scarf resting on her shoulders. "I'll let you in on a little secret, Mr. Fullerby." Her voice turned into a whisper. "I love books." She let out a jolly laugh and said, "So what brings you here today?"

"There's another old novel calling me."

"Which one?"

"*Citadel Fallen.*"

Myrtle clapped her hands. "Ah! Another classic. A good choice. Shall I find her for you?"

"No need, I know exactly where she's sitting." Bob turned away from the counter and headed for the steep staircase.

"Mr. Fullerby, wait!" Myrtle said. "I found a book you really should read."

Bob didn't want to linger in the store too long. Also, he was anxious to retrieve Richard's secrets. "Thanks, Myrtle, but it's *Citadel* that's on my mind. Maybe next time."

Myrtle persisted. "You don't understand, Mr. Fullerby. There may not be a next time. You see, this book I speak of, it's not a classic, so its odds of surviving another week are slim."

The words, *no thanks*, sat on the edge of his lips, but her sudden change in mannerism—from carefree to impassioned—made him hold his tongue. "Okay, Myrtle, show me what you got."

A look of relief reflected in her eyes. Something was up. This was more than a sales pitch. Myrtle spoke with authority. "As a collector of great literary works, you really shouldn't be without what I'm about to show you. If you like *The Voyages of Renn* and *Citadel Fallen*, then this tale is for you."

He followed Myrtle to a shelf near the counter. She removed a paperback book from a rack. Bob read the title: *A Ship Came to Harbor*. "I've never heard of it, Myrtle."

"The ink is of poor quality," she said. "Come this way. The lighting is better over here."

She led him to a spot away from shelves and furniture. In a whisper, she said something strange. "I know about you, Mr. Karther, and the chimney."

"Pardon me, ma'am?"

Myrtle opened the book. She pointed to a random spot on a page. "Richard is scared. He's hardly slept in weeks. You see, Mr. Fullerby, I know a man in trouble when I see one. Poor Richard isn't made for a life of danger. He's a good soul, a kind soul."

"Myrtle, how do you know him?"

"Not many people know this, you understand. Richard's father, Adam, and I were … involved. It was long ago when Adam was in the navy. Richard was just a boy at the time. Adam introduced me to Richard. Adam, bless his heart, called me *a friend*." Myrtle's voice turned dreamlike. "Adam was a young man a long way from home when we met. He'd just returned from an extended tour of duty. I was barely a woman, away from home for the first time. When my friends and I learned the ships were returning to port, we joined the welcome wagon. The second Adam's eyes met mine, well … you know. We saw each other for five months. Then we both came to our senses and called it off. Every now and then, though, I'd hear from him. Things picked up when Richard went to college. Adam would visit him … and me, but platonically, you understand. I saw less of him after Richard graduated, but still, every now and again, I'd get a letter or call. I was devastated when Adam died. I love my late husband, God rest his soul, but Adam and I shared something two people rarely find. A connection existed between us. It was simply there, no matter what. Then, one day, after all those years since Adam's death, Richard walks in the door of Book Nostalgia. He recognized me instantly even though he hadn't seen me since I was a rather young woman. I recognized him, of course. After all, he's the defense secretary and always in the news."

Bob took the book from her hands. "Myrtle, you wrote this novel, didn't you?"

"I did. It's based on the love Adam and I shared, but I changed many details so it wouldn't point to him and me. There's a boy in this story. He's modeled on Richard."

"Well, Myrtle, you talked me into it. I'll take this book and *Citadel Fallen*."

"Mr. Fullerby, I didn't mean to speak to you about my novel—well, maybe a little—but I'm worried about Richard. He needs to be free of this mess. I fear he's in grave danger."

"I'm afraid you're right, Myrtle. I'll see what I can do about giving him a warning."

"Thank you, Mr. Fullerby." She took *A Ship Came to Harbor* from his hands. "I'll wrap this for you." Myrtle walked away.

Bob climbed the winding staircase to the third floor. He pulled the oversized, leather-bound novel, *Citadel Fallen*, from a stack of old books. Next, he took folded papers from the hiding place in the chimney. He was about to leave, but he didn't. There was one more thing he had to do. Bob found a stray piece of paper lying on the floor. He scribbled a note, telling Richard Karther to ease up on his battle with the Freedom Party and the Back-to-Basics Club. The situation had grown too dangerous. Bob hid the note behind the bricks of the chimney and then made his way down the winding, former-bell-tower staircase.

As Myrtle handed him his wrapped books, he whispered, "I left a note for Richard."

She smiled. "Thank you, Mr. Fullerby."

Bob left the bookstore and made his way down littered streets to the Sunshine Diner.

The workday breakfast crowd had dwindled. A waitress led Bob to a corner table.

He didn't risk damaging the fragile pages of *Citadel Fallen*; instead, he browsed Myrtle's book about a young woman who had an illicit affair with a married sailor. If Myrtle's writing depicted the truth, her relationship with Adam had a spiritual bend more than a physical one. She described the young boy in the story, based on a child-aged Richard, as a sensitive kid who moved earthworms off sunbaked sidewalks and onto shady dirt. An epilogue claimed Richard joined the navy not because he wanted to, but because his father did, as did his grandfather, and his grandfather's father and grandfather.

The time had come to put aside Richard's childhood and focus on his secrets as Cadona's defense secretary. Bob unfolded the papers that Richard had left in the chimney dead drop. The creased sheets contained a surprise. Instead of rows of Richard's neat handwriting, the papers enveloped a miniature slip disk.

Bob unrolled his computer and slid the disk into a dash slot.

Myrtle was right about Richard being in danger. His plans included a public announcement about Flight 1070 and treaty-breaking, Cadonan military activity in Izvyona.

Richard's other notes hit closer to home; Cookie Davis had some explaining to do.

Bob Fullerby stepped into the back room of the print shop. Cookie, Angela, Rona, and Kever were seated around the wooden table.

Cookie jumped up. Her voice sounded frantic. "Mr. Fullerby, do you have news about Leeha?"

"Sort of. I have information that may help us figure out her connection to the Guiding Light."

"What did you learn? Please, tell me!"

Angela looked up from her computer. "Cookie, let Mr. Fullerby get settled. He just walked in the door."

"It's all right, Ang," Bob said. "I have urgent questions for her."

Cookie appeared desperate. "Anything! Ask me anything if it'll help Leeha."

Bob took a seat by the table. Cookie plopped into a chair next to him.

Rona's voice sounded like gentle rain compared to Cookie's gale. "Mr. Fullerby, would you like coffee or tea? We have both brewed."

"I could use a shot of java, Row, thanks."

Rona filled a cup for him.

Cookie wiggled to the end of her chair. "Mr. Fullerby, what's going on?"

Her emotions seemed genuine, but he wanted to gauge her reaction when he showed her a picture. "Do you know this woman?"

Cookie studied the image. "She kind of looks like me, but it's not. Who is she?"

"No one seems to know. We've been referring to her as the Sohn-Suran woman."

"Why do you call her that?"

"Because no one knows her name. She's on the list of missing persons from the one-thousand-three Mik-la-tah Tsunami. Some people think her death was faked."

"Mr. Fullerby, do you think the woman in the photo is me?"

"I don't. This image was taken after we brought you here to the print shop. You can't be in two places at once. Cookie, this is very important. Are you sure you don't know who she is?"

"No! How many times must I tell you?"

Kever said, "Cookie, take a deep breath and clear your mind."

Whatever magic Kever possessed worked. She relaxed. "Sorry, I'm just so worried."

"We know you are," Kever said. "Take a moment to think. Have you seen this woman around Leeha's apartment or anywhere you and Leeha hung out?"

"No, I'd remember a woman who looks so much like me." Her eyes grew wide. "Wait ... Mr. Fullerby, you may not think she's me, but *somebody* does, don't they?"

"I'm afraid so. A contact I trust told me that plastic surgery could make you look like this woman and vice versa. Even simple techniques like temporary Probane treatments and light-scattering filters would do the trick. If someone saw you with Leeha, they'd have reason to believe you are this woman and not *Cookie Davis*."

"Mr. Fullerby, I'm confused. What does this woman have to do with Leeha?"

"The woman's DNA was found in Leeha's apartment and in your motel room at the Roadside Inn."

The shock in Cookie's eyes seemed authentic. "Mr. Fullerby, if she was in either place, I wasn't there when she was."

"Here's the other twist, Cookie; your DNA was erased from both Leeha's apartment and the motel room."

"Mr. Fullerby, how is that even possible?"

"Short of serious disinfection that would wipe out all trace of anyone, the only way to do it is with very sophisticated equipment. Someone went through a lot of trouble to replace your DNA with the woman's in this photo. Cookie, do you know Captain Timothy Becker?"

"Is he the guy who's missing? Rosie Stanton's fiancé?"

"Yes, do you know him?"

"Not personally. I heard about him on the news. Ang reported that he disappeared and nobody's telling Rosie where he is. Why do you ask about him, Mr. Fullerby?"

"He belongs to a group called the *Cadona Guardians*."

"Who are they?"

"A defector group opposed to the Freedom Party and the Back-to-Basics Club."

"Mr. Fullerby, what do the Cadona Guardians have to do with me?"

"They may have been involved with replacing your DNA with the Sohn-Suran woman's."

"Why?"

"I was hoping you could tell me. Allen Bosswell was a Guardian."

"Wow! I have no idea what's going on."

"Cookie, does the name *Verona Vondelle* mean anything to you?"

"No, who's she?"

"Verona is connected to Timothy Becker and the Cadona Guardians."

Cookie looked on the edge of tears. "I'm sorry, Mr. Fullerby, but I don't know Verona Vondelle. I only know Captain Timothy Becker from the news. I don't know anything about the Cadona Guardians.

Look, I know you're suspicious of me. I don't blame you; I've done some stupid things, like sneaking to Leeha's apartment and forgetting to tell you about Allen Bosswell. This whole thing with Leeha stealing an important document ... it's so surreal." She pressed her face into Kever's shoulder. "Mr. Fullerby, I'm so worried about Leeha! I can't believe Toofy and Mrs. Furley are dead. They were good people. I'm afraid I'll lose Leeha, too. I'm afraid she'll die in that horrid, dark prison cell at Hansen Hills."

Kever wrapped his arms around her. "Cookie, for what it's worth, I believe you're telling the truth. I cannot imagine how crazy this must seem to you. You haven't walked in this world of spies and deception like we have."

Bob also found himself believing her. "Cookie, you may not have walked in our world before, but you're walking in it now. If there's anything you can think of, anything at all, let us know at once. The slightest detail may aid us in helping Leeha."

Cookie raised her head. Tears had left a wet spot on Kever's shirt. Watery streaks glistened on her cheeks. "I will. Mr. Fullerby, if it's okay, I'd like to lie down."

"Go ahead, get some rest."

She sobbed as she staggered to her bedroom. The door slid shut.

Angela said, "Mr. Fullerby, it was Richard Karther who gave you the info about Cookie and the Sohn-Suran woman, wasn't it?"

"Yep."

"Did he tell you anything else?"

"Yeah, he did. He's planning a press conference. He's going to tell the world everything he knows about Flight Ten Seventy and Timothy Becker. And there's more. He's going to explain how General Willirman fabricated a reason for Izvyonsk forces to cross the Bakhadaree ceasefire line. When Willirman, Fischer, and Rineburg learn what Richard knows, our defense secretary is going to find himself in a whole lot of trouble."

◈

Cadona City, Cadona
SATURDAY, MAY 13, YEAR 1007 EE
5:30 A.M., EAST CADONA TIME

Bob Fullerby paid for the taxi ride with his personal device.

Maatus said, "Mr. Fullerby, too much! You pay too much!"

"You've earned it, Maatus. Westville is a dangerous neighborhood. Not to mention you stayed up with me all night at the murder scene."

"So, Mr. Fullerby, dead man on train track is Defense Secretary Karther?"

"Unfortunately, yes, it was Richard Karther."

"Too bad. He good guy."

"Yes, Maatus, he was one of the good guys."

Bob climbed out of the taxi. "Get some rest, Maatus, you had a long night."

The taxi left. The empty street darkened.

Only a few lights gleamed from the building housing Andecco News Service's main office.

Bob felt the weight of Richard's death as he staggered down the wide walkway leading to the front entrance. With each step, he wondered if he'd fall to his knees, but he made it to the door.

An eerie quietness hung in the ground-floor lobby. Three bored security guards watched as he scanned his nodes and press badge. The chief guard said, "Mr. Fullerby, we heard about Defense Secretary Karther. Terrible news."

"Yes, indeed. We've no shortage of disasters."

Bob headed to the elevators. The doors to one of the lifts slid open with a ping. The happy chime and shiny mirrors didn't fit with the tragic events of the previous night.

He stepped inside and pushed the button for the twentieth floor.

The elevator came to a smooth stop. The doors opened with another cheery ping.

He found the reception area dark and empty, but light poured through the doorway of Bill Marantees' office.

Bob stood by the office door, but Bill didn't see him. Bill was sitting at his desk and reading an autopad. Bob knocked.

Bill looked up. "Morning, Bob."

"Morning, Boss. I take it you read my report."

"Yes, I did. Bob, I need you to back off on your assassination theory."

"Theory? You call it a theory? Richard was assassinated. Did you read the evidence? Did you look at the video?"

"Bob, of course I did. Like you and Detective Brunish, I also believe the Freedom Party and Back-to-Basics Club are involved. The killing has all the hallmarks of the Soldiers of God Justice Group."

"If you agree with me, then why not publish the evidence supporting assassination?"

"Please, Bob, take a seat. By the way, grab some coffee. You look like you could use some." Bill raised his mug. "I'm on cup number four myself."

Bob filled a cup with strong, black coffee. His back ached as his body crumpled into a chair. "I apologize for the outburst, Boss, but I'm getting tired of withholding information from the public."

"I know it's frustrating, but something else happened last night you don't know about. I just got word from a trusted source in the National Police ...."

"What word?"

"It's Barry Kingle. He's dead."

"What? How?"

"The National Police are about to publish a lie, Bob. The cover story is that a manhunt began when Barry failed to appear for a summons. The story goes he was under suspicion of spying for Domataland. The authorities caught up with him in an abandoned building in the industrial sector by the Helmsey District. National Police officers killed him in a shoot-out."

"Barry in a shoot-out? That's absurd!"

"I know it's absurd, Bob. My source claims Barry did respond to the summons. He was interrogated and died in the process."

Bob's stomach burned. "Let me guess; he was interrogated to death at Hansen Hills."

"Yep, you guessed right. He had no legal representation and no rights."

"Boss, this whole thing is fricked up. If only Barry stayed with Andecco ....
I'll never understand why he went to work for News, News, News."

"Bob, you're mistaken if you think we're safe because we work for
Andecco. Fischer, Rineburg, Willirman, and Walls attack all who refuse
to tow the Freedom Party line. Stephen Hutchinson can only do so much
to protect us, no matter how rich he is, and, don't forget, Senator Rineburg
is richer. If Stephen sells his Andecco shares, and if Bradley Seldortin loses
the election to Mitch Fischer, it's all over for us. Free press in Cadona will
die a quiet death."

"Boss, free press will only die a quiet death if we remain silent."

"When we were young, Bob ... and foolish ... we thought we'd save
the world. We're not young anymore. We know better. We know our limits. Look, Bob, I know Barry meant more to you than just a fellow reporter.
I'm very sorry. But we need to look at our situation realistically. Barry's
death proves the press is in more trouble than ever."

"So, what will our report say about his death?"

"We'll report the official position of a shoot-out—"

"What! Boss, we can't do that! We owe Barry that much. He gave his
life for our freedom."

"Hold on, Bob, let me finish. We'll counter the shoot-out scenario
with unfounded charges of spying for Domataland and his subsequent
death at the hands of overeager law enforcement. But we won't mention
the involvement of the Freedom Party, the Back-to-Basics Club, or the
Soldiers of God Justice Group."

"And what about Richard? What will our report say about him?"

"Well ... I'm ... I'm still working on that."

"In other words, Boss, we're going to bury our heads in the sand." Bob
rose from his chair.

"Sit down, Bob, I can see you're upset."

"I am, but I have appointments."

"Okay, I understand."

Bob headed toward the office door.

Bill said, "Bob, remember your team. Angela, Kever, and Rona are
top-notch news people. We need to protect them."

"I know, we do need to protect them. But I can't help but ask … who protected Barry? Who protected Richard? I'll check in with you later, Boss."

As Bob made his way out of Bill's office, he wondered what *protection* meant. Did *protection* mean preservation of life in its rawest sense? Didn't a reason to be alive mean as much as naked survival?

He needed to go somewhere to think. Two people who fought for justice and morality had left this life. How might the nation persevere without Richard Karther and Barry Kingle being there to light the way?

Bob took the elevator to the eighteenth floor.

Many seats were taken in the Andecco cafeteria. He did his best to remain incognito as he made his way to a table for one facing a window. A waitress with weary eyes took his order. She stumbled away as if she might fall asleep on her feet.

He stared out the window at a depressing scene. Far below, trees and lawn space had been ripped away to make room for yet another Rineburg Industries building.

Food arrived. He chewed a piece of breakfast potato as memories of a luncheon date with Barry Kingle played in his mind. Barry had made a brave decision: he'd changed jobs in the hope that he would encourage News, News, News employees to protect freedom of the press. That move cost Barry his life.

Bill Marantees was right, of course; Senator Mitch Fischer, Senator John Rineburg, General Douglass Willirman, and Pastor Leon Walls took bold steps to control the press. Andecco News Service also once took daring action, but nowadays the agency cowered like a frightened child. Maybe today was the day to rediscover courage. Bob took his last drink of apple juice. He must return to the print shop.

Bob Fullerby opened the back door of the print shop building.

Angela, Rona, Cookie, and Anson were seated at the wooden table. Kever was standing by a wall monitor and pointing at a map.

Kever looked toward the door. His eyes grew wide. He rushed to step in front of the viewplane. His tall body hid most of the map, but Bob saw enough of the image to know that the map was an aerial view of Hansen Hills.

Rona switched off the monitor.

Angela said, "Sorry, Mr. Fullerby, we didn't expect you to arrive yet. We know you don't want to be involved with our plans to spring Leeha."

Anson and Cookie didn't say a word. They probably anticipated a lecture.

"Row," Bob said, "bring that map back up."

Rona obeyed.

Bob took a seat. "I hope it's not too late for me to join you on this adventure."

Kever gave him a surprised look. "Mr. Fullerby, are you serious?"

"Very, I've had a change of heart."

Angela said, "What made you change your mind?"

"Richard Karther and Barry Kingle. I have bad news. Both men are dead, and guess who took them out? Rineburg, Fischer, Willirman, and Walls."

"Mr. Fullerby," Rona said, "how did they die?"

"Richard was assassinated. Barry died after being interrogated at the Hills. The boss tells me that all reporters who don't do the Freedom Party's bidding will be targeted. If Andecco is going to go down, then let's go down standing up for those who can't stand up for themselves. Let us go down to protect liberty and justice. Richard and Barry can't help us anymore. It's our turn to be bold."

A look of pride covered Angela's face. "That's the Mr. Fullerby I admired when I was a kid."

"Mr. Fullerby," Kever said, "with you on our side, our plan will work."

Bob hadn't felt a burst of energy like this in a long time. "Tell me about this plan of yours to rescue Leeha."

◉

Hansen Hills, Cadona
SATURDAY, MAY 13, YEAR 1007 EE
7:30 A.M., CENTRAL EAST CADONA TIME

Senator John Rineburg opened the door to Dr. Ellen Palchero's office. Her piercing, dark eyes met his. "Senator Rineburg, good morning." Her attention shifted to an old geezer with a crew cut. "Sir, would you mind if we continue our conversation later?"

The old man stood. "Not a problem, Doctor. My apologies, Senator Rineburg." The man rushed out of the office.

Ellen's red lips glowed as she smiled. "Come in, Senator."

John stepped inside and shut the door behind him.

Ellen leaned back into her chair. The pose she struck revealed the firm curves of her slender figure. "What can I do for you?"

He took a seat. "My dear, you gave me everything I needed, and you did it all night long."

"So, John, does that mean you enjoyed yourself?"

"Almost as much as you did."

"Ah, the mighty senator is sure of himself. I assume this visit has a purpose?"

"I thought I'd say goodbye before returning to Cadona City. It may be a while before I can see you again. Those fricken protesters are causing havoc. Another convoy of rabble-rousers is on the way. Those jerks are making it hard to come and go."

Ellen crossed one long, sexy leg over the other. "The demonstration will fizzle."

"But when? And at what cost? Maybe we should find you another facility. A locale closer to Cadona City would be nice."

"Why, John, does that mean you'll miss me?"

"You know I will, babe, but I was speaking more generally. Your work is very important to our cause. You're too good at extracting critical information. We can't afford to lose you."

"Thank you for the compliments, but I prefer to stay put for now. I'm close to pulling the truth from Leeha Ritsagin. That bitch is tougher than she looks. She withstands more punishment than most, but she's breaking."

"Are you sure she hasn't spilled her guts already?"

"Oh, I'm positive. She's mixing truth with lies. There's a whole lot about the Guiding Light she's not telling. Her story about Jenton's Auto Body and Repair is fabricated—of that, I'm certain. We're about to start another round of interrogations. Are you sure you don't want to hang around a bit longer and watch?"

"I'd love to, but Senator Seldortin's announcement about Hansen Hills and Mind-One is creating a stir."

"Well, John, things should go more smoothly with the defense secretary out of your hair."

"It will once the fervor settles. His temporary replacement isn't a loyal, but he's weak and green. I have a feeling Dougy will be able to control him." John stood. He longed to turn the bolt on the door and have one more round, but he had crises to deal with in the capital, and Ellen had an interrogation to conduct. "Think about what I said. Maybe after Ritsagin breaks, we can get you to a safer facility."

Ellen rose. "I'll think about it." She straightened her tight, white dress. "John, you be careful."

"You as well, babe." He walked out of the office and signaled his aides to arrange for his return to Cadona City.

Hansen Hills, Cadona ...

Leeha Ritsagin didn't realize two guards had entered her dark cell until strong hands hoisted her up by the arms.

"What's going on?" she asked.

No one spoke.

She struggled to keep her footing as the guards dragged her down the hall.

The door to the torture room opened. They pulled her to the table with the straps. Leeha recalled water dripping on her face.

She heard footsteps. The doctor-in-white said, "Tie her down."

"No! No! I won't let you put me up there again."

"Too bad," the doctor-in-white said, "you brought this on yourself. You've been a naughty girl."

Leeha's vision narrowed. Time slowed. All pain vanished. She hurled a dirty foot into the knees of the guard to her right. His body flopped onto the floor.

The second guard reached for her.

Her right palm smashed against his nose. His midriff was unprotected. She jammed an elbow into his fleshy side. He fell onto his back. Blood poured from his nostrils.

The first guard rose to his hands and knees.

Leeha didn't know where the power came from. She kicked the guard between the legs. He grabbed himself and rolled onto his side.

The doctor's eyes widened from fear. The shock didn't last. An expression of cold confidence replaced her look of terror. She raised a weapon. It resembled a toy gun with a badminton birdie stuck in the barrel.

Leeha felt a prick to the neck.

Something was wrong; her head flopped to the side. She couldn't swallow. Her tongue and lips wouldn't move. All strength left her legs. Her body crumpled to the floor. She tried to blink, but her eyelids refused to flutter. Breathing grew labored.

The doctor-in-white shouted at the guards. "You call yourselves men? You let a fat girl bring you down. Get up, act like soldiers, and strap Ritsagin to the table."

Leeha felt hands on her shoulders and legs, but she was unable to move a muscle. Even her fingers refused to wiggle. Breathing grew more difficult.

The doctor-in-white spoke again. "Get me a respirator before she suffocates."

Leeha's vision blurred. A diamond-shaped device approached her face. Something scraped the back of her throat. Her chest rose, but she wasn't breathing on her own.

A fuzzy view of the doctor's face loomed above her. "Ritsagin, I'll return when you can speak." The face disappeared.

Leeha heard footsteps. A door closed.

Try as she might, nothing moved—not fingers, toes, lips, or tongue. Her brain told her to scream, but she couldn't make a sound. Saliva pooled in the back of her mouth. The liquid bubbled each time the breathing machine pumped oxygen.

Her vision darkened.

Leeha awoke with a jolt. Pain bolted through her head.

Her condition had changed. Images came into focus. Her eyelids fluttered. An itch trickled through her arms and legs. It felt like colonies of ants were crawling on her, but she couldn't move to make it stop.

Bit by bit, life returned to her fingers and toes.

Something in her mouth made her gag. Her tongue explored the obstacle. It felt like a tube.

She figured out what was going on. A machine was pumping oxygen into her lungs. Her own breath fought to take on a different rhythm. She felt dizzy. She bit the tube, but the air kept coming.

People entered the room.

The diamond-shaped object lifted away from her face. She gagged as the tube slid out of her throat.

The doctor-in-white said, "Ritsagin, do you know why you couldn't move?"

She coughed as she spoke. "No … I … don't."

The doctor-in-white held a tiny, badminton-birdie-like device. A needle poked out from one end of it. "This is a paralysis dart. The Ostollians perfected them for crowd control and terror attacks. A high dose suffocates the victim." The doctor rotated the dart in her long, bony fingers. "Lovely thing, don't you think?"

"Not really."

"I see you haven't lost your bitchy sarcasm, Ritsagin. But, you see, you're weaker than you let on. Do you want me to shoot you with one of these goodies again?"

"No."

"I won't if you honestly answer my questions. Who gave you the Guiding Light?"

"Three ladies. I never knew who they were."

"Where did they give the document to you?"

"In front of Hatchets Bar."

"When did this happen?"

"March twenty-sixth. I think it was about eight o'clock in the morning."

"Did Randy Altholder tell you what to do?"

She'd no choice but to stick to the story that she told while under the influence of Mind-One. "Yes."

"Did he ask you in person?"

"Yes."

"Did you deliver the document to him in person?"

"No."

"How did you deliver it?"

"I copied it and sent it to him on my personal device."

"Where was he when you sent it to him?"

"I don't know."

"Has he contacted you after you sent him the document?"

"Only to tell me he received it."

"Ritsagin, tell me what you did with the printed Guiding Light."

Leeha felt a tickle in her throat. Her chest ached. She coughed. It got worse. One cough followed another and another.

The doctor's voice was screeching. "Guards! Untie her and sit her up."

Waves of coughs racked her body. Sitting upright helped a little. Something pricked her arm.

Another dart! Leeha jumped off the table. Two guards grabbed her. A third guard stood nearby.

She waited for paralysis to set in.

The doctor-in-white said, "Stop fussing, Ritsagin. I gave you something for the cough. Guards, give her shoes, socks, and another blanket or two and take her back to her cell."

LET'S GO GET LEEHA

Cadona City, Cadona
WEDNESDAY, MAY 17, YEAR 1007 EE
6:00 A.M., EAST CADONA TIME

Bob Fullerby watched as Kever Carsen stuffed high-tech equipment into his backpack. "Kever-o, are you sure you have everything? Did you remember the node-dampening devices?"

"I have everything Row set out for me, Mr. Fullerby. I'm pretty sure the node dampeners are in there."

Bob checked the time. "Speaking of Row, she's late. I hope she didn't run into trouble."

Angela Thirgal rinsed out her teacup and said, "I'm sure she's fine, Mr. Fullerby. She and Anson are picking up a few more things for the trip."

"Is Cookie with them?"

"No," Kever said. "She's in her room. She's probably still praying. Cookie's really into the Kettish thing."

Bob was sure they were forgetting something. "What about the sign in the reception area?"

"Don't worry, Mr. Fullerby," Angela said. "Row already put the *closed for remodel* notice in the front window. We're all set."

Security lights flashed. Bob saw Anson Dailey and Rona Betler on the security monitor. The back door to the print shop opened.

A radiant smile covered Rona's face. "Morning, all."

Bob noticed her slim satchel. "Is that all you're taking, Row?"

"It's all I'm taking with me to cover the protest at Hansen Hills. I left other stuff, including stuff for Leeha, in Anson's car. That way, he, Kever-o, and Cookie can take it straight to Forest Falls. Is that okay, Mr. Fullerby?"

"It is, Row. Good thinking. How about you, Anson? Is your gear in the car?"

"Yep, I'm packed and ready to go."

The door to Cookie's bedroom opened. As she walked toward them, she guided a Kettish prayer medallion beneath the loose neckline of her baggy, gray shirt.

Bob wasn't sure if her serious expression meant determination or fear. "Cookie, how are you holding up?"

"Okay, but I'm worried about Leeha. I'm so glad you agreed to help us save her, Mr. Fullerby."

These young people put too much faith in his skills. "I'll do what I can to help."

Angela filled a to-go cup with coffee. "Row, are you ready to head out?"

"Yep, let's get down there. More protesters are pouring in. We shouldn't miss anything."

Bob felt a sense of trepidation creep over him. "You ladies be careful. Drive safely, and remember, no heroics. Don't do anything but report the news until checking with me first."

Angela tossed a sweater over her arm. "We'll be careful, Mr. Fullerby."

Anson put his hands on Rona's shoulders. "Row, don't forget; big crowds can get out of control, and the military or National Police may decide to strike out at the protesters."

Angela said, "Don't worry, Anson, I'll keep an eye on her. We'll see you at the cabin tonight."

Rona and Angela left through the print shop's back door. Bob watched on the security monitor as the ladies settled into Rona's little car. The vehicle drove away.

Kever slung his backpack over his broad, square shoulders. "I'm ready to roll. Cookie, Anson, how about you guys?"

Cookie picked up her travel bag. "I'm ready; let's go get Leeha."

Kever followed Anson and Cookie toward the exit. Before shutting the door behind him, Kever said, "Hey, Mr. Fullerby, when can we expect to see you in Forest Falls?"

"Tonight, around five o'clock, Forest Falls time."

"Why so late?"

"The boss wants to see me before I leave town, and I'm planning to stop at the Hills to evaluate the situation there before heading to the cabin."

"Gotcha," Kever said. "See you down there, Mr. Fullerby."

The print shop's security cameras showed Kever getting into Anson's car. The vehicle drove away.

Alone in the room, Bob's sense of unease grew. Would they all make it back alive and in one piece? Something else haunted him as well—many secrets lay hidden in the print shop.

He pulled a hollow rod from his military-style cot. Inside the rod rested papers, slip disks, and memory sticks. The media contained information from several informants, including Pastor Mark Walzelesskii, Detective Carl Brunish, and the late secretary of defense, Richard Karther.

Bob sealed the papers and devices in a tracking-resistant bag and then hid the package in an unused heating duct embedded in the print shop's walls. With luck, no one would find the hiding place, and, with more luck, he and his team would return safely after freeing Leeha Ritsagin from the Hansen Hills Federal Facility.

It was time to go. His first stop was Book Nostalgia, in the Langlire District.

Bob parked his old, maroon-colored car along a street a few blocks away from Book Nostalgia. He secured a thick, old book under his arm. The restored *The Voyages of Renn* would be a gift to someone he knew was

346 ◈ C. N. SKY

grieving. Parting with the antique text pained him, but the leather-bound stack of paper might bring a bit of joy to a broken heart.

He climbed out of the vehicle. The acrid odor of industrial fumes wafted on the slow-moving air. Sticky humidity added to the unpleasantness. The old bookstore, although cluttered, was one of a handful of niceties in this exhaust-stained neighborhood.

Bob walked into the sprawling shop. Nothing had changed since his last visit. As usual, Myrtle stood behind a counter. She wore a dark dress. He noticed her red-rimmed eyes.

"Good morning, Mr. Fullerby," she said. "I have another book I think you may enjoy."

He followed her through a maze of shelves. She pulled a random novel from a bookshelf. "Thank you, Mr. Fullerby."

"For what?"

"For daring to report that Richard Karther may have been murdered. I know in my heart that the Freedom Party had him killed. You'd better be careful yourself. I heard the news about that reporter, Barry Kingle. Did you know him?"

"I did. We used to work together. He was my friend as well as my colleague."

Myrtle dabbed away a tear. "The Freedom Party gives us plenty of reasons to mourn, don't they?"

"They sure do. Politically motivated mayhem is as pandemic as the J2 virus. We live in dismal times. Say, Myrtle, I brought you something that may cheer you up, at least a little." Bob handed her *The Voyages of Renn*.

Her eyes widened. She embraced the book as one would coddle a baby bird. "Such a job they did! The quality of the restoration is incredible."

"I had it done at Gold's Antiques and Collectibles. It's a bit pricey, but worth every coin."

"I am so thankful *Renn* found you, Mr. Fullerby. You are truly a patron of the written word." She offered him the book.

"Myrtle, *Renn* is yours."

"I can't accept this."

"Yes, you can. In fact, you deserve it more than I do. You are an author, after all."

"How can I repay you, Mr. Fullerby?"

"By doing all you can to protect written art. Freedom Party attempts at censorship are truly frightening."

"I shall cherish this gift forever, Mr. Fullerby. Will you be browsing for another good read?"

"Not today; I have a meeting with the boss, and then I'll be out of town for a few days. But after that, I hope to take some time off and do a whole lot of reading."

"Excellent! Then I'll be seeing you soon, Mr. Fullerby."

After coffee and apple pie at the Sunshine Diner, Bob drove to downtown Cadona City.

A swarm of humanity had engulfed the lawn in front of the Andecco News Service headquarters.

As Bob walked along a footpath, he picked out three groups of people. Some visitors were hungry for information; they wondered how two public figures died back-to-back under mysterious circumstances. Freedom Party supporters complained about Andecco's innuendos of foul play in the deaths of Defense Secretary Richard Karther and investigative journalist Barry Kingle. Allegiance Party backers urged Andecco to expose the crimes committed by Senator Mitch Fischer, Senator John Rineburg, General Douglass Willirman, Pastor Leon Walls, and their Back-to-Basics Club thugs.

Police in riot gear manned barricades at entrances to the tall building. Bob showed his press badge to a burly security guard. Several seconds passed before the front door opened.

The ground-floor lobby bustled with activity.

Bob wormed his way into an elevator.

As the lift rose, a cloud of despair fell over him. Cadona, the nation he loved, was tearing itself apart.

The elevator doors opened on the twentieth floor. Andecco employees zipped about as they sought to make sense of recent events.

He elbowed his way through the crowd.

Bill Marantees' office door was closed.

Bob was about to knock, but the door swung open. A young fellow bolted out. Bob recognized the man's face but didn't recall his name. The man's voice carried a cheery ring. "Good morning, Mr. Fullerby. Mr. Marantees is anxious to see you. I wish we had time to chat; I could use advice, but there's no time."

"What are you up to?"

Youthful excitement animated the man's face. "I'm on my way to Pokerk. Lots of stuff going down in Izvyona and the Bakhadaland Region. I'm hoping to get permission to cross into Domataland and set up a base of operations in the Port of Naltuk, but the Domataree government isn't too keen on letting Cadonans in at the moment."

Bob recalled days when he, too, was able to run across deserts, trudge up steep mountains, or battle beating waves to escape a foe who didn't like snooping reporters. Age, however, had stolen such abilities. "I'll see if I can pull some strings for you. Remind me of your name."

"*Arthur Keller.*"

"I'll see what I can do, Mr. Keller."

"Awesome! Thanks, Mr. Fullerby." Arthur darted away.

Bill said, "Come in, Bob."

He walked into his boss' spacious office.

Stress and fatigue showed on Bill's face. "Bob, shut the door and have a seat. I'm afraid I have more bad news."

Bob settled into a chair. "What's happened?"

Bill drew a deep breath before speaking. "It's Scott Walters. He's been arrested."

"Arrested for what?"

"Spying for Domataland."

"That's insane! Where is he being held?"

"We don't know, but I have a good guess."

"I bet your guess is the same as mine. If I were a gambler, I'd bet they took him to Hansen Hills."

Bill nodded.

"Well, Boss, I sent Ang and Row to the Hills to report on the protests. I'm heading down that way myself. We'll nose around for Scott."

Bill didn't say a word. He seemed preoccupied with wantonly fingering the edge of a spongy desktop pad.

"Boss, is something wrong?"

"Bob, you've been my friend, colleague, and counselor for many years, but this enemy is greater than any we've ever faced. Until these terrible days befell us, our foes infested other lands. Back then, we always had our home base. Our country stood behind us. We don't have that home base any longer, Bob. Cadona was a light to the world. Look at us now; Cadona's beacon of freedom has gone out."

Bob understood Bill's sullen mood; if not for Angela, Kever, and Rona, he would've abandoned hope, too. *"Though dark these times seem, if the tiniest shred of will to resist remains, the war is not yet lost."*

A weak smile tugged on Bill's lips. "I recognize those words. Thomas Fillimore wrote them. The passage is from the *Treacherous Chronicles*."

"Things are hard today, Boss, but they weren't easy during Fillimore's time in the Awakening Epoch either. Look what followed: many in the world consider Cadona the place where freedom was born. True, we lost good people. Richard and Barry risked their lives and lost them. At the moment, the situation doesn't look good for Scott. But Senator Bradley Seldortin and Detective Carl Brunish are still with us, and I must add Angela, Kever, and Rona to the list, not to mention my Drop Case informant. Also, the young man I just ran into, Arthur Keller, seems motivated. Good people always die prematurely in dire times, but it's often those deaths that inspire a new crop of leaders to fight for justice. What I'm trying to say, Boss, is that we haven't lost yet."

"Don't underestimate the Freedom Party's attack on the press, Bob. Andecco is the last bastion. Our competition has fallen into Back-to-Basics Club hands. Barry's murder proves their purge is nearly complete. The

Freedom Party is coming for Andecco now. I doubt Scott will be the only victim."

"Boss, that's why we mustn't delay. We must expose the crimes of Fischer, Rineburg, Willirman, and Walls."

Sorrow filled Bill's eyes.

The desperate stare reminded Bob of an incident from long ago. He recalled wandering across a blighted Fletish landscape in search of people who had experienced a rebel onslaught. He came upon the ruins of a temple. Only steps remained. A woman sat there, lost in grief. Insurgents from the north had taken hostages; her son was among those captured. *It's too late for my boy,* she'd told him. *He's already left this life. You are an important man, Mr. Fullerby. Please don't let another mother lose her child to terror.* Try as he might, he was unable to convince her that her son might still be alive.

Bob now saw the same hopeless expression in Bill's eyes.

"Bob," Bill said, "watch yourself out there. You may be a popular figure, but the protection that popularity gives you has limits. You are a Freedom Party enemy. Make no mistake; you are a prime target."

"You be careful as well. Sitting behind a desk won't keep you safe. I'll nose around for Scott when I get to the Hills." Bob stood. "I should get going. Anything else, Boss?"

Bill shook his head.

Bob left the quiet office and walked into the bustling reception area.

He snuggled into a private spot along a wall and sent a message to Angela Thirgal; she must know Scott Walters had been arrested and was likely detained at the Hansen Hills Federal Facility. His next message went to an old friend at the Andecco news desk in Pokerk, Republic of Ostollia: *I need a favor. A young reporter, Arthur Keller, is seeking access to the Andecco news center in Naltuk, Domataland.*

With the messages sent, Bob left the building and jumped into his car.

He headed for his apartment to grab his suitcase. The extra stop delayed his departure, but a few moments of peace would be a welcome respite from assassinations, angry mobs, stinky air, and littered gutters. He pictured his cramped, eighty-sixth-floor apartment. It would be quiet inside, or as quiet as Cadona City could be. A strong cup of home-brewed coffee also sounded good. With luck, he might see a pigeon or two atop a neighboring roof.

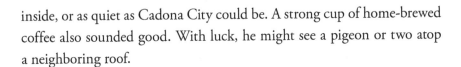

Dense traffic hampered his commute, but he was almost home.

Bob turned onto a concrete ramp. A striped security gate slid open. It closed behind him as soon as he pulled into the tenant parking garage.

A wave of peace came over him. Outside, on the streets, engines rumbled, but inside the shadowy garage, cars slumbered in tidy rows.

The drive to Hansen Hills would be a long one, so he parked in a slip near the stairwell. A walk down the steps would offer at least a bit of exercise before a lengthy journey.

Bob trotted down the stairs.

The last bend in the staircase was just ahead.

He turned the corner and froze. Two men stood in front of the elevators. The strangers' dark clothing and hairstyles were dead giveaways; the men were National Police investigators. No doubt they were there for one reason—to haul him away as they did Scott Walters.

Bob backstepped around the corner and tiptoed up the stairwell. If he could get to his car, he might be able to make it to a garage exit. After that, he'd sneak to his attorney's office.

He climbed the last flight of stairs.

His car was waiting for him.

He heard footsteps. His pursuers were closing fast. He touched his personal device. It sent an emergency signal to Bill Marantees. He tapped the device again to transmit the same signal to Angela Thirgal. Something was wrong; the touchpad felt blank beneath his fingertips. He glanced at the viewplane. It was dark.

"National Police! Stop right there, Mr. Fullerby. Place your hands on your head."

He obeyed.

"Very slowly, Mr. Fullerby, I want you to turn around. Slowly! No sudden moves."

When he turned, he saw the same two national policemen who had been standing by the elevators. "What can I do for you, gentlemen?" Bob asked.

"You'll be coming with us," the older of the two men said.

"Who are you?"

"I'm Agent Barness, and this is Agent Hooper."

Bob hoped Bill received his emergency signal. If not, no one would learn of his plight for several hours. Angela and Rona were not expecting him to arrive at Hansen Hills until later in the day. "What do you fellows want with me?"

"We'd like to ask you a few questions."

"Okay, ask away."

"We're taking you to an interrogation facility, Mr. Fullerby."

"Gentlemen, you may question me right here."

"No, this may take a while," Agent Barness said.

Agent Hooper approached. He grabbed Bob's right wrist and then his left.

Cold cuffs dug into his flesh. "Am I under arrest?"

"Not if you cooperate," Agent Barness said. "If you don't cooperate, we'll be having a different conversation."

"I want to call my lawyer."

"You won't be calling anyone, Mr. Fullerby."

"I have a right to have an attorney present."

"Not when there's a grave threat to national security. Your right to legal representation is waived."

The agents guided him to a sturdy car. The vehicle's opaque windows were as gray as its paint.

◉

Hansen Hills, Cadona ...

Leeha Ritsagin pulled the quilts away from her ears. Something was going on in the hallway beyond her dark cell. The sounds of several people running reverberated through the floor. Men were shouting, but she couldn't make out their words.

Shivers ran through her. She draped a quilt over her head. The gurgle in her chest reminded her that she was ill.

The noises from the hall faded, but a realization coalesced in the dark and dank surrounding her. She should've been terrified, but, instead, the sensation brought clarity. The truth was clear and simple; if she remained a prisoner, only two outcomes were possible: she'd die before revealing the location of the Guiding Light document, or she'd die after telling her captors that the document was hidden beneath the kitchen cabinets in her apartment. All reasons for not attempting an escape dissolved. She'd likely be killed trying, but she was as good as dead anyway.

More sounds resonated through the floors and walls. The situation at the prison must've changed. Maybe the discord would offer a chance for freedom.

ESCAPE PLANS

Hansen Hills, Cadona
WEDNESDAY, MAY 17, YEAR 1007 EE
6:00 P.M., CENTRAL EAST CADONA TIME

Angela Thirgal looked into the camera that Rona Betler had set up. They didn't need to insert a backdrop; a barbed-wire-topped fence enclosed drab, military-style buildings and a yard that resembled the surface of the moon. The scene would convey the ideal mood to viewers.

Rona gave the signal.

A green light flickered. "This is Angela Thirgal, reporting from the Hansen Hills Federal Facility. Another bus carrying protesters has just arrived, adding to the already huge crowd of civilians massed outside the austere military base. However, we've seen little in the way of security forces. A few hours ago, a military convoy arrived. The armored vehicles entered through the east gate and then disappeared into the cliff. Since then, the compound has remained quiet. The military has been unwilling to tell the public what is really going on inside the mountain. Are people being interrogated here as Senator Bradley Seldortin has claimed? Speculation abounds that Scott Walters, an Andecco News Service reporter, is one of several prisoners. Andecco News has repeatedly asked General Douglass Willirman's office for answers. So far, General Willirman has not responded."

Rona flashed another signal.

Angela knew it was time to end the report. "As the sun sets behind rocky hills, one is left to wonder if the sun is also setting on a cornerstone of Cadona's freedoms: a justice system that gives each citizen equal access to a fair trial and quality legal representation in an unbiased court of law. This is Angela Thirgal of Andecco News Service, wishing you a good night."

Rona folded the camera equipment. "Ang, I'm really worried about Mr. Fullerby. He's *way* late. I think it's weird Mr. Marantees hasn't returned our calls. You'd think he'd be concerned if Mr. Fullerby went missing."

"I'm worried, too, Row."

"Ang, maybe we should call Kever-o. Mr. Fullerby may have gone directly to Forest Falls."

"No, Row, let's keep radio silence as we planned—no signals to or from the cabin."

A crowd was forming along the northern side of the Hansen Hills yard. "Let's go have a look over there, Row. People are trying to rip down the fence."

Angela watched as a protester attempted to cut a wire with long-handled clippers. The tool flew from his hands. People clustered together to plan their next move.

"Hey, Row," Angela said, "are you picking up any nanoprobes or unusual signals?"

Rona pulled a tiny scanner from her purse. She stared at the viewplane. "Nope, nothing." She slipped the instrument back into the handbag. "Ang, where do you think Kever-o got this scanner? I've never seen anything like it."

"Who knows with Kever-o. I wouldn't be surprised if he slept with a techy at the Defense Department to get it."

"I don't think Kever-o would do something like that," Rona said. "You know what? When he broke up with Roberta, I thought you might be next in line."

"Ain't happening! Kever-o and I are never going to be an item, so you can quit waiting."

Rona didn't look convinced, but she changed the subject. "Ang, where do you think the guards are?"

"They're probably holed up inside the mountain. If they want to keep this prison secret, they'll need to be careful. They wouldn't want the public to see too many soldiers and weapons."

Sparks danced in the fading light. Three protesters flew backward, as if swatted by an invisible hand.

"I think you're right, Ang. The fence could've had a much bigger charge. The military's being careful about what they let people see."

Angela's personal device vibrated. "Finally! Mr. Marantees is calling." She put the microphone close to her lips. "Hi, Mr. Marantees. Have you heard from Mr. Fullerby?"

"I have. Earlier, he sent me an emergency signal."

"What type of emergency signal?"

"The code meant he was in imminent danger of capture …. I'm sorry."

"Mr. Marantees," Angela said, "what exactly did Mr. Fullerby say?"

"Nothing, I don't think he had time to speak."

"Who got to him?"

"That's why I didn't call you right away, Ms. Thirgal; I wasn't sure. Detective Carl Brunish tracked down what happened. The National Police have him. He's being held in one of the interrogation facilities in Cadona City. We don't know which facility, but it doesn't appear he'll be shipped to Hansen Hills."

"I can see why," Angela said. "Protesters have the Hills surrounded. I bet our show of force is what kept Mr. Fullerby from joining Scott Walters. Is Mr. Fullerby accused of spying for Domataland, too?"

"I don't know. Detective Brunish didn't have details."

"Does he know when Mr. Fullerby will be released?"

"No, and I'm worried, Ms. Thirgal. I called Bob's lawyer. She hasn't heard from him. My guess is the National Police denied him the right to legal counsel. I've told Senator Seldortin what happened."

Angela felt a tug on her sleeve. "Ang," Rona whispered, "what's going on?"

"The National Police took Mr. Fullerby."

Rona's healthy, pink tones drained from her face. "Has he been arrested?"

"We don't know, Row."

Mr. Marantees said, "Ms. Thirgal, I'll let you know when I learn more. Be careful with this information. I can tell by your voice you're upset; so am I. But if you overreact, you'll put yourself, Ms. Betler, and Mr. Carsen in danger."

Angela bit her lip. Mr. Fullerby wouldn't want her to call Bill Marantees a chickenshit. "I understand, Mr. Marantees. Please keep us informed."

The line fell silent.

Rona's eyes were wide. "Ang, tell me, what did he say?"

"Not much, Row."

"What does he want us to do?"

"He told me to be careful; don't stir the pot. The normal blah, blah, blah and sit on our hands and keep our mouths shut."

"What! We can't just sit here, Ang. Mr. Fullerby's in trouble."

Angela fought to control brewing rage. "Mr. Marantees is worried about us, Row. I get that."

"Ang, no! They have Mr. Fullerby. We can't let this slide."

"You're right, Row, we can't. Set up the camera. It's time for an Andecco News alert: Bob Fullerby is missing. I'll make the announcement right here by the fence."

Rona punched the air with a tiny fist. "All right!"

Cadona City, Cadona ...

Bob Fullerby adjusted a stained pillow. The new position didn't relieve the ache in his neck. Lumps in the thin mattress poked into his back. He twisted and turned to get more comfortable, but his elbow banged against the steel frame that fastened the bed to a concrete wall.

His army surplus cot in the print shop offered more comfort than did this prison bed.

To make matters worse, National Police officers had confiscated his personal device, so he had no idea what time it was. He hadn't seen a single window since arriving, so he didn't even know if it was day or night.

Worry consumed him. Had Bill Marantees received his emergency signal? Had authorities also arrested Angela Thirgal, Rona Betler, Kever Carsen, Anson Dailey, and Cookie Davis?

He could do nothing but wait.

To distract himself, he stared at an amorphous water spot on the gray ceiling.

A clanging sound came from the direction of the prison bars. Two guards walked into the cell.

One of the men said, "Mr. Fullerby, stand up, please."

Pain shot through Bob's back as he rose to his feet.

The guard said, "Turn around and place your hands behind your head."

Cold cuffs bound Bob's hands together. "Officer, where are you taking me?"

"A detective has questions for you. Let's go."

The guards led him down a gray hall and into a compact room containing a single table and three rudimentary chairs.

One of the guards removed the handcuffs and said, "Sit here and place your hands on the table."

Bob sat down. The men cuffed his wrists to a metal bar sticking up from the tabletop.

The guards left.

Alone in the room, Bob studied his surroundings. Two long, skinny lights were embedded in the ceiling. The ceiling itself, as well as the floor and bare walls, were made of gray concrete. The surface of one wall, though, was smoother than the others. He guessed this wall, when viewed from the other side, functioned as a window.

A man in a cheap suit strutted into the room. His testosterone-driven arrogance matched that of other National Police investigators Bob had met over the course of many years. Was this official in cahoots with the Soldiers of God Justice Group? Bob figured he was about to find out.

"Mr. Fullerby, I'm Detective Antonio Stromer. I'm here to ask you a few questions."

"All right, detective, but first, can you tell me where I am?"

"You're in the National Police Northwest Holding Facility."

"So, I'm still in Cadona City?"

"You are."

"Thank you, detective. What are your questions?"

"Do you know Scott Walters?"

"If you mean the Andecco reporter, yes, I know him."

"What can you tell me about Mr. Walters' anti-Cadonan activities?"

"Nothing. I know of nothing he's done that can be construed as anti-Cadonan."

"Are you aware he's spoken to Domataree officials, including people we suspect are intelligence operatives?"

"I'm sure he has spoken to such persons, so have I. So have most journalists who report on international news."

"Mr. Fullerby, was Mr. Walters acting as an agent for Domataland?"

"I'm not sure what you mean by *agent*, but if you mean, *is he passing Cadonan secrets to Domataree spies*, my answer is—not that I know of. He hasn't done anything to make me suspect such activity."

Detective Stromer set an autopad on the table. "Mr. Fullerby, does this statement look familiar to you?"

Bob read the text. "Yes."

"Mr. Fullerby, do you know who wrote it?"

"I do. Scott Walters did."

Anger crept into Detective Stromer's words. "So, you're telling me you know Mr. Walters penned this statement, yet, just moments ago, you said that Mr. Walters, to the best of your knowledge, had never committed an anti-Cadonan act."

"Detective, perhaps you showed me the wrong article. The piece I just read was about the True Followers of God Church, and how the church professes beliefs that are a danger to the civil rights of many Cadonan citizens."

Detective Stromer pushed the autopad away with a force that almost sent it sailing off the table. "What was your relationship with Barry Kingle?"

"Well, currently, he's my dead friend."

"What was the nature of your relationship with Mr. Kingle before his death?"

"We were coworkers and friends for many years."

"You didn't answer my question: what was the nature of your relationship with Mr. Kingle?"

"I did answer your question."

"How close was your friendship?"

"We sometimes hung out after work and bounced ideas off each other, if that's what you mean. I saw him less frequently after he left Andecco and went to work at News, News, News."

"Are you aware of Mr. Kingle's violent tendencies?"

"No."

"Mr. Fullerby, do you know how he died?"

"I'm aware of the phony story of how he died."

"Tell me, Mr. Fullerby, how do you think he died?"

Bob realized he needed to be careful. If he divulged too much information, it might put his sources in danger. "Seeing that he died at the hands of the National Police, you are the one who needs to tell *me*."

"Mr. Fullerby, what do you know about Mr. Kingle's unpatriotic behavior?"

"I've never known Mr. Kingle to espouse unpatriotic behavior."

Detective Stromer slid a sheet of paper across the tabletop. "Do you recognize this article?"

"I do."

"Mr. Fullerby, do you not consider this ... this slander unpatriotic?"

"If you pardon me, detective, you are confused about what constitutes unpatriotic or anti-Cadonan activity. Barry Kingle was investigating illegal transport of Cadonan weapons to Estdevent terrorist cells in Domataland and to the Izvyonsk military. Scott Walters wrote a piece about separation of church and state, and how the True Followers of God Church is trying to worm its way into our political process. Detective ... Barry's and Scott's words are the epitome of patriotism and *pro*-Cadonan activities."

A muscle twitched in Detective Stromer's jaw. "Mr. Fullerby, we know the press corps in this country is crawling with Domataree agents. We know Sohn-Sur and other nations are establishing their own networks of spies. Give me names. Who are the spies?"

"I don't know of any spies working in our press."

"So, there's not a single spy working at Andecco News Service?"

"There may be; I've been around long enough to know that foreign agents find it useful to place spies in media agencies. In fact, Cadona isn't innocent of this behavior. We make it a regular practice to plant agents in the press of other nations."

"Mr. Fullerby, are you telling me you are unconcerned about spies in our press?"

"That's not what I'm telling you. I'm saying I know it happens around the world. I'm also telling you I don't know of any spies at Andecco or any other media agency in Cadona."

"You can't give me one single name of someone you even remotely suspect is working for a foreign intelligence service?"

"Your statement is correct. I suspect no one."

"What about Arthur Keller?"

"What about him?"

"You contacted the Andecco office in Pokerk on his behalf. The Republic of Ostollia is right by Domataland. From word that's reached my ears, Mr. Keller is mighty keen to visit Naltuk. Are you telling me you don't find it a bit suspicious?"

"Why should I? Mr. Keller wants to report on the Izvyonsk-Bakhadaree conflict. Crossing into Bakhadaland from Domataland is a safer journey than crossing from Izvyona. Look, detective, Mr. Keller strikes me as a young man hungry for a story. Most youthful journalists long to record the story of the century."

Detective Stromer pressed a button next to the doorframe. "Send in the guards."

Bob stretched his sore arms as far as the cuffs allowed. "Am I free to go?"

The detective struck an overbearing pose. "No, you'll be staying with us awhile."

Bob knew he had his answer; this National Police unit, at least Detective Antonio Stromer, was in league with the Soldiers of God Justice Group.

Forest Falls, Cadona
WEDNESDAY, MAY 17, YEAR 1007 EE
10:00 P.M., CENTRAL EAST CADONA TIME

Angela Thirgal squeezed Rona Betler's little car into a narrow parking space. "Well, Row, here we are. We'd better get to the cabin; I bet Kever-o, Anson, and Cookie heard our broadcast about Mr. Fullerby. They'll be worried about him—and us."

Rona stretched her back and yawned. "I'm sure they are worried. It's going to be weird going to the cabin, and Mr. Fullerby won't be there."

"Yeah, it will be strange." Angela switched off the headlights.

In the distance, yellow flickers sparkled.

"Hey, Ang, get a load of all the campfires! Way more people pitched tents here than at the Hills."

"It's safer here. If the military decides to move against the protesters, the first targets will be those near the Hills itself."

"Makes sense," Rona said.

Angela climbed out of the car. Cool, dry air brushed her cheeks.

Rona stepped out from the passenger side. "Hey! I hear people singing. It's a nice song—kind of sad, but peaceful."

Angela listened to the tune. "I remember it from when I was a kid."

"What is it?" Rona asked.

"It's an anti-war song from the last time we were tangled up in the Ostollian wars. The song's based on passages from *On the Arrogance of Man*."

"Isn't that a Thomas Fillimore book?"

"Sure is. Funny how words written way back in the Awakening Epoch still make sense in our time."

The melody faded.

Angela pulled a satchel from the back seat. "I'll carry the equipment, Row. You've been lugging it around all day."

"Thanks. I'm tired. I'm looking forward to a hot drink and a soft bed."

"So am I." Angela pointed her personal device luminaire toward a path heading away from the campground. "This trail leads to the cabin. Let's get going."

With each step upon the dry earth, dust puffed into the air. Fine, gritty rocks covered the path at the place where the trail curved downhill. Glimmers from the campfires dimmed.

Rona stared at the sky. "Clouds must've rolled in. Not all of the stars are out."

"Those aren't rain clouds, Row. It's smoke from the fires down south."

Rona said, "It's still nice to be able to see some stars. I haven't seen them in a long time. Ang, what's making that noise?"

"Crickets."

"I like the sound," Rona said. "I've never heard them before. Have you?"

"A couple of times, on assignments outside of Cadona City."

The insect chorus sang as she and Rona strolled over gentle rises and falls in the trail. Outlines of mountains and contours of trees formed jagged silhouettes against a navy sky.

"Ang, what smells so good?"

"Woodsmoke and plants, like pine and juniper."

"You know what?" Rona said. "I like it here."

"Me, too." They trekked to the top of a rise. Patches of amber lights glowed in the darkness. "We're almost to the cabin, Row. Ours is the one farthest back and to the left."

They reached the cluster of homes. Dim, outdoor lamps cast faint light on narrow, gravel roads. Every now and then, a shrub or stand of tall grass shook or rustled.

"Hey!" Rona said. "I thought I saw something jump into that plant."

"Yeah, it's hard to believe, but some wild animals still live here."

Angela checked her personal device for directions. She turned down an even narrower street. Beyond a plant-filled yard, tiny night-lights glowed from a broad deck. "We're here, Row," she said. "This is our cabin. Let's use the side entrance. The front door is too exposed."

She led the way to an enclosed porch at the side of the house. Short, stout trees cast heavy shadows. "Be careful of your step, Row. It's really dark."

Angela pointed her luminaire downward as she and Rona climbed a series of wooden steps made from bisected logs. A hinge let out a squeak as she pulled open a screen door.

They walked into a dusty, bucolic storage room. Floorboards creaked beneath their feet.

Unlike the rickety porch, the door to the house appeared sturdy. Angela knocked.

Light poured out. Kever stood in the doorway. "Hi, ladies, we heard your broadcast about Mr. Fullerby. I'm glad you're safe. Here, let me take your gear."

Angela wiped her feet before following Kever down a hall and into a broad living room filled with rustic furniture. Anson and Cookie were standing next to a long sofa.

Cookie's eyes were red from tears. "Thank goodness, you're here! We were so worried."

Anson draped a shawl over Rona's shoulders. He said, "We were watching the news. The situation at Hansen Hills was looking dicey. I was thinking about running over there to look for you ladies."

"We're fine," Angela said. "Sorry for being late. Michele and Blake got held up in traffic."

"Michele and Blake?" Cookie asked. "Ang, who are they?"

"Other Andecco journalists. Mr. Marantees wants to keep around-the-clock coverage at the Hills."

Kever's voice sounded deeper than usual. "Ang, how will we know if new info comes in about Mr. Fullerby?"

"Mr. Marantees will keep us informed, but we're on radio silence at the cabin, so we'll need to run over to the campground to get his messages."

Cookie burst into tears. "How … how … are we going to rescue Leeha without Mr. Fullerby?"

"I was thinking about that myself," Anson said. "Maybe we should postpone rescuing Leeha and focus on freeing Mr. Fullerby first."

Cookie's eyes widened. "No! We can't. Leeha will die."

Angela knew what Bob Fullerby would expect of her: make decisions in his stead. "Freeing Mr. Fullerby first is a tempting idea, but we can't change our plans now. He would want us to move forward without him. We need to find out what happened to the Guiding Light document."

Kever said, "I agree with Ang. It's what Mr. Fullerby would want. The Hills is under assault. It's vulnerable. Besides, we don't know where the National Police are holding Mr. Fullerby. We know where Leeha is."

Angela missed her boss' leadership. He'd be disappointed if she failed to assume command. "We're all upset about Mr. Fullerby, but Mr. Marantees, Senator Seldortin, and Detective Brunish are working together to free him. The five of us will focus on Leeha."

Hansen Hills, Cadona …

A narrow beam of light seared Leeha Ritsagin's eyes. In a flash, all light vanished.

She crawled out from beneath the quilts and felt her way to the door. A sandwich and a cup of water sat on the ground.

After eating, she listened for noises. At the moment, she heard nothing, but bursts of activity in the hallway had been increasing. Also, besides being tossed food, no one had bothered her for what seemed a long time.

So far, an avenue of escape had not materialized, but one day an opportunity would come. She must be ready.

A shiver racked her body. Leeha returned to her smelly bedding and wrapped herself in quilts. She must stay warm. The rattle in her lungs had died back to a mild flutter, but to manage an escape, she must get stronger.

She pictured the layout of the prison—the halls, doors, and torture rooms. She recalled where the guards wore their weapons and where the doctor-in-white carried her medical equipment.

Leeha wished she could practice the self-defense maneuvers that Grandpa Ritsagin had taught her, but she was too weak. For now, visualizing the fighting moves would have to do.

The bad guys would return. When they did, she'd pounce on the first chance to break free.

34

RESCUE LEEHA

Forest Falls, Cadona
FRIDAY, MAY 19, YEAR 1007 EE
5:50 A.M., CENTRAL EAST CADONA TIME

Angela awoke. A big hand tapped her shoulder. She opened her eyes. Kever's face hovered above her.

"Ang, sorry to wake you, but there's something you'll want to watch."

She sat up on her cabin bed. The warm, soft quilt rolled off her body. Chilly air penetrated her nightshirt. "Kever-o, what's going on?"

"In a few minutes, General Willirman and Senator Rineburg are going to make statements."

"About what?"

"We don't know."

"Okay, I'll be right there."

After Kever left, Angela stuffed her feet into a pair of thick socks, stood, and pulled on the sweatshirt that she had worn the previous day. She glanced in a mirror. Her hair was a bit of a mess, but she didn't feel like primping. Instead, she ran her fingers through her curls and headed out of the bedroom.

She found Kever, Rona, Cookie, and Anson in the living room. They were huddled around a viewplane.

Cadona City, Cadona
FRIDAY, MAY 19, YEAR 1007 EE
7:00 A.M., EAST CADONA TIME

General Douglass Willirman took his place behind the podium. Senator John Rineburg stood next to him.

Doug hated this part of his job. He'd rather face down hostiles on the battlefield than a room full of wannabe movers and shakers. Most of the reporters in the crowd, though, were sympathetic to the Freedom Party and the Back-to-Basics Club. On this day, the nastiest of the nasty couldn't hound him. The National Police had locked Bob Fullerby behind bars, Scott Walters faced interrogators at Hansen Hills, and Angela Thirgal was out of town covering protests. A few scoundrels from the general public, however, found their way into the briefing room.

John cleared his throat.

Doug understood the cue; the time had come to speak. "Good morning. By now, many of you have heard that Bob Fullerby of Andecco News Service was taken into custody. The reports are untrue; Mr. Fullerby is not under arrest, nor is he suspected of any crime. Mr. Fullerby is fully cooperating with the National Police. He's working with federal officers to identify traitors in the ranks of the media. As you may recall, the police had recently apprehended an Andecco News Service reporter, Scott Walters. Mr. Walters stands accused of spying for Domataland. Bob Fullerby is assisting law enforcement with identifying other journalists working for foreign powers."

A loudmouthed woman in the crowd didn't wait for question-and-answer time. "General Willirman, what proof do you have that Scott Walters is working for Domataree intelligence?"

Doug's cheeks grew warm; this stupid woman didn't understand basic rules. "You are speaking out of turn, ma'am, but I will address your question anyway. Due to the sensitive nature of the evidence, I cannot provide details, but—"

A murmur buzzed through the riffraff standing in back of the room.

Doug's anger grew. "Listen! If I release such information, our methods of operation will be at risk, thereby threatening the security of our nation and endangering the lives of our agents in the field. I will say, however, that the hunt for traitors continues. As I've already made clear, Bob Fullerby is willingly assisting us in this effort."

A young man stepped into an aisle. "General, if Bob Fullerby is not under arrest, why has he not been seen in public? Why have we not heard from him?"

Doug scowled at the man before speaking. "I would like to remind everyone there will be a question-and-answer period at the end of our briefing."

The man in the aisle raised a fist over his head. "Free Bob Fullerby! Free Bob Fullerby!"

A few other people added their voices to the call. Capital Guard officers ushered the noisy rabble out of the room. Finally! Someone had the guts to get rid of the troublemakers.

"The other news we'd like to report this morning is the status of the Hansen Hills Federal Facility," Doug said. "Senator Rineburg will fill you in."

Doug felt a weight lift from his shoulders as he stepped away from the podium.

It was now John's turn to deal with the riffraff.

"Good morning, my fellow citizens and esteemed members of the press. It is with a heavy heart that I stand before you today to share this news. Our nation is under siege. Domataland is taking unprecedented steps to compromise Cadona's security. As General Willirman explained, we flushed out a spy: Scott Walters, of Andecco News Service. Unfortunately, Mr. Walters is only one of several traitors in our media. To make matters worse, Domataland is not alone; several other nations, including Sohn-Sur and Fletchia, have stepped up hostile intelligence operations against us. And, beyond the press, anti-Cadonan agitators have infiltrated our military, our intelligence agencies, and private corporations. In response to these growing threats, we have temporarily—I emphasize *temporarily*—resumed incarcerations at Hansen Hills. This I promise—and Senator Mitch Fischer promises—Hansen Hills will revert to a sole function of urban warfare training once the threats to our nation are contained. Now, we'll take your questions."

A man in the crowd shouted without being called upon to speak. "Why was Senator Bradley Seldortin not involved in the decision to reopen Hansen Hills? As a member of the intelligence and finance committees, he should've been engaged the entire time. Yet, Senator Seldortin was surprised when discrepancies in budgets arose."

"You'll need to ask Senator Seldortin," John said. "However, as I have stated on previous occasions, since he launched his campaign for president, Senator Bradley Seldortin has neglected his senatorial duties. I would like to add that Senator Mitch Fischer—unlike Senator Seldortin—has remained fully engaged in the security of our great nation."

A poor excuse for a young man darted into an aisle. "Senator Rineburg, you're lying. You, General Willirman, and the military apparatus are intentionally keeping Senator Seldortin in the dark."

John's words blared through the room. "Security, remove that man."

Capital Guard officers dragged the scruffy guy toward the exit, but the nutcase continued his incoherent rant. "Hansen Hills is a Back-to-Basics Club scheme. Check the news! Even President Meyfeld wasn't aware."

The room fell silent after the guards shoved the wack job out the door.

John pointed to an attractive, well-dressed, young woman. "Ma'am, what's your question?"

She stood. "Thank you, Senator. I'm honored to be recognized. The young man they took away makes a valid point. Why was our president unaware of what was happening at the Hills?"

Doug noticed sparkles in John's eyes as he stared at the pretty blonde.

"Ma'am," John said, "President Louis Meyfeld, since early in his term, has been out of touch with threats to our national security. As foreign powers ransack our nation, he's attending a World Assembly summit in Visstel. While our sitting president consorts with the enemy and Senator Seldortin puts all his energy into benefitting himself, Senator Fischer remains focused. Mitch has not forgotten our nation. He puts Cadona first!"

Many people in the room rose to their feet and clapped. Security hauled the naysayers away.

Doug applauded as well. John sure could think on his feet! It was a brilliant tactical maneuver. Coverage of the conference would show a video of a crowd praising the reopening of Hansen Hills.

The briefing ended. "Good job, John. You made our opposition look like raving idiots."

"Thanks, Dougy. We may have gained points with our friends, but Seldortin won a victory of sorts himself; our opponents will be wilder than ever. We need to clear the mob away from the Hills. The J2 virus is spreading. Let's make the public think the disease is showing up among the protesters. Heck, it just may be true."

"Good idea, John. J2 should scare them off. I'll take care of it."

John patted him on the back. "Thanks, Dougy. I'll see you later."

"Where are you off to?"

"I'm going to see if I can track down that blond reporter."

"Ah, I know the pussy you're talking about. Talk to you later, John." Doug rushed to a private, backstage room. He sent a message to loyals: *announce incidence of J2 infection among protesters at Hansen Hills.*

Forest Falls, Cadona
FRIDAY, MAY 19, YEAR 1007 EE
6:30 A.M., CENTRAL EAST CADONA TIME

Angela Thirgal scooted her derrière over the thick, living room rug and rested her back against the side of a soft sofa. "I can't believe what Willirman and Rineburg just said! If the National Police didn't arrest Mr. Fullerby, why would he send an emergency signal to Mr. Marantees?"

Rona sat down next to Anson. She said, "It's not like Mr. Fullerby to just vanish. He would've called us if he could."

Kever paced back and forth in front of an unlit fireplace. "Another thing doesn't make sense. Willirman said Mr. Fullerby was helping weed out reporters who are traitors. Mr. Fullerby would never throw a fellow reporter off the cliff for some trumped-up, Back-to-Basics charge."

"No kidding," Anson said. "Nothing about what happened sounds like willing cooperation. At least they're not holding him in Hansen Hills. Thank goodness for the protesters, or he'd be a prisoner there just like Scott Walters."

Cookie's body slumped into the thick cushion of a sofa. "I'm getting really scared. What if Mr. Fullerby disappears for good? What if he winds up dead like his friend, Barry Kingle?"

Kever sat next to her and slipped his arm around her shoulders. "Cookie, you're tired. You've been through a lot. Fatigue is talking. I'll make you avavarian tea. It'll help you relax." He stood and headed for the kitchen.

Angela's frustration rose. Kever was babying Cookie again. Why did such a crybaby rate special treatment? On the other hand, why did she care whom he babied?

Kever stopped walking. "Hey, Ang, I'll get tea for you, too. You haven't gotten much sleep lately."

So he knew she existed after all. "Thanks, Kever-o."

The rumble of angry voices poured from the sound array.

Rona said, "Check it out! Look how big the crowd outside Hansen Hills is now!"

Angela rolled her head against the armrest so she could see the view-plane. Andecco reporter Michele Collins spoke into a microphone. In the background, protesters swarmed the fence.

Kever set a steaming cup of fragrant, avavarian tea on the coffee table. "You know, Ang, you played a big part in inspiring all those people to come out and challenge the Freedom Party."

"Lots of people were involved, but thanks for saying so, Kever-o."

She sipped tea as she watched protesters mob the tall, wire fence.

"Something on your mind, Ang?" Kever asked.

"Yeah, I was thinking tonight may be the ideal time to spring Leeha. The crowd is huge and angry. And now that Rineburg and Willirman have admitted that Hansen Hills is a prison, the military can tighten security without worrying about making the public suspicious. We may never get another chance to rescue her."

Ver-Nuvelin, Domataland
FRIDAY, MAY 19, YEAR 1007 EE
8:00 A.M., CENTRAL FEWWOK TIME

President Demnar Tarish sat at the conference room table. He studied the face of each key staff member. Their emotions ranged from ire to discouragement to worry. He understood the concerns of his team. Since the rise of the Freedom Party, Cadona has antagonized Domataland on every front.

"Minister Henik," he said, "are Izvyonsk forces still in Bakhadaree territory?"

Anger showed in Rivar's eyes. "Yes, Honorable President. Izvyona has withdrawn most of the strike troops from the May tenth incursion, but a few units—about three hundred troops total—remain in the Tratrebulin Valley. In addition, Izvyona used this opportunity to sneak an estimated one hundred fifty mercenaries into Bakhadaland. These forces are augmenting established guerrilla cells operating west of the Satur River."

"What about naval and air bombardment?"

"No forays within the last four days, Honorable President. However, naval assets continue to patrol the Strait of Tears in numbers above ceasefire limits. Aerial patrols have dropped to ceasefire levels, but tactical air units remain on high alert in eastern Izvyona."

Foreign Minister Intam Takee spoke without being recognized. "Honorable President, we must extricate ourselves from the World Assembly. They refused to condemn Izvyonsk military action in Bakhadaland. Heck, they wouldn't even consider our petition to discuss the issue. The Assembly is worthless. Cadona and Visstel have a stranglehold on it."

"Minister Takee," Demnar said, "we expected this reaction from the World Assembly."

"Yes, Honorable President, we did. What I don't understand is why we continue to waste our time dealing with such a worthless international body."

Science Council Chief Madrik Meppatch pounded his fist against the tabletop. "Hear! Hear!"

Demnar said, "Minister Takee … Chief Meppatch, we continue our participation because the World Assembly keeps records. Such archives may one day inspire other nations to stand against Cadona and Visstel. Minister Takee, file an appeal to reverse the decision. Bakhads were killed, facilities have been destroyed, and transportation in western Bakhadaland is disrupted."

"Understood, Honorable President."

"Chief Kolensha," Demnar said, "do you have further insights into why Izvyona attacked Bakhadaland?"

"Our conclusion remains the same, Honorable President. Cadonans across the political spectrum hate us. The Freedom Party wants to distract people from internal problems. The Bakhadaree conflict is the perfect tool to do just that."

Demnar glanced around the room. "Anything else about the Izvyonsk assault?"

No one spoke.

Rozula raised her hand. "Honorable President, when you have time, I have updates for you on other topics."

"I have time now, Chief. Everyone else is dismissed."

The room cleared.

"What are your updates, Rozula?"

"Contrary to what General Douglass Willirman told the Cadonan press, Bob Fullerby is under arrest. Ruzhman Fullerby hasn't spoken publicly, nor has he contacted his team or his attorney."

"Is he at Hansen Hills?"

"No, Cadona City. It sounds like they won't be taking him to the Hills because of the protest. There's something else; I've received word that his team is moving forward with their plans to free Leeha Ritsagin. There's a good chance they'll make their move this evening."

"Keep me informed, Rozula."

"I will, Honorable President."

A CLIMB TO FREEDOM

"If you are looking for great rock climbs, there's no need to risk dangerous company roads to visit Sand Dome Tower. Nor is there need to battle the Antropkan heat. Neither must you travel afar to the Shinchik Territories. Instead, visit the beckoning cliffs of Hansen Hills and Forest Falls."

"World's Best Ascents"
Cadonan Outdoor Life News
Year 1005 of the Enlightened Epoch

Hansen Hills, Cadona
FRIDAY, MAY 19, YEAR 1007 EE
7:30 P.M., CENTRAL EAST CADONA TIME

Leeha Ritsagin awoke with a jolt. An alarm was blaring.

The world fell silent.

A few seconds passed. Another alarm shrieked.

She heard people running down the hall that lay on the other side of her cell walls.

The alarm screeched three more times. The footsteps faded.

She heard another sound. Someone was unlocking her cell door.

Light burst into the dark room. The doctor-in-white and a guard walked in.

The door closed, but Leeha didn't hear the clinking noise of the lock.

A tiny light gleamed from a headlamp strapped to the doctor's forehead. She balanced a long, shallow tray on her left arm.

The guard held a folding table and chair in one hand and his pistol in the other.

The doctor-in-white said, "Ritsagin, get up."

Leeha stood. Cold air swirled around her.

The doctor-in-white pulled a dart gun from her belt. "If you try anything, Ritsagin, I will shoot you." She wiggled the gun. "Do you remember what this is?"

Leeha recalled a prick to the neck and then paralysis. "Yes, I remember."

"Good, I'm glad we understand each other." The doctor-in-white reattached the dart gun to her belt. "Weber, set up the chair and table."

"Yes, ma'am," the guard said. He holstered his handgun.

Leeha watched as he unfolded the table and chair.

Was this her chance? Maybe she could escape through the unlocked cell door before Weber and the doctor-in-white could grab their weapons.

He finished setting up the furniture. He drew his weapon from his holster. If this had been her chance at freedom, the opportunity had passed.

The doctor-in-white pointed a bony, long finger at the chair. "Ritsagin, sit."

Leeha sat down. The cold, metal seat chilled her bottom.

The doctor-in-white set the tray on the tabletop. She yanked away the mesh cloth that had been concealing the tray's contents. Pointy, surgical instruments gleamed in the light coming from her headlamp. "I've had enough of these charades, Ritsagin. You are going to tell me everything you know about the Guiding Light document. You are going to tell me what Randy Altholder plans to do with it. And you are going to explain how the Sohn-Suran woman contacts you."

As if anticipating the taste of luscious chocolate, the doctor wrapped her fingers around a needle-like instrument. Her sigh bordered on eroticism. "Ritsagin, will you tell me everything I want to know?"

"I've already told you everything. Please just kill me and get it over with."

The doctor-in-white swung the instrument from side to side. "Uh-uh, no can do. Do you know why?"

"No."

"You are not telling me the whole truth, Ritsagin. You are threatening the security of Cadona. You will not be at rest until—"

Rage contorted the doctor's face; she shook the chair. "Until you spill your guts."

Her loony eyes gazed once again at the pointed object. Her voice softened. "Pretty, isn't it? Shocking such a lovely thing can cause so much damage to human tissue. And, oh, Ritsagin, it can cause so much pain."

"I don't want more pain, but I can't tell you what I don't know."

The doctor's eyes were like those of an obsessed cat savoring a senseless attack on an innocent mouse. "There's one little problem, Ritsagin; you're lying, and I know it."

As if a puppeteer pulled on a string, the doctor's spine popped pole-straight. She kicked the chair. "Weber, secure Ritsagin."

Leeha felt the guard's hands on her right forearm. A band dug into her flesh as he strapped her right wrist to the rear, right leg of the chair. He strapped her other wrist to the left chair leg.

The doctor-in-white put the shiny needle back onto the tray. She tapped a finger on one instrument, and the next, and the next. Her fingers settled on a black cube. "We'll start here. Open your mouth, Ritsagin."

Leeha clenched her teeth. It did no good; the doctor-in-white forced her mouth open.

Squish, squish, squish. With each sound, her mouth opened wider. Her jaw ached. On the left side, her tongue squeezed against her teeth. The taste of blood filled her mouth. Saliva pooled in her throat.

The doctor-in-white held up another tool. A drill at the tip whirred. She tapped a molar. "Now, we are going to have some fun, Ritsagin."

Leeha feared her lower lip might tear away from her gums as the doctor-in-white pushed the tool into her mouth.

The drill whined. The odor of ground tooth wormed its way into her nose.

The drill hit a nerve. Her body shook. The chair wobbled.

Something had changed; her right wrist no longer pressed against the chair leg. Her hand was almost free of its bond.

More pain. She tugged at the ties as her body shuddered.

Both hands broke free, but she pretended that the bonds still held.

She might never get another chance. She eyed the paralysis dart gun on the doctor's belt and the shiny needle on the tray. What about Weber's weapon? She guessed it was in the holster on his right hip.

The drill bounced off her tooth and cut her gums.

Glee filled the doctor's voice. "This has got to hurt. It's time for a new spot."

Leeha had enough. It would be escape or death.

Time slowed. Her left hand yanked the dart gun from the doctor's belt. Her right hand grabbed the needle from the tray.

The needle glided into the doctor's neck.

The doctor's eyes grew wide. Her mouth gaped. She hadn't seen the attack coming.

Sounds came from behind the chair. Weber had a gun; he mustn't get a chance to fire it.

Leeha pressed the dart gun against his right thigh. She pulled the trigger. Weber groaned in shock and pain. He would try to call for help; she mustn't let him.

But how might she stop him? The element of surprise had ended. Using a medical instrument wouldn't suffice. He was too strong, and the paralysis drug, though fast-working, wasn't fast enough.

She knocked the table out of the way as she stood.

Weber seemed confused.

Leeha ripped the communication device from his uniform and tossed it aside.

She went for his gun. She wasn't fast enough. Weber grabbed his weapon.

Leeha dived into the darkness. She knew every feature of this cell. She didn't need light to navigate in it, but Weber did.

He might try to grab the doctor's headlamp, but he wouldn't have much time. The paralysis drug would take effect soon.

Bang! Bang! Bang! Weber fired three shots. None hit her. Perhaps he pulled the trigger as an SOS signal.

Leeha lay motionless on the floor.

Several seconds passed. No one came. No footsteps or voices echoed from the hall.

Her jaw ached as she pried the cube from her mouth. She tasted blood, but she'd worry about her injuries later. Escape was all that mattered.

The doctor's headlamp cast stray beams of light in Weber's direction. He was dragging himself along the ground. No doubt he was searching for his communication device or maybe a respirator.

His movements slowed. Then he lay stone still.

Leeha peeled herself from the cold floor. She tiptoed up to Weber. He didn't move. She took his weapon. From his web gear, she stripped off a spare energy clip. She shoved the clip into her pants pocket.

Time to go.

She was about to leave, but thoughts of suffocation haunted her.

It was a bad idea, but she pulled the respirator from the doctor's belt. Leeha shoved the tube into Weber's mouth and pressed the mask onto his face. His chest didn't rise. She found a button on a tiny box attached to the end of a cord. She pushed the button. His chest rose and fell.

It was past time to go. She practiced pulling the spare energy clip from her pocket. Now, she was ready.

Leeha walked to the cell door. Once she opened it, she'd either find a way out, or she'd die. Either way, her torturers must not get their grubby hands on the Guiding Light.

She opened the door just a crack and peered out. The bright hall was void of people.

Which way should she go?

Each time they took her to a torture chamber, they'd turned right. She'd seen no exits. This time, she'd go left and into unexplored territory.

She crept down the empty hallway.

It ran straight for a long way. Cell doors lined both walls.

She paused when the hall curved to the left.

Hearing nothing, she kept going.

The doors were different here. They were white and marked with black numbers.

The bow in the hallway ended. The corridor ran straight again.

Then she saw it! The hall ended at a deserted security desk.

Leeha squeezed into a cubbyhole next to a drinking fountain and studied her surroundings. Viewplanes flashed from consoles behind the security desk, but the chairs were empty. Past the desk lay tall windows and glass doors.

What was on the other side of the windows?

Outside! The windows faced outside! Night had fallen. Beyond the glass, a few stark lights glared from atop tall poles.

Movement!

From the far end of the security desk, two men appeared. They looked like soldiers. They wore camouflage and carried weapons. The men rushed across the security area. They were heading in her direction.

They knew! They were coming for her.

Her hands cradled the gun; its smooth surface settled into her fingers. In seconds, the encounter would be over.

The soldiers were almost on top of her.

They didn't stop running. They passed by! Their footsteps faded. The men hadn't seen her.

Leeha's head fell back until it rested on the wall. Her knees went weak, but she must stay alert. By no means was she safe. If not for the nook, the soldiers would've spotted her.

She gathered her strength. The exit was close, just two hundred paces away. She readied herself to make the dash.

Advice from long ago rang in her ears. She was a child; Grandpa Ritsagin was teaching her how to protect herself. *Your greatest ally in a dangerous situation is a cool head,* he had instructed her. Was she calm now? Heck no, but where might she go to collect herself? *Be aware of your surroundings,* Grandpa Ritsagin used to say. She scanned the hall, the security desk, and each door. Nothing presented itself as a solution. This was one of those times when *winging it* was the only option; she'd make it outside, or she'd die.

As she stepped away from the drinking fountain, she took one more look to the right.

How had she not seen *that*? Next to the drinking fountain stood a door. The word, *WOMEN,* was written on it in black letters. She pushed on the door handle. It turned! She walked in and locked the door behind her.

The restroom contained one toilet stall and one sink, all in white. The sterile cleanliness of the simple fixtures contrasted with the stench of her cell as a clear, mountain lake contrasted with a cesspool.

She leaned against a wall and allowed her body to slide to the floor.

Tears poured down her cheeks, but crying was a luxury. She must focus on escape. She couldn't hide in the bathroom forever.

Leeha wiped tears from her face and pushed herself to her feet.

She was not alone!

A woman glared at her. The lady was a horrid sight; she resembled the bag ladies who loitered in CadTranS stations. Blood dribbled from the woman's swollen lips. Her mussed, tangled hair clumped together like muddy wool sheared from a drowned lamb. Leeha aimed her gun.

The woman also raised a weapon.

Something was weird. The woman's face bore familiar angles.

Leeha lowered her pistol. So did the bum.

No one occupied the room with her. A mirror mounted above the sink reflected her own ghastly self.

She staggered to the mirror. How could this horrific image belong to her? Layers of ground-in dirt soiled pallor skin. Purple bags drooped under red-rimmed eyes. She tugged on the bottom edge of her shirt. Her clothing appeared pulled from an oil-saturated mud puddle and hung up to dry in a dust storm. Blood stained the crotch of her light-colored jeans. She looked every bit as downtrodden as the vagabonds who slept in Helmsey District gutters.

Leeha locked herself in the toilet stall and pulled down her pants. Her panties and crotch were a disgusting mess. Gobs of toilet paper did little to clean the pungent filth. She needed soap.

Low-hanging pants hobbled her legs as she shuffled to the sink. Reams of paper towels, water, and soap lessened the mess.

She washed her hands. They were still gross. She washed them again. Still dirty. She pumped a mound of foamy soap into her palm and scrubbed her hands a third time.

Clean hands contrasted with the rest of her filthy body. Leeha removed her shirt and shoved her head under the faucet. Warm water rolled over her face and scalp. In the basin, blood from her mouth mingled with water.

Three rounds of scrubbing soothed her wounds and puffy eyes, but a sponge bath with paper towels didn't get rid of the stink coming from her underarms.

She leaned over the edge of the sink. Water flowed directly onto her stinky armpits. Rubbing and plenty of soap got rid of most of the pungent odor.

Grit on her shirt scratched her clean skin as she dressed, but she didn't have anything else to wear. Dirty clothes would have to do.

Once more, she looked into the mirror. Even after a good washing, the light, reddish-brown color of her hair carried a gray tinge. Her hair was a tangle of knots. A comb might never free the strands.

A tapping noise echoed in the restroom.

She grabbed her gun, but then relaxed. Gurgling water made the sound. Soldiers had not found her. But they would. She'd lingered in the restroom too long.

Leeha pressed her cheek against the door. Not a sound met her ears.

She readied her weapon and opened the door just a crack.

No one stirred. No noises rolled in.

She stepped through the doorway.

The cubbyhole protected her from prying eyes, but it blocked her view. She gripped the gun with both hands. One! Two! Three! She lunged into the hallway. It was empty.

Leeha dashed toward the security desk—and the exit.

She reached the desk. A sheltered spot beneath the counter offered a place to hide.

Although lights and images flickered on various pieces of equipment and monitors, the chairs sat vacant and askew, as if the people who sat in them had scurried off in a rush.

She studied outdoor images on the viewplanes. Pictures showed the nighttime grounds as they would appear in brighter lights. Crates, storage containers, and bleak buildings filled a vast, lifeless yard. A tall, wire fence loomed in the distance. Not a single soldier was in sight.

Leeha stood and took one last look around. A hall extended both to the left and right of the security desk. Both corridors were void of people. She saw no exits except for the glass one in front of the counter.

She dashed to the door.

If she pushed on it, would an alarm sound? Her fingers trembled as she pressed the handle. No sirens wailed. The thick glass slid open.

Cool, outdoor air brushed against her cheeks. The odor of engine grease swooped into her nostrils, but the breeze also carried fragrant scents. She caught the smells of pine, greenery, and dry earth. A picture flashed through her mind: the family farm.

She shook her head to chase away the image. Even if she survived the night, she'd never see the rolling fields and groves of trees again, for the beauty of Oakwood had been stripped away years ago.

Leeha stepped outside. The door closed behind her. She was out of the building, but she still had to find a way out of the compound.

The nearest structure was a tall wooden crate. She ran to it and hid in its narrow shadow.

What should she do next?

She needed a plan.

A thought came to her. When she was hiding by the security desk, she had studied images on the viewing monitors. One of the monitors showed images of a fence and a gate. The gate would be in front of her and to the right.

Her plan—head for the gate.

She darted to another crate and then to a storage container.

As she slipped around a corner of the massive box, she heard faint, undulating sounds. Dim shimmers of light appeared and vanished like ghostly wisps of fog.

The noises and lights weren't coming from the direction of the gate. Perhaps a change of plan was in order. Maybe if she headed toward the lights and noise, she'd find a better way out of the compound.

Leeha rushed to a single-story building. Holes pocked the concrete walls as if the structure had suffered a barrage of weapons-fire. She hugged the shadows and peeked around the corner.

Spotlights flooded the distant scene. People dressed in civilian clothes massed along the outside of the fence. On the inside of the fence, handfuls of soldiers and a few boxy vehicles faced off against the mob. Most of the commotion was taking place in one spot. But why?

The fence had a hole in it, that's why!

A trickle of civilians sprinted through the breach. None made it far. Some people fell to the ground as if swatted by an invisible monster. Others flew into the air as if thrown aloft by a great wind.

For the first time since her abduction, hope filled her soul. The opening in the fence was her ticket out of this terrible place. She had no idea where she was, but outside the fence had to be better than inside. Her new plan was a promising one; she'd slip through the rip in the fence and get lost in the crowd. Then she'd be free!

A noise crept through the darkness. This sound was close. It came from behind her. After experiencing a pitch-black prison cell, blindfolds, and torture chambers, she'd learned what muffled, human footsteps sounded like.

She strained to listen but heard nothing else.

Perhaps she'd made a mistake. Filtered starlight hinted at trees and cliffs. Wildlife might live here. Maybe an animal lurking in the night made the noise.

Once again, she turned her attention to the mob at the fence. She must get closer to find a way to escape.

Leeha searched for her next destination.

Just ahead, three storage containers rested side by side. Long shadows provided cover, and no one was in sight.

While the path to the three containers seemed safe, the darkness behind her did not. A tingle ran through her, like walking in a house rumored to be haunted. Someone or something unseen and unwanted might be watching.

She readied her gun.

A strong hand grabbed her wrist. The pistol tumbled to the ground.

Another hand covered her mouth. A strong arm pulled her against a hard body.

She fought like Grandpa Ritsagin had taught her.

Nothing worked. The attacker anticipated every move.

She had one more trick to try; she bit the fingers that covered her mouth. It did no good. The man wore gloves.

He spoke. His voice didn't sound cruel or angry. "Leeha Ritsagin, my name is Kever Carsen. I'm here to help you."

He dragged her into shadows. "I know what you're thinking, Leeha; you're planning to escape through the hole in the fence. You'll never make it. I have another way out, but you have to trust me. If I release you, will you listen to what I have to say?"

The man's grip loosened, but only enough for her to give a nod.

"Don't try anything, Leeha. I have a weapon, and I know how to use it. Do you understand?"

She nodded again.

"I'm going to let go now, Leeha."

Cool air filled the void as his body pulled away from hers.

In the low light, she discerned the shape of a tall, slender man with wide shoulders. He bent down and picked up the weapon that had fallen from her hand. He wiped off the gun with a tiny piece of fabric and tossed the gun aside.

The wounds caused by the doctor-in-white's dental instruments made it hard to talk. "Why did you do that?"

"It's an army-issue weapon," he said. "They build tracking mechanisms into them. I cleaned it up to get rid of your prints and DNA." He pointed toward her hips. "Give me the spare clip in your pants pocket. The military tracks clips, too."

Her fingers brushed his gloved hand as she gave the spare ammunition cartridge to him.

He cleaned the clip and flung it away. "I take it you know how to shoot?" he asked.

"Sort of. My grandpa taught me when I was little." Nothing was making sense. "I'm confused. Where am I? What is this place?"

"The Hansen Hills Federal Facility."

"Hansen Hills? Why am I here?"

"We'll fill you in later, Leeha. We've got to go."

"Who are you?"

All his attention focused on her. "Like I told you, I'm Kever. Most people call me Kever-o. Cookie Davis is my friend. I work for Bob Fullerby."

"Bob Fullerby! Why does Bob Fullerby care about me?"

"Many things have happened, Leeha. We can't talk about it here. We've got to go."

"Go where?"

"Do you want to get out of here, Leeha?"

"Of course." She glanced at the crowd and the gaping hole in the fence.

"Leeha, you'll be caught if you go that way. I have a safer way out, but we have to hurry. The military will restore perimeter security soon. I don't intend to get trapped in here. Come with me, or do it your way. It's up to you."

Kever slipped away. He was not a small man, but he vanished into the night like a tiny bat.

Who was this guy? Did he really work for Bob Fullerby? Was it a trick? Were her captors using another tactic to make her reveal her secrets?

Leeha watched a civilian run through the opening in the fence. The person didn't get far. His body flew backward as if thrown by an unseen giant.

Perhaps Kever was right. Heading to the commotion by the fence might not be a good idea. For better or worse, she'd follow Kever Carsen.

Leeha picked her way through the darkness. Where had he gone?

She heard his voice. He was standing nearby. "Leeha, glad you decided to come along. Put this on."

He handed her a flexible, curved object. "What's this?"

"Night vision goggles." He helped her position the object over her eyes.

"Wow! I can see lots of stuff."

"Leeha, are your nodes in your left arm?"

"They used to be. I think someone cut them out. Why do you ask?"

"Hmm, that would explain why I didn't pick up communication signals from you." He handed her a stretchy, cloth band. "Just in case, put this over your arm."

She obeyed. "Where are we going?"

He pointed to a secluded edge of the compound. "We've cut an opening. You ready?"

Kever might end up being a bad guy, but out of Hansen Hills was *out of Hansen Hills*. Out was better than in. "Yes, I'm ready."

She followed him into heavy shadows near the fence. Kever leaned close to her. He smelled good, like pine needles. His breath smelled of spearmint. "Leeha, a friend is waiting on the other side. Don't hurt him, please."

"Hurt him? How could I hurt him?"

"You can fight. He doesn't know how skilled you are."

Her? A skilled fighter? "I'll try my best not to hurt him, Kever-o."

"You know, Leeha, I was wondering if you were worth it … worth the risk of breaking you out. I've just decided you are worth it. I like you."

Kever slithered in snakelike fashion to a tiny slit in the fence. He pushed up a section of wire. "Leeha, crawl through. My friend will help you."

Coarse sand scratched her hands and arms as she dragged her body under the fence.

Sleeved arms and gloved hands reached from the darkness. Whoever Kever's friend was, he was strong. He grabbed her by the shoulders and pulled her into a cluster of rocks and shrubs. The man crouched next to her. He spoke in a deep voice. "Stay still. Be quiet."

She'd lost sight of Kever, so she pushed aside a tangle of twigs. She spotted him. He'd crossed through the fence, but he was hunched on the ground. "What's he doing?"

The man said, "Patching the fence."

"Why?"

"When perimeter security is restored, the patch will delay detection of the breach. Now, be quiet."

Whoever this guy was, he lacked Kever's amicable style. Yet, the man's voice sounded familiar, but she didn't know why.

"Sir, how long will it take him—"

"Quiet!"

At last, Kever crawled away from the fence. He joined her and the other guy among the boulders and bushes. Kever set a hand on her shoulder. "How are you holding up, Leeha?"

"Okay."

"Good. Leeha, this is my friend, Anson."

"Hi, Anson."

Anson gave her a nod, nothing more. He said, "Kever-o, I'll scout ahead."

Kever tapped him on the back. "Go, buddy. Be careful."

Anson's powerful shoulders pushed through the shrubs without making a sound.

"Here, Leeha," Kever said. "Put this by your ear."

She took a small device from his hand. "What's this?"

"It's an ear-piece. You'll be able to communicate with Anson and me."

Anson's voice came through the device. "All clear."

She felt Kever's strong hand on her back. "Okay, Leeha, let's go."

Kever led her along a faint trail littered with rocks and knots of plants. Tree needles grazed her arms as she stumbled along. An unexpected thought popped into her mind. These trees, like people, fought for a right to live, a right to grow, a right to enjoy one more day of sunshine or rain.

Anson's voice flowed through her ear-piece. "Overlook reports hostiles approaching from the north and east."

Kever grabbed her wrist. "Leeha, we need to pick up the pace."

They headed uphill and away from the fence. The vegetation thickened. The faint path diminished as they tromped over a clutter of boulders. Shrub and tree branches slapped her face. "Kever-o, why did we leave the trail?"

"We didn't. Focus on where you step. The ground is rough."

What an understatement!

Bushes released a spicy aroma as she and Kever plowed into a thicket.

The patch of brush ended. Up ahead, a narrow path wound between two columns of rock.

Leeha heard Anson's voice. "I'm in position. It's clear."

"We're right behind you, Anson," Kever said.

She followed Kever along the meandering, earthen path.

He stopped walking.

Leeha willed herself to stop, too, but her weary legs didn't obey. She smashed into him. His solid body didn't budge. She forced herself to pull away from the comfort of his shoulders.

They stood in a sheltered clearing at the base of a giant cliff. Anson stood near the rock wall, his gaze fixed upward. He wore a funny-looking helmet.

Leeha scanned the terrain around her. Stone and interwoven plants encircled the clearing. "Why are we stopping here?"

Kever's breath tickled her ear. "This is where we go up."

"Up? We've been going uphill for a long way."

"Do you climb, Leeha?"

"What ... what do you mean by *climb*?"

"Have you ever rock climbed?"

What sort of nutty question was that? "No, of course not."

"That's okay, we figured you weren't a climber."

Anson's hands caressed the face of the cliff as tenderly as a mother squirrel's tongue preened the fur of her child. "What do you think, Kever-o, can she use ascenders?"

"Yeah, she seems okay."

Anson pulled things from a backpack. "Good, that'll make it go a lot faster." He handed the items to Kever.

"Here, Leeha," Kever said, "put these on."

Leeha recognized one of the objects: a helmet like the one Anson was wearing. She set it on her head. The other object was a bit of a conundrum. She rotated a twisted, thick, fabric band in her hands.

Kever fastened a similar contraption around his hips. "You ready, Leeha?"

"What is this thing? I don't know how it works."

"It's a harness. I'll help you." Her whole body jerked as Kever adjusted the bands. "There, that should do it."

He pulled the helmet from her head. "You've got it on backward. See, this piece goes in front." He plopped the helmet on her head and fastened the strap. "Leeha, why don't you rest a bit?" He tapped a flat boulder. "Here, have a seat."

She sat on the boulder and rested her back against the vertical cliff. Her eyes closed as she breathed in the scents of soil and greenery.

A clinking sound roused her from her trance. She looked around. "Kever-o, where's Anson?"

Kever's eyes were angled upward. "He's leading first."

"Leading?" She saw Anson's muscular form scaling the cliff like a spider. "Kever-o, why is he going up there?"

"He's setting the first anchor."

Why on earth would he do that?

She heard Anson's voice through the ear-piece. "Anchor one is set. Send her up."

Kever held another strange contraption. This one was made up of two strips of cascading fabric loops. An odd, metallic gadget topped each strip. "Leeha, you'll go up next."

"Kever-o, you ... you want me to go up there, where Anson is?"

392 ◆ C. N. SKY

"Yes, don't worry, it's an easy climb. If bad guys weren't hanging around, it'd be a route Anson and I would use to warm up."

Her eyes followed the cliff. Up and up, it went. The wall didn't end until her head tilted back as far as her neck would bend. Far above, the rock face met a starlit sky. Her pulse pounded in her neck. "I don't know how to climb."

"You won't need to rock climb. These are ascenders. It'll be just like climbing a ladder. All you need to do is scoot these up the rope like this." He pushed what looked like a giant, deformed safety pin up along a rope. "Instead of rungs on a ladder, you'll step into these stirrups."

"I'm … I'm scared of heights."

"Don't look down."

"What if I fall?"

"The rope will catch you. Come here, I'll hook you in."

Running away seemed a good alternative. "I can't do this, Kever-o."

"Leeha, you can do it. If you get tired, take a break."

"We're not going all the way to the top, are we?"

"Yep. Friends are waiting for us up there."

"Kever-o, how are you getting up?"

"When you reach the anchor, I'll climb next. I'll set the second anchor. Anson will set the third. Anson and I will each lead three times. We'll alternate. Got it?"

"No!"

"You'll be fine, Leeha. Remember, it's just like climbing a ladder."

The impatience in Anson's voice was audible even through an earpiece. "Kever-o, what's the delay down there?"

"We're ready, Anson. She's on her way."

Kever touched her back. He had removed his gloves, so warmth from his palm penetrated her shirt. "Sorry about all this, Leeha. The military is patrolling the roadways and the main trailheads. They don't have the manpower to cover climbing routes, but that'll change soon. More forces and equipment are coming. When that happens, there'll be no way out."

"I understand, Kever-o, but I'm still scared." She stepped into a cloth loop and pushed one of the safety-pin-like gadgets up the rope as he had shown her.

"Good job, Leeha. Push up with one hand, then step up. Repeat on the other side."

Kever was right; the motion mimicked climbing a ladder. An old barn on her family farm had wooden rungs nailed to an interior wall. As her toes hit the solid wall of the barn, so now did her foot tap solid rock. However, this contraption of ropes and loops swung to and fro against an uneven surface. With almost every step, a sharp stone poked an elbow or knee.

She heard Kever's voice through the ear-piece. "Stop and catch your breath if you need to, Leeha." She wanted to keep going. Her arms were tiring, but resting delayed reaching the top.

The failure gave no warning. Ropes flung her body sideways. Her left foot slipped from its rung. Her right leg slid through a cloth loop.

She did what Kever told her not to do; she looked down. The ground lay far below. She saw the top of Kever's head. He was so far away! "I'm scared! I'm going to fall."

Kever's voice, calm and soothing, came through the ear-piece. "It's okay, Leeha, you won't fall. Focus on breathing. Let your body relax. The rope will hold you. When you catch your breath, concentrate on getting your body back into position."

She drew one breath and then another. Both inhalations were shallow, but the third pushed air into her lungs. The fourth breath expanded her belly. She noticed the scent of the rock. It smelled good, like real earth. She shook her right hand and then the left to loosen her rigid fingers. A smidgeon of strength returned to her limbs.

Leeha longed to return to flat ground. She preferred to take her chances dodging the enemy through the valley forest, yet she did as Kever asked.

Each foot found a loop. After a few wobbles, she was standing once again in this weird apparatus Kever called *ascenders*.

Cheery tones filled his voice. "Good job, Leeha. Your body alignment is stable. Try going up again. Pace yourself."

The sway of the rope took on a rhythm as she climbed.

A glint caught her eye. "There's something shiny up here. There's a rope going through it."

Kever said, "It's a piece of protection that Anson put in. It's what catches us if we fall. You're not at the anchor yet, but you're almost there. Then you'll get a nice break."

Up she went, concentrating on each move. Right side. Hand up. Foot up. Left side. Hand up. Foot up.

The sway of the rope changed. Rather than long, fluid moves, the rope jerked in short, quick wiggles.

She glanced upward. "Kever-o, my rope is going through weird spikes."

"You've reached the anchor, Leeha. Rest now. I'll see you soon."

She clutched the rope below the anchor. Squeezing it gave her a sense of comfort—a sense of attachment to the earth—even though she dangled from a skinny cord high up on a cliff.

A shuffling sound came from her right. Anson hung alongside her. His body appeared as relaxed as if he were sitting in a lounge chair.

"Anson, what … what are you doing up here?"

He let out a laugh. "I'm glad you kept a sense of humor, Leeha."

She hadn't intended the question as a joke, but it was nice to know he wasn't stone-cold serious all the time.

His smile faded, but compassion colored his words. "How are you holding up?"

"Um, okay. I do want to get to the top, though."

"I know what you mean. Having bad guys running around down there does take the fun out of a pleasant climb."

Pleasant climb? Did such a thing exist?

Faint tapping sounds came from below. Leeha looked down. Kever was scaling the wall. No tension contorted his lean, long body. He reached and stepped with the grace of a dancer.

He joined them at the anchor. "How's it going, Leeha?"

"Okay. How long do I need to wait here?"

"Not long. I'm going to set up the next anchor. Anson will stay with you."

Kever was on his way again. Most of the sounds he made traveled through stone rather than air.

Images from old movies ran through her mind; a tracker would press his ear against the ground to listen for movement.

Leeha rested her cheek against the chilly cliff and imagined lying on level land. She'd be listening for fun. No one would be chasing her. Hansen Hills would be far away in both distance and time. She and Kever would be playing hide-and-seek. Except for a dusting of unspoiled earth, she'd be nice and clean. Then she'd find him in a hiding place next to a giant evergreen tree. He'd take her in his arms—

Anson's deep voice shattered her fantasy. "Leeha, Kever-o has the second anchor set. You can start climbing."

She pulled herself into position.

"Keep your backside tucked in," Anson said. "It'll help you stay balanced."

Once again, she focused on sliding the safety-pin gadget along the rope. Only one time did her body wag to the side.

She met Kever at the second anchor.

He gave her a giant smile. "You did awesome, Leeha. You're a natural."

Ha! So not true! The compliment was nice, though. "What happens next, Kever-o?"

"We'll wait for Anson. He's going to set the third anchor."

She recalled something Kever had told her: *he'd lead three times, and Anson would lead three times.* Relief flowed through her like a blast of cold water on a scorching day. "When Anson gets done, we'll be at the halfway point, right?"

"Right!" Kever tossed something into his mouth and chewed.

How on earth could he eat while hanging on the side of the cliff? He and Anson had odd ideas of what constituted fun. However, as frightening as climbing was, her dark, cold prison cell was worse. Unpleasant—and recent—memories flashed through her mind: a needle piercing the doctor's neck; a guard lying on a concrete floor, gasping for air.

"Hey, Leeha," Kever said, "what's wrong?"

"Hansen Hills is right down there. It's so close."

"Yes, but we'll get you away from here soon."

Even in this precarious situation, she noticed how sexy Kever was.

Reality struck. Leeha rested her cheek against the stone. What a fool she was to fantasize about him! For all she knew, he might be a bad guy trying to get information about the Guiding Light document. If he did work for Bob Fullerby, why on earth would he be interested in her? She was no raving beauty before going to prison, but now, she was this god-awful mess. Someone as splashy as Kever would never fall for someone like her.

"Leeha, why don't you tell me about yourself."

"Like what?"

"Like, what's your favorite dessert?"

"I like lots of desserts."

"If you had to pick one favorite, what would it be?"

She recalled the dessert Randy Altholder bought for her in her secondary school days. "I'd have to say strawberry milkshakes."

"What about strawberry milkshakes do you like?"

She mustn't tell him about Randy. In case Kever was a bad guy, she didn't dare mention anything related to the document. If he was a good guy, the worst thing to do was talk about another good-looking man. Randy was splashy, but as hard as it was to believe, Kever was even better looking. "I like strawberries and vanilla ice cream. The two go good together. What's your favorite?"

"Chocolate with black walnuts."

Leeha pictured walnut trees on the family farm. "When I was growing up, I used to help my mom and grandma pick walnuts. A lot of different types of trees grew on our property."

"Sounds like a nice place."

"It was. The trees are gone now, though. Just about everything nice is gone."

"When was the last time you had a strawberry milkshake, Leeha?"

The last time had been with Randy. She would leave such details out of her answer. "I ... it's been a long time. When did you last have chocolate with black walnuts?"

"Oh, let's see ... the day before yesterday."

Despite the many terrible things that had happened, Leeha felt a smile creep across her face. The wounds on her lips and gums prevented the grin from stretching as far as usual. "Wow! You must be really keen on chocolate with black walnuts."

"You betcha!"

Anson's voice came through the ear-piece. "The anchor is set."

She was surprised how chatting with Kever made time fly. She said, "I'm off to the halfway point, right?"

"You sure are, Leeha."

She headed toward the next anchor.

After several steps, the rock changed. The surface had roughened. Grains ran left to right rather than in vertical columns. The stone smelled of chalk.

The texture of the cliff smoothed again a few steps before anchor number three.

Anson was waiting for her. He reached for her arm. "Leeha, let me help you get into a more comfortable position." He then spoke through the ear-piece. "She's secure, Kever-o."

Echoes of Kever's movements reverberated through the stone. The vibrations were mesmerizing, like the sound of tinkling wind chimes on a warm, summer night.

Kever stopped climbing when he reached her side. "You still holding up okay, Leeha?"

"Yeah." She didn't tell him about a twinge in her right calf.

"I'm off to set the fourth anchor, Leeha. If you get bored, tell Anson about strawberry milkshakes."

Bored? He must've been thinking *scared*, but he was being nice.

Kever went on his way. His climbing moves seemed effortless, as if he were strolling along a flat street.

She glanced at Anson. His attention was fixed on everything but her. She doubted he'd want to chat about desserts. By the look of his massive muscles, she wondered if he'd ever tasted sweets.

Far below, flickers of light bounced about in the forest around the Hansen Hills compound. "Anson, I ... I see lights down there."

"I see them, too. I've been watching them."

"What's making the lights?"

He paused before answering. "Probably soldiers."

"Are they looking for us?"

"I don't know, Leeha."

She looked up. Kever hadn't yet stopped to set the fourth anchor.

"Anson, do you think Kever-o knows about the lights?"

"He does."

She rested her forehead against the rope. She wished to blend into the rock to stay out of sight. Anson, too, didn't make a sound.

If Kever feared the lights, it didn't reflect in his voice as it flowed through the ear-piece. "Anchor four is set. Come on up, Leeha."

Her body ached as she pulled herself into position. With each step, her muscles weakened. Instead of knee-high strides, each step equated to the length of a hand.

It took forever, but at last she met Kever at the anchor. "Leeha, are you okay?"

"Yeah."

"Are you getting tired?"

"Yeah, in the legs."

"Remember, Leeha, pace yourself. Don't burn out."

He didn't mention the flashing lights in the valley.

"Kever-o, there are lights in the forest. Anson thinks soldiers are down there."

"I know, Leeha."

Distant whistles echoed in the night. "Kever-o, was that gunfire?"

"Yeah, standard military issue M-R-Tens. None of the shots came in our direction. You look tense, Leeha, try to relax."

She pointed her toes to stretch.

A cramp seized her right calf.

Something weird happened. She felt weightless. Her body fell backward. She saw sky, ground, then rock. The harness tugged at her hips. Her left shoulder slammed into the cliff. She clutched tiny lumps of stone with her fingertips. Her arms trembled.

Kever slid down the rope like a spider from a web. "Leeha, are you hurt?"

"I'm going to fall!"

"Leeha, you're not going to fall. The rope caught you." He touched her hand. "You can let go; relax your fingers."

"I'll fall!"

"You won't fall, Leeha."

She released her grip on the tiny bits of rock. She didn't fall.

"Leeha, what happened?"

"I got a cramp in my leg. The pain's gone now."

"Where was the cramp?"

"Right calf."

He reached for her leg. Strong fingers massaged her muscles. "There, that should loosen it up a bit." His hands grasped her waist. "Let me help you get back into position."

Anson soon joined them. "Is everything all right, Kever-o?"

"Yeah, she got a cramp. She's okay now."

Anson said, "Don't worry, Leeha. Cramps happen sometimes. See you at the next anchor." He was off again, climbing without even a hint of weariness.

A cool blast of wind slapped her body. Another gust followed. Each blast threatened to knock her off balance. "Kever-o, it's getting windy."

"We're close to the top. We've less shelter up here."

"It's kind of scary. It's hard to hold on."

"Hang in there, Leeha. Anson's about to set his last anchor. After that, we'll be at the top."

"You know, even though I'm scared up here, it's better than prison. I'd rather fall to my death than live another day in a cell."

"Leeha, let's hope neither happens. You're doing great. I'm impressed how well you're taking all this."

Anson's voice came through the ear-piece. "Anchor five is ready. Send her up."

Kever spoke in his cheery voice. "This is it, Leeha. Next stop after this is the end of the climb. Take your time. Pace yourself. We'll get through it."

She headed toward the next anchor. She didn't like the wind. Just when she thought it had died down, another gust would slap her body.

A long-ago memory popped into her mind. She was hiking with Grandma and Grandpa Chavatan. A trail switchbacked up a hillside covered with trees and rocky outcroppings. Her short, seven-year-old legs fumbled over teensy bumps, that, at the time, seemed like giant steps. The sun was setting. Terror filled her child's heart at the thought of being out after dark. Dangers of many sorts prowled at night. *Don't worry, Leeha,* Grandma Chavatan had told her. *We have headlamps, and your grandfather and I know the way. We won't get lost, so there's no reason to be afraid. We're with you, little angel.*

Weapons-fire whistled. Flashes flickered against the cliff. Stone groaned and crackled. Rock trembled against her body. The sound echoed through the rock like deep, growling thunder.

Leeha didn't need an ear-piece to hear Anson's shout. "Rockfall!"

Hundreds of crackling sounds came from above. She looked up. Chunks of stone were silhouetted against the star-speckled sky. The black clumps grew larger as they plummeted toward her.

She closed her eyes and pressed her body against the cliff.

Another volley of whistles rang out.

She heard Kever's voice. "Leeha—" If he spoke more than her name, she didn't hear the words. A new rumble ran through the mountain. More debris plunged from above.

When the rockfall had zoomed by, she glanced upward. A large object loomed overhead. This object was different from the others; its edges appeared rounded rather than sharp.

The object was a man!

She scanned the cliff for Anson. No sign of him; she saw only the tumbling, human form.

The body bounced to a stop at the end of a skinny rope.

She heard Kever's voice through the ear-piece. "Anson, can you hear me?"

"I hear you, Kever-o. I'm okay. The last protection was blasted from the rock, but the lower pieces appear intact. I'll put in some lateral protection and check out the conditions. We may need to veer to the right."

Kever spoke again. "Leeha, were you hit?"

A few chunks of debris had clanked against her helmet, but all of the stones were small. "I'm okay, Kever-o, but I don't understand what's going on."

"Weapons-fire knocked out some of the protection Anson had set. He's setting new positions."

Time crawled. She didn't like hanging there all alone. Gusts of wind whooshed by, careening like a demon dragging his claws along a fence to terrorize innocents cowering in midnight shadows.

She sensed another presence in the twirling gusts, this one peaceful, as if the wind carried her father's voice. *My sweet little girl, your resolve is strong. Your tenacity and independence are among your greatest strengths, but these same strengths are also your most dangerous weaknesses. Self-reliance saved you in Hansen Hills, but it will not save you now. Leeha, the time has come for you to forge partnerships; I know this has always been difficult for you, but I also know you can do it. You are my daughter!*

Through the ear-piece, she heard Anson's words. "Anchor reset."

Kever's voice followed. "Leeha, you can climb again."

Every movement hurt. Her whole body felt stiff. Perhaps fear or the chilly air caused it. Or maybe adrenaline, which had propelled her to great feats, had become a liability. Whatever the reason, she couldn't take one more step. The doctor-in-white had broken her will; torture left her body broken. Sobs caught in her throat and strangled her speech. "I'm sorry, Kever-o. I can't do this anymore."

"Leeha, did you say something?"

Again, she heard her father's voice. *Think about the poem, Leeha. Remember how scared you were? You had to memorize a poem and recite it in front of the entire class. I remember how worried you were as you practiced; you kept forgetting the lines, and you feared when the time came to stand before the students and the teacher, they'd laugh at you, point at you, and call you bad names. My little angel, do you recall what I told you to do to relax?*

She remembered. Her dad had told her to sing her favorite kiddy song: *The Adventures of Baby Duck.* Baby Duck's momma said it was time to leave the nest. Baby Duck didn't want to; the nest was soft and warm. Mommy and Daddy promised to protect him as they left their home behind. Baby Duck faced many ordeals: rough grass, sticky mud, cold water, dense reeds, scary eyes glowing in the dark, and, finally, the currents of a wide river.

The ascender would rise no farther. She'd reached the anchor!

Anson's words had a raspy edge. "Leeha, how ya doing?"

"I'm okay. Just tired."

A glossy patch on his back glistened in the dim light. "Anson, what's that on your shirt?"

"I got grazed by a bullet."

"Are you bleeding?"

"Probably, but it's not bad."

"Not bad? Are you crazy? If that's blood, it's a big spot." She leaned back as far as she dared. "Anson, you have a big tear in your shirt. Do you have first-aid stuff? Maybe I can do something."

"Thanks, Leeha, but Kever-o's almost here. I'll have him take a look."

Kever hurried up the cliff. He reached the anchor. "Leeha, are you okay?"

"Yeah, but Anson isn't. He was shot. Look at all the blood!"

Kever studied Anson's back. "That's a long gash you have there, buddy."

Anson seemed calm, but his voice betrayed him; he was in pain. "I don't think it's deep."

Kever hooked a pouch to the anchor. "Leeha's right. There's a lot of blood. I'm going to have a look." He cut Anson's shirt with thin scissors. "The wound's not too deep, but it is long. I'll pin you up. Will you be able to climb by yourself?"

"Yep, I'm just a bit sore is all."

Kever closed the wound with long, skinny bandages. "That should hold you for now. How does it feel?"

"Not bad."

Kever stuffed the first-aid pouch into his pack. "This is it, Leeha. Next stop is the top. It'll be like before; I'll set up an anchor. You'll climb to it. Once you're up, Anson will join us."

Seconds later, Kever transformed into an undulating shadow on the rock face above.

He reached the top! His voice came through the ear-piece. "Okay, Leeha, come on up. This is the last leg."

She was about to climb, but she wasn't sure if leaving Anson alone was a good idea. "Are you sure you're okay here by yourself?"

"I'm good enough, Leeha. Don't worry."

Fatigue had taken a toll, yet she mustn't screw up. The sooner they reached the top, the sooner Anson could get to a doctor. She focused on every move.

"You're almost up, Leeha." It was Kever's natural voice; the words didn't come from the ear-piece.

Her eyes peeked over the lip of the cliff. She'd made it!

She flung her right arm onto the flat ground. Her strength failed. Rock and grit dug into her fingernails as she slid off the ledge. "I'm falling!"

Kever's voice was calm. "You're not falling. You're tied in. I'll help you up."

The harness tugged at her hips. Her body rose. She scampered over the sharp, rough lip of the cliff.

At last! Her belly pressed against level earth.

A glance to the right reminded her that the cliff lay just a mouse's tail away. On hands and knees, she scrambled away from the edge.

Kever helped her to her feet. "Give me your ear-piece," he said. "We're safer without them. Someone might pick up a signal."

Her legs wobbled as she handed him the device.

He swung an arm around her. "Come on, let's get you to the brush line. You can rest there."

She pulled away from his embrace. "I can make it myself. Go help Anson."

Her legs shook, but she made it to a long thicket filled with dense shrubs, clingy vines, and tall grasses.

She pushed her way into the fragrant vegetation. A thick mat of branches and twigs cushioned her back. Her jail cell felt light-years away even though the hellhole lay at the bottom of the cliff she'd just scaled.

Gentle whispers of nature soothed her mind and her aching muscles. Newfound calmness, though, allowed cold air to penetrate her lightweight clothing. As she did in her dank cell, she wrapped her arms around her legs to retain any remnants of warmth. But, unlike prison, the air smelled of evergreen and wild herbs.

She rested her head on her knees. The stench of her dirty clothes reminded her yet again of her ordeal. She willed herself to not cry. Her best efforts failed. Leeha pulled the night vision goggles away from her face and sobbed into the worn, dirty fabric of her jeans.

What was she doing? Now was not the time for crying. She must stay alert.

When she raised her head, she saw dust dancing in filtered light. Morning had dawned!

Leeha reset her goggles to keep dust out of her eyes. She pushed aside a tangle of branches.

What a glorious sight! The sun had risen. Pale rays streaked through dips in distant, rough mountains.

Nearer to her, from the direction of the cliff, came the sound of metal on stone. She saw Kever. He was kneeling down and looking over the edge. Anson hadn't yet reached the top.

Doubt returned. As nice and brave as the two men seemed, did they really know Bob Fullerby? Or was it a trick to get her to tell the truth about the Guiding Light?

A thought crossed her mind; Kever and Anson were preoccupied. This might be the ideal moment to sneak away.

But what about her father's warning? Dare she ignore his advice about forming partnerships?

What was she thinking? Her dad was long dead. However real his advice felt, he didn't climb the cliff with her. She'd conjured up both his presence and his words. She mustn't let her own wild imagination guide her.

On the other hand, if she chose to leave, where would she go? She had no clean clothes, no personal device, and no map. Even worse, bad guys were searching for her. Kever and Anson might be bad guys themselves, but, at the moment, they pretended to be good; she might find at least a smidgeon of comfort before things turned nasty.

She slumped deeper into her living cushion. For good or ill, she'd be traveling with Kever and Anson awhile.

Through a slender gap in the vegetation, she watched as Anson dragged his muscular body onto flat ground. Kever helped him walk to a stubby, fat juniper tree. Anson leaned against the thick trunk as Kever folded ropes and stuffed gear into a backpack.

He flung the pack onto his back. The weight of the pack failed to shorten his strides as he trotted toward her hiding place in the brush. "Leeha, we're all set. Let's go. Our people are waiting for us by the ridgeline."

She crawled out from the thicket. Her legs trembled as she stood. "Is it far?"

"No, and Overlook tells us the coast is clear. Let's go."

She followed Kever and Anson as they weaved among boulders, brush, and trees.

The men led the way through a thicket.

The brush line ended.

She stumbled into a dark, barren clearing. An old man and a pretty, young woman stood beneath overhanging stone.

The woman dashed to Anson's side. "How badly are you hurt?"

"It's not bad, Row. I'll be okay; Kever-o patched me up. Take care of Leeha."

The woman's green eyes met hers. "Leeha, I'm Rona Betler of Andecco News Service. Please step under the arch."

Leeha had never seen a structure like it. It resembled a giant birdcage. "What does it do?"

"It'll tell us if you have active nodes or tracking devices anywhere in your body."

Leeha stepped into the birdcage-like arch. A rubbery floor flexed beneath her feet. A soft hum emanated from the thin, wire walls.

Rona said, "Leeha, please remove the dampening device from your arm."

Leeha pointed at the black, stretchy band that Kever had given her when she was still inside the Hansen Hills compound. "Do you mean this?"

"Yes."

She slid the band from her arm and handed it to Rona.

The steady hum coming from the arch stopped. Numerous squeaks, pops, and groans followed.

The old man spoke for the first time. "She's clean."

Rona said, "You may come out now, Leeha."

Leeha stepped off the rubbery surface and onto hard earth.

Rona's voice oozed femininity. "Professor, are you sure you don't need help taking the arch apart?"

"I've got it covered, Row. Look after your friends."

Kever emerged from shadows at the periphery of the clearing. "Thanks, Professor. We appreciate your help."

"You're welcome. When you get news about Bob, please let me know."

"We'll keep you informed, Professor."

Leeha felt Kever's hand on her back. Warmth from his palm flowed through her shirt. "Come on, Leeha. It's time to go."

"Go where?"

"A place where you can get something to eat, clean up, and rest."

She followed him along another faint path. Rona and Anson trailed behind.

They reached a clearing hidden beneath overhanging tree limbs. Anson said, "Kever-o, I'm holding you guys up. Get Leeha to the van. Don't wait for me. Row and I will make sure no one's tracking you."

A look of concern covered Kever's face. "Anson, if you're feeling worse, I don't want to leave you."

Rona said, "I'll stay with him, Kever-o. Leeha needs to get warm; she's shivering."

"Okay," Kever said, "call me if you need help. Come on, Leeha, let's go."

Kever walked along the flimsy trail without a misstep.

Leeha struggled to keep up, reaching for any available branch or stone to keep her balance.

He disappeared into a knot of greenery.

She plowed her way through it and froze. A van was parked in a narrow clearing. This was how the nightmare had begun: she was thrown into the back of a van.

Kever's hands rested on her shoulders. "It's okay, Leeha. It's safe. The professor assured us it's clean of tracking devices."

A door on the side of the van opened. While layers of dust covered the scratched exterior of the vehicle, the interior was spotless and filled with fluffy, folded blankets.

A book she had studied in a college literature class haunted her: *A Poison Gift*. The old classic described the downfall of Barmadosa. The mighty, ancient Fewwoki kingdom came to a sudden and tragic end when a delegation from an enemy kingdom presented the Barmadosan king with a peace offering. The gift was a royal cape—a tribute fit for a sovereign. But the offering was not what it seemed; the cape was infected with a deadly scourge that had swept through a part of the world that was now the Domataree Lowlands. Was Kever's invitation to enter a warm, clean van a poison gift?

His breath tickled her ear. "Leeha, is something wrong?"

"When … when they took me, they threw me into a van. They did something to me; I only remember bits and pieces, but I do remember a van."

"Leeha, you have nothing to fear from us. We want to help you."

The urge to fight and run away picked at her. After all, she'd taken down two guards in a torture chamber at Hansen Hills. She'd stabbed the doctor-in-white. She'd shot the doctor's guard with a paralysis dart. She possessed the skills.

Who was she kidding? Her legs struggled to support her. Shivers racked her body.

Warm air wafted through the van's open door. She climbed inside. Kever followed.

"You may lie here if you wish. This pad may not look like much, but it's comfortable. Oh, give me your goggles and helmet. You won't need them anymore."

She handed him the items and snuggled into the soft mattress. Her head sank into a squishy pillow. He draped a thick quilt over her. She caught a faint scent of lavender. For better or worse, she was at his mercy.

The warmth and cleanliness of the bedding coaxed her to sleep.

Leeha awoke to the sound of footsteps. She pried open her eyes and saw Anson and Rona. The vehicle pitched as the couple climbed into the van.

Someone hovered over Anson's wounded back. Leeha wasn't sure if the caregiver was Kever or someone else. She was too tired to give it more thought.

The vehicle backed up and turned hard to the left. It then drove away over bumpy ground.

The rocking and rolling revived memories from long ago. Thoughts came and went in snippets, as if a damaged recording hopped from one random film-fragment to the next. She was a child. She was sitting next to her father as he drove an old pickup truck along a rough, country road. His strong and calloused right hand rested on the gearshift. His feet, encased in worn work boots, pressed floorboard pedals. Sun streamed through the dusty windshield, and the wholesome scent of late-summer crops poured in through the passenger side window. While the recollections were old, her father's words were new. *Don't be afraid, my Leeha. Don't curse the trials you face. Tribulations teach us lessons so we can fulfill our reasons for being born. Don't let difficulties defeat you as I did. When your time comes to leave this*

world, I pray, my daughter, that you will have accomplished your mission. Be
strong, for more trials await. More lessons must be learned. You have much
yet to do, my angel. Stay strong, and know I am proud of you.

A big, strong hand shook her shoulder. She heard another pleasant, male
voice. "Sorry to wake you, Leeha. You need to get up now."

She opened her eyes. Kever was leaning over her. Dishwater blond hair
hung alongside his handsome face. He'd changed outfits. Gone were his
dark, prowler clothes; he now donned earthy-colored outdoor wear.

"Kever-o, where are we?"

"Near Forest Falls. We need to get you inside."

"Inside where?"

"A vacation cabin. It belongs to one of Mr. Fullerby's friends.
We've secured the place, so we don't need to worry about government
eavesdropping."

"Is Bob Fullerby here?"

She sensed an uneasy pause before Kever answered. "Mr. Fullerby is
in Cadona City."

Distrust returned; did Kever and Rona really work for Andecco News
Service?

"Kever-o, how long will I be here?"

"We don't know; we need to play it by ear."

The van door slid open. Despite sunshine, the air still carried a chill.
She longed to remain snuggled in the quilt, but Kever said, "Let me help
you up."

Her legs wobbled as she climbed out of the van. Her feet landed on a
pebble footpath. The walkway stretched across a yard filled with junipers,
pines, and hedges. Leggy flowers danced in gusts of dry air. The path
ended at broad steps leading to a wide, covered deck.

Kever whispered in her ear. "I think you'll like it here, Leeha."

He steered her away from the path. Instead, he guided her along a
gravel driveway that led to a roofed parking area at the side of the house.

Rugged trees shaded a small, rustic porch. Rough-hewn log steps ended at a screen door. The door gave a creak as he pulled it open.

Aged floorboards groaned as she followed him inside. Firewood was stacked to the left. Tools of various types hung from the walls. The porch reminded her of her father's old toolshed.

Kever opened another door—this one sturdy. Warm air gushed out, as did the smells of baking bread and spices. He escorted her down a short hall and into a big living room filled with rustic furniture. Wood paneling and beams gave off a soothing, amber glow in the soft lighting.

A pretty, slender woman in casual clothing approached. Gentle rays of light reflected on her dark, shiny curls. Clear, olive skin framed her ebony eyes. Despite her petite build, she had a solid, athletic look. "Leeha Ritsagin, I'm Angela Thirgal of Andecco News Service. It is an honor to meet you."

Something didn't seem right. Angela Thirgal, *the* Angela Thirgal, was honored to meet her? Without doubt, this lady looked like Angela, but was she really the famous reporter from Andecco News? "Thank you, Ms. Thirgal, I'm a big fan of Andecco."

Even the woman's voice sounded like Angela's. "Please, Leeha, call me *Ang*. Everyone else does."

A wail shot across the living room. The voice belonged to someone Leeha didn't expect to see: Cookie Davis.

Cookie's huge, dark eyes were wet and wide. "Leeha! Oh, my God, Leeha!" She said something else, but sobs distorted her words. She tiptoed forward as one might when approaching the ghostly apparition of a dearly departed soul. "My God, Leeha! What did they do to you?"

Leeha recalled her mirrored reflection. Ratty hair, bloodshot eyes, and swollen lips made her a ghastly sight. "I know I'm a mess, but I'm not as bad off as I seem."

Cookie didn't speak. All she did was stare.

Leeha recalled a similar expression on a teacher's face. It happened in physical education class. Leeha had run away from a ball that she was supposed to catch. Teammates jeered her for losing the game, and a pity-staring teacher consoled her. Now, the pity stare filled Cookie's eyes.

Out of nowhere, Cookie's arms swung around her. "Oh, Leeha, I was so worried! I didn't think I'd ever see you again."

Cookie's grip tightened. Leeha thought her feet might leave the ground. Kever came to the rescue. "Leeha, would you like something to eat?"

"Yeah, I'm starving, actually."

Cookie released her. "Good! I'm glad you're hungry. Row and I prepared a bunch of food. We didn't know what you'd want. We made stew and baked bread—the dark, heavy kind you like."

Without warning, Cookie grabbed her by the arm and dragged her around a counter.

A chair squeaked as Cookie pulled it away from a table made of thick, blond, knotted wood. "Here, Leeha, sit!"

A bowl of steaming stew appeared on the tabletop, as did a plate of buttered bread, a glass of cold water, and a cup of hot tea.

Leeha picked up a fat spoon. Wounds on her lips made it hard to dump food into her mouth.

Cookie handed her a small spoon. "Here, Leeha, try this one."

"Thanks. It's kind of hard to eat with my mouth messed up like this."

"I know, Leeha. Remember how my face looked after my ex beat me up? I had trouble using big spoons and forks for a while."

Until now, she hadn't considered how Cookie might view the situation. Cookie had experienced her own share of loss and pain.

Leeha scooped up the last of the stew.

"Goodness," Cookie said, "you finished it off fast! Do you want some more?"

Leeha looked up. Something odd was going on. Cookie, Kever, and Angela were watching her, and not just watching, but gawking. "Um … maybe more tea."

Cookie brought a fresh pot.

Leeha held her cup in both hands, savoring the heat and healing fragrance. She considered asking why everyone was staring at her, but she decided to ask more pressing questions instead. "How ... how long was I in Hansen Hills?"

"Two weeks," Cookie said, "but you were gone almost a week before you arrived at the prison. We were frantic with worry."

Angela blinked away a long stare. "Leeha, do you remember where you were before the Hills?"

Memories of being strapped to a gurney flickered in her mind, but until she was sure *this* Angela was *the* Angela, she dared not say too much. "I'm ... not sure. They gave me a drug. I think I slept a lot. I'm pretty sure I was in some kind of big vehicle. You know, in some ways, it seems I was gone for years, yet, in other ways, it feels like a couple of days."

No one spoke.

She asked another question. "I'm really confused. Cookie, how did you find Angela ... er ... Ang?"

Cookie's lips trembled, as if tears would pour from her eyes at any second. "The day you were kidnapped, I saw three goons shove you into a van. I ran to Mrs. Furley's unit—"

Kever cleared his throat.

For a moment, Cookie stopped talking. "Anyway ... Mrs. Furley and Toofy weren't ... around. I chased the van, but it disappeared around a corner. I lost my PD, so I was running to the Happy Day Diner to get help. A car pulled up to the curb by our apartment building. Kever-o and Ang were in the car. That's how they found me."

Leeha took a sip of tea to buy time to frame her next question. The story wasn't making sense. "Ang, why were you and Kever-o at the Pineland Apartments?"

This time, it was Angela who paused before speaking. "Kever-o and I were looking for you."

"For me? I don't get it, Ang, why would you guys be looking for me?"

"You know what," Kever said, "perhaps we should wait until Doctor Platcher examines Leeha before bugging her too much. He's almost finished working on Anson."

Leeha recalled the giant splotch of blood on Anson's shirt. "I forgot ... Anson ... how is he?"

Kever spoke in a calm voice. "He's doing fine, Leeha. The wound is long, but not deep. Doctor Platcher just wants to make sure it's really clean."

"Thank goodness! I saw lots of blood."

Tears rolled down Cookie's cheeks. "It's so like you, Leeha, to worry about others even after what you went through …." Cookie sobbed into a napkin. "S … sorry. It's been … so … hard. You … you're so … brave, Leeha!"

Brave? Guys in suits drugged and kidnapped her. How was that bravery? "Um … no I'm not. I'm a chicken, actually. Um … where's the bathroom?"

Cookie dried her face. "It's right down the hall. I'll show you." Cookie led the way to a bright bathroom with big mirrors. The scent of honeysuckle filled the air. "This will be your bathroom, Leeha, so you can have privacy. I know how important that is to you."

"Cookie, is it okay if I take a shower?"

"Of course!" Cookie opened a drawer. "If you need more towels, there're extras in here. Oh, we brought clothes for you. I'll get them."

She dashed off and returned with a stack of folded fabric. "These should fit." She set the pile on a corner table. "Everything should be here: shirt, pants, socks, underwear, bra. Goodness! I forgot the slippers!" She ran off again and returned with a pair of house shoes. "There's other stuff for you in your bedroom, too. It's the room at the end of the hall." Cookie pushed the shower curtain aside. "I'll get the water started so it gets nice and warm."

Soon, the sound of gushing water filled the room. "Leeha, do you need anything else?"

Leeha shook her head. This cabin was more like a fancy house than a vacation getaway in the country. As nice as it was, she missed her little apartment in the Warrenton District. "Thanks, Cookie, so much."

"You're welcome, Leeha. It's so good to have you back."

"Oh, Cookie, there is something else."

"What's that?"

"When can I go home?"

Cookie's full lips pursed, as if to hold back tears. "I don't know, Leeha. I've been wondering the same thing. I want to go back to Pineland, too. When things settle down, we'll need to talk to Ang and Kever-o about it."

Leeha knew Cookie wasn't telling her everything, but the water had warmed. "Okay, Cookie, we'll chat with them later."

Cookie lifted a bucket from the tub. "Leeha, let me know if you need help."

"I will, but what's with the bucket?"

"It's been drier than usual here, so we collect water and pour it on the plants outside."

"Oh, that's a good idea."

"Remember, Leeha, call me if you need anything. I'll wait right outside the door."

Cookie left.

When the bathroom door closed, Leeha stripped off her smelly clothes and stuffed them into a garbage can. She climbed into the shower. Never before had spraying, warm water felt so good. She scrubbed her face and all those places that were hard to reach when bathing by a tiny sink.

Her hair was the worst; it was hopelessly tangled. Three applications of conditioner didn't undo the knots.

When she was as clean as she was going to get, she reached for the faucet.

Her fingers didn't make it to the handle. Tears burst from her eyes. Her body crumpled to the bathtub floor.

She willed the sobs to stop. The last thing she wanted was for Cookie, Angela, Rona, Anson, and especially Kever, to see her in such a pathetic emotional state. She raised her face. Pulsating water rinsed tears from her cheeks. She must get control of herself. Pretty, feminine Cookie bawled her eyes out, not her.

The time had come to leave the shower. Her rescuers, if they were rescuers, would find it odd if she hung out in the bathroom too long.

Leeha pulled herself to her feet, turned off the water, and pushed the shower curtain aside. She dried herself with a plush towel and stepped onto the warm floor.

She stared at her reflection in a full-length mirror. Bruises of black, blue, purple, red, green, and yellow dotted her face, hands, arms, and legs. She knew the cause of a few of the marks, but the origins of most of the wounds were a mystery.

Not everything about her reflection was bad; she looked better than she did in the bathroom at Hansen Hills. Also, the bruises on her face drew attention away from her zits. In fact, her blemishes had lessened in intensity while imprisoned.

A knock rattled the door. Cookie said, "Leeha, are you okay? Do you need help?"

"I'm fine. I'll be right out."

Leeha dressed. She must hurry, else Cookie would barge in.

The clothes were a bit on the baggy side. She checked the label on a pair of soft jeans. The pants were her size. Perhaps she'd lost weight in prison.

She found a comb and brush on a table next to the sink. No amount of combing undid the knots in her hair.

Leeha opened the medicine cabinet. Cookie had thought of everything! A concealer makeup stick sat on a shelf.

She made up her face—Kever would see her, after all.

Prepared or not, she must engage with a group of strangers. She drew a deep breath and opened the bathroom door.

The moment she stepped through the doorway, Cookie swung an arm around her shoulders. "Come on, Leeha, there's someone here to help you."

Just great! Someone else to bug her. She peered down the hall. Angela and Rona were by the kitchen table. Anson was there, too. He was eating. It was the first time she'd gotten a good look at him. It wasn't only his voice that seemed familiar; he looked familiar as well. Someone else was also there. An old, balding guy stood by the counter. His drooped shoulders and hawkish nose gave him an evil-scientist appearance. Kever, however, was nowhere in sight.

Cookie steered her down the hall. Just as they entered the kitchen, Kever appeared. He dropped a spoon into the bowl he held. "Wow! Leeha, what a difference! Look at you!"

"Thanks. The shower felt good."

Kever gestured toward the old man. "Leeha, this is Doctor Platcher."

The guy's kind voice didn't match his scary appearance. "Leeha, I just finished patching up Anson. Would you mind if I have a look at you?"

Kever must've picked up on her suspicions. "It's okay, Leeha. Doctor Platcher and Mr. Fullerby are longtime friends."

"Well ... um ... okay." Certainly, he didn't intend to examine her in front of everyone. "Um ... where shall we go?"

"Leeha," Cookie said, "do you remember where your room is?"

"Yes, you pointed it out to me."

Doctor Platcher's voice contained an *I pity you* tone. "All right, Ms. Ritsagin, lead the way."

SOUNDS OF NATURE

"Ang, here is a pic of my friend's cabin. Full security sweeps have been conducted. It's a safe place to hide Leeha Ritsagin."

Andecco Journalist Bob Fullerby
Message to Angela Thirgal
Year 1007 of the Enlightened Epoch

Forest Falls, Cadona
SATURDAY, MAY 20, YEAR 1007 EE
9:20 A.M., CENTRAL EAST CADONA TIME

Cookie Davis watched as Leeha and Dr. Platcher disappeared behind the bedroom door.

"That poor woman!" Cookie said. "She looks half dead. I almost didn't recognize her."

Cookie leaned against a wall; the charade of hiding the shock she felt had sapped her energy. She buried her face in her hands. "Leeha knows! She knows I was alarmed by how she looks. I feel so bad!"

Angela poured herself a cup of tea. "She's free now. She'll be okay."

"How do you know, Ang? You know what happens; you and Mr. Fullerby report on stuff like this all the time. When someone goes through something horrible, they may never be the same. They get all weird and paranoid; they can't sleep, can't hold down a job. Lots of people can't handle real life and end up committing suicide."

Kever took a seat at the table and buttered a slice of bread. "Sometimes bad stuff changes people for the better, Cookie."

Anson winced in pain as he leaned back in his chair. "I agree with Kever-o. As a cop, I've dealt with people who've gone through all types of stuff. Some come out the other end better than ever. There's this one lady who was held captive by a gang of crazies for over a week. She's now one of our best hostage negotiators. She's saved many lives."

Cookie believed Anson's story, but he and Kever didn't know Leeha as she did. "Leeha doesn't like danger. She wants a nice, peaceful life where she spends lots of time at home."

"You know what, Cookie," Kever said, "I just met Leeha, but she strikes me as one tough lady. I'm guessing she has what it takes to pull through." He pushed a chair away from the table. "Cookie, sit down and have something to eat. Leeha's going to need you over the next few days. She's in good hands with Doctor Platcher right now, so take this time to catch your breath."

Cookie took her last bite of stew. "I was hungrier than I thought. Thanks, Kever-o, for reminding me to take care of myself." She glanced around the room. "Hey, where's Ang?"

"She stepped out," Kever said.

"Oh, no! I hope I didn't hurt her feelings! I jumped all over her when she told me that Leeha was going to be okay."

He laughed. "Good luck with hurting Ang's feelings."

Rona said, "Don't worry, Cookie. Ang left to check in with Mr. Marantees. She also wants to make sure her friends from the shooting range are okay. One of them got hurt trying to keep security forces away from us."

Time crept. The silence hurt Cookie's ears. "Doctor Platcher's been examining Leeha for a long time. I hope it doesn't mean something's wrong—I mean, badly wrong."

Kever tossed an orange slice into his mouth. He opened a printed periodical. "Cookie, there're books and old magazines in the living room. Maybe you can find something to read to pass the time."

"I can't concentrate on reading. I'm worried about Leeha, and I'm starting to worry about Ang. She's been gone awhile."

The side door opened. Angela walked in and took a seat at the kitchen table. "Any word on Leeha?" she asked.

"Not yet," Cookie said.

Kever closed the magazine he'd been reading. "Ang, did your buddies get out okay?"

"They did, but as they were pulling out, they saw military and National Police reinforcements moving in. Hansen Hills is arming up."

"Ang," Rona said, "what about Mr. Fullerby? Any word on him?"

"Unfortunately, no, but Mr. Marantees did hear interesting news about the Hills. A source from the military said a doctor and a guard were killed in a prison cell. The doctor was stabbed with a medical instrument. Here's the weird part; the guard was hit with a paralysis dart. He was wearing a respirator, but it ran out of power before he was found. The military thinks an escaped prisoner killed them. The National Police have launched a manhunt. And, get this, they found the guard's sidearm on the ground in the west yard."

"Wow!" Cookie said. "I wonder who killed them?"

Kever's eyebrows rose. "Cookie, it might have been Leeha."

"No, way! Leeha isn't capable of killing."

"Kever-o," Angela said, "why do you suspect Leeha?"

"When I found her, she was wandering around in the west yard holding a military-issue handgun. I cleaned it for DNA and prints and left it on the ground."

Angela's eyes widened. "Kever-o, Leeha was outside when you found her?"

"Yep, gun in hand. She was heading toward the north yard, toward the breached fence. Because she was armed, I grabbed her from behind. She's strong; she put up quite a fight. The thought crossed my mind that she might gain the upper hand and shoot me."

Cookie said, "What a crazy thing to say! Leeha wouldn't shoot or stab anybody. Maybe she had help getting out, and whoever killed the doctor and guard gave her the gun."

"If she did have help," Angela said, "Mr. Marantees' source didn't know about it. The source reported one escaped prisoner. Kever-o, did you see anyone else in the west yard?"

"Nope, only Leeha."

Cookie jumped to her feet. "You people have lost your minds! Leeha's not capable of things like this."

Anson appeared sore as he shifted in his seat. "Cookie, you'd be surprised what people will do in extreme situations, and I can't think of anything more extreme than being tortured in an illegal prison."

Cookie's urge to protest got the better of her. "Leeha would never hurt—"

The door to Leeha's bedroom opened. Dr. Platcher walked out. At a sloth's pace, he shuffled down the hall.

Cookie dashed toward him. "Doctor, how is she?"

"Considering what she's been through, remarkably well. Let's go to the kitchen so I can fill all of you in." He ambled to the table.

"Doctor," Kever said, "will Leeha be okay?"

"If we can get her respiratory infection cleared up, she should be."

"What type of infection?" Angela asked.

"I'm pretty sure it's caused, at least in part, by water torture. I've seen it before in war zones. She also has irritation in her throat, as if an emergency breathing support tube had been used. I became suspicious because inserting a tube like that implies something very serious had happened. I ran some tests and found a compound in her system that I hadn't seen used since the Ostollian wars."

Cookie said, "What … what kind of compound?"

"Paralysis Elixir."

"What's that?"

"Nasty stuff. It's banned internationally. As its name suggests, it causes paralysis. The effects wear off, but the Elixir, among other things, temporarily obstructs lung function, meaning the patient can't breathe. Without respiratory support, a victim will die. I'm sorry to say the young lady did tell me that a so-called *doctor* shot her with a paralysis dart."

Cookie felt her body sway. She clutched Kever's arm as she took a seat. "Oh, my goodness! Leeha went through all those terrible things?"

"And then some," Dr. Platcher said. "Her samples also contain traces of Mind-One. It's the drug that Senator Seldortin was talking about; the truth serum that's being created at Hansen Hills."

"What about her wounds and bruises?" Anson asked.

"I'm pretty sure dental instruments caused the injuries to her lips, gums, and a tooth. By bruising patterns on her arms and legs, I'd say she was tied up a number of times. She has other bruises consistent with squeezing, punching, and falling. Fortunately, there are no signs of a concussion or internal injuries."

"Doctor," Rona said, "what do we need to do for her?"

"I gave her injections and left pills on the nightstand in her bedroom. It's very important that she takes her meds every six hours until all the tablets are used. I also left medication for pain. Other than that, she needs to get lots of rest, drink water regularly, and eat healthy food. It's best if she's not moved unless absolutely necessary. Keep her as calm and relaxed as possible. I hope to return on Tuesday to see how she's doing."

"Thank you, Doctor," Angela said. "Is there anything else?"

Doctor Platcher reached into a deep pocket of his baggy overcoat. He placed a bottle of pills on the table. "Ms. Davis, these meds are for you. They'll help you relax."

"I can't take drugs. I need to look after Leeha."

Rona spoke in a soft voice. "I'll look after her while you rest, Cookie. I need to keep an eye on Anson anyway."

"There you go, Ms. Davis," Dr. Platcher said. "Problem solved. A good, long sleep will do you a world of good."

Angela stood. "I'll see you out, Doctor."

"No need. I know the way. I'm sure you folks have a great deal to discuss. I ask, though, that you keep me updated on Bob."

Angela sat down and said, "We'll do that, Doctor."

He left through the side door.

Angela filled a cup with tea. Cookie noticed the drink was the kind that kept one awake.

Steam rose when Angela blew into the cup. A life-or-death expression covered her face. "We did the impossible; we got Leeha out of Hansen Hills. She's free, but not safe. The protesters are keeping the security forces busy right now, but the protest won't last forever. Because of Leeha's health, we need to stay here for as long as possible, so we have to be extra careful about keeping a low profile. We mustn't do anything to draw attention to the cabin. Kever-o, we'll need to prepare for the worst; we need to be ready to move Leeha to another location at a moment's notice."

"I agree," Kever said. "We'll also need to figure out when to question her about the Guiding Light document." He counted on his fingers. "We need to figure out what she did with the original, printed version; to whom she sent copies; how, and if, Randy Altholder and the Sohn-Suran woman are involved; and what she told her interrogators."

Cookie watched as Angela looked at each person at the table. "Here's what we'll do …. Anson, take my bedroom; it's next to Leeha's. That'll make it easier for Rona to look after both Leeha and you. Cookie, you'll take one of those pills Doctor Platcher gave you and lie down. Kever-o and I will update our contingency plans."

Anson pushed against the tabletop as he stood. "Thanks, Ang. I have a feeling I'll be much better in two or three days. Let's hope the bad guys don't catch on to us before then." Rona followed him to his bedroom.

Cookie grabbed the medicine bottle. She dropped one tiny, white pill into her palm. Once she swallowed it, nothing would prevent drowsiness. She plopped the pill into her mouth. "Kever-o, Ang, see you guys later."

She headed down the hall. The door to Anson's room was open. Rona was checking his bandages.

Cookie peeked into Leeha's bedroom. Enough light shone in to highlight Leeha's body as she lay beneath fluffy quilts. "God, watch over her," Cookie whispered.

Ver-Nuvelin, Domataland
SATURDAY, MAY 20, YEAR 1007 EE
8:20 A.M., CENTRAL FEWWOK TIME

A light blinked on President Demnar Tarish's office desk. He heard Presidential Assistant Druzha Timkensha's voice. "Honorable President, Intelligence Chief Kolensha is here. She wishes to see you."

"Send her in, Druzha."

Rozula opened the door. She still wore purple in honor of those killed on the Goodwill Ship. She bowed. "Good morning, Honorable President."

"Good morning. Please come in and have a seat."

She smiled as she settled into a high-backed guest chair.

"From the look on your face, Rozula, I take it you have good news."

"Yes, Honorable President, for once I do. Bob Fullerby's people rescued Leeha Ritsagin from Hansen Hills. They're hiding her in a cabin near Forest Falls."

"Excellent news indeed! How is she?"

"Ill, but expected to recover. She's not out of danger, though. The National Police have launched a manhunt. When she escaped, a doctor and a guard were killed."

"Did Ruzhman Fullerby's people kill them?"

"No. We don't know what happened for sure, but we suspect Lady Ritsagin did."

"Hmm, Leeha Ritsagin is no ordinary person."

"No, Honorable President, she's not."

"Rozula, what about the Guiding Light?"

"One of my agents will question her about the document when she's strong enough."

"Any idea how long that will be?"

"We're hoping in a few days, maybe Tuesday."

"Thank you, Rozula. Please keep me updated on developments."

"I will, Honorable President."

Forest Falls, Cadona
SATURDAY, MAY 20, YEAR 1007 EE
4:20 P.M., CENTRAL EAST CADONA TIME

Leeha Ritsagin awoke to the sound of a soft voice. "Leeha, Leeha, wake up. You need to take your medicine."

She opened her eyes. Rona hovered over her.

Dim light glowed on Rona's pretty face and smooth skin. She flashed her pixie smile. "How are you feeling?"

Leeha sat up. "Not too bad. This bed is comfortable."

"Yeah, this is a swift cabin." Rona handed her two pills and a glass of water.

Leeha popped the pills into her mouth and took a long drink. "How's Anson doing?"

"He's a bit sore, but his wounds aren't serious. He should feel better in a few days. Do you need anything else, Leeha? Are you hungry?"

Leeha pictured bread soggy with butter, but these people had done enough for one day. "No, I'm good, Row."

"If you need anything, Leeha, just push this button. Else, I'll see you in six hours for your next round of meds."

"You know, Row, I can take them myself."

"I know, but we want to make sure you're okay. I'm looking after Anson, too. You guys are on the same medication schedule."

"Thanks, Row."

"No problem. Do you want the night-light on or off?"

Leeha had enough of darkness. "On, please."

Rona tiptoed toward the door.

"Hey, Row, wait ... there is one thing ... I was wondering about my mother. Bad guys are looking for me; I'm worried they'll hurt her."

"I'm sorry, Leeha, you can't talk to her; if you did, your mother would be in trouble for sure, and so would we. They'll trace the call and find all of us. I'll talk to Ang; we might figure out a way to check up on her."

"Thanks, Row."

"I ... I wish I could help, Leeha. The Freedom Party, the Back-to-Basics Club, the True Followers of God Church ... they're turning this country ... they're making it dangerous for many of us."

"You are helping, Row. Just listening makes me feel better."

"Rest now, Leeha. Remember, ring if you need anything." Rona walked away and shut the door behind her.

Leeha heard fluttering sounds coming from outside. Birds sang.

Living things! How wonderful it would be to see them! She reached up and pushed aside the edge of a printed curtain, but wooden shutters shielded the window glass.

As shutters blocked daylight, so did a shadow creep over her soul.

Tears paid another visit. Despite the soothing, warm air and comfy bedding, her heart yearned for the narrow bed and thin mattress in her own apartment. She longed to open her eyes and find herself in her own bedroom.

As the inside of the cabin fell silent, a haunting fear picked at her. Would she ever again see her home? Had the Pineland Apartments era of her life drawn to a close?

Beyond the cabin walls, gusts of wind whistled in trees and rattled tall grass. Birds chirped and cawed. From far away, a horse whinnied. She hadn't heard many of those sounds since childhood, but her time as a little girl on the family farm had also slipped into the realm of history.

She brushed away tears. The time had come to stop her endless sniveling. She had many questions. Who were her saviors? The one named *Ang* sounded and looked like Angela Thirgal, but why in the world would a famous person be interested in *Leeha Ritsagin*, a nobody? Rona Betler seemed like a sweet, young girl, but did she really work for Bob Fullerby? And where was Bob, anyway? Why did people act uneasy whenever his name came up?

Another thing didn't fit: why would two gorgeous guys rescue her from Hansen Hills? Anson looked darn familiar, but she couldn't place him. She remembered overhearing someone say that he was a cop. Why would a police officer get involved with her rescue when police departments had ties to the bad guys? One thing was for sure, Kever Carsen was way splashy, yet he was gentle and kind. Nice and good looking rarely came in one package. Was the attention he gave her an act?

The strangest thing of all: Cookie Davis entered her life shortly after the Guiding Light appeared in the back seat of her brown Monarch. Was Cookie really her friend? Or was she pretending to be to learn about the weird document?

Leeha had told her kidnappers many things about the Guiding Light. Some things were true, others tales. Until she knew with certainty that her rescuers were Bob Fullerby's friends, she must keep her stories straight. She mustn't tell them that the document was hidden beneath the kitchen cabinets in her little apartment in the Warrenton District.

In the meantime, she'd enjoy the comforts of this cute cabin, the good food, the companionship, and, most of all, Kever Carsen's alluring eyes and spellbinding smile.

A grin tugged at her lips. She nestled into the spongy mattress as sounds of nature lulled her to sleep.

ABOUT THE AUTHOR

C. N. Sky is a former US Army Intelligence officer with a degree in political science. Sky loves nature and is especially fond of flying squirrels.

Printed in the USA
CPSIA information can be obtained
at www.ICGtesting.com
CBHW031737160224
4401CB00038B/413